LOVE BLOSSOMS AT PUDDLEDUCK FARM

DELLA GALTON

Boldwood

First published in Great Britain in 2023 by Boldwood Books Ltd.

Copyright © Della Galton, 2023

Cover Design by Alice Moore Design

Cover Photography: Shutterstock

Every effort has been made to obtain the necessary permissions with reference to copyright material, both illustrative and quoted. We apologise for any omissions in this respect and will be pleased to make the appropriate acknowledgements in any future edition.

A CIP catalogue record for this book is available from the British Library.

Paperback ISBN 978-1-80280-915-2

Large Print ISBN 978-1-80280-916-9

Hardback ISBN 9978-1-80280-914-5

Ebook ISBN 978-1-80280-918-3

Kindle ISBN 978-1-80280-917-6

Audio CD ISBN 978-1-80280-909-1

MP3 CD ISBN 978-1-80280-910-7

Digital audio download ISBN 978-1-80280-911-4

Boldwood Books Ltd
23 Bowerdean Street
London SW6 3TN
www.boldwoodbooks.com

For my lovely Aunt Pat, my biggest fan, with my love

1

'Did you know guinea pigs come from deepest darkest Peru, where they are not pets but a source of protein and they can even *break-dance*?' Young Archie Holt paused for breath and looked at Phoebe, who was kneeling on the lawn beside him.

She raised her eyebrows, taking all this in, as Archie lifted a plump brown guinea pig out of its pen, which was in front of them, and plonked it onto Phoebe's lap. His dark eyes were expectant.

'I didn't know they could breakdance,' Phoebe replied, running her fingers over the sleek brown coat and decidedly curvy belly of her patient.

It was not the most orthodox of consultations, kneeling as they were out in the early April fresh air on the bowling-green grass of the beautiful back lawns of Beechbrook House. Phoebe was more used to examining her patients in her spotless consulting rooms at Puddleduck Vets, which was at Puddleduck Farm next door, but she would have forgiven ten-year-old Archie for most things. She'd had a soft spot for him for even longer than she'd been dating his father, Rufus Holt, who was currently ensconced in his home office, oblivious to the goings-on in his back garden.

'Can this guinea pig breakdance?' Phoebe asked Archie cautiously.

He grinned at her and then shrugged. 'Maybe. I've never seen her. But I saw one do it on TikTok.'

Of course he had. TikTok was Archie's current favourite social media platform.

Phoebe glanced back into the pen where she could see at least two of Archie's other guinea pigs, Elastigirl and Edna – he was a fan of *The Incredibles* – before returning her attention to the one on her lap. 'She's new, this one, isn't she? What's her name?'

'Violet.'

He was still on the same theme for names then.

'Archie, did you realise that Violet was pregnant?' Phoebe looked at him curiously. As far as she knew, Archie didn't have any male guinea pigs; certainly, none he'd registered with Puddleduck Vets. Mind you, she hadn't seen Violet before today either.

Archie nodded. 'Yes, I know she is. Lucius is the father.'

Phoebe seemed to remember Lucius was a character in *The Incredibles* too.

'And where is Lucius?'

'He's not here. He belongs to my mate Jack.' Archie grinned. 'We're sharing the profits when the little pigs are sold. We've set up a spreadsheet to factor in the costs of food and hay and stuff. Jack isn't getting as much of a cut as me – technically, I could just pay him the stud fee seeing as I've got all the responsibility, with Violet being the brood guinea pig.'

'I see.' Phoebe wondered if Rufus knew about any of this. She'd been under the impression that he'd been trying to keep the lid on Archie's ever-increasing menagerie – he had two rabbits as well, both males fortunately – but then maybe Rufus figured letting Archie breed guinea pigs was a good way to teach his son entrepreneurial skills.

'Guinea pigs have an average gestation period of sixty-nine days,' Archie continued knowledgeably, 'and when the little pigs are born, they have all their fur and teeth and stuff and can run around in the first hour.' He hunkered back on his heels, frowning slightly.

Phoebe nodded. From what she could remember about guinea pigs, Archie was spot on. There was a grass stain on his cheek. She resisted the urge to lean across and wipe it off.

'Do you know how old Violet is?'

'Four months,' Archie said promptly. 'It's the ideal breeding age for a sow because once they go past six months of age, parts of the pelvis fuse up and then they can't give birth.'

Phoebe suppressed a smile. He was correct about that too. Mind you, she would have expected nothing less. Archie didn't do anything by halves. Why would his breeding project be any different?

'Do you know how long Violet's been pregnant so far?' She was no expert, but she'd have said Violet was about to pop.

'Seventy-one days.' Archie rubbed his nose, a gesture that Phoebe knew meant he was slightly anxious. 'I was wondering if she might need some vet help.'

'She doesn't look as though she needs any help just yet. But you were right to get me to have a look. And you will need to keep a close eye on her over the next couple of days.' It was a good job it was the Easter holidays. In four days' time it was Good Friday but Archie's school had a two-week break. Archie must have planned ahead.

'I should probably transfer her to the nesting cage now then,' Archie said solemnly. 'Do you think that's a good idea? My book says she needs to be separated from the others when she has her litter and for some time after the babies arrive, to keep them all safe. I've got it all ready. I've put in chippings and stuff.'

'Now is probably the right time,' Phoebe said. She wasn't a bit surprised that Archie had it all planned out. He loved animals and, unlike some kids Phoebe encountered in her work, he was totally focused on their care.

But she was even more sure now that Rufus couldn't have sanctioned this. He'd always seemed keen to curtail Archie's plans for a guinea pig emporium. And he certainly hadn't mentioned Violet's imminent litter. On the other hand, why would he? He had an estate to run. He tended to leave all things Archie to Emilia, Archie's Swiss German nanny.

There was only one way to find out. Phoebe took the bull by the horns. 'Archie, does your dad know about this, er, enterprise with Jack?'

Archie's cheeks reddened. 'No.' There was an awkward pause. 'You're not going to tell him, are you?' His voice was pleading. 'Can't it be our secret? Please, Phoebe, please don't tell Dad?'

She took a deep breath. Out of the corner of her eye she had just spotted movement. She turned to look. Emilia had just come out onto the terrace at the back of the house, now she shielded her eyes and looked out across the grass. Her slim figure was in profile to them briefly. Then she saw them and began to march across the lawn, her blonde ponytail swaying crossly from side to side.

Archie spotted her too. 'Uh-oh,' he muttered.

This was a sentiment with which Phoebe agreed. Despite her best efforts to be friendly towards the younger woman – Emilia was twenty-nine to Phoebe's thirty-six – Emilia had never been more than cool towards Phoebe and her attitude had become even more glacial when she'd discovered that Phoebe and Rufus were an item. They'd begun dating last summer, eight months ago, and although they'd kept it low-key, Emilia clearly did not approve of her boss's new girlfriend.

In the beginning, Phoebe had put this down to her being overprotective, of both Archie who she'd looked after since his mother had died nearly four years ago and also perhaps a little of Rufus, formerly known as one of the most eligible bachelors in the New Forest, being both a rich widower and in line to be the next Lord Holt.

But Phoebe was no longer sure if it was just overprotectiveness. When Rufus was around, Emilia was friendly and pleasant but as soon as he was absent, she found fault with everything that Phoebe did or said. If she hadn't known better, Phoebe would have said Emilia was ragingly jealous. She'd recently wondered if Emilia had had designs on Rufus herself. She hadn't mentioned this to Rufus – and as far as she could see, Rufus was never anything other than professional towards Archie's nanny, so it seemed unlikely, but Phoebe couldn't think of another explanation.

Phoebe wasn't the type to get intimidated by people who didn't approve of her, but it was hard not to feel slightly unnerved by the nanny's unfriendly manner. And by the look of Emilia's body language as she strutted across the lawn towards them, she wasn't very happy today.

Phoebe was gently lifting Violet back into her pen when Emilia arrived.

'Archie, there you are. You must tell me if you are vanishing from house. I worry.' She looked down her nose at Phoebe which wasn't difficult as Phoebe was still on her knees. 'I did not know you were here.' She made it sound as though Phoebe should apologise for not informing her, which Phoebe had no intention of doing. 'Is this visit of the professional or the personal?'

'A bit of both,' Phoebe said equably. 'I was in the vicinity...' That was obvious, she worked next door, '...when Archie texted me.'

'About the mini pig, ja?' Emilia glanced into the pen. 'Archie – if the vet is called you must tell me. These things are expensive.'

'There won't be a charge,' Phoebe said quickly.

Ignoring her, Emilia went on, 'Should the mini pig be this heavy? That is not right. Wait.' Her eyes narrowed suspiciously. 'Is this mini pig with babies, Archie?'

Archie, who'd got to his feet when Emilia had arrived, put his hands in his pockets and after a moment's hesitation he nodded. He seemed to realise that there wasn't much point in denying it. Especially as Violet was now waddling her way across to see her companions, her brown belly swaying very obviously.

'Pfff,' Emilia said. 'How did this happen?'

Phoebe winced.

Emilia pffed again. 'You knew about this?' She turned her laser gaze on Phoebe. 'You have come without Rufus knowing to check pregnant mini pig.'

Phoebe stood up. On her feet she was taller than the haughty blonde nanny, which helped equal things out a little. 'I'm just going to talk to Rufus now,' she said, realising that if she told Emilia she hadn't known about Violet's condition, she'd be dropping Archie in it, and if she said she *had* known then she'd be giving Emilia all the evidence of collusion she needed.

She was definitely going to have to tell Rufus, though. However much Archie had planned to keep this under wraps, it couldn't stay a secret any longer.

Archie had suddenly become very interested in something on the lawn and was scuffing at it with the toe of his trainer. Behind him in the distance, Phoebe saw one of the gardeners come out of the shed on the sit-on mower and reverse it into position. At the same time, her mobile buzzed in her pocket.

Phew. Saved by the bell. Phoebe hooked it out just in time to see the name Anni Buckland flick up on the screen. Anni Buckland, owner of Anni's Alpacas, was a new customer but Phoebe had given Anni her direct number because she'd been over there a few times lately to treat an old cat.

'Sorry,' Phoebe told both Archie and Emilia, 'but I need to get this.'

* * *

Twenty minutes later, Phoebe was driving her Lexus between the newly planted lavender fields on either side of the quarter-mile drive that led towards the gatehouse of the Beechbrook Estate. The lavender bushes, planted in dozens and dozens of straight rows, were a new venture for Rufus. They wouldn't bloom until June, ready for their first harvest in July, but they would look and smell stunning when they did. Rufus had plans for upmarket skincare products and had negotiated a deal with an artisan co-operative.

She drove past the gatehouse and on beneath the high stone archway, topped by a life-size sculpture of a stag, and off the Holts' land. It still felt a little bit surreal coming in and out of the estate as though she lived there when up until last year she'd spent her whole life wondering what lay beyond the imposing brick wall that circled it.

Phoebe had only got the chance to see Rufus very briefly – he'd been on an extended phone call himself – but she'd waited until he'd ended it, and then given him a quick update on Archie's breeding enterprise. He'd reacted with a mixture of frustration and amusement. As Phoebe had suspected, Archie hadn't mentioned his guinea pig breeding project to his father but she'd got the impression when she'd filled him in that Rufus was secretly quite proud of his son's ingenuity.

'I'd have said no if he'd asked me,' Rufus had said, smiling ruefully. 'Which is of course why he didn't ask me. But maybe it's not such a bad thing. At least he'll have done it all properly. Conscientiously, that is, as far as the animal is concerned.' He'd flicked a glance at her. 'Thanks for coming over. Was the guinea pig OK?'

'She was fine. You're right. He had done everything by the book.'

'I will tell Archie that he can't just go calling you whenever he feels like it, though. He can't just get free veterinary advice whenever he likes just because we're friendly.'

'Actually, he can,' she had said, smiling. 'I don't mind.'

'Well, I do. It's a boundary. Besides, it would be good for him to learn that veterinary advice is a cost he needs to factor into his business plan. Did you say he'd set up this breeding programme with Jack?'

'Yes. Apparently they have a spreadsheet.'

Rufus shook his head. 'Amazing. OK. I'll speak to him. Thanks for the heads-up.'

She had moved across to his side of the enormous walnut desk where he was sitting and kissed him on the nose. 'I've got to go – I've got a call. If there are any problems with that guinea pig, let me know, but fingers crossed there won't be.'

Rufus nodded. 'Thanks again. I will. See you later.'

'I'm looking forward to it.'

Something Rufus said had niggled Phoebe as she drove towards Anni Buckland's, which was on the Lyndhurst side of the New Forest, about half an hour away, but it wasn't until she was almost at the farm that she realised what it was.

'Archie can't get free veterinary advice whenever he likes just because we're friendly.'

It was the word 'friendly' that was bothering her, she realised. Was that how Rufus saw their relationship? Friendly? She'd rather hoped he saw it as a bit more than friendly.

He was just as attractive to Phoebe as he'd been on that very first kiss but she was beginning to wonder if the chemistry had faded for him. Part of the problem was that they were hardly ever alone. They still only saw each other a couple of times a week. This despite the fact that Phoebe lived at Woodcutter's Cottage, a ten-minute drive away from Beechbrook House, and she worked next door. The problem was that – relationship or no relationship – Phoebe had her own vet practice and Rufus had a son, and a huge estate to run, and neither of them could spare much time away from what was effectively a 24/7 commitment.

Phoebe knew they were no nearer to resolving the problem of not enough time than they'd been on their first Christmas together, when thanks to a dozen 'impossible to break' prior commitments, they'd barely seen each other.

She shook her head. Of course Rufus didn't see them as just friendly, Phoebe told herself firmly, it was a turn of phrase, nothing more.

With a small sigh, Phoebe parked below the painted sign that proclaimed you'd reached Anni's Alpacas and checked to make sure she had no more messages. She'd recently taken on a newly quali-fied vet, Max Jones, to work full time at her surgery. Max was hugely enthusiastic, passionate about animal welfare and she already trusted him enough to leave him and her senior vet nurse, Jenna, holding the fort while she did the farm callouts.

She had to admit she was loving the freedom of getting out and about. Small animal practice was great, but it consisted mostly of dogs, cats and the occasional rabbit, with allergies, digestive prob-lems and minor injuries. Much of it was routine and it was nowhere near as varied as going out to farms, seeing the animals on their own turf – literally usually – and never being quite sure what you would find.

Phoebe found two messages on her phone. One was from Marcus, her receptionist, asking if Anni had got hold of her about an alpaca that was off its food. Phoebe texted back to say she was there now.

The other was a message from Archie with a link to a TikTok video, headed up 'Bill the Brilliant Breakdancing Guinea Pig'.

It was very hard to resist the temptation to open the link immediately.

2

Phoebe had been introduced to Anni Buckland by Maggie Crowther, her grandmother. Maggie was the owner of Puddleduck Farm, which for the last fourteen years had been an unofficial animal sanctuary, taking in waifs and strays from the surrounding New Forest villages. Last year, with Phoebe's help, it had become more official. It had been rechristened Puddleduck Pets, and now did animal sponsorship as well as animal adoptions and it was slowly becoming a more sustainable charity.

Last year, Phoebe had also had an old barn at her grandmother's farm converted into a modern vet unit, with consulting rooms and operating theatre, and she now rented the space from Maggie, which helped both of them. It meant that Phoebe could keep an eye out for the old lady – although Maggie would have denied she needed any eyes kept out for her – and it also meant that Phoebe had achieved her dream of owning her own veterinary practice.

Prior to this, Phoebe had worked thirty minutes away at Marchwood Vets, a big practice on the New Forest side of Southampton, where Seth Harding, who owned it, had become her good friend and mentor. He'd been thrilled when Phoebe had set up her own practice and had even cut the ribbon at the official opening. The two practices, Marchwood and Puddleduck Vets, worked closely together, doing each other's out of hours cover and passing on clients in each other's areas.

There was a lot of word-of-mouth business in the New Forest. And there were a lot of families who had been there for years. The forest people, especially the farmers, looked out for each other. They were a close-knit community.

Anni Buckland had rehomed a border terrier from Maggie several years ago, and although the dog had since died, the two women still kept in touch.

'Anni's a quirky old soul,' Maggie had told Phoebe before she'd set off on her first visit to Buckland Farm. 'I'd go as far as to say she was totally bonkers. But she's got a good heart. I'll say that for her.'

'Takes one to know one,' Phoebe had quipped. 'On both fronts, I mean...' She'd slanted a glance at her grandmother, who insisted on being called Maggie by everyone, even her granddaughter, but Maggie had rolled her eyes and refused to rise to the bait. 'You'll see what I mean when you meet her,' was all she would say.

Anni Buckland, Phoebe had discovered, looked like an old-fashioned Romany gypsy, which she'd later discovered was precisely what she was. It was hard to tell how old she was – somewhere between her late sixties and mid-seventies. She had dark eyes, olive skin and gorgeous ringleted black hair, very gently touched with grey, and if you were to glance at any of the dozens of framed pictures around her spacious hall, which Phoebe had on the first occasion she'd visited, you could see that it was a look that had come down through the generations. Glamorous women, handsome men, and beautiful sloe-eyed children smiled or gazed broodingly out from family scenes.

Anni was proud of her Romany ancestry and happy to chat about it. Her grandmother had told fortunes and read tarot on the beach in high season at Scarborough apparently and there was a line of the family that had inherited the gift and were still in great demand.

'Madam Kesia was the real deal,' Anni had told Phoebe proudly the first time they'd met. 'None of your pseudo nonsense with wigs and gold earrings. No, no, no. None of that. Madam Kesia read the palms of the stars. Hugely well-known celebrities who paid a fortune – if you'll excuse the pun – for her skill.' She had reeled off a list of people who Phoebe had never heard of, but had pretended to know because Anni was a sweetie and she liked her.

'Did you inherit the gift?' Phoebe had asked, fascinated, and Anni had laughed.

'No, no, no, although I do get the occasional insight. If you were to bring round a prospective life partner to see me, I'd probably be able to tell you whether he was "the one" or whether you should be running for the hills.'

'Would you?' Phoebe's thoughts had flicked instantly to Rufus, and she'd berated herself. She was already sure he was 'the one' – she didn't need confirmation from Anni.

'Oh, yes, definitely.' Anni's eyes had sparkled. 'But you'd need a bit more than the occasional insight to read palms for a living. Alpacas are a better bet.'

She'd confided she'd been proud of her heritage, but had traded it in to marry a New Forest farmer, four decades ago. 'Nick came from three generations of sheep farmers,' she'd told Phoebe. 'But we switched to alpacas a few years ago. They're our retirement project.'

Anni liked to chat – boy did she like to chat – and Phoebe, who liked people nearly as much as she liked animals, luckily, was happy to listen.

Besides, chatting was good for business. If the customer was happy and relaxed, they tended to invite you back – this was

Phoebe's third visit to the farm. The first one had been a few weeks ago to stitch a wound in a farm cat's neck and the next to administer antibiotics when it wouldn't heal properly.

'A run-in with a rat, I expect,' Anni had told Phoebe. 'Reuben's getting on a bit lately – he ain't so good at despatching rats as he used to be – but in his head he's still a youngster.'

She'd been right about the rat bite in Phoebe's opinion and the antibiotics had seemed to do the trick.

Phoebe had half expected, when she'd seen Anni's number flash up today, that she was being called out to see Reuben again. The cat must have been about sixteen and he wasn't much bigger than a large rat himself.

But as it turned out, today's patient wasn't Reuben. Anni had said when they'd spoken that she had an alpaca that was off colour.

Phoebe had been called to see more and more alpacas lately. There was a trend in the UK for keeping them. They made great pets and were easy to keep. They were also renowned for disliking foxes so quite often hobby hen keepers or smallholders kept them to protect their flocks of free-range chickens.

They didn't have many health problems and Phoebe wasn't expecting this alpaca to be any different. Anni loved her animals and was the kind of owner who'd call the vet at the first sign of a problem.

But when she met Phoebe at the door, her usual smiley face was sombre.

'Hello, love, thanks for coming out so quick. I'm worried about Cindy.'

'Oh dear,' Phoebe said, clutching her vet bag and following her client past the gallery of pictures and along a narrow hall that smelled of cats, through the old farmhouse kitchen and out of the back door once more.

'What seems to be the problem?' Phoebe asked, as they tramped across a yard, and down the track which led to the alpaca field, stopping briefly for Anni to grab a bucket and halter.

'I'm not sure, but she's just not her usual self. She's off her food – not like her at all – and she seems a bit – tired – not bouncing around full of beans.' Anni frowned. 'Nick said I was imagining it at first, but I knew I wasn't. I'll show you.'

They paused at the five-bar gate of the smaller field. The Bucklands had fourteen Suri alpacas, which were the type with the corkscrew coats, and the herd was split across their seven acres of land. During the time they'd been in business, they'd bred several greys, which was the most coveted colour of fleece, Phoebe had learned, but they also had other colours, ranging from fawn to dark brown to black. They mostly sold fleeces but they also bred beautiful alpacas to sell on. There was a scattering of small trees currently bedecked in pink blossom, looking like giant sticks of candyfloss dotted across the fields. It was the most idyllic scene, like something out of *The Darling Buds Of May*, Phoebe thought, as she looked out across the smallholding.

Today, six of the alpacas including Cindy were grazing at the far end of the smallest field. Phoebe shielded her eyes against the midday sun to look. Patients on farms were always at the far ends of fields, Phoebe had learned. And if they weren't when you arrived, they soon put themselves there. Animals had an unerring instinct for knowing when the vet was around and putting as much distance as possible between them. Or maybe it was the vet bag they recognised. Either way, they didn't hang around to say hello.

Anni climbed over the fence, agile as a cat, the bucket and halter in one hand, and Phoebe followed suit. They'd had a lot of rain in April and the ground by the gate was sodden and muddy. Thankfully it wasn't raining now.

As they approached, Anni banged the bucket, and a couple of

the alpacas began to amble over. 'Cindy's the black one on the right,' Anni pointed out. 'She's not very old. I hope she's OK.'

From a distance, Cindy didn't look much different from the rest of the herd but as they got closer, Phoebe could see she did seem quieter than the rest.

Neither was she as interested in the bucket Anni carried, although she did accept a handful of oats.

'Cindy's as tame as a dog anyway,' Anni told Phoebe. 'We've had her since she was a tiny cria, so I didn't think there'd be a problem catching her.' She slipped a halter over the alpaca's nose. 'Do you want her inside or can you look at her here? The others will sod off once the bucket's empty.'

'Here should be fine, thanks.' Phoebe unpacked a stethoscope from her bag. 'Are you all right to hold her while I examine her?'

'Of course.' Anni held the alpaca's halter and buried her hand in the thick black fleece of her neck in a little gesture of affection. 'But I don't think she'll move far.'

She was right. Cindy didn't object to having her heart rate checked or to having her temperature taken. Both were just slightly out of the normal range, but not wildly.

'How long has she been off her food?'

'A few days, maybe a week. I wasn't too worried at first, but it's going on a bit now. And I don't think she's as lively as usual. Some days she seems OK, but others not. What do you think might be wrong?'

'I'm not sure yet. Has she been wormed lately?'

'Yes, I think so.'

While Anni held Cindy securely, Phoebe checked the obliging alpaca's eyelids and saw they looked a little paler than they should have done.

'She's slightly anaemic,' she told Anni. 'I'm going to take a blood test and then we can send it to the lab to confirm and test for what might be causing it.'

'Will that be expensive?' Anni looked alarmed.

'Not too bad, but I think it's necessary. If she is anaemic, we need to find out what's causing it, don't we?'

'I suppose we do. How long will it take?'

'About a week.'

'OK. If that's what we have to do.' Anni still sounded reluctant, and Phoebe wondered, not for the first time, how much of a shoe-string the alpaca farm was run on. OK, so she knew the Bucklands weren't far off retirement but everywhere you looked there were signs of decay. The fencing in the alpaca field was good but there were bits in the unused fields alongside it that were broken and rotting. The barn they'd collected the bucket from had been falling down and the farmhouse looked as if it needed a new roof. The whole place reminded Phoebe of how Puddleduck Farm had looked when she'd first moved back from London.

Maggie had let things go at Puddleduck Farm because she was struggling for money.

Phoebe wondered if the Bucklands were doing the same. Anni had paid her cash for Reuben's treatment, counting the notes out from a tin in her kitchen.

'Don't tell Nick how much it cost if you bump into him,' she'd quipped, but Phoebe had caught the underlying seriousness of her words. 'He's always on at me for spending money on the animals.'

There was a world of difference in cost between treating an alpaca and a cat. Phoebe found herself hoping fervently that what-ever was wrong with Cindy wouldn't take long to diagnose and wouldn't be too pricey.

She took the bloods from the long-suffering Cindy, not a totally simple matter when you had to get through the thick fleece first, and popped the blood tube safely in her bag. 'We'll soon get you sorted out,' she murmured, as much to reassure Anni as for the animal's sake.

She turned back to Anni. 'I'm going to prescribe some iron supplements. I can get them dropped off to you later on or you can come into the surgery to pick them up in about an hour. She'll need to be started on them straight away. Try not to worry. I'm sure we'll soon get to the bottom of this.'

Anni nodded. 'OK, I'll come and get them. That will be quicker. Thanks.' She sounded relieved. 'How's your grandmother?' she added as they got back to the five-bar gate.

'Away on a cruise around the Caribbean,' Phoebe replied.

'She never is.'

Anni looked at her in amazement and Phoebe paused for dramatic effect before saying, 'No, you're right, she's on a canal boat in the Norfolk Broads but she told me to say she's cruising in the Caribbean, should anyone ask.'

Anni laughed. 'I don't blame her. I'd probably do the same. Not that there's anything wrong with a canal boat on the Norfolk Broads. Has she gone on her own? Who's looking after the animals?'

'Natasha, her manager, is living onsite temporarily and no, she's gone with a friend.' Phoebe decided not to elaborate on this. Maggie had actually gone with Eddie, who back in the day when Puddleduck had been a working dairy farm had worked as a farm hand. The two of them had always been firm friends but last year, to Phoebe's delight, they'd got closer than friends.

Her grandmother had spent fourteen years alone, since the death of Farmer Pete, who'd died just after their retirement. Phoebe was thrilled that she and Eddie had decided to start stepping out, as Maggie called it.

'Well, I hope she has a wonderful time,' Anni said and Phoebe realised they were back at the yard. 'Give her my best when you see her. I'll see you at the surgery in about an hour.'

'I'll have the prescription ready for you,' Phoebe said.

'Thanks, love. And thanks for coming so quickly.'

'No problem. And don't worry. I'm sure we'll soon get to the bottom of this.'

'I'm sure you will too.' There was a mixture of gratitude and trust in Anni's dark eyes and Phoebe really hoped it wasn't misplaced.

3

Phoebe was back at Puddleduck Farm just before 5 p.m. As she let herself in through the glass double doors of Puddleduck Vets, she saw Max talking to a pretty dark-haired woman with an absolutely irresistible golden Labrador puppy in the waiting room alongside reception.

Max Jones may have only worked for her for three months, but he was already a big hit with Phoebe's female clients. He wasn't your classic heart-throb, with his sandy-coloured hair and Roman nose, but he was a very snappy dresser. Verging on preppy, he was a big fan of designer labels, he wore Ralph Lauren shirts to work under his scrubs, and he had a voice to die for. Phoebe would have described it as Oxbridge, plus sunshine – he sounded exactly like Hugh Grant, but in a very good mood. He was also incredibly kind and passionate, and he took the time to make every patient, or rather patient's owner, feel special.

Right now, he was crouched in the middle of the waiting room petting the pup's head and the owner, kneeling opposite, was gazing at him adoringly, eyelashes fluttering, and looking like she'd have liked a bit of head petting from Max herself.

'Every puppy is different,' Max was saying. 'Some pick it up straight away and some take longer, but Sammy's an intelligent little chap. I'm sure he'll get it in no time. The thing to remember is that they have very small bladders at this age so the occasional accident is inevitable.'

'I see,' the woman was saying. 'Yes, of course.' Her face was rapt, as if a discussion about house training her puppy was the most fascinating thing she had ever heard. 'So you wouldn't be putting a time limit on it then?'

'No, definitely not. It's like potty training a toddler. They all learn at their own pace.'

'Have you got toddlers then?' More eyelash fluttering. 'You don't look old enough to have any kids of your own.'

Max chuckled. 'Thank you, and no, I don't have any. But my sister does. So I do know a bit about it.' More chuckling.

More eyelash fluttering.

Phoebe wondered if Max realised he was being checked out and chatted up. Behind him she could see Marcus, her receptionist, who was behind the desk, rolling his eyes. Marcus Peterson, who was twenty-nine, three years Max's junior, wasn't bad looking himself. But he wasn't a woman magnet. Marcus had intense brown eyes, a crew cut and always wore a suit to work. Marcus was definitely high street, not designer. Buttoned up would have been a good description for Marcus – or at least Phoebe had thought that about him when she'd first offered him a job and he'd insisted on calling her Miss Dashwood and Maggie, Mrs Crowther.

Once he'd loosened up a bit, she'd discovered that behind his formal exterior lay a very sharp wit and a fine sense of humour. He was also passionate about animals. But he didn't have the same effect on women that Max did, that was for sure.

Phoebe exchanged smiles with both Max and Labrador lady, who got up when they saw her and began to move towards the door, still chatting, still flirting, or at least the woman was still flirting. She clearly didn't want to leave.

Phoebe went across to join Marcus behind reception.

'Everything OK here?'

'Everything's cool.' He frowned and nodded towards the couple at the door. 'What does *he* have that I don't?'

'I've no idea,' Phoebe lied as convincingly as she could. 'But it's obviously good for business. Has she been here long?'

'Her appointment finished ten minutes ago, but she was the last.'

The woman was laughing now. 'Oh, you're so funny, Mr Jones,' she said when she finally paused for breath. 'That's priceless. Have you ever considered doing behavioural training as a sideline? Or writing a book?'

'I think being a vet is probably enough.' Max managed to sound both self-deprecating and pleased as the client and her puppy finally left and he shut the door behind them. As he strolled back towards the reception desk, Marcus pointed at his mouth with two fingers and mimed retching. 'How does he do it? Phoebe, do you think I should get a Ralph Lauren shirt?'

'It's not the shirt.' Was Max actually blushing? 'Miss Harper was just keen to get her puppy sorted out.'

'Keen to get in your trousers, you mean.' Marcus gave a mock sigh.

Max shook his head. 'No, I really don't think so. I think she was genuinely interested in the best way to house train her puppy.' He looked at Phoebe. 'We should offer that service, Phoebe, don't you think?'

'House training puppies?'

'No, pet behavioural training. There's a huge demand for it and I think it's something that your grandmother would find useful too, for animals that come into the sanctuary. What do you think,

Phoebe?' Warming to his theme, he continued before she could answer, 'Dogs and cats are often given up because they have behavioural issues. If we were affiliated with a behaviourist, we could iron out any issues before animals were rehomed and pre-empt any future problems.'

Phoebe bit her lip, but she didn't interrupt. Max looked so enthusiastic that she didn't want to burst his bubble. And it certainly sounded like a good idea on paper. The sanctuary rehomed lots of animals and he was right – they often came in with behavioural problems.

Saddam, a huge ginger tom, who roamed free on the farm, except when the small dogs were being exercised, was a classic example. He'd been dumped in a taped-up box by the gate a few years earlier. Half feral and totally furious, he'd exploded from his prison when Maggie had opened the box, scratching her on the way, and no one had been able to tame him since.

Saddam hadn't become too much of a problem, though, until he'd started terrorising the small dogs. So last year they'd hired Catty the Cat Whisperer to come out and see him. That hadn't gone well. So now he had to be kept in the barn when the small dogs were out and about.

'And if the practice could recommend a good behaviourist,' Max was saying now, 'it would be an extra service for our customers.'

'The sanctuary has tried a behaviourist before,' Marcus chipped in, resting his elbows on the desk and giving Max a challenging stare. 'It didn't go well. Catty the Cat Whisperer lasted about five minutes before Saddam sent her packing. Legging it on her high heels with a torn stocking.'

'How did you know about that?' Phoebe stared at him in surprise. 'You weren't even working here then.'

'Saddam's a legend,' Marcus said happily. 'I've heard all about his exploits from Maggie and Natasha.'

His voice softened as he mentioned Natasha, the sanctuary's young manager, and Phoebe gave him a quick glance. If she wasn't mistaken, Marcus had a soft spot for Natasha.

'A behaviourist with high heels and stockings was obviously the wrong kind of person,' Max said quickly. 'Maybe someone here could do a course.'

'I'd be up for a course,' Marcus offered instantly.

'It's certainly something I'd consider,' Phoebe said. 'Let's talk about it properly when we've got some more time. I need to sort out some iron tablets for an alpaca. The client's coming in for them in a minute. And these bloods need to go off for testing. Did you arrange the lab courier?'

'Yep.' Marcus looked at the clock. 'He'll be here in ten minutes, and I need to tell you about a weird call I had earlier.'

Phoebe's ears pricked up. 'Oh?'

'Long story short, it was from a man who wants to register two Kunekune pigs while he's on an extended break in the New Forest.'

'What was weird about it?'

'The guy, really. He wanted me to give him your mobile number, which I didn't, obviously, but I did promise you'd phone him back personally.'

'Why does he want to speak to me?'

'Well, for a start, he wanted your personal reassurance that we don't film consultations.'

'I assume you'd already told him that we don't.'

'Yes, of course I did, but he wants a personal reassurance from you – if not a signed affidavit,' Marcus said, arching an eyebrow. 'I think the guy was a bit paranoid. Er, understatement.' He looked at the bit of paper in front of him. 'His name's Mr B. That was another weird thing.'

'Bee, as in honey bee?'

'No, just the letter B. No first name either. Or at least not one he'd give to me. I didn't push him.' Marcus grinned. 'He sounded harmless enough, just a bit eccentric. To be honest, I quite like eccentrics.'

Phoebe had to admit she did too. They had a few on their books. From the enigmatic Miss Alice Connor who called all of her male animals Boris, after Britain's erstwhile prime minister, to the completely deaf Dusty Miller, who communicated in sign language and was an octogenarian protester.

Mr B and his Kunekunes would probably fit in well.

Shaking her head, she went through to the back to get the iron tablets.

By the time Phoebe had caught up with Max, written up her call notes on the computer system, given Anni her iron tablets and locked up, it was just gone six.

She sat in her Lexus outside Puddleduck Farm and checked her messages. There was one from Rufus:

Thanks again for coming out to see Violet. No news yet!!!!! Apologies, but I've got to head out to a meeting – Dad was going to go, but he's not feeling well. Can we take a rain check on tonight?

Hoping there wasn't too much wrong with Lord Holt, she tapped back a reply.

Of course we can.

But she felt deflated. This happened way too often. Their plans were either cancelled or delayed. It wasn't always Rufus, just as often it was her. But if they couldn't even fit in a two-hour date, how were they ever going to properly jigsaw their lives together? She consoled herself with the thought that at least they were going to spend Easter together.

Max was on call for most of the Easter weekend, so although she was working Saturday, she had Friday, Sunday and Monday off. Three glorious days.

On Sunday, Rufus and Archie were coming to meet the Dashwoods for lunch. The Dashwoods being her parents, James and Louella Dashwood, Frazier, her brother, and Alexa, her sister-in-law, and their twins. Maggie, who'd be back by then from the canal trip, was even bringing Eddie. The Dashwoods didn't usually do a lot for Easter but this year they'd decided to push the boat out – her parents were eager to meet Rufus properly and her mother had offered to cook a big Sunday roast with all the trimmings. Phoebe knew it was because they were so happy for her and she loved them for it. She was lucky enough to have been brought up in a very close-knit family. She'd always felt loved and supported by all of them and she still felt like that now.

Rufus had not been so lucky. His mother had died when he was four years old and Rufus barely remembered her. His father, who'd never married again, had struggled to bring up his son so had eventually sent him away to boarding school, which Rufus had hated.

Stiff upper lipped and dictatorial, Lord Alfred was not a touchy-feely kind of father, so even when Rufus was at home he had felt isolated and ignored. He'd grown up feeling alone and unloved.

The old lord had softened a bit when Rufus had married Rowena, the daughter of a very wealthy family of bankers, and they'd had Archie. Rufus had just begun to finally feel part of a family when tragedy had struck.

By some terrible twist of fate, history had repeated itself. Rowena had died in a riding accident when Archie was barely six. Rufus had been watching his wife at a cross country event and had witnessed the whole thing, and he still suffered PTSD around horses. Because of his own experience, and despite what his father had advised, Rufus had refused to send Archie away to school – he went to a local private school – and had instead hired the tetchy Emilia to look after him.

From what Phoebe had seen, Archie was amazingly well balanced, and although he often complained about his nanny, and regularly dodged her, Phoebe suspected that he secretly respected Emilia and was actually quite fond of her.

But Phoebe did ache sometimes for the autonomous little boy, growing up without a mother. He was so grown up, so responsible, his focus so inward and serious. The first time she'd ever met him he had been playing chess on his own on the terrace of Beechbrook House. She'd since discovered that it was something he often did – in a bid to improve his game. But it had seemed a too solitary pursuit in her eyes.

At least if he was breeding guinea pigs with his friend Jack, he would be connecting with kids his own age. Remembering the link he'd sent her, she clicked on it and was transported to what turned out to be a thirty-second video of Bill the Brilliant Breakdancing Guinea Pig.

Bill turned out to be a white guinea pig with a black patch over one eye jumping up and down to breakdancing music while a teenage boy laughed uproariously in the background. It was the laughter that was the funniest part. No wonder Archie had loved it. There was nothing wrong with his sense of humour. That was for sure. Phoebe headed home feeling uplifted. If she wasn't going to see Rufus, she'd get a bath and an early night. She could do with a good night's sleep.

4

The blare of Phoebe's mobile woke her up at 3 a.m. She'd been in the middle of a garish dream about a Kunekune pig called Boris and a breakdancing animal behaviourist in red stilettos.

She answered her phone blearily. Being on twenty-four-hour call was one of the downsides of being a vet, although to be fair there weren't many callouts in the small hours.

'Puddleduck Vets, can I help?' She forced herself to sound wide awake and energetic.

The woman's voice was quiet but full of urgency. 'Hi, Phoebe, it's Sarah Mansfield from Middlebrook Farm at Burley, I'm so sorry to get you up but we've got a difficult calving, it's a breech. She's struggling. Our dairyman's tried but he can't manage. We're worried we're going to lose her.'

'Absolutely no problem.' Phoebe was already pulling on her work clothes, folded by the bed ready, in case of emergency. 'I can be with you in just over half an hour.'

'Great.' The woman sounded heartily relieved. 'I'll get my dairyman to meet you at the gate.'

Middlebrook Farm was a huge dairy farm on the edge of Burley. It was just a nineteen-minute drive from Woodcutter's Cottage where Phoebe lived. The advantage of no traffic was negated by the fact she had to take extra care, animals were harder to see on the forest roads in the darkness.

Fortunately, it was a clear night with a full moon and Phoebe drove as quickly as she dared and was at Middlebrook just inside half an hour.

As Sarah Mansfield had promised, there was someone waiting to meet her, flashing a torch as she approached the gate, and a few minutes later they were both tramping across a field. 'I'm afraid she's outside,' the dairyman filled her in as they went. 'I tried to get her in earlier, but it was too late. Can you do a C-section in the field?'

Phoebe swallowed. 'Yes, if we have to.' There was higher risk of infection in a field. Higher risk of injury and death, but if the dairyman said it was too late to move the cow, it probably was.

'I've tried a normal delivery. It's not happening. Even if she wasn't breech, the calf's too big.'

Phoebe didn't argue with him. She knew they'd have tried everything before calling her. Sometimes she wished farmers didn't try quite so hard and leave things quite so long before calling her out, but she knew why they did. The difference between breaking even and making a profit these days was narrower than it had ever been before.

Thankfully there was a full moon and Phoebe could hear the diesel thrum of a tractor, the harsh glare of its headlights shining out in the dark, so she wasn't expected to work by moonlight, then. Phew! As they got closer, Phoebe heard her patient too. A low desperate mooing. She was tied to a gate and there was someone holding her head too. A slim figure silhouetted against the bars who she realised was Sarah Mansfield, the owner of the farm. The cow was on her feet but her head was low and every so often she let out a heartbreaking groan.

'OK, I just need to check progress.' Phoebe barked instructions as she opened her vet bag, and pulled on gloves. 'Can you get her moved round into the light and hold her tail aside?'

'You're wasting your time,' the dairyman replied, doing as she asked with bad grace.

Phoebe didn't doubt he was right, but experience had taught her always to check. It was possible a farmer had misread a situation and she wasn't about to carry out a C-section in the middle of a field unless it was absolutely essential.

'Let her get on with it, Daniel.' Sarah spoke for the first time. 'Thanks for coming out so quick, lovey.'

Phoebe acknowledged the farmer with a grateful nod. But a few minutes later she'd confirmed that on this occasion Sarah's dairyman was right. There was no way this calf was coming out the normal way. Even if it hadn't been breech, it was big.

She could feel sweat pouring down her forehead, despite the coolness of the night. She wished Seth, her ex-boss and mentor, was here. But even Seth would have seen this situation as a challenge.

'You're up for this, though?' Daniel asked her gruffly and Phoebe could hear the doubt in his voice. 'You've done them before?'

'Of course she's done them before,' Sarah Mansfield spoke firmly. 'I bet you've done dozens, haven't you, Phoebe?'

'I've done them before,' Phoebe said, getting out a local anaesthetic from her bag and administering several shots to her patient in the area she wanted to numb. The truth was she'd done two, and both of them had been carried out in nicely lit, dry stables. The first had been as a student vet and the second had been when she'd assisted Seth, who'd had years of experience with big animals.

The weight of responsibility hung heavy. If this went wrong, both the cow and the calf would die. It wasn't going to go wrong. Sweat poured in her eyes and she wiped it away.

'Do you need her on the ground?' Sarah asked.

'No, she's fine on her feet. We just need to give that a few minutes to take effect.'

'This cow'll be dead in a few minutes,' Daniel said unhelpfully. 'We haven't got time to mess about waiting for things to take effect.'

'While we're waiting, we can shift her into the right position so she's side on to the lights,' Phoebe told him. 'I need to be able to see exactly what I'm doing. I'll need you to scrub in too and help me. And I need somewhere clean to open the C-section kit. We need to keep this as sterile as possible.'

Daniel did as he was bid, more amenable now he had something to do. They both scrubbed up and donned gowns and Phoebe shaved off a large area of hair on the cow's skin, through which she would make the incision, and scrubbed it with iodine.

She left it as long as she dared before making the cut. Thank God for fast-acting anaesthetics. The cow was distressed enough but she wouldn't feel a thing with the amount of anaesthetic that had just gone in. Act confident, Phoebe, she told herself. Acting confident and being bold was half the battle. It helped both the client and their animals to trust you if they thought you knew exactly what you were doing.

At least going in from the side there was room to work – the trick now was to get the calf out and the cow stitched up again as quickly as possible. The faster this happened, the less chance there was of a problem. Working mainly by feel, Phoebe found the outline of the hooves, and the bulk of the calf in its amniotic sac. She freed them quickly, the next problem was getting a good grip, as amniotic fluid spewed everywhere. Then it was a matter of strength. Pulling the calf out was a two-person job and time was of the essence. No way could she do it alone.

She shouted instructions at Daniel and to her huge relief he didn't argue. But even with two of them tugging on a foot each, it was a tough call. Big calf, small space. They could not fail now. Phoebe knew that fear powered them both as they hauled together to bring the baby out of its sanctuary and into the night. For a few terrible seconds, she thought it wasn't going to happen. Then, with one huge final effort, the calf was finally out and onto the ground. It was moving, that was something.

'Is it OK?' She was only half aware of Sarah bending over the black and white newborn, its tongue lolling from its mouth, as she turned her attention back to the mother and the placenta. 'The quicker I get this out and her stitched back up, the less chance of infection. Daniel, I need your help here, please. We're not finished yet.'

Again, he followed her instructions to the letter, holding the heavy uterus in place while she stitched, his face a study of concentration. They were both sweating profusely despite the chill night air.

'It's a fine bull calf.' She heard Sarah's voice tinged with pride and full of relief. 'Well done, Phoebe, I was worried there for a minute.'

'You and me both. But we did it.' Phoebe swallowed her elation – she didn't want to tempt fate – and focused on stitching. 'I hope she takes to him. They don't always bond so well after a caesarean. Sarah, can you milk her – the calf needs the colostrum and the quicker we can get it into him the better.'

She'd seen the vet doing a caesarean in *The Yorkshire Vet* on Channel Five. That had been in a nice warm stable, well lit and clean. A world away from a muddy midnight field. The Yorkshire

Vet had said afterwards that his mission was to stitch up the mother before her calf had managed to get to its feet for the first time. This wasn't a bad ambition, Phoebe thought, redoubling her efforts, as Sarah huddled beneath the cow to milk her.

And in fact, Phoebe was only just behind him. Mum was stitched up and sluiced with antibiotic spray by the time the calf was staggering around attempting to find out how his legs worked.

Now, finally, Phoebe felt the wave of elation and the pure joy of a safe delivery as she looked at the bull calf. Euphoria rose in her as she turned towards the old dairyman whose face had transformed from grumpy and sceptical into an expression of wonder, and his eyes were full of new respect. 'Well done, Daniel. Good job.'

He nodded, acknowledging the praise. 'I think I'll try and get them both across to the barn if I can,' he said, looking up at the sky which was still inky black. 'Just so I can keep an eye on her for a day or two.'

'You need any help?' Sarah asked.

'No, you go on. I'm in no rush.'

'Phoebe, you'd better come in and have a sluice down,' Sarah said, wrinkling her nose. 'I can't have you going off in that state. Not after you've just saved the life of my best cow.'

Everyone laughed and Phoebe knew it wasn't just her, they were all high on adrenaline. Despite the fact that she was freezing cold, covered in gunk and stunk to high heaven, she didn't think she had ever felt so happy. As she followed Sarah back towards the farm-house, she saw that the sky was just starting to lighten in the east. Grey streaks were painted across a charcoal backdrop and the stars were beginning to fade.

Soon, another day would be starting. She'd be expected to be at the surgery, bright eyed and bushy tailed, sorting out dogs and cats' annual vaccinations and injured paws. Giving advice on neutering and diet. She wondered how Archie's guinea pig was doing. There had been no more messages from him. But then she doubted that Violet's delivery would involve the high drama of the last couple of hours.

Hopefully not, anyway.

By the time she'd showered off in a downstairs wet room in the farmhouse, gratefully borrowed a spare jumper from Sarah and gulped down a mug of tea that had helped to defrost her fingers, the sky was almost fully light. She diverted back to the barn to check the calf had bonded with its mother and was pleased to hear from Daniel that he had. She knew there was no point in going back to bed, even for an hour. She might as well head home, grab another change of clothes, pour a bucketload of coffee down her neck and then drive to the surgery for an early start.

* * *

At Beechbrook Estate, at more or less the same time as Phoebe left for work, Rufus Holt was summoned by Archie to witness the miracle of Violet's brand-new family of five.

Having only just eaten his breakfast, he was rather relieved he hadn't been summoned to witness the miracle of birth. Archie had, apparently, been overseeing that bit since 6.30 a.m.

'How did you know she was so close to having them anyway?' he asked his son as they stood by the guinea pig hutch. 'Were they due this morning?'

'Giving birth isn't an exact science, Dad. But I did know they were due soon. Phoebe confirmed that yesterday. So I've been checking them every few hours.'

'At night-time as well? That's keen.'

'I checked them at midnight – then Emilia checked them at five thirty and she spotted the signs and alerted me.'

'Archie, what were you doing up at midnight?' Rufus berated. 'You should have been asleep.'

'It's the holidays, Dad. Besides I was too excited to sleep.'

'And it's not Emilia's job to be getting up at five thirty to check on guinea pigs. She's here to look after you, not be on call all hours of the day and night.'

'Emilia doesn't mind. She gets up early anyway. She likes it.'

Rufus made a mental note to ask her about this, but Archie was way too excited to look even slightly chastened now. He was pointing into the hutch. 'Look, Dad, mother and babies are all fine. Although I'm not sure what sex they are – I might need your help with that, Dad. Jack says that guinea pigs can mate at a very young age, often with the siblings and they need to be separated promptly. Otherwise, it can all go wrong. Interbreeding isn't recommended. Do you think we should try and find out now, Dad?'

'I think we've probably got a bit of time,' Rufus said, alarmed. 'They're only a couple of hours old, aren't they?'

Archie frowned. 'Yes, that's true. We should be OK for a while, I should think. Do you think I should get Phoebe out to check them over?'

'No, I don't,' Rufus said. 'They all look fine.'

He was feeling guilty enough about Phoebe already. It had been lovely of her to come out to see Violet yesterday. He'd planned to thank her properly when he'd seen her last night.

'I think she'd like to see them, though.' Archie had his most pleading expression on. 'We could invite her over to wet the babies' heads, couldn't we?'

'I think that tradition is more for real babies than guinea pigs, son.'

Archie's face fell and Rufus thought, what the hell? It would be great to see Phoebe later. She was always telling him to be more spur of the moment.

Maybe for once he should follow his son's lead and do something totally spontaneous.

'I'll definitely call her,' he told Archie.

5

By the time Jenna, her vet nurse, and Marcus arrived – both of them tended to get in early – Phoebe had already been at work for an hour and a half.

'You look tired,' Jenna said, eyeing her keenly, as she shrugged off her coat, hung it on a hook and tucked her lunchbox in its place under her desk.

Jenna had two kids of fourteen and twelve, and she said while she was doing their lunch boxes, she might as well do one for herself. She was incredibly efficient, but also warm and down to earth and had once worked for Seth at the Marchwood Practice.

When Phoebe had first opened Puddleduck Vets, there had just been her and Jenna, with Maggie doing part-time reception cover.

Phoebe knew she would have been lost without Jenna, who aside from Maggie was the oldest member of her team. Jenna was forty-six and didn't look it, but she was one of those people who seemed to have a natural inbuilt wisdom.

'You look like you've been up all night,' Marcus added, glancing at Phoebe.

'Was it a hot date with Rufus?' Jenna quipped. 'Weren't you seeing him last night?'

'Actually, it was a hot date with a cow at Middlebrook Farm,' Phoebe said, not wanting to admit Rufus had cancelled. She told them about the C-section, adding as an aside, 'I think that experience has to go down as one of the most stressful events of my life. But it was also amazing when we got the calf out. I don't think that will ever get old – helping to birth an animal.'

'Rather you than me,' Jenna said. 'I bet it was freezing.'

'It wasn't too bad. I was too stressed to be cold. Not to mention the fact that it's physically really hard work. To be honest, I wouldn't have coped without the help of the dairyman. I worry about that sometimes. Not being physically strong enough for the job.'

As she spoke, Max came in through the door. 'Morning, all. What aren't you strong enough for, Phoebe?'

She told him and he shrugged. 'I wouldn't worry. I think getting a calf out's a two-person job however you look at it. And at least you have height on your side.'

'That's what Seth always says. He was a jockey, before he was a vet,' she told Max, who hadn't yet met Seth face to face.

'If you're worried, you could join a gym and do some upper body training,' Jenna offered.

'Yes, I'll just slot in a few gym sessions in my spare time. In between work, keeping an eye on what my grandmother is up to, and having a life,' Phoebe said. Wow, she must be tired, she didn't usually do sarcasm. 'Sorry,' she added quickly.

'Fair point, though,' Jenna said, unfazed. 'And talking of Maggie, isn't she back today?'

'Has she been away?' Max looked surprised.

'She's been on a canal boat break with Eddie,' Marcus told him. Marcus knew everything that was going on at Puddleduck Pets, partly because he talked to Natasha a lot, and partly because he had a photographic memory and never forgot anything that anyone told him.

'Yes, they've been WhatsApping me photos,' Phoebe said. 'Or at least Eddie's been WhatsApping me photos. Maggie is still of the opinion that mobile phones are the spawn of the devil. But Eddie's quite a keen photographer.'

He might be keen but he definitely needed some practice. Most of his pictures were slightly out-of-focus shots of pints of beer.

The phone rang and Marcus answered it. 'Puddleduck Vets, how can I help you?'

He listened to what sounded like an extended tirade before saying, 'Of course, sir, I'll see if she's available now.'

He put the phone on hold. 'It's that Mr B fellow again, Phoebe, do you want to talk to him? Or shall I tell him you'll phone him back?'

'No, it's fine, I'll talk to him.'

Phoebe still felt as though she was buzzing. After the dramatic events of the night, talking to a new customer about a couple of Kunekune pigs should be a walk in the park.

She took the phone from Marcus. 'Phoebe Dashwood here. Who am I talking to, please?'

'My name is Mr B,' said a rather more cultured voice than she'd been expecting. 'Am I talking to the head vet of the Puddleduck Practice?'

'Head vet and owner,' Phoebe said peaceably. 'How can I help?'

'Ahhhh.' He let out what sounded like a purr of relief. 'Allow me to introduce myself. I'm an award-winning chef and I'll be moving into the New Forest in June on a temporary contract in order to assist an hotel to gain a Michelin star. I'd like to clarify one or two things if I may? Do you have time now?'

'I have a few minutes.'

'That should suffice. First and foremost, I'd like to confirm that you don't film your consultations, not just the ones on your premises, where of course you'd be perfectly at liberty to film if you wished – that being your property and where possibly you might have to do it for insurance reasons – but I'd also like to confirm that you wouldn't ever on any occasion film or record a callout to a client.'

Phoebe hesitated.

'Ah-ha,' said Mr B. 'It appears that it's a good job I asked. There might be an occasion, might there?'

'I can't think of an occasion where we would film or record a callout to a client's property,' Phoebe said quickly. 'We certainly wouldn't film any consultation at the practice. Let me reassure you about that. For one thing we don't have the means.'

'You don't have CCTV?'

'Well, yes, we do have CCTV on the premises, but it wouldn't be used to record clients once inside the practice. It's more for security purposes.'

'Could it be switched off when I have an appointment?' he asked.

'Um.' Phoebe was slightly taken aback. 'I suppose so.' She glanced at Marcus who was looking at her with raised eyebrows and a rather smug 'I told you so' expression on his face.

'I don't think we've actually registered you as a client, have we?'

'Not yet,' Mr B swept on regally. 'I have not yet confirmed my wishes to be registered with your practice.'

'That's very true,' Phoebe conceded. She wasn't sure whether to cut the conversation short straight away and tell him they weren't taking on any new clients – Mr B might well be a step beyond eccentric even for her liking – or to humour him. She decided on the latter. It seemed a bit mean to cut him off before she'd actually heard him out. She'd promised him a few minutes and luckily her first appointment wasn't for a while.

'I understand you have Kunekune pigs,' she said.

'You understand correctly. Portia and Percy.' His voice both softened and warmed up a shade as he said their names. 'I do hope you'll forgive me for being something of an aristarch, but I've learned that there are numerous ninnyhammers, morosophs and zounderkites in the veterinary profession – and indeed every profession – so I probably err on the side of overcaution.'

'Overcaution is preferable to being slapdash,' Phoebe said, picking up on one of the few words that made sense in his last sentence. 'I prefer clients to be overcautious when it comes to their animals.'

'Then we are in agreement. Fabulous.' His voice warmed up another two shades. 'I'm extremely fond of Portia and Percy.' He paused. 'Question number two: are you au fait, as it were, with common Kunekune ailments?'

Oh, lord, were they only on question two? Phoebe wondered how many there were as she glanced at the practice clock. Marcus had given up listening and was tapping something into the computer system.

Max and Jenna had disappeared into the consulting room at the other end of the surgery.

'I'm not an expert,' Phoebe admitted, 'but I have a working knowledge and if I was to see a patient where I was unsure about a diagnosis, I do have many resources to go to and of course there is always the option of a second opinion or a referral to a specialist.'

'Excellent,' said Mr B. 'In that case, I would like to register Portia and Percy as patients. Can I do that with you?'

'Er, yes,' she said, relieved that there did only appear to be two questions after all. She took him through the process, noting down name, age, breed, weight and previous medical history of his animals, all of which he had off pat.

'Thank you, very much, Ms Dashwood. I don't need to book an

appointment now. I won't be moving into the area until June, so I will say au revoir for the time being.'

'Mr B, I'm also going to need your full name and address,' Phoebe said swiftly before he could hang up.

'I'm afraid that kind of information has to stay confidential. To guard against identity theft, you see. They don't need much these days. They can hack into systems from afar and before you can say zounderkite – they know everything about you.'

'Who can?'

'The Chinese. They get in via cameras, record systems, mobile phones, where there's a WiFi there's a way. Therefore, I wouldn't want anything on record about myself. Just the barest minimum. As a precaution.'

'A precaution,' Phoebe echoed uncertainly.

'Exactly that. I could take you through it if you like – how it's done. I have considerable expertise – I've studied the subject at length. Would you like to hear?'

'No. That's fine. I won't put your name and address,' Phoebe interrupted hastily. 'I'll just put your phone number down if that's acceptable? So we have some details on our system, and can confirm it's you, should you need to make an appointment.'

'I suppose that's acceptable,' Mr B agreed. 'Should we have a code word?'

Code word? Was he serious? Phoebe kept expecting him to say that this whole call had been a wind-up and for him to burst out laughing. Or for his voice to morph into the voice of her brother, Frazier. It was the kind of phone call he might make for a laugh, but neither of those things happened.

'I don't think a code word's necessary,' she told him. 'We have you registered, Mr B.' She thanked him and finished the call before he could get going on another rant.

'Phew,' she said, as she put the phone down and Marcus spun around lazily in his office chair.

'Told you he was bonkers, didn't I? Did he mention the Chinese by any chance?'

'He did. And a few words I've never heard before. What's a zounderkite when it's at home?'

'A bumbling idiot,' Marcus said promptly. 'It's Victorian. Did he say, "Where there's a Wi-Fi there's a way?"'

'Yes, he did. How do you know what zounderkite means?'

'Retaining useless information is my superpower. I think I heard it in a quiz once.'

'Remind me to ask you if I ever need a quiz partner.'

'I will, boss.'

Phoebe blinked. She felt gritty-eyed and she could see her first client, complete with a white pug, on the other side of the glass door. Then it opened and all thoughts of crazy Kunekune owners were swept away as the day progressed.

At lunchtime Phoebe had a text from Rufus.

Five guinea pigs have arrived safe and sound. PS Any chance you fancy a celebration drink out later – if you're not too busy?

Fantastic news. Never too busy for a celebration drink.

Great. Would you like to come by at seven for a look at the GPs first?

Absolutely.

His message powered her through the afternoon. She felt tired – missing a night's sleep wasn't as easy as she remembered it being when she'd been in her twenties – but she could catch up tonight, and she was really looking forward to seeing Rufus and Archie and hearing all the details about the baby guinea pigs. She bet Archie was full of it.

Max and Marcus had left for the day, Jenna was packing up her things and Phoebe was just about to lock up – it was five past six – when she saw a figure approaching the glass doors of the practice at great speed. Her heart sank. People only ever rushed like that if it was an emergency.

Suppressing a sigh, she opened the door wide to allow them access and realised with a little shock that the tall dark-haired figure in the wax jacket was familiar. It was Sam Hendrie, one of her oldest friends, and his face was grim. He was carrying a cat box. Through the grating-style front cover, Phoebe caught a glimpse of black fur.

'Oh, Sam, what's happened? Is it Snowball?' He'd had that cat for years, no wonder he looked serious.

He nodded, clearly out of breath. 'Yes. I'm sorry not to ring, Phoebe, I just wanted to get him here as quick as possible. I think he's been hit by a car.' On the last words, his voice cracked a little and Phoebe felt her heart go out to him.

'Bring him in. Let's have a look at him. Try not to worry.'

She ushered him through to the consulting room, switching the lights back on as they went.

6

Jenna appeared at the door. 'Do you need me to stay?'

Phoebe glanced at her gratefully. 'Yes, please – I think I might.'

Jenna nodded, and without a word of complaint took off her coat, while Sam put the cat box on the examining table and gently lifted out the fluffy black cat. Snowball was panting and there was blood on the side of his face.

Phoebe examined him quickly and carefully and felt her anxiety growing. Apart from the obvious injuries to his face – he'd cut his jaw and lost a couple of teeth – Snowball had all the telltale signs of a traffic accident: scuffed claws and, to her concern, pale gums. Although there were no immediately obvious fractures, she was pretty sure that he had internal damage.

'I think you're right about the car accident,' she said, finishing her initial examination and looking up into Sam's worried blue eyes. 'Sam, I'm not sure about the extent of his injuries but I have to warn you it doesn't look that good. I'm going to give him some pain relief.'

Jenna held the cat while she sorted that out, and Sam rubbed his forehead and swore softly. 'Thank you. He never usually goes on the road. He's got such a big garden to play in.'

Phoebe knew. Sam had bought the maisonette he lived in because of its hugely long tree-filled garden. Sam preferred the outdoors to being inside – he was a keen horseman and was happiest when he was either riding his horse, Ninja, in the New Forest or pottering outside in his garden.

'Have you any idea when it happened?' Phoebe asked him.

'No. He was hunched up by the cat flap when I got in from work. I don't know how long he'd been there. If only I'd come in earlier.'

'Sam, don't beat yourself up. It may have happened five minutes before you got there.'

'I hope so.' Sam stroked Snowball's head, with gentle, slightly trembling fingers.

Inside, Phoebe could feel herself trembling too. She knew how much this cat meant to Sam and she had a feeling it was going to take a miracle to save him.

'Cats are a law unto themselves,' Jenna said in that lovely calm way she had which was such a balm with both owners and pets alike. 'Ours have a big garden to play in too but they still occasionally go out on the road. You can't keep them locked up, can you? It wouldn't be fair.'

'No.' Sam shoved his hands in his pockets. He was clearly struggling. His Adam's apple bobbed as briefly he turned away.

Phoebe gave him a few moments to gather himself before saying softly, 'I'm going to do an ultrasound and X-ray which will give us a bit more information. But he's not in pain at the moment, Sam. That's a good thing. Would you like to sit in the waiting room?'

He nodded and turned away and when he'd closed the door, Phoebe looked at Jenna and shook her head slightly.

'You're thinking internal damage?' Jenna said quietly.

'He's certainly bleeding inside and I'm a bit worried he may have fractured his pelvis. But we won't write him off just yet, eh?'

'Are you sure you're up for this? You didn't sleep last night, did you? Shall I call Max?'

'No, I think we need to move quickly. I'm fine, Jenna. Really.'

* * *

In the waiting room, Sam sat on an uncomfortable green plastic chair and put his head in his hands. It was some time since he'd seen Phoebe and he wished it were in happier circumstances. He had known her forever and she had been one of his closest friends for as long as he could remember. Their mothers were close friends too, and had been before they were even born, both women working in the small market town of Bridgeford on the banks of the River Avon at the edge of the New Forest.

Sam's mother, Jan, owned and ran Hendrie's, the village post office and stores, where Sam also worked, and Phoebe's mother, Louella Dashwood, was a teacher at the local school.

Sam, Phoebe and her younger brother Frazier, and Tori, who was still Phoebe's best friend, had lived a stone's throw apart from each other since the year dot.

They'd all gone to the same first and middle school and they'd all played together, building camps and tramping around on Puddleduck Farm – back when it had been a dairy farm, populated by dozens of gentle Friesians and owned and run by Phoebe's grandparents, Farmer Pete and the indomitable Maggie Crowther.

Farmer Pete was gone now but Sam's memories were of a gruff but kind man, and Maggie Crowther was still every bit as tough and determined as she had always been.

In those long-ago golden days of childhood, the sun had always been shining and the sky had always been blue – or at least that's how Sam remembered it. They were days that stood out as being amongst the happiest in his memory.

Life had played out in a halcyon bubble of warmth and safety within the confines of the farm where there was freedom yet also firm boundaries and as they got older the forest became part of their playground too so they could stretch their wings and fly without danger.

Both Maggie and Farmer Pete were of the opinion that children shouldn't be mollycoddled too much but allowed to make the occasional mistake – scraped knees, stinging nettle fingers and torn filthy clothes had all been shrugged off as occupational hazards. The only time Sam could remember them getting into real trouble was when they'd decided to have a picnic in a field of cows. That time, Farmer Pete had come charging over with a shotgun, threatening to shoot them for trespassing. Phoebe had sworn blind that he hadn't realised it was them, but Sam had been certain he had known and had just wanted to frighten the living daylights out of them so they'd never do it again and risk getting trampled by a herd of cows. He'd certainly succeeded there. They hadn't ever gone wandering about in the cow fields again without asking.

Phoebe hadn't been scared of animals even then. She had always wanted to be a vet and she'd had the drive and academic brilliance to do it. Sam had watched in awe as she'd pursued her dream with a dogged determination and he hadn't been a bit surprised when she'd got into the London Vet School and then qualified with a first-class honours degree. He'd been thrilled for her, even though he knew their lives were destined to diverge.

Besides, the fact they would tread very different paths had been clear since they were kids. Sam wasn't daft but he'd never been academic and ambitious like Phoebe. They were totally different.

Sam was a 'content with his lot' kind of person while his best friend would always be aiming for the stars and beyond.

The door opened, interrupting his thoughts, and jolting him back from the past. Sam stood up hastily, unsure of how long he'd been sitting there. Long enough for his legs to have stiffened up he realised as he stumbled slightly, but when he looked at the clock, he was amazed to see it had been nearly an hour.

He'd always been an expert at reading faces and he knew at once that it wasn't good news.

Phoebe came across the room and touched his arm. 'I'm afraid Snowball is quite badly injured, Sam. I think he has a ruptured liver which has caused some bleeding inside and he also has a fractured pelvis. I think I can sort out the liver, but the pelvis is more difficult. There's not much we can do for a fractured pelvis except give it the time to heal. That would mean he'd have to be kept still – or at least contained, most likely in a crate, for several weeks in order to allow the time for it to heal.'

Sam nodded, images of his beautiful exuberant cat flooding through his mind. Snowball wasn't and never had been a house cat. Sometimes he disappeared for days, out hunting, mousing, whatever cats did and only occasionally checking in for meals. Sometimes when Sam got in, he'd meet him at the front door, winding around his legs, meowing a greeting. Other times he wouldn't bother.

Sam lived in a maisonette with stairs from the ground floor that led up to his flat door, so it meant the cat wouldn't even be able to be outside in a crate, although that in itself might be tortuous for him – seeing the great outdoors through bars but not able to be part of it.

Sam hesitated and Phoebe said softly. 'How old is Snowball now?'

'Thirteen,' he answered.

'And he's had a very good life.' There was a pause. 'It's up to you, Sam. Some owners may opt to have an animal put to sleep in these circumstances. Getting him well again is a huge amount of effort and commitment. It might be different if you were at home all day, but I know that you work full time. And then some,' she added softly.

She was right there. He worked nine till five at Hendrie's and he spent the rest of his time teaching at the stables or looking after his own horse, Ninja. Generally speaking, Sam was in his own flat purely for the odd meal and to sleep.

A little like Snowball.

Sam knew that Phoebe was giving him a get-out clause and that if he took it she wouldn't judge him. And he loved her for that.

'But you can fix the liver and if we could get him through the fracture he would be totally OK again?' he asked, meeting her hazel eyes. 'He wouldn't be lame or anything?'

'No promises, but yes, I think we can fix the liver and yes, I think he would be fine as long as the fracture healed properly. Shall I give you a few moments to think about it?'

Sam thrust his hands deep in his pockets. 'No. I don't need to think about it. I want you to do it. I know the recuperation bit will be difficult, but I'll manage. It's not as though I live very far from work. I can pop back at regular intervals and Ma would help. Pa too, probably, he's out and about. In fact, thinking about it, I could probably put Snowball in a crate at the back of the shop.' He was thinking on his feet now. 'It'll be quiet enough there and we've got a tiny bit of yard out the back. We could probably make that secure with netting so he's got a bit of outside space and he can see the sky. Do you think cats need to see the sky?' He looked at her, noticing for the first time the dark shadows beneath her eyes. She looked exhausted. 'Are you OK to do it, Phoebe? You look tired out?'

'I had a late-night calving,' she told him. 'But yes, I'm fine.' A new light flickered in her eyes and Sam realised it was relief. She'd been expecting him to say no. She'd thought he'd be put off by the commitment.

'Then I'd like you to operate,' Sam said firmly. 'And thank you, Phoebe.'

'You can thank me later,' she said lightly, turning to go. 'You don't need to wait, Sam. I can phone you if there are any updates. And I'll let you know how it went as soon as we're done.'

* * *

To Phoebe's huge relief, Snowball's injuries weren't as extensive as she'd feared. The tear in his liver was small and she was able to fix it and there was no reason to suspect it wouldn't heal very nicely. The fracture should heal too, given enough time and care.

As she and Jenna lifted him carefully into a preprepared night crate where he could recuperate and gently come round, she let out a small sigh of relief.

'I think he's been very lucky,' she said to Jenna. 'Another couple of centimetres and his liver would have been past repair.'

'He's very lucky to have Sam as an owner, that's for sure. Did you tell him what he was taking on?'

'Yes, he knows. I was very clear about it. It sounds as though he can take Snowball into work with him, so he'll be able to keep a close eye on him.'

'Sam's a friend of yours, isn't he?' Jenna asked curiously.

'Yes, I've known him all my life. He's a great guy. I've always loved him. Not in that way,' she added hastily. 'I mean that we're mates. Very good mates.'

'Yes, well, you've got the sexy lord of the manor.' Jenna winked.

'Tall, dark and handsome and heir to a title and a grand estate. It would be difficult to top that.'

'Oh, my God, Rufus.' Phoebe's hand shot to her mouth and she swore. 'I'd planned to go round and see Archie's guinea pigs at seven and I completely forget to tell him I wouldn't be there. I need to go and phone him. Are you OK to clean up?'

'Of course I am. It's part of my job description, isn't it? Mopping up mess.' Jenna smiled. 'What are we doing about post-op checks and overnight checks on Snowball?'

'I'll stay here at the farmhouse. Maggie should be back by now. Although I'm surprised she hasn't been down here already making a nuisance of herself.' Phoebe chuckled to soften her words. 'That way I can keep an eye on him through the evening and I can set my alarm for the night-time checks.'

Jenna paused midway between the operating table and the sink. 'Phoebe, are you sure? You were up most of last night. Could we not ask Seth's practice for help – they might have someone on night duty at Marchwood.'

'No, it's fine. They're half an hour away and I'm quite happy staying over here. I'm very good at sleeping in short bursts. And I'm on call anyway. On Thursday I'm handing over to Max. I am so looking forward to that. It's Easter so chances are he'll be busy.'

Phoebe never had quite got her head around the fact that vets – like hospital A&Es – tended to be busier over the holiday times, but they often were. Maybe it was simply the fact that humans tended to be up and about so they noticed if anything cropped up with their pets.

Leaving Jenna to clear up, she changed out of her work clothes and went to find her phone. There were two missed calls and a voicemail from Rufus, which said, 'Phoebe, I'm guessing you must have had an emergency call. But if you happen to pick this up, I'm taking Archie to the Jugged Hare for our celebration drink. Meet us there if you can. We'll probably be there an hour or so.'

He'd left the message at seven twenty. It was now just gone half nine. Phoebe phoned Sam and updated him as she'd promised. It was lovely to hear the relief in his voice. Then, because she wanted to speak to Rufus out of earshot of Jenna, she left Puddleduck Vets and walked round to the farmhouse.

7

As Phoebe approached, she could see several of the lights were on, sending squares of warm light out into the night. They included Maggie's bedroom light, which probably meant Maggie and Eddie were back then. She was pleased. Not that Maggie would have minded if Phoebe had made use of the spare bedroom Natasha wasn't using.

Puddleduck farmhouse had always been her second home. But it would be lovely to see her. It had only been ten days since Maggie and Eddie had set off on their canal boat holiday, but it seemed much longer than that.

Phoebe hesitated beside the corner of the building. Close to the back door and standing there in the shadows, she hooked out her phone and dialled Rufus. It went straight to voicemail. He was either on another call or he had no signal. She redialled a couple of times with the same result and on the third time she left him a message.

'Rufus, I'm so sorry. I feel terrible about letting you and Archie down. Please can you apologise to him too? I had an emergency and

I ended up in the operating theatre. I'll phone you back soon – or if you pick this up maybe you can call me.'

Her last few words were drowned out by a deluge of barking. The kitchen door opened and two dogs came hurtling around the corner in her direction. Strictly speaking, only one of them hurtled, and that was Tiny, Maggie's Irish wolfhound. The other one's gait could be described as more of a brisk hobble. That was Buster, who was so ancient and arthritic that Phoebe was convinced he was only still alive by the sheer force of his will.

Both of them stopped barking when they saw her and set up a tail-wagging duet instead, their tails banging against the brick walls of the house, which Phoebe stopped quickly because every time Tiny did that, he ended up injuring his tail and making it bleed copiously.

Close behind them she saw the diminutive figure of her grandmother wielding a baseball bat and a torch. 'Who's there? Show yourself or I'll set the dogs on you.'

'It's a bit late for that,' Phoebe called out. 'If I was a proper intruder, they'd have already torn me limb from limb.'

'Good dogs. That's their job.' Maggie shone the torch at her. 'What are you doing skulking around out there? Why didn't you just come in?'

'I was on my way. I just wanted to phone Rufus.' Phoebe shook her head. 'I've been doing emergency surgery on a cat. It's a long story.'

'Well, come and tell it to me inside. It's too cold to stand around gossiping out here.'

Despite her brusque words, Phoebe could hear the warmth in her grandmother's voice and she felt unexpectedly emotional.

'I've really missed you, Gran.'

'I've only been away for five minutes. And don't call me Gran.

You know it makes me feel old. Come in, love. I can't see you properly out here.'

A few moments later, both dogs and humans had gone back through the wooden stable-style back door that led indoors. The wonderful Aga warmth of the farmhouse kitchen wrapped Phoebe in a huge hug that felt almost human. With its flagstone floors and Welsh dresser and its great solid oak table that was too heavy to move so had been in the same place for ever, Puddleduck Farm kitchen was as familiar and as comforting as a mother's arms. It was a warm balm of a kitchen. Gloriously cosy, despite its generous size. Phoebe longed for a hot chocolate with marshmallows, which was her latest comfort food.

Reading her mind, Maggie said, 'I've got some hot chocolate if you fancy it? Or do you need something stronger? An Irish coffee maybe? Eddie and I have been having one as a nightcap before we go to bed. It's a bad habit we picked up on our trip that I'd like to continue.'

'I'm on call so I'd better not have whisky, but I'd love a hot chocolate.' Phoebe pulled out a chair at the farmhouse table and sat down while her grandmother went to the fridge, got out a carton of milk and poured it into a small pan which she put on the Aga hob.

'Is Eddie still here?'

'No, he's gone off back to his son's. I said he could stay, but he was adamant he went back to Jonathan's – he doesn't agree with living in sin.'

'How did that work on the canal boat?' Phoebe asked. 'Did you have separate rooms? Separate boats even? I thought barges were quite small and intimate.'

'Never you mind what we did on the canal boat – they're not called barges, you were right the first time – that's between ourselves.'

Phoebe suppressed a giggle. Five minutes of her grandmother's company and she felt so much better already. The exhaustion, the intense focus and the rollercoaster of emotion of the last twenty-four hours, all of them felt as though they were retreating. Backing off like morning mist when confronted with midday sunshine.

Maggie came across to the table and put two mugs in front of them. Phoebe saw hers had tiny pink and white marshmallows floating in it and her grandmother's was topped with cream. She caught a waft of whisky fumes across the table.

'Thank you,' she said, and for no reason she could put her finger on, she felt tears gathering at the backs of her eyes. The emotion hadn't held off long then.

'My, my,' said Maggie, who missed nothing, 'you really are tired out. Or has something happened? Is everything OK with your Rufus?'

'Yes, I think so. Well, apart from the fact that we keep having to cancel our plans.' Phoebe brought her up to date on what had been going on and Maggie smiled as she heard about Archie's guinea pig project and the midnight calving and then frowned when she heard about Snowball.

'Sam would never have had that cat put to sleep,' she commented. 'You do know that, don't you?'

'I think I did. But he's got so much on his plate – I didn't want him to feel pressurised. It really is going to be quite a tough call getting Snowball healthy and fit again. I remember we had a client once before in London whose cat had similar injuries from an RTA. It was a beautiful Burmese and they said they were happy to do the rest and recuperation thing, but the cat kept escaping – don't ask me how – and making the injury worse. In the end it took nearly a year to get it right again.'

'Sam's a man of integrity, though,' Maggie said, 'and highly committed. I don't imagine he's the kind of young man who'd mess about when it came to an animal's welfare.'

She sounded very sure of herself and Phoebe knew she was right. Sam wouldn't mess about – once he was set on a course of action, she didn't imagine much would deter him – and he was one of the few people she'd ever met who loved animals as much as she did. Lots of people said they loved animals but there was a limit on their love. In Phoebe's experience, it was usually a limit that was governed by either money or effort.

'Yes, I know he is,' Phoebe said quietly.

There was a gap in their conversation, filled by the sound of Buster's snoring and the ticking of water pipes in the old house and from somewhere outside the distant sound of a dog barking.

'I'd better go and check on my patient,' Phoebe said. 'I was planning to make use of your spare room if that's OK with you? Then I can keep an eye on him through the night.'

'Of course it's OK. You never need to ask.' Maggie sipped her Irish coffee, wiped off a moustache of cream with her index finger, and eyed Phoebe over the rim of her mug, her hazel eyes a mirror image of her granddaughter's. 'I'll not be going to bed before midnight. I want to catch up on some paperwork for the sanctuary. Natasha said there were a few emails that needed my attention when I spoke to her. I can do a couple of checks for you later if you like? Then you can go and get your head down.'

'Get you and your emails,' Phoebe teased. 'Since when did you even know what an email looked like?'

'You cheeky mare.' Maggie took a mock swipe across the table which Phoebe deftly ducked. 'Eddie's been giving me some lessons. He's an expert emailer – amongst other things which we won't mention.' She looked shifty and didn't elaborate and Phoebe resisted the temptation to ask. Not that Maggie would necessarily have given her any more details.

'Seriously though, thanks, Maggie.' Phoebe got up from the table. 'I'll go and check on Snowball now, make sure his vitals are

OK. But it would be lovely if you don't mind doing the later checks. I'll get up at 6 a.m. and do the early ones.'

'No need for that either. I'm sure Natasha will help. I'll give her a ring. She's here before six most days.'

Phoebe was about to protest that poor Natasha had been on 24/7 call for ages already when Maggie raised her hands, palms forward. 'No arguments. I'm happy to help. And grab yourself a sandwich and some soup before you go to bed. I bet you haven't eaten, have you? There's home-made soup in the freezer. It just needs defrosting.'

Phoebe went and checked Snowball, who was fine, and when she came back, she found that Maggie had already defrosted some soup in the microwave and it was now steaming in a sunshine-yellow bowl on the table with a chunk of warm bread topped with melting butter on a plate alongside it. The fragrance of smoked paprika, cinnamon and garlic hit her nostrils and her mouth watered. Her grandmother made amazing soup.

It wasn't the big dramatic gestures that made up love, Phoebe thought with a dart of realisation. It was the little things. Heating up a bowl of soup, offering to help with a sick cat, lying about staying up late to check emails. She was pretty sure that her grand-mother had no such plans. In fact, Phoebe was pretty sure that emails were still as much of a mystery to her as the planet Jupiter.

Maggie was now sitting down again at the table, the dogs sprawled around her feet. She was reading *New Forest Views*, which was the local free magazine, owned and edited by Phoebe's best friend Tori Williams.

For a while there was peace as Phoebe devoured the soup and the bread – she'd been much hungrier than she'd realised – and Maggie flicked through pages. She was the first to speak.

'How's Tori doing these days anyway? You haven't mentioned her much lately.'

'I haven't seen her much lately,' Phoebe admitted. Her friendship with Tori was another thing that had suffered since she'd been having a relationship with Rufus. There just weren't the hours in the day. Although this wasn't all down to her. Tori's job at the magazine also involved long hours and deadlines and was pretty full-on. Not to mention the fact that Tori was having a full-on romance with Harrison who just happened to be Rufus's groundsman and best friend.

Phoebe had thought when she'd started seeing Rufus that this might actually be an advantage – two best friends seeing two best friends. She'd thought they might end up doing couples evenings, meals or cinema visits. But this hadn't worked out as she'd hoped. Organising four busy people to be in the same place at the same time was even harder than organising two busy people.

'I think Tori's fine, though,' she told Maggie now. 'She's all loved up with her boyfriend.'

'It must be serious then,' Maggie remarked. 'I don't think I've ever known her go out with the same chap for more than six months.'

'You and me both. I keep expecting her to tell me he's proposed and rush round to show me her ring.'

'Can't women propose to men in these enlightened times?' Maggie asked idly.

'Yes, they can.' Phoebe had thought that herself, but she suspected that deep down Tori was more traditional than she let on. That was something else they had in common.

'I think I might go up to bed if that's OK,' she said. 'Are you sure you don't mind doing Snowball's late checks?'

'I wouldn't have offered if I did. Be off with you. If there are any problems, I'll wake you up. I promise.'

'Thank you.'

'It's no problem, love. Strolling over to the surgery will give me a break from sitting down looking at emails and getting that screen, um, burnout, tiredness thing from looking at a bright screen.' Her face went ever so slightly pink, Phoebe thought, or maybe that was just a trick of the light.

It was only when she was tucked up in bed, wearing one of her grandmother's old pairs of stripy pyjamas, which felt as if they were made of softest brushed cotton and smelled of fabric conditioner, that Phoebe realised that Rufus had never called back or even sent her a text message.

She contemplated trying to phone him again but decided against it. She was too exhausted to make much sense. She would apologise properly to him and Archie tomorrow. In a few days it would be Easter. She would make it up to them then and on Sunday they would all be going to her parents' for a family meal. She couldn't wait.

8

To Phoebe's huge relief, she didn't have another callout on Tuesday night and, even better, there were no problems with Snowball.

Sam came in, just after close of business on Wednesday, to collect him. 'Phoebe, I'm so grateful,' he said as they stood in the empty reception area with the fluffy black cat, safely inside the same cat basket he'd come in, nestling beside Sam's feet.

He got out his wallet. 'What do I owe you?'

Phoebe told him and he frowned. 'That seems awfully cheap considering it was an out of hours emergency.'

'Mates' rates,' she said, giving him a quick smile. Sam wasn't broke, but she knew he wasn't flush either. One of the reasons he taught kids to ride at Brook Stables where he kept Ninja was so he could subsidise his own horse's keep.

'I don't want you doing me any favours, Phoebe.' He looked at her sternly. 'Seriously, give me the full price. Otherwise, I'm paying double what you just told me.'

She upped the price a bit. That was so typical of Sam, wanting to pay his way. Wanting to do the right thing. A man of integrity, Maggie had called him. She was spot on about that.

'Get you, wanting to pay me double,' she quipped as he put his card in the machine on the front counter. 'What's going on? Have you met a rich woman?'

'That's for me to know and you to find out when we invite you to the wedding,' Sam said, keeping a totally straight face and then ruining it by winking.

'You have, haven't you? I can tell. You're blushing. You have met someone.'

'No one new,' he said cryptically, and she did a double take. She'd been half joking but there was definitely something in his eyes.

But however much she pushed him, he refused to say anything else. He asked about her Easter plans instead and she told him she was taking Rufus and Archie to meet her parents and have Sunday lunch.

'He's not met them yet then?' He sounded surprised.

'No, or at least not as my partner. Maggie's met him, of course.'

Rufus was Maggie's landlord. Well, technically, his father, Lord Alfred Holt, was her landlord, which in Maggie's eyes amounted to pretty much the same thing. Maggie owned Puddleduck Farmhouse and the outbuildings and some of the land, but she rented some of her acreage from the Holts.

Sam nodded and Phoebe couldn't read his expression. She knew he hadn't had a very high opinion of Rufus for years, considering him an elitist arrogant nob. Last year, due to a misunderstanding between the two men, things had deteriorated. There had been one drunken occasion which Phoebe knew Sam deeply regretted when he'd tried to start a fight with Rufus in a pub and had warned him off dating Phoebe, having claimed that he, Sam, was her boyfriend. This hadn't been true. Phoebe and Sam had only ever been friends, although there had been a time when Sam had wanted them to be more.

But since then, Sam had apologised and had done his best to make amends to Rufus. Sam might be prone to act on his emotions, but he always put his hands up and apologised when he was wrong.

'So what are you doing over Easter?' Phoebe asked Sam now in one last attempt to fish about his love life, but he didn't play ball.

'I think I'm going to have my work cut out taking care of this one here.' Sam indicated Snowball. 'As well as the usual routine.'

'Good luck. Any problems, let me know.' They said their good-byes and Phoebe put the closed sign up, before heading to find Maggie to say another thank you to her too.

She found her grandmother talking to a woman who wanted to rehome a fluffy Pomeranian that her grandchildren were allergic to. The woman, who was elderly and wearing a fawn-coloured hat which was a very similar colour to her dog, had it in her arms and there were tears in her eyes.

Puddleduck Pets was technically closed but Maggie would never turn away an animal in need. In the end, Maggie took the dog and the woman walked away without looking back.

'How sad,' Phoebe said, 'and what a difficult choice to make.'

'Her daughter was putting pressure on her,' Maggie said. 'Get rid of the dog or you can't see the grandchildren any more. It's scandalous. That woman's had this little dog for ten years and the grandchildren haven't had a problem until last week. But the daughter's been looking for an excuse to get rid of it for ages apparently and now she's found one. If it had been me, I'd have got rid of the daughter.'

Phoebe knew she wasn't entirely joking. There were sparks of anger in her eyes. Maggie hated bullying.

Maggie went off to settle the Pomeranian, whose name was William, into a kennel, and Phoebe headed for home.

She finally caught up with Rufus, having missed a call from him at lunchtime, and apologised for messing him and Archie about the previous evening.

'Don't worry at all. I guessed something like that had happened,' he'd told her. 'I'd have got back to you sooner, but I didn't see your message until it was quite late.'

'Maybe I could pop over in a bit and say sorry to Archie?' she suggested.

'I'd have liked that. But we're not at home. We're en route to an Easter egg hunt at the Priory Manor with my father. It's owned by one of his cronies.' There was a pause and then he'd added, 'If you'd have phoned half an hour earlier, we could have picked you up en route – we went past your cottage.'

'I'd have loved that,' Phoebe said wistfully. 'I finished work late.'

'That's a shame.' Did Phoebe detect a hint of relief in his voice or was she imagining things that weren't there?

'How about Good Friday?' she suggested. 'Could we do something then?' Puddleduck Vets was closed for routine appointments on Good Friday, Easter Sunday and Easter Monday. But they were open for emergency cover which was being shared between Marchwood and Puddleduck. Phoebe was incredibly relieved that it was Max, not her, who was doing their side of it. They were open for business as usual on Saturday.

'Archie's going riding on Friday,' Rufus said, 'and I think I've got an Easter function.' Phoebe heard Lord Alfred's voice in the background, asking him something, and Rufus's brief reply that he wouldn't be a moment.

She'd been about to say they could make a plan for Good Friday evening instead when Rufus said, 'Never mind. We'll see you on Sunday anyway, won't we? For lunch with your parents. We're both really looking forward to it.'

He'd hung up before Phoebe could say anything else. She drove home feeling sad. She'd barely been home lately, what with the late-night callout and then staying at Puddleduck, and she supposed it would be good to just be in her own space for a while and regroup. Woodcutter's Cottage wasn't hers – she rented it from Tori, who'd been given it by her grandparents – but it was the kind of place that Phoebe would have bought if she'd been in the market for buying. It was a whitewashed cottage with a green front door. A tiny two-up, two-down, seventeenth-century cob cottage with a thatched roof, tucked away up an unmade road near Linwood. It was next to a woodland, and had presumably once belonged to a woodcutter, although perhaps the name was just whimsical.

Location wise, Woodcutter's Cottage was close to Puddleduck Farm, so handy for work, although when Phoebe had first rented it, she hadn't known she would one day be working there – or for that matter seeing the lord of the manor next door. Not that she had seen very much of him lately, she thought ruefully. Back then, she'd just wanted to live near enough to keep an eye on her grandmother.

Phoebe let herself in and switched on the heating. The place felt cool and unlived in. Thick cob walls were brilliant both in summer because they kept out the heat, and winter because they kept it in. The cottage was small enough to warm up quickly when the wood burner was on, but it hadn't been on lately. She hadn't been in enough. It was nice to be home though and fingers crossed there would be no calls on her time tonight. Phoebe made herself coffee and sat in the lounge to drink it.

Her mind flicked back to the conversation she'd had with Sam earlier, and his surprise that Rufus hadn't yet met her parents.

She supposed there were extenuating circumstances. Archie was one of them – understandably Rufus was very protective over Archie. He'd been six when he'd lost his mother and Rufus hadn't had any kind of relationship since. It wasn't surprising that Rufus was reluctant to dive into meeting her family when their relationship was still relatively new. Rufus was very keen that Archie shouldn't have any more disruption in his life. He wanted stability for his son and that must be incredibly hard to maintain.

If you also added into the mix the fact that the Holts and the Crowthers (Maggie's family name) had history and it wasn't a very comfortable history, it was easy to see why Rufus was keen on taking things slowly.

Until just over a century ago, Puddleduck Farm and all of its land had been part of the Beechbrook Estate. But in 1905, Walter Holt, the firstborn son of Lord William Holt, the holder of the hereditary title, had gambled it on a hand of poker and lost it to Maggie's grandfather, Henry.

After that, relations had soured between the two families. They'd spoken to each other as little as possible across the years and although it wasn't exactly the kind of feud that had been immortalised by the Capulets and the Montagues in *Romeo and Juliet*, the families hadn't been on very good terms.

Maggie still wasn't very comfortable around Rufus Holt, although she was always polite and cordial.

Archie's love of animals had meant that Maggie got on much better with him than she did with the adult Holts. Maggie would have been the first to admit that with a few notable exceptions, she much preferred animals to people, but she found Archie endearing and on a similar wavelength to herself. Neither of them had any compunction whatsoever about breaking a few rules. Particularly where animals were concerned. Archie had sneaked out of the Beechbrook Estate on more than one occasion to see the Puddleduck donkeys without his father or Emilia's permission. Phoebe knew Maggie probably wouldn't have admitted to it, but she was pretty sure that this had elevated the little boy into hero status where her grandmother was concerned.

Rufus was a different kettle of fish entirely, though. He was naturally more reserved, and Phoebe wasn't sure how much her grandmother approved of her choice of boyfriend.

She was equally sure that Rufus's father didn't approve of her either.

Phoebe had met Lord Alfred Holt soon after she and Rufus had first started dating. She had been introduced as a friend, which she supposed had been a pretty accurate description back then.

She had at least understood why Rufus had said friend and not girlfriend. It had been early days, there was Archie to consider, and he already knew Phoebe as his father's friend.

Rufus had introduced Lord Holt as 'my father', and Phoebe had asked the older man, there and then, how he liked to be addressed. She liked to know where she was with people and she had thought it best to get that straight from the beginning.

'Alfred will be fine,' he'd told her. 'The title's a formality in this day and age. Hardly anyone uses it.' He'd held out his hand.

A handshake like a dead fish was a massive cliché but this had been exactly what it had been like. There was no warmth in his eyes either, Phoebe had noticed, although he had given her a slight smile.

Slightly taken aback, she'd swallowed and taken a step back after the handshake. She felt as though she had somehow been put in her place without a word being spoken.

'He's just reserved,' Rufus had said later when they'd talked about it. 'He's old school and he was brought up like that. Stiff upper lip – never show any emotion. He'll warm up when he's known you for a while.'

Phoebe had hoped he was right. But there had been no sign of any warming up so far. Once or twice, when she'd been up at the house with Rufus and Archie, she'd tried to engage Alfred Holt in conversation, but they'd never got past the weather or some non-controversial item on the news. It was as though he had put up an impenetrable glass wall between them. She could see and hear him perfectly but not touch or connect with him. Neither had he ever eaten with them, although Rufus had invited him once or twice, to tea on the terrace. Either Lord Holt was still harbouring some simmering family rivalry or he wasn't happy about his son dating a woman below his pay grade.

She sighed and wandered back into her kitchen and washed up and then made herself more coffee. She knew things were going to be very different with her own parents. They would welcome Rufus and Archie as warmly as if they were long lost relatives. So would her brother and sister-in-law. Phoebe was pretty sure everyone would love Archie because he was very loveable and they would welcome Rufus because he was Phoebe's choice – it was what her family had always been like. Totally supportive. She knew it was rare and she was incredibly lucky.

But she was disappointed that she wouldn't be seeing Rufus until Sunday.

9

On Easter Sunday, Rufus called for Phoebe at eleven thirty as planned. Or, to be more precise, Archie called for her. When she answered the door, having been ready and waiting for about ten minutes, it was Archie who stood on the doorstep, looking very smart in grey trousers and a maroon waistcoat and beaming from ear to ear. Rufus was just shutting the driver's door of his silver Mercedes, which looked as though it had been polished for the occasion.

'Hello, Phoebe.' Archie was practically jumping up and down in excitement. 'Do your mum and dad like lavender wine?'

'Lavender wine, yes, I expect they do.'

She looked over his head at Rufus, who was approaching more slowly. 'Where did you find lavender wine?'

'Harrison tracked down a supplier – we're not planning on producing it ourselves. Ours is destined to be soaps and skin care, but it's fun to experiment. I brought along a few bottles. There's a soft drink version too. For the drivers.'

He bent to kiss her cheek. He smelled divine and her tummy somersaulted. He'd had that effect on her from the very first kiss and it showed no signs of abating. Absence makes the heart grow fonder. Phoebe could have added a line to that old cliché. Absence makes the chemistry stronger. Or at least it had on her part.

'You both look very smart,' she said. Rufus looked great too. No waistcoat but dark grey trousers. Rufus always looked classy – even when he was in his oldest gear – Tori had told her that was one of the advantages of designer labels.

'We're not overdressed, are we?' Rufus asked.

'Not at all. But it wouldn't matter what you wore. Seriously. Jeans would be fine too.' She'd opted for a dress, which didn't happen very often. And she was glad she had now. They looked like a unit. A family unit, offered up a small voice from her heart, and in that moment she felt gloriously happy.

Today was going to be perfect. She knew her family would make Rufus and Archie feel very welcome. They were like that. They were lovely.

It was only a twenty-minute drive to her parents' house. They lived in Godshill on the edge of the New Forest and usually Phoebe would have picked up Maggie en route but today she was going over with Eddie, his son Jonathan had said he'd give them a lift, so they'd arranged to meet there.

On the way, Archie talked nonstop about Violet and the babies and how well they were doing and how he'd already found homes for three of the babies, and Phoebe was glad of his chatter because despite the fact she was really looking forward to this, she had butterflies too.

When they got to number five, Old Oak Way, Phoebe saw that Frazier's car was already in situ – her brother and Alexa and the twins had probably arrived early so they could help with the meal. She guessed Maggie and Eddie would be here too.

Rufus – unusually for him – took two goes to park in a space outside on the unmade road.

'Are you nervous?' Phoebe asked, slanting him a glance.

'Terrified.' He swallowed. 'Can't you tell?'

'They're really lovely,' she reassured.

'I don't doubt it. They produced you, didn't they?' His dark eyes were warm and Phoebe felt a rush of pleasure. Of course he didn't see them as 'just friends'. No way would he have agreed to come to lunch with her parents and brought Archie if he had.

She grabbed his hand. 'Mum's a great cook too. We're going to have a lovely time. Come on, guys.' She smiled at Archie, who was sitting expectantly in the back beside a box of lavender wine and a bouquet of flowers that Rufus had also brought. 'Come and meet the Dashwoods.'

The front door was open before they'd got anywhere near it and Phoebe could see her father, James Dashwood, standing in the opening with a big beam on his face. He was wearing an apron that said *Keep calm and eat cake* which Phoebe knew belonged to her mother, but beneath it she could see that he had dressed for the occasion too.

'It's such a pleasure to meet you both,' he said, his gaze flicking between Rufus, who was carrying the wine, and Archie, who was half hidden behind the bouquet. 'We've heard so much about you from our Phoebe. All of it good.'

'Likewise,' Rufus said, manoeuvring the box of wine under one arm so he could hold out his hand, which her father grasped warmly. 'Thank you for inviting us. We've been so looking forward to it.'

There was nothing dead fish about Rufus's handshake, Phoebe thought joyously. And then her father was shaking Archie's hand too – Archie had impeccable manners – and she was hugging her father and they were inside and heading along the short hall to the kitchen which was where the whole of the family tended to gather because it was big and had a breakfast island with stools that invited you to sit down and chat.

She saw she'd been right about everyone being there already. Frazier was stirring something fragrantly savoury in a pan on the sunshine-yellow range oven. When had her brother started helping with the cooking? – that must have been since the twins had been born – and Alexa was chopping up some herbs on a board and looking overheated. The whole kitchen was full of the aromas of rosemary and garlic and roast dinner.

Through an archway that led into the snug next door, Phoebe could see her mother kneeling on the floor playing with the twins, who'd just started walking, well, Bertie had. Flo apparently had such a good grasp of language that she hadn't bothered learning to walk yet – according to her doting parents, she just demanded, and got, whatever she wanted.

Maggie and Eddie were sitting in armchairs. Maggie appeared to be polishing cutlery and Eddie was talking loudly about canal boats – Eddie was quite deaf.

It was the warmest of family scenes, albeit slightly chaotic, and as they went fully into the kitchen the noise slowly hushed.

Rufus paused for a moment and Phoebe knew that from his perspective this must all seem pretty overwhelming. Impulsively she grabbed both his hand and Archie's in each of hers. 'Everyone, this is Rufus and Archie. Rufus and Archie, this is everyone. You can meet each other properly over dinner, one by one, but for now maybe everyone could just wave.'

Everyone waved with great enthusiasm – even Bertie and Flo, with some encouragement from the nearest adults. The thrum of chatter restarted again and Phoebe knew instinctively that the wave ploy had been the right thing to do. They had the whole day to get to know each other. She didn't want there to be any pressure. She didn't want Rufus to turn tail and bolt like a frightened horse. The irony of Rufus bolting like a frightened horse wasn't lost on her, in view of the fact that the PTSD he suffered from was triggered by horses.

Sunday lunches at the Dashwoods' had always been a warm and slightly chaotic affair where everyone laughed a lot, let their hair down, and ate too much. Louella Dashwood loved feeding people and she was a great cook. Having had Maggie as her role model, she wasn't a prescriptive, 'stick to a recipe' kind of cook, but more of a 'taste it and see' kind of cook. She was a great baker and always erred on the side of making too much.

Today was no exception. Louella had gone to town on the food and had done two roasts. A whole free-range chicken and a side of roast beef which went down very well with everyone. Alexa had brought all the accompaniments apparently like the home-made stuffing and the cranberry sauce and the horseradish made from a root from her garden. She had made the puddings too – bread and butter pudding and two different flavour cheesecakes – she said it was just as easy to make two cheesecakes as one.

Alexa was the archetypal earth mother. Phoebe had no idea how she had time to make anything from scratch when she had the twins to look after. She was in awe.

The subject of time management came up over coffee. Every-one, or at least everyone who wasn't retired, had time-intensive jobs.

Louella was a teacher.

'Contrary to popular belief,' she said, 'teachers do actually work quite long hours. The problem is that no one ever takes into account the lesson plans and the marking. Not to mention the endlessly tedious paperwork we have to do, these days, most of which is utterly bureaucratic and doesn't benefit the children one iota.'

It turned out that Rufus was quite interested in this, his father was on the board of governors of the school where Louella taught, and the chat went back and forth.

Then they moved on to solicitors and Phoebe's father and brother, both of whom worked for the same family law firm, argued that their profession was much more time intensive than anyone imagined. 'Better paid, though,' Louella argued. 'If you're looking at it overall.'

'Oh, I don't know. I'd say vets are better paid than us,' Frazier said, with a challenging look at Phoebe. 'A friend of ours just paid an extortionate amount for an operation on his dog the other day. Alexa, do you remember what it cost?' He turned towards his wife. 'A cruciate ligament operation on a cockerpoo?'

Before Alexa could answer him, the electronic Alexa on the sideboard piped up. 'The average cost for a cruciate ligament operation on a cockerpoo is £9,000.'

Everyone chuckled. This was an occupational hazard when Alexa the human was around, and Alexa the virtual assistant had been left switched on. Archie chuckled the loudest. It transpired that there was no Alexa – or any other kind of virtual assistant – at Beechbrook House because Lord Alfred didn't like the idea of a machine listening to everything anyone said. He'd get on well with Mr B, Phoebe thought fleetingly.

So, after that, there was no sensible conversation to be had. Archie did his best to get the word 'Alexa' into every sentence he could. Then Flo joined in – what she lacked in walking skills she made up for in talking skills – and the conversation, aided by glasses of lavender wine consumed by the people who weren't driving, degenerated into silliness.

Eddie and Maggie, who were both fluent in British Sign Language, or at least a version of it, taught anyone who was interested – Archie was very keen and there was a lot of laughter and a great deal of noise.

At around four thirty, Maggie and Eddie started making going home noises. Phoebe, Rufus and Archie, having tried to help with the clearing up but been denied access to the kitchen, weren't far behind them. Rufus and Archie thanked Phoebe's parents profusely and Phoebe could tell from the sparkle in her mother's eyes that Louella had taken quite a shine to Rufus and his son. The day had been a great success.

Because Phoebe wasn't on call or driving and had actually been one of the partakers in the lavender wine experiment, she didn't look at her phone until they were back in Rufus's car. But when she did, she found she had two voicemails from Anni Buckland, left an hour apart.

'Phoebe, I'm so sorry to bother you on Easter Sunday, but I think Cindy's taken a turn for the worse. I've also got another alpaca with similar symptoms. Can you give me a call as soon as possible, please?'

Phoebe frowned as she read it. That was not good news. She'd assumed that the iron supplements had helped as she hadn't heard anything from Anni since she'd been out to the farm last Monday. Thanks to the bank holidays, the results of the blood test she'd taken wouldn't be back till Tuesday and hopefully that would give them a clue as to the cause. But there was very little else she could do until then.

'Is everything OK?' Rufus was looking at her and she realised she must have sighed aloud.

She told him what had happened. 'It's a client who has my mobile number, but I'm not on call. I'll just give Max a quick ring if you don't mind. He's the on-call vet for this weekend. Just to check that she's been in touch with him too.'

'Of course I don't mind. Go right ahead.'

Phoebe phoned Anni and discovered to her relief that she had got hold of Max and in fact he was still at the farm examining the two ill alpacas. She disconnected, feeling a bit more reassured. Maybe Max would spot something she hadn't.

Rufus seemed happy enough. As they approached Woodcutter's Cottage, he said that he and Archie had had a delightful day and that Phoebe's family were absolutely lovely. His voice had sobered a little and his eyes had gone distant for a moment afterwards. Phoebe had wondered if he was remembering Rowena and the time when he'd been part of his own little family.

Or maybe she was reading too much into it. There was certainly no ambiguity in Archie's voice when he said he was now going to learn sign language and then asked her when she was going to come over and see the baby guinea pigs.

She'd been about to say she could come over now if they liked – it was still only just before five and there was no reason to end the day this early – when Rufus intervened.

'I think Phoebe may have seen enough of us for one day.'

'Oh but, Dad, we do need to see which ones are male and which ones are female,' Archie begged. 'So we can separate them.'

'I will come and look at them first thing tomorrow,' Phoebe promised, and was pleased when Rufus said, 'Thank you. That would be perfect.'

Besides, she may not be on call, but she still wanted to phone Max and see what he'd thought about the alpacas.

When she did phone Max a bit later on that night, she discovered he was as mystified as she'd been. It had been pointless to take blood tests on a bank holiday as the lab was closed, but he'd arranged for them to go back on Tuesday morning to do some more.

Unsettled, Phoebe said goodbye and disconnected. It had been such a lovely day. It was a shame that it had ended on such a worrying call.

10

On Easter Monday, Phoebe finally got to meet the guinea pigs and told Archie which were boys and which were girls. She also checked in with Sam, who said, to her relief, that all was fine with Snowball.

On Tuesday, her mother phoned, buoyed up with enthusiasm about how lovely Rufus and Archie were. She'd been thrilled to receive a hand-delivered thank you card. Which was so like Rufus, Phoebe thought, smiling.

And on Wednesday, Phoebe had a WhatsApp and a selfie from her best friend Tori. She was holding up a copy of that week's version of *New Forest Views*, the magazine she owned and edited, and making a silly face.

I'm sending a photo to remind you what I look like. I can't believe how long it is since we met. I'm SO sorry. I meant to catch up over Easter. When are you free for a girlie catch up?

Feeling a rush of warmth, Phoebe replied.

I'm just as bad. Sorry, I don't know where time goes. How about Friday night? We could meet at the Brace after work. 7ish?

Done.

The reply flew back.

Phoebe was on call on the Friday she was meeting Tori, but she rarely drank anyway, and never when on call, so that didn't matter.

She got to the Brace of Pheasants, which was local to both her and Tori, at just after seven. The olde worlde country pub was in Godshill, near to where her parents lived, but it was off the beaten track, so mainly attracted locals.

Its main claim to fame was its fabulous home-made pies and Phoebe's mouth watered every time the kitchen door opened and a delicious waft of pastry and rosemary drifted out.

Tori arrived a few minutes after Phoebe had found a table and they hugged and then stood back to look at each other.

'I think I had almost forgotten what you looked like,' Phoebe said, taking in her friend's glowing complexion, shoulder-length red hair and sparkling green eyes. 'You look amazing. What have you been up to?'

'Lots of things I shouldn't,' Tori quipped. 'No change there. I will tell you all – but let's get some drinks in – are you eating? I want to know all about what's happening with you and especially with Rufus. I've got a gossip column to write.' She saw Phoebe's face and added quickly, 'I'm kidding. Don't look at me like that.'

They got drinks in, ordered pies, and sat opposite each other at a table with the inglenook fireplace on one side and a window with a view out over the pub garden on the other. There were two magpies on the lawn, strutting about in the golden light of early evening.

'So, what do you want to know about Rufus?' Phoebe asked curiously. 'I thought you'd have seen him on a fairly regular basis. What with Harrison being in and out of the big house.'

'Harrison's hardly ever at the big house. He's outside all the time – doing whatever groundsmen do all day.' Tori shrugged. 'Chopping down trees and stuff – I watched him do that once. It was hot. There's something about a bare-chested man chopping wood.' Her eyes gleamed.

'Stop there.' Phoebe put up a hand. 'I don't want images in my head of Harrison with his top off.'

'That's probably just as well.' Tori giggled. 'Although it is quite a popular spectator sport. I don't mean Harrison, but did you know there's a guy on TikTok who's got half a million followers and all he ever does is post videos of himself chopping wood? He's called WoodMan.' She made the word sound even more outrageously suggestive than it was probably designed to sound.

TikTok had a lot to answer for, Phoebe thought, raising her eyebrows in amazement.

'I can't say as I watch that much TikTok' (Breakdancing Bill sprang into her head), 'but if he's got that many followers, maybe Harrison should try posting some videos himself. It sounds like a profitable sideline. Think of the advertising revenue.'

'No, he couldn't. I don't want other women/men/non-binary – whoever they may be, these days – swooning over my man. I want to keep him all to myself.'

They both giggled.

'Anyway,' Tori said, 'enough of wood for now. Although we could come back to it later if you like.' She winked. 'How's it going with you and Rufus? Tell me all your news. You've been very quiet lately. Is that because you're wrapped in a rose-tinted bubble of romance? Am I looking at the future Lady Holt? Lady... Phoebe...

Holt.' She rolled the words around her mouth. 'It does have a certain ring to it, doesn't it?'

Phoebe dropped her gaze from her friend's. 'To be honest, I've mostly been quiet because I'm flat out with work.'

'But that's great news, isn't it?' Tori's eyes grew more curious. 'Puddleduck Vets is a success. That's brilliant.'

'Yes, it is.' Phoebe could hear the hesitancy in her own voice. 'And I'm thrilled. Don't get me wrong. But when it comes to Rufus, I... I guess I just thought things might have progressed a bit faster than they have.' She paused.

That was one of the funny things about talking. When thoughts were running around in your head, they didn't have so much weight – but when you voiced them aloud to your best friend, they became terribly real. She felt a wash of sadness.

Tori looked concerned. She rested her chin on her elbows on the table and leaned forward. It was bad timing. A waiter chose that moment to arrive with their pies.

By the time he'd sorted them out with knives, forks and servi-ettes, Phoebe almost regretted saying something. She felt as though she'd be being disloyal to Rufus if she carried on, but she had opened Pandora's box. She wasn't going to get away with backtracking now.

Tori ate a few mouthfuls of pie and then said thoughtfully, 'You did realise I was joking about you being the next Lady Holt, didn't you?'

'Yes, I did.' Phoebe wondered how much she should say. But for once Tori wasn't pushing her and that somehow made it easier.

She ate some of her own pie, which still smelled delicious but had somehow turned to dust in her mouth and washed it down with a gulp of Diet Coke. She was very aware that Tori was still waiting for her to say something.

The muted chatter of other pub goers surrounded them as the

pub filled up around them. So it all felt quite private and anonymous.

'Put it this way,' she began. 'Rufus is very cautious. I know a lot of that is to do with Archie. He doesn't want his son to be hurt so he can't just go charging into a new relationship. I do get that.'

'But Archie already knows you – and he likes you.' Tori's eyes were troubled.

'And Rufus is still grieving for his wife,' Phoebe rushed on. 'Their whole world fell apart when she died.'

'Wasn't that nearly four years ago?'

'Yes, but sometimes things take longer. And there have been other problems.' She realised she had never told Tori about the PTSD that Rufus suffered. She had never told anyone about that, although Sam knew because he had worked it out for himself. Sam had taught Archie to ride and had seen Rufus on a professional level at Brook Stables.

'Rufus has PTSD that's triggered by horses, and I feel terrible telling you because I know he's ashamed of it.'

'Having PTSD's nothing to be ashamed of. And I'm not surprised he's got it. His wife died in a horse-riding accident, didn't she? And he was there watching. Harrison told me. That kind of stuff has far-reaching effects.'

'Yes, you're right.' Phoebe was relieved she didn't need to explain. 'As you can imagine, it's very difficult, but he's getting there. He does see someone about it.'

'Bless him.' Tori's voice was compassionate. 'I didn't realise he was so damaged, although it does explain a lot.' She'd finished her pie now and she pushed her empty plate aside. 'He's lucky to have met you. But I do get that it's difficult having a relationship with someone who has so much baggage. I don't mean that in a bitchy way,' she added quickly. 'I just mean it's difficult.' She bit her lip.

'I'm preaching to the converted, aren't I? You lived with Hugh for six years.'

Phoebe smiled despite herself at the mention of her ex, who'd been so buttoned up, thanks to both his parents being cold to the point of freezing, that he'd been unable to get properly close to any human being. Although he'd managed to get close enough to Melissa, their ex-boss!

'Ouch. But yes, you're right. I've had plenty of practice. Not that Rufus is anything like Hugh. At least he's had a relationship. He knows how they work. And I think he really does want this one. I mean, he didn't have to ask me out to dinner, did he?' She wasn't sure whether she was trying to convince herself or Tori.

'And how are you getting on with Emilia?' Tori asked, ultra-casually. But her words were like another arrow in the heart.

'Bloody Emilia.' Phoebe hadn't realised just how much the woman irked her until she'd said her name aloud. 'She clearly can't stand me. She tries to cause trouble every time I'm at the house. The latest fiasco was with Archie's guinea pigs...'

Tori put her hand up. 'Hold that thought. I'll go and get us another drink. And then you can tell me all about it.'

Phoebe rehearsed the words in her head while she waited for Tori to come back from the bar. She didn't want to sound sniping and mean but it would be quite good to let off steam about Emilia. She couldn't do it with anyone else. And Tori, despite being a journalist and despite her mention of gossip columns, was actually the soul of discretion when it came to personal things.

Tori put their drinks back on the table with a clunk. 'Two Diet Cokes with ice and a slice,' she muttered. 'In the old days it would have been G&Ts. Get us being all grown up and sensible.'

'In the old days we didn't have grown-up jobs and responsibilities,' Phoebe said. 'We were both what my mum used to call fancy free.'

'Yes, that's true. Anyway, back to Emilia. What's she been up to?'

'Well, first I need to get you up to speed on Archie's latest enterprise.' Phoebe told her about the guinea pig enterprise and how he hadn't told Rufus and had asked her not to tell him either, and how Emilia had more or less accused her of keeping things back deliberately from Rufus too.

'The truth is I didn't actually know what Archie was up to either,' Phoebe said. 'Well, not until I got there and realised he had a guinea pig about to give birth. But Emilia told Rufus that I'd known all along and that's why I'd come round – in my veterinary capacity to see if there was any progress.'

'Did Rufus believe her?'

'I don't think so but I couldn't make too much of it because I didn't want to get Archie into trouble with his dad. Anyway, that's just one thing in a long list. I popped in over Easter to see the baby guinea pigs and she and Archie were discussing the possibility of bringing Lucius – that's Daddy Guinea Pig, he belongs to Archie's friend, Jack – round to see Violet and the babies. Which would actually be a very bad idea because (a) Violet could get pregnant again, and (b) Lucius might hurt the babies.'

'So why was she suggesting that?'

'She told Archie I'd said it would be OK. But what I'd actually said was that guinea pigs are incredibly social and in the wild they live in family groups. When I reiterated that, Emilia said she'd misunderstood and blamed the language barrier. I feel bad saying it out loud, Tori. It all seems a bit petty and nitpicking, and maybe it's true about the language barrier.'

'I bet it isn't. She's spoken perfectly good English every time I've met her. Harrison says she's a manipulative witch too, when it suits her. Anyway, what was she even doing there at Easter? I know she lives there but I thought she usually went back to her family at holiday times?'

'Only on the longer breaks apparently.' Phoebe sighed. 'They all live in Zurich. The worst thing is that when I leave messages, she doesn't pass them on. She sometimes answers Rufus's phone – his personal mobile, I mean.'

'Really, doesn't he mind?'

'I don't think so. But I've noticed that every so often when I phone the call gets declined. You know you get an option, accept or decline, and if you decline, it just beeps in your ear. Well, that's happened a few times and I mentioned it to Rufus once and he blamed it on the signal being variable in different parts of the house.'

'Maybe he was right?'

'It's possible but I don't think so. It was Archie who told me that Emilia sometimes picks up Rufus's phone when it's ringing and he's not around, and she presses decline.'

'Do you think you need to tell him?'

'Well, I could but I think she only does it when she sees my name. Archie says she does answer the phone too – and take messages for Rufus. And Rufus is quite happy with that.'

'The conniving cow.' Tori looked outraged. 'And they're just the things she does that you know about.'

'I know. And I'm sure Emilia has nothing to do with the fact that Rufus still wants to take things slowly.'

'But she certainly isn't helping.' Tori's voice softened and her eyes were serious. 'You probably do need to find a way of talking to Rufus about her.'

'I've thought about it, but I don't want to stir things up and I know she won't be there for ever. Archie's going away to school in September. To boarding school, I mean, and when he does, Emilia won't be needed any more.'

'So it has a natural end in sight. Yes, I see your point. But

September is still five months away. She could do untold damage by then.'

'I know. I probably do need to say something.'

'How about after sex?'

'After sex?' Phoebe met her friend's direct gaze, a little shocked.

'Yes. You know... that time in the afterglow when they're lying beside you, all happy and spent and you could ask them to do anything – fly to the moon and get you a moon rock – and they'd say yes. Although, I suppose, bringing up another woman's name when you're lying in your lover's arms might not be the ideal time. Hmm.'

Phoebe bit her lip and dropped her gaze and there was an awkward little silence.

'You *are* having an afterglow, aren't you?' Tori's eyes widened and her face changed and Phoebe knew that it was pointless to lie to her friend. She had hoped to steer clear of this conversation, but it was too late. They were slap bang in the middle of it. Bang being the operative word. Or not being the operative word, as it happened – in this case.

'I told you. We're not rushing into anything. And Archie's around.'

'Doesn't Rufus come and stop at Woodcutter's though?'

'He hasn't stopped over yet.' Phoebe felt her eyes fill with tears. For a few moments, she couldn't speak.

She heard Tori's chair legs scrape the floor as she got up abruptly and came round to Phoebe's side of the table. She hunkered down and took Phoebe's hands in hers. 'Oh, Pheebs, I'm so sorry. Me and my big mouth.'

'It's OK.' Phoebe grabbed a serviette off the table and wiped her eyes. 'Actually, I feel better for talking about it. I didn't realise quite how much it's all been getting to me.'

'Why don't we go back to mine?' Tori suggested. 'Or yours. I know you can't drink in case you get a call, but we can relax a bit more at home.'

Phoebe nodded. On the grass through the window there was just the one magpie now, strutting about on its own. The other had flown away.

11

Rufus had suffered from insomnia on and off ever since he'd lost his wife. Bartholomew Timms, the therapist he'd seen and still saw sometimes, had told him that insomnia was a symptom of PTSD. But Rufus didn't remember ever having slept that well, even before Rowena had died. He'd certainly never been a heavy sleeper. Not like Harrison who'd said that when he was a kid the house two doors down from them had caught fire and eight fire engines had come screaming into the cul-de-sac to put out the blaze and he hadn't woken up.

Rufus didn't mind too much about not sleeping. He kept an iPad in his bedroom which meant he had access to his emails, and when he couldn't sleep, he sometimes used the time to go through them and clear the endless list of work emails. One night he had got the shock of his life when he pinged off an email at 4 a.m. to the vice chair of the tenant/landlord association and five minutes later got an answering ping in reply from Ms Cynthia Winterbottom. Clearly he wasn't the only person who had a nocturnal working pattern. After that he stopped sending emails in the small hours. He still wrote them, but he scheduled them to go out the next morning during business hours.

He felt isolated enough waking up in the dead of night, but if no one else knew he did it, he could pretend that it wasn't happening.

Pretending something wasn't happening had become a coping strategy. Rufus was aware that it was probably a bad one. But it worked for him. Or at least it had done until recently.

Since Easter – or more specifically since meeting Phoebe's family at Easter – his insomnia had got even worse. He was pretty sure the two events were connected. Although he hadn't quite worked out why. They'd been lovely. They had welcomed him and wrapped him in warmth, and he'd felt for that brief afternoon as if he belonged somewhere. As though he was part of a family.

So why the hell had there been such a kickback? For a night or two afterwards, he had barely slept at all. Then things had settled down again and he'd gone back to his usual sleep broken routine, napping just enough to get by on. But that had been nearly two weeks ago and his eyes had pinged open at 2.30 a.m., always the worst time to wake up, and Rufus had felt wide awake, his thoughts churning.

He climbed out of bed, pulled a robe from the back of a chair, he usually slept naked, and went over to the bedroom window. Looking at the stars sometimes helped. When Rowena had first died, he'd told Archie that she was now a star in the sky – a brightly shining star lighting up the space all around her, just as she'd always done when she was alive.

He pulled back a drape. There weren't a lot of stars tonight. It was cloudy. Somewhere on the estate an owl hooted. A haunting sound, the epitome of loneliness.

Rufus rubbed his eyes, which felt gritty with exhaustion.

It wasn't Rowena who was on his mind tonight. It was Phoebe.

While his late wife's face was growing harder and harder to recall as the years went by, Phoebe's face was ever present. An image of her flew into his head now. Those beautiful hazel eyes, that slightly upturned nose, her lips.

Rufus cut off the image before it could get any further. His heart was beating so loudly in his ears that it drowned out his thoughts. All at once, he knew why he felt so terribly conflicted. Why he hadn't been able to sleep since he'd met Phoebe's parents. It was guilt that had stolen his sleep. Guilt that although on the outside they must seem the perfect couple, they weren't a couple. He had stopped them being a couple because he'd prevented their relationship from going any further.

Not because he didn't want it to go further. There had been evenings when he'd had to force himself to shove his hands in his pockets and practically run out of Woodcutter's Cottage, because he'd known they would end up in bed if he hadn't.

Rufus clenched his jaw as beyond his window a cloud moved back to reveal a bright star high in the sky. If he took Phoebe to bed, he knew he would feel as though he was betraying Archie's mother. Betraying Archie too. In his head, there was a memory of a dusty church with sunlight pouring in through stained-glass windows swirling dust motes in its light – 'until death us do part' – and although death had parted them, death hadn't severed the connection between them.

Only Rufus could do that. And he wasn't yet ready to take that step.

* * *

Sam had spent several sleepless nights since the Easter weekend too. But for quite different reasons to Rufus.

Some of them had been related to Snowball. As he'd suspected, his black cat had not appreciated being contained in a crate. Sam had bought two crates – the kind used by dog owners when they were house training puppies. The kind that were easy to pack up and move because Sam knew they were in this for the long haul and he wanted to make the practicalities as easy as possible. One of the crates was set up in the room at the back of the post office so that he and his ma could keep an eye on the cat during working hours. Sam had set the other crate up in his bedroom at home so he was close to hand if there was any problem in the night. At least he could be a friendly voice.

There was ample space in the crates for Snowball's litter tray and food and his comfy cat bed, but not enough space for Snowball to move around and damage himself. It was the perfect recuperation solution.

Snowball had not appreciated all this effort one little bit. He hated the crates and swung between clawing at the bars and yowling discontentedly to sulking. It wasn't so bad when he was in his daytime crate because there were lots of people in and out of Hendrie's Post Office and Stores and many of them popped out to say hello to Snowball and give him treats taken from a bowl that Jan Hendrie kept on the front desk.

The nights were a different matter. Snowball had always been a vocal kind of cat and for the first couple of nights he'd shown his disapproval by howling miserably for what had seemed to Sam to be much of the night.

'It's for your own good, mate,' Sam had said, knowing it was fruitless and that neither of them was going to get any sleep.

On the third night, he'd hardened his heart and moved the crate out of his bedroom and into the kitchen. With a few walls and a staircase between them, at least the impact of the yowling was lessened. He'd also had an ulterior motive.

He hadn't been making it up when he'd hinted to Phoebe that

he was seeing someone. A couple of months ago, he'd bumped into an old flame, Judy, and somehow, slightly against Sam's better judgement, they had started seeing each other again.

Judy was the only person Sam had ever met who was as besotted with horses as he was. They'd originally met a few years ago when they were both out riding in the forest and they'd fallen into conversation. She'd been riding a classy black thoroughbred called Delilah, with a coat that gleamed in the morning sunlight and the kind of lines that Sam knew came from generations of careful breeding.

As soon as Judy had opened her mouth, Sam had realised that she too was the product of generations of classy breeding – although he knew that was something he'd never say aloud. She had the plummiest of voices and the confidence of someone who's been brought up in a life of privilege.

Much later, Sam had found out he was right. Judy Barker was the daughter of two stockbrockers. Her father was as rich as Croesus and her mother was the most upmarket woman Sam had ever met – and he met quite a few upmarket women at Brook Stables. Mostly the mothers of the kids he taught to ride.

But Judy was no snob. On that first meeting, she had told him with passion in her voice that she would rather be riding her horse through the New Forest than doing anything else in the world and Sam, who burned with the same passion for horses, had told her he felt exactly the same way.

They had started a relationship and Sam had thought he'd met the woman he'd marry. But then, when they'd been dating for around eight months, Judy had taken him to meet her parents. Sam had known straight away that her parents didn't like him. Or, more to the point, they didn't think he was good enough for their daughter.

They weren't rude to him, they were just cool and they made it clear that they lived in different worlds. The Barkers were the kind of people who had houses in four countries with staff to maintain them and a superyacht moored off an island in the Caribbean. They owned the island as well as the yacht.

They were occasionally photographed at celebrity weddings and rumour had it that they'd once had the young Prince Charles and Lady Diana, as the couple had been then, round for dinner.

Although the Barkers never said it outright, they managed to show it in a hundred different ways. Sam was not of their world. They could accept him as a friend of their daughter – at a push. But no way would their future son-in-law be the son of a postmistress and a chippy.

Sam had known all this before Judy had even been fully aware of it, and in the past he'd made a decision to end their relationship because he had never wanted her to have to choose. Him or her parents.

So when they'd met again, this time at a pony club show where she'd been watching a young cousin compete and he'd been accompanying one of his Brook students, Sam had been cautious.

Judy less so. He'd bumped into her three times at the show, once at the ringside and twice in the coffee queue, and in the end, she confessed it was deliberate.

'I've missed you, Sam,' she had said candidly. 'Shall we have dinner some time? Just for old times' sake. No strings, nothing heavy.'

One dinner couldn't hurt, Sam had thought in a weak moment. And she'd looked stunning and the truth was he had missed her too. But of course it hadn't ended at dinner. Before he'd had time to say, 'This relationship has no more future than it did last time,' they were in bed again.

They did of course have to sleep at Sam's because of Snowball. Judy liked cats and as soon as she'd found out what had happened, she'd proclaimed that Sam was a complete hero and that she'd be happy to help him nurse Snowball.

'I wanted to be a vet when I was small,' she told him. 'But I think I'd have been too soft to do it. You have to be fairly hard-headed to do that as a career, I think.'

Sam thought of Phoebe, who was the least hard-headed person he knew, and shrugged noncommittally.

But Judy, to give her credit, was wonderful with Snowball. She was gentle and calm and endlessly patient and seemed quite happy to always come to Sam's and to cut short dinners and trips out because he was anxious to get back to the cat.

It meant that they spent a lot of time at Sam's and quite a lot of that time was in bed. Bed was another area where they'd always been totally compatible. That hadn't changed. If anything, it was better than he remembered because they had history.

Sam felt torn in two. He knew deep down that their relationship didn't have a long-term future. As a couple, they were just as compatible and perfect as they'd always been, but their backgrounds and families were just as incompatible and imperfect as they'd always been. Judy couldn't change her upbringing and he couldn't change his. Their relationship really didn't have a long-term future – not unless they ran away together, and Sam knew he had no way of supporting her and her lifestyle.

Judy still had two horses at livery in a posh stable on the other side of the forest. Sam knew his wages from the post office wouldn't even cover one of their liveries. It was impossible. He'd have to win the lottery or inherit a fortune, neither of which had a cat in hell's chance of happening.

But Sam didn't want to end their relationship again either. It was one of the truly bright spots in his life. So he buried all these uncomfortable thoughts and did the only thing he could do and still keep sane. He threw himself totally into living in the moment. His eyes were wide open about the possible heartbreak ahead, but he decided he would deal with the future when it arrived.

Right now, he was having a ball living in the present.

12

Phoebe was not feeling very confident about either the present or the future. After her chat with Tori, she had felt relieved that she'd shared what was going on between her and Rufus. Or more to the point what was not going on between them. It felt like less of a dark secret, but it still felt like a dark shadow.

The answer, Tori had said, was to talk about it. 'Obviously I mean with Rufus, not me,' Tori had added hastily. 'Pin him down – I don't mean physically – although actually that might be a good idea.'

They had both giggled at the thought of that, and Phoebe had been amazed that they could laugh, but then that had been a lot later and by then the whole subject had felt less taboo and shameful. Although she wasn't sure exactly why she felt ashamed about the fact that they hadn't made love. Because it certainly wasn't because *she* didn't want to.

But talking about it with Rufus was a lot easier said than done. Her night out with Tori was four weeks behind them. It was now the middle of May, but Phoebe had only seen Rufus a handful of times since Easter.

And when she did see him, the last thing she wanted to do was to start a heavy conversation. No matter how much she thought about it, she couldn't think of a way of keeping it light.

'Hey, babe, so when am I going to get you into bed then?' No, too coarse and they didn't really have pet names for each other. Rufus wasn't a pet names kind of guy.

'Rufus, I'd really like to move our relationship on a step.' No, that sounded like she wanted to get engaged.

'Rufus, can I ask you something? It's a bit sensitive. Do you find me attractive/sexually attractive/hot/sexy?' None of those words seemed appropriate.

Besides, what if he said, 'No'?

In her heart she knew that the answer wasn't no. She could feel that in him. The chemistry still sparked between them on the rare occasion they were alone – surely she wasn't imagining that.

Or maybe she should simply just wait until the next time he came round and say, 'Rufus, why don't you stay over tonight?' Part of the problem was that he didn't come round very often. Because of Archie, she tended to go to Beechbrook. Occasionally, Rufus came and picked her up from Woodcutter's and they went somewhere else. But quite often he had Archie with him. They had become more of a unit of three than a couple, Phoebe realised. She didn't mind this. Archie was great and she loved being with the pair of them, but it did make life tricky on the romance front.

Archie didn't always tag along, of course. Sometimes it was just the two of them but on those occasions, Rufus was keen to get back for Archie's bedtime.

It was crazy. Especially when he hired a live-in nanny to look after his son, but it was how it had been.

'But surely you stay over at Beechbrook?' Tori had said to her when they'd discussed it.

Phoebe had confessed that she never had. That Rufus had never invited her. It wasn't a normal setup. Rufus lived with his father and his son and a nanny. And yes, they might live in a manor house with God knows how many bedrooms, Phoebe didn't want to admit she didn't even know how many, but it would still have felt a bit strange to be making mad passionate love with so many other people under the same roof. Or maybe she was just making excuses for him.

Phoebe decided that she would ask him to dinner at hers. And she would ask him to come on a night when it was convenient for him to stay over. She would definitely do it in the next couple of weeks.

Thankfully, her work didn't leave much time for angst. Puddle-duck Vets was incredibly busy. Sam had been in with Snowball for an X-ray four weeks after she'd done the surgery and to Phoebe's relief, the fracture in the cat's pelvis was healing nicely, so Sam wouldn't have to keep him in a crate for too much longer.

He'd looked pretty tired, but when she'd commented on it, he'd remarked that it wasn't just Snowball who'd been keeping him up at nights. Then he'd told her he'd started seeing an old flame again. A woman called Judy who was apparently as obsessed with horses as he was.

She'd told him she was really pleased for him, which she was, even though she had a vague memory that they'd split up last time because Sam had felt that Judy's parents didn't approve. Phoebe didn't feel it was appropriate to ask him if anything had changed there. Sam would tell her in his own good time if he wanted to.

Phoebe had spent quite a lot of time at Anni's Alpacas lately. She had got into the habit of dropping by when she was in the area. Not on an official callout that Anni would have had to pay for, but just to keep an eye on the situation.

Fortunately, she was in the area often because it was about half-way, and also directly en route, between Puddleduck Vets and the Marchwood practice, which she visited often to see Seth and his staff. They updated each other on cases and needed to be in close touch.

To Phoebe's relief, things seemed to be improving at Buckland Farm. Cindy and the other alpaca, Jenson, that Max had looked at were both doing well on the iron tablets. The good news was that their bloods had tested negative for all of the more serious things that caused anaemia in alpacas. Phoebe was quietly optimistic.

She had also got quite friendly with Anni herself, who despite all her chat was quite a private person.

On this particular afternoon, she did have an excuse to pop in to Anni's. The last of the results had just come back from the lab and Phoebe decided to pop in personally to tell her.

Anni, as always, was pleased to see her, although she looked more tired than usual. Phoebe wasn't surprised. Neither she nor her husband Nick were as young as they'd once been. This place was a lot to cope with and they had no help as far as she could gather.

'Hello, Phoebe, nice to see you. Is this an official visit? Or were you just fancying another one of my home-made scones?'

'Is it that obvious?' Phoebe covered her mouth with her hands in mock horror. 'It's semi-official. I've got a few more results for you – all good news. But if there did happen to be a scone...'

'There's one with your name on it,' Anni said, ushering her in through the hall and into a kitchen that wasn't totally dissimilar to Maggie's, albeit slightly smaller and slightly shabbier. The wooden work units looked as though they'd been fitted in the eighties, and the cupboard under the sink had a wonky hinge so it was slightly askew.

There were no dogs, but it was a working kitchen with a stone tiled floor and a row of muddy boots lined up by the back door. The smell of baking was sweet, though. Phoebe sniffed appreciatively.

'Tea or coffee?' Anni offered as she put two pale golden scones on a plate and pushed it towards Phoebe.

'Whatever's easiest,' Phoebe said.

'Tea because then I can practise reading the leaves,' Anni told her.

'I thought you didn't inherit the gift,' Phoebe said, looking at the older woman, surprised.

'No, no, no, I didn't, but anyone can learn to read the leaves – I do it when I'm a bit worried and want some reassurance.'

'And you're worried about something today.' Phoebe left the question hanging in the air. She didn't want to push it if Anni didn't want to talk. But she knew that she probably wouldn't have mentioned it if she didn't.

'A little.'

Anni made two cups of tea and brought them back to the table: the white china cups clinked a little in their white saucers.

Phoebe waited, knowing that was the best way to let Anni talk. A comfortable silence was the best way to let anyone talk in her experience. She wondered if Anni was still worrying about the alpacas. That would be normal. Deep down, she was a little bit worried herself, even though all the results had come back clear.

But when she did start to speak, Anni didn't talk about her worries. Instead, she stirred her tea slowly and said, 'Buckland is a Romany name. It's the only thing I kept when I married Nick. I said I wouldn't be giving up my name. We even changed the name of the farm. This farm used to be called Knightwood Farm, after the Knightwood Oak, have you heard of the Knightwood Oak? It's supposedly the oldest tree in the New Forest. It's rumoured to be between 450 and 600 years old. That dates back to the times royalty used to hunt regularly in the forest.'

'I have heard of it, yes. It's not that far from here, is it?'

'Three or four miles as the crow flies. This farm was called Knightwood Farm for generations. Nick wasn't keen on changing the name, but I insisted. I gave up everything when we got married.

But I didn't want to give up my name. So he agreed that the farm would become Buckland Farm. Although in a way I have given up my name.' There was a faraway light in her eyes. 'I was born Anselina Buckland. But everyone except my mother called me Anni because it was less of a mouthful.'

'Wow.' Phoebe sipped her tea which was black and tasted strong. After a moment, she said, 'Did you know that Puddleduck Farm used to be called something else too?'

'Yes, I did. Maggie told me. It was named Puddleduck after her great-grandmother was given a pair of ducks as a wedding present by her maid of honour. Wasn't she a fan of Beatrix Potter?'

'That's right,' Phoebe confirmed.

'There's a tradition too, isn't there? That as long as there are puddle ducks on the farm, the farm will prosper.'

'Yes. And one of the puddle ducks has to be called Jemima. And there are still puddle ducks there. And one of them is still called Jemima.'

'These traditions are important,' Anni said. 'Or to be more precise, the beliefs behind the traditions are important. Beliefs are very, very important. Beliefs shape our world.'

'I think I'd agree with that.'

Anni spread butter and jam on one of the scones on her plate and then pushed the butter and jam towards Phoebe. 'We should probably eat these before they get cold. Have you finished your tea?'

'Almost.'

Phoebe followed suit with the butter and jam, she couldn't see any cream, and there was another small silence as they both ate scones and sipped tea and Phoebe thought what a very English tradition that was. And how had it crept into this Romany kitchen in the heart of the New Forest?

The scones were delicious, the melt in your mouth variety, and

Phoebe, who'd only planned to eat one, found that she couldn't resist and ate both of them.

Anni, who'd only eaten one, finished first and brushed crumbs from her mouth onto her plate. 'Now I'm going to read my leaves,' she said.

She picked up the teacup by its delicate bone china handle, swirled it a couple of times with her eyes closed, and then opened her eyes and inverted it onto her saucer.

She left it there for maybe a minute. Then she slowly righted the cup.

Phoebe watched in fascination as Anni stared into her cup without speaking. Despite having come from a background of science, she was fairly open minded about fortune telling, whatever its form. She'd had friends at school and college who'd sworn by it and often visited tarot card readers, although it wasn't something Phoebe had ever relied on.

Anni's dark eyes were hard to read and her face was still. Then, after a couple of minutes of intense concentration on her cup, she nodded a couple of times and said, 'Mmmm.'

'What did you see?' Phoebe asked, desperate to know.

'Things I wish I hadn't, really.' Anni frowned. 'There's trouble ahead.' She sighed. 'There is always some kind of trouble ahead, of course. That's life. But this is of the worst kind, the emotional kind. A heartbreak of some kind.'

'Oh, no.' Phoebe hadn't been expecting that. She wanted to say something to make Anni feel better. For a second there, the older woman's face had been so shadowed and sad. But she didn't know what she could say to offset something that Anni so clearly believed in, realising after such a reading that most things would seem trivial.

She fell back on science. 'I don't think it's anything to do with the alpacas. I got the last of the results back yesterday from the lab and they're all clear.'

'Well, that's good news at least.' Anni shrugged her shoulders as though she was shrugging off a coat. 'I'll park that for now then.' She leaned forward, and a ringlet of dark hair fell across her face. 'Would you like me to do yours?'

Phoebe swallowed. 'If there's heartbreak ahead, I'm not sure if I want to know.'

'Don't worry. There'll be joy as well. The two things go hand in hand. They have to or the world would be unbalanced. Yin and yang. One can't exist without the other.'

'OK,' Phoebe said impulsively. 'Then, yes, please. Read mine.'

13

Phoebe expected Anni to take her cup, but she didn't. Instead, she instructed her on what to do.

'Have you finished your tea?'

'Almost.'

'There should be only a couple of teaspoons of tea and leaves left in the cup.'

'There are,' Phoebe said, feeling a knot of anticipation forming in her stomach.

'OK, well, try and clear your mind of any preconceived ideas, and then see what thoughts rise to the top. Maybe there's a pressing question that's been bothering you. If there is, let it come.'

Phoebe did what she was told. Rufus sprang instantly into her mind. He was never far away. Does he fancy me? Do we have a future? Is it really a good idea to push him or should I let things evolve naturally?

'Try not to have too many questions swirling about,' Anni said, almost as if she were reading Phoebe's mind. 'That can muddy the waters. Try focusing on just the one.'

'Right.' Phoebe felt herself blushing. She truly hoped Anni couldn't read her mind. That would be highly embarrassing.

'Now, as you're doing that, pick up the cup with your left hand and slowly move it in a counter-clockwise direction so the tea leaves swirl about inside.'

Phoebe picked up the cup and swirled. Her finger and thumb felt slightly sweaty on the handle. Rationally and logically, she might not be giving much weight to fortune telling, but she knew there was a part of her mind that was giving it plenty. The power of belief, huh.

'Now invert the cup onto the saucer,' Anni instructed. 'And leave it there for a minute or two.'

Phoebe did as she was told.

While they were waiting, the back door opened and Nick appeared. He was dressed in an ancient greatcoat, fastened with orange bailing twine and his grey hair was windswept.

'Oh, hi there, Phoebe. I didn't know we had company. Did we call you out for an animal?' He exchanged glances with his wife.

'No, I was just passing.' She saw the flicker of relief cross his face.

'Good job – we've spent enough money this month already.'

'She fancied one of my scones and a cup of tea, love…'

Anni tailed off and Nick glanced at the table and took in the inverted cups. 'Ah, say no more.' He rolled his eyes. 'I'll grab a flask then and I'll leave you ladies in peace.'

He was gone a few seconds later.

'Doesn't he approve?' Phoebe gestured towards the cups.

'He has his beliefs and I have mine. It's the only way marriages work,' Anni said. 'Cooperation and patience. I put up with him and he puts up with me. Right then, are you ready? Shall we have a look at those leaves?'

'OK.' Phoebe's mouth felt dry.

'So this is how it works. The rim of the cup shows the present day. The sides of the cup show the medium term and the bottom of the cup shows the far future.'

Phoebe looked into her cup. As far as she could see, there was just a mess of tea leaves against the white china, more dotted up one side than the other with a few blobs in the base. Anni had used the type of cups where the sides sloped outwards a little towards the rim, which she assumed made it easier for the leaves to stick.

'It can sometimes take a while for what's there to become clear,' Anni said. 'At first it can all look a bit messy, but the more you look, the more you see.'

She pointed at a cluster of leaves near the rim. 'There we are. Can you see that shape there – an upside-down triangle, not properly filled in?' Frowning, Anni leaned closer. 'Ah, I see it now, not a triangle. It's the letter A. There's someone in your life whose name begins with A who's significant at the moment. Does that ring a bell?' She glanced at Phoebe.

'Well, I guess that depends on how much in the present we're talking about,' Phoebe said. 'Maybe it's you. Or maybe it's an alpaca. That would make sense. Given the amount of time I've been spending here lately.'

'Maybe,' Anni said, not looking particularly convinced. 'And that shape there, do you see, as we go further down, directly below the handle of the cup? It looks a bit like a crown.'

All Phoebe could see was a blob, although she supposed it could have had a couple of spikes on the top.

'The crown signifies success. Often success in a venture. Ah...' Anni broke off and paused.

'What?' Phoebe said eagerly. Her intention to stay coolly detached and not to put too much stock in any of this was vanishing fast. 'What have you seen?'

'A little bit in the future, but not too much. There's the shape of a house. You can see that, right?' Anni pointed.

Phoebe looked. This time she had to admit she could see the shape of a house. A little wonky maybe but definitely a house shape.

'A house is one of the symbols of family.' Anni broke off and looked directly into Phoebe's eyes. 'You're going to be part of a family – in the future, but not that far in the future. It's crystal clear.'

'I'm part of a family now,' Phoebe said. 'We all are, aren't we? We have mums, dads, brothers and sisters, nieces, nephews.'

'We are. We arise from families and then we have children of our own.' Anni looked back into the cup. 'I take it you're not planning to have a baby?'

Phoebe wanted to say definitely not, but Anni was still talking. 'Yes, I think there's a baby there – so if you're not planning one, you should take care.'

If only she knew, Phoebe thought, that right now there was as much chance of her getting pregnant as there was of her growing wings and flying to the moon.

'Yes, definitely a baby.' Anni paused again. 'Although there is love there too. It's the biggest symbol here. And the strongest. The heart shape in the bottom of your cup. It's so big I didn't see it for what it was at first. You are very much loved, Phoebe. I'm talking in a romantic sense here. A big heart can sometimes denote one great love, or... it could also mean there's more than one suitor.'

Just for a second, Phoebe thought of Sam. There had been a time a couple of years ago when she'd first come back from London when Sam had told her his feelings had changed from deep friendship to something stronger. And she had told him, as gently as she could, that hers hadn't changed. Then last year, just before she'd got together with Rufus, she'd had a suspicion that Sam still felt the same way. There were things he'd said and done that had backed this up. Tori had thought the same thing. But Phoebe had finally dismissed it. Because Sam had pushed her towards Rufus. When Sam had been injured in a show-jumping accident at the New Forest Show last year, Phoebe had run to his side, alarmed at the strength of her feelings for him. For a few seconds, she'd been terrified that he might die. He had been badly injured. He'd been stretchered out of the show ring by two paramedics. Phoebe had followed them to the ambulance.

But Sam had virtually chucked her out of the ambulance. He'd told her he was fine and that Rufus needed her more than he did and this had turned out to be true. Phoebe had found Rufus in the middle of a full-blown PTSD attack, triggered by Sam's show-jumping accident, and poor Archie, who'd been with him, had been sobbing his little heart out because he hadn't known what to do.

'I don't want to pry...' Anni's soft voice interrupted Phoebe's train of thought. 'But some of what I've said is ringing a bell with you, isn't it?'

'Yes, a bit.' Phoebe was flustered. 'I'm glad I'm loved. That's really nice to hear.' She forced lightness into her voice, wanting to change the subject of love back to less disturbing territory. 'It's all good then. You can't see any bad news ahead?'

'Nothing too major. There are always difficulties, obviously...'

'Part of the yin and the yang,' Phoebe repeated what Anni had said earlier.

'Exactly.' Anni smiled at her.

* * *

Phoebe was still feeling unsettled as she drove back to the practice. She wasn't sure exactly why. Anni hadn't really said anything that unsettling. It was the kind of innocuous information Phoebe knew a fortune teller would tell people, the kind of thing she imagined Anni's grandmother Madam Kesia had told the stars. Classic stuff about pregnancies and love affairs and having successful ventures. Nothing too specific. Although the A had been specific. Then again, Anni had been fairly safe with that – being as it was the first letter of her name. How had she known it was an A anyway, Phoebe wondered. It could just as easily have been a V.

V for Violet. That would make sense – Phoebe's head spun. V for Violet and Violet's babies, all of which had been rehomed now, although Archie hadn't made as much profit – if any – as he'd planned because the baby guinea pigs had been sold to friends of his and Jack's at school and they'd all battered him down on price.

'Archie will need to develop a more ruthless business head for his future ventures,' Rufus had joked when they'd all been talking about it.

Phoebe braked sharply to avoid a pigeon that was slow to take off on the forest road. Pigeons were so far away from aerodynamic that sometimes she wondered how they ever managed to take off at all. She waited for it to get properly airborne before her thoughts drifted back to Archie.

Oh, my goodness. Archie. What if the A in the tea leaves was for Archie? Why hadn't that struck her before? Suddenly all of the pieces jigsawed together in her head and made a complete picture. Archie and Rufus, two of the most important people in her world.

The family, the huge love, even the unplanned pregnancy. She felt a prickle of excitement run down her spine. Not that she was in the market for an unplanned pregnancy, but she was definitely in the market for the actions that could lead up to one. So maybe the whole of her reading had been to do with Rufus and Archie. Maybe that was what Anni had seen in the tea leaves, without knowing any of the background or any of the details. Wow. Phoebe blinked a few times. She liked and trusted Anni or she would never have got involved in a reading, however light-hearted it was. But she'd been sceptical, still. Now she wasn't so sure. Maybe there was something in it after all. Maybe Anni had read her future.

Phoebe decided it didn't matter whether she had or hadn't. It was the shove she needed to talk to Rufus. Suddenly she knew that the timing was right. As soon as she finished at the practice for the day, she would pop round and see him. She would pin him down on a date where he could come to hers and stay over. She felt excitement spark through her. She knew she'd been putting it off because she was scared to upset the status quo and risk rejection. But now that Anni had seen it in the tea leaves, it felt like a sign from the universe. Phoebe felt full of hope. Whatever else had happened in the Buckland kitchen, one thing felt certain in her heart. The stars were clearly aligned.

14

'Rufus, he is not here.' Emilia had answered the front door on her second ring and Phoebe wished she had followed her instincts and gone round the back.

She'd done that once or twice lately to avoid having to navigate her way past the guard dog of a nanny. But she wasn't totally comfortable about it in case she bumped into Lord Alfred. She had a horror of him thinking she was sneaking around without anyone knowing.

'His car's here,' Phoebe pointed out reasonably. 'Can you tell him I'm here, please?'

Emilia spread her hands out in a gesture of bemused puzzlement. 'He is not in house. Maybe he go to some place outside. I cannot know always his movements. You tell him you come, ja?'

She was interrupted by a shout from behind her. 'Phoebe. Dad didn't say you were coming round to see us.'

Thank goodness for Archie. Ignoring Emilia pointedly, Phoebe greeted him warmly. 'It's a surprise visit. Do you know where your dad is?'

'Yep. He's talking to Harrison in the garden. I'll show you.'

Emilia bristled and her ponytail bristled with her, but she couldn't do much about it and she was forced to step aside and let Phoebe pass.

A few minutes later, Phoebe and Archie were crossing the expanse of lawn towards a shed at the far corner where Rufus and Harrison were deep in conversation.

The gardens looked beautiful. Purple, lilac and pink delphiniums filled the beds around the lawn, in a gloriously pink and purple haze, reminding Phoebe that soon the Beechbrook fields would be lilac with lavender. In the woods beyond the gardens, Phoebe could see clusters of bluebells beyond the trees too. It was as though everywhere you looked there were echoes of the purple harvest that was to come. Or maybe she was being too fanciful.

Despite Emilia's frostiness, she still felt warm with anticipation, although she was going to need to drag Rufus away from Harrison for a bit – and Archie too, come to that. She couldn't say what she had to say in front of either of them.

Rufus turned at the last minute and the smile that lit his face was reassuring.

'Hey, Phoebe, I didn't know you were here. Is everything OK?'

He stepped forward and pecked her cheek.

'Yes, it's fine,' she said, as Harrison nodded in her direction. He didn't look that thrilled to see her, but, from what she could gather, Harrison never looked particularly thrilled about anything. Morose was a word that could have been made for Harrison. Brooding if you were being generous. Phoebe had found it difficult to understand what Tori saw in him the first time she'd met him and to be honest she still did.

'I don't want to hold you up, if you're busy,' she said, looking at Rufus. 'I just wondered if you were free for a quick coffee.'

'Yeah, yeah, I am.' Rufus looked at his hands, which were earthy, and rubbed them on his jeans. 'We're about finished here, aren't we?'

Harrison nodded.

'Archie, have you done your homework?' Rufus called to his son, who having delivered Phoebe to his father had wandered off towards the edge of the woods.

'Nearly,' Archie called back.

'Well, don't leave it too late, will you.'

'OK, Dad.'

Rufus gave a rueful shake of his head. 'Emilia's supposed to make him stay inside till he does it, but he's very good at finding excuses to slip away.'

'My fault today then,' Phoebe said.

'Mmmm, I doubt you had much to do with it. Archie could teach masterclasses in how to get out of doing homework. He'd much rather be outside. I can't really say I blame him on an evening like this. It's beautiful, isn't it?'

He paused and gestured around him. They were in the middle of the lawn which had recently been mowed. It had lines on, Phoebe noticed. Perfectly straight and ordered that echoed the straight lines of the house, which was a long pale grey three-storey building with a parapet roof and a colonnaded terrace.

'We've got a new gardener.' Rufus noticed her noticing. 'I'm not sure if I like the lines or not. What do you think?'

'It is a bit formal. Although the flowerbeds aren't. They're a riot of colour.'

'Yes, they are. Apparently it's all about contrasts,' Rufus said. 'Ordered lawns and chaotic flowerbeds. He wanted to cut back some of the bluebells – they encroach onto the edges of the grass. I drew the line at that.'

'Good,' Phoebe said, horrified.

The birds were singing, the air was warm. It had been a beautiful May. It was hard to imagine that this green and purple English garden was only a short distance from the wild and ancient forest beyond the estate boundaries.

'Shall we have our coffee out here?' Rufus suggested.

'That sounds lovely.'

A few minutes later, they were sitting on the terrace. The same terrace where Phoebe had first met Archie. She'd been in hot pursuit of three of Maggie's donkeys who'd escaped during a storm and she'd found them here with Archie who'd been feeding them bread from a bag.

But now, sitting here with Rufus, that time seemed part of another world. Years away from the present day. Phoebe sipped her coffee and wondered how to broach the subject of Rufus coming for a stopover.

She didn't want to change the lovely peace that had settled between them. But it was the perfect opportunity to ask him and if she didn't do it now, she knew she would kick herself later.

'I thought I might cook you a meal at the weekend,' she said. 'Friday or Saturday, whichever night's easiest. At Woodcutter's, I mean.'

'Sounds nice. Can we do Saturday? Is it a special occasion?' Inadvertently he'd given her the perfect opening.

'It could be,' she said softly. 'I was hoping you might stay over the night with me. At Woodcutter's.'

She watched his face. He was looking down, both hands clasping the mug in his lap. Was there the tiniest flicker of tension? It was so hard to tell with Rufus. Archie might be able to teach a masterclass in how to get out of doing homework, but his father could have taught one in the art of not showing emotion.

The only time Phoebe had seen him losing control had been when he'd been in the midst of a PTSD attack and that was hardly normal life.

'That sounds like a plan,' Rufus said and Phoebe felt a stab of disappointment.

'I have to say that I'd hoped for a slightly more enthusiastic response than that, Rufus.'

'I'm sorry.' His apology was immediate. 'Of course I'd love to come. What shall I bring?'

'A nice bottle of wine. Seeing as neither of us will have to drive.' She wasn't sure why she felt the need to hammer the point home, but she did.

'Great. Consider it done.'

'Do you like oysters?'

'Er – not much. Why?'

Did she really have to explain? Phoebe took a deep breath. But before either of them could say anything else, Emilia appeared through a door that led out onto the terrace.

'Rufus, there you are. Your father is wanting to speak with you. He said it's urgent. If you're not busy.' She flicked a triumphant glance at Phoebe. 'Also, I cannot find Archie? Did he go into the woods?'

Rufus began to get up and Phoebe knew it was pointless trying to stop him. She had to pick her battles where Emilia was concerned and she had already achieved what she'd come to do. At least when they were at Woodcutter's, just the two of them, there could be no interruptions. No reason not to do what new couples were supposed to do.

She got up too. And she was about to say goodbye to Rufus when a thought struck her. Aware that Emilia, who was hovering, could probably hear every word she said, she leaned in closer to Rufus. 'I'd like it to be just the two of us on Saturday. Is that OK?'

'Yes, it's fine. I think Archie's seeing Jack anyway. No doubt hatching a plot about which two guinea pigs will be the most compatible for the next pairing.'

Phoebe nodded. The irony of this didn't escape her. But Rufus, if he thought the same thing, gave no hint of showing it. Not even a wink.

She felt strangely deflated as she kissed him goodbye – with Emilia still hovering unnecessarily – and left for home.

* * *

'That is flaming awesome news,' was Tori's response when Phoebe, unable to keep it to herself, phoned her that night. 'Did I actually just say awesome?' she added almost immediately.

'You did,' Phoebe said. 'But you're right. It is.'

'You don't know yet. He might be terrible in bed or have a tiny willy or an inappropriate tattoo on his backside. Have you actually seen his backside? No. Don't tell me that. It's too much information.'

'I shan't be telling you any details,' Phoebe said, laughing despite herself. 'That would be utterly inappropriate – we're not teenagers any more.'

'Oh no, we're grown up and sensible women now, aren't we? I forgot. On reflection, I think it was more fun being teenagers.' She gave a dramatic sigh. 'Seriously though, Phoebe...' Her voice sobered. 'I'm really pleased you got that sorted. Maybe he just needed a little prod.'

'I thought that was me. But I'm definitely not after little. I'm after lengthy...'

'I thought we weren't allowed to talk details.'

'I don't mean that sort of lengthy. I mean timewise.'

'You mean stamina? I bet he's got plenty of that. What with that awesome self-control of his. Harrison once told me that if there was an Olympic medal for self-control, Rufus would have the gold. And he should know. He's his best friend.'

'No, I don't mean stamina either. I mean tender and gentle and not wham bam, thank you, ma'am.' Phoebe paused for thought. 'What if I've waited all this time and it's all a big disappointment? Or it doesn't work out. Or he doesn't want to?'

'You're definitely overthinking it now. He's a man and we know he's not gay. And we know he fancies you. Or he wouldn't be dating you. Honestly, Phoebe, stop second-guessing it. If you want my opinion, I think you were right about what you said before. He's only been taking it slowly because of what happened with Rowena. When you told me about the PTSD, it made a lot more sense.'

'Yes. Thanks. I'll stop overthinking it. How's everything going with you and Harrison?'

'It's great. Everything's great.' Tori paused and for a second Phoebe thought she was going to add something else, but she didn't. She changed the subject back to Phoebe's love life instead.

'I know you're not going to tell me any actual details. Obvs. As that would be massively inappropriate, not to mention immature and we're all sensible and grown up, etc. But maybe on Sunday morning, you could just send me a number via text.'

'A number?'

'Yes, a number between one and ten. One being, needs a bit more practice, and ten being, bloody hell, that was the most amazing night of my life.'

'No, I could not.'

'At least give it some thought.' Tori snorted with laughter.

'I'm hanging up,' Phoebe said. But she was laughing too.

15

There were three whole days before Saturday, so Phoebe had plenty of time to prepare, but she still felt slightly panicky. She wasn't sure why. That was plenty of time for a wax and a manicure. It wasn't enough time to lose any weight, but she was fairly trim anyway. Rushing around and skimping on meals because she was busy saw to that.

As for the house, she was barely ever at Woodcutter's so it wouldn't need much of a tidy up and she had cooked for Rufus before. They'd had casseroles that had been in the slow cooker all day made with carrots and potatoes Rufus had brought her from his father's vegetable patch. Phoebe hadn't even known Lord Alfred had a vegetable patch until that point but apparently he loved the outdoors as much as Archie.

Phoebe had wondered if that love of outdoors had skipped a generation. Rufus spent so much time holed up in his office. Although he'd had a tree house when he was young, which was still there, deep in the silver birch wood. They'd once sat in it and eaten chocolate. That day also seemed like it had happened in another lifetime.

Maybe Rufus was just too busy to spend much time outdoors. He had told her that he'd taken over more and more of his father's responsibilities when it came to the running of the estate, and that even managing the family investments was a full-time job. Dealing with tenants and being on the management committees of the many meetings his father was on was all work he had to do on top of this.

And he had Archie, of course. Yes, he had the annoying Emilia to take care of his son, but Phoebe knew that Rufus took his duties as a father very seriously.

It brought her back to time and the fact that they had so precious little of it together. What if making love with Rufus turned out to be so amazing that they couldn't keep their hands off each other after that but they had no time together? That would be utter torture. Now she really was overthinking it.

'Earth calling Phoebe,' said Jenna's voice in her ear and Phoebe remembered where she was – which was at work – just about to start her Tuesday afternoon's appointments.

'Sorry, I was daydreaming,' Phoebe said.

'No kidding. That's the third time I've asked you the same question.'

'Sorry. What question?'

Jenna rolled her eyes and repeated patiently, 'Sam Hendrie is due to bring Snowball in for a check-up and I wanted to make an appointment for when you're here. As you did the surgery.'

'Of course. That would be great. I'm in every morning the rest of this week, I think.'

'Thanks. I'll phone him back and book one first thing tomorrow or Friday. Just in case you get called out.'

'Brilliant.'

'Oh, and Max wanted to know when would be a good time to arrange a meeting between himself, you and Maggie.'

'Why does he want to arrange a meeting?'

'He's been in touch with an animal behaviourist – it's his pet project at the moment. Do you remember he was talking about it before? The possibility of sharing one between Puddleduck Vets and the sanctuary. Or at least having one we could recommend.'

'I do. And I don't think Maggie will be too keen.'

'Apparently this particular guy is becoming a bit of a celebrity on YouTube and he's happy to come and do a free half-hour demonstration. On condition that he can film it and use it on his social media channel. That's if we had any suitable candidates in the sanctuary. Max thought that Saddam would be the perfect choice. But he'll need to run that by Maggie, and he thought maybe it would be better if you spoke to her first.'

'I bet he did,' Phoebe said, picturing her grandmother's reaction. 'OK, I'll ask her. Did he say when the behaviourist could come?'

'I think he's quite flexible,' Jenna said. 'Which makes me wonder how much work he actually gets. But we don't really have anything to lose, do we? I've got some details somewhere. Max gave me a card.'

Rather to Phoebe's surprise, Maggie was a lot less resistant to the idea than Phoebe had expected.

She popped in to see her after work and now they were standing in the over-warm kitchen. One of the advantages, but also the disadvantages of having an Aga as old as Maggie's was that you couldn't turn it off. Well, you could, but it took several hours to warm up again and as it was her only way of cooking, turning it off was pretty inconvenient.

'You're saying that this animal behaviour chap wants to come and work his magic on that reprobate cat and that it won't cost me a penny,' she asked, turning the business card that Phoebe had given her, over and over in her hand.

'That's exactly what I'm saying,' Phoebe confirmed. 'And he also wants your permission to film it.'

'Does he now?' Maggie's eyes gleamed with amusement. 'I assume he has a glamorous assistant for that bit, does he? Being as it'd be quite tricky to film yourself.'

'I'm sure he will have.'

'And he does know about Saddam's little habit of attacking first and asking questions later? And the fact that he chases dogs for fun.'

'I'm not sure exactly how much Max told him, but apparently he told Max that he's an expert with feral cats.'

'Oh, is he now? An expert on feral cats? Well, I can't wait to see him in action.'

'So you're happy for us to make an appointment when you're here?'

'Indeed I am. It cheers me up every time I think about Catty the Cat Whisperer.' She smirked. 'I'm going out with Eddie tomorrow afternoon but other than that I'm free. Any evening's good for me. If you and Max are going to be there, I'm assuming it would be an evening?'

Phoebe nodded.

'Don't rush off, love. There's something I want to talk to you about.'

Phoebe hesitated.

'I'm all ears.'

'Do you want a cuppa? Tea or coffee?'

'Coffee, please.' Phoebe wasn't sure whether she'd ever be able to drink tea again, or at least not the kind made with leaves. She hadn't told anyone about that. Not even Tori, she realised. She'd been waiting until they spoke face to face.

Maggie brought the coffees and they settled opposite each other at the kitchen table. 'It's about Buster,' Maggie began and Phoebe heard the seriousness in her voice. 'He couldn't get up this morning and he messed his bed. He was so upset, bless him.' She paused. This was obviously difficult for her. 'I know his arthritis is bad. Most of the time I think he's younger than he is because we've got that so well under control. But he's nearly thirteen and I know he's not going to live forever.'

Phoebe nodded. She could see her grandmother's heart was breaking at the thought of losing her beloved black Labrador. Buster had been around for almost the entire time Maggie had the sanctuary. He'd arrived as a tiny pup, the only surviving one of a litter that someone had left in a box on the recycling lorry. Maggie had nursed him and trained him and cosseted him with love and he'd grown into a beautiful dog with a sleek coat and a penchant for biscuits. Since then, he'd been a black Labrador shadow at Maggie's side.

Before Buster there had only been farm dogs at Puddleduck. But he'd arrived just after Farmer Pete had died. Phoebe was pretty sure that like Neddie, the first donkey who'd arrived at the farm, Buster had given Maggie a reason to go on living when she lost her husband. Buster and Neddie had helped to fill the space that would otherwise have yawned achingly before her.

Maggie cleared her throat. 'It's the first time anything like this has happened. Maybe it's just his medication that needs changing? Or do you think I should be preparing myself to let him go? I can't bear the thought of him being in pain.'

A tear ran down her face as she glanced at Buster, who was at the moment lying flat out by the Aga beside Tiny, snoring softly, oblivious to the chat about his future that was going on over his head.

'Let's not make any hasty decisions before we know the full story. I will look at his medication, and I'll examine him properly. Do you want to do that now? Or you could bring him in to the surgery tomorrow and I can give him a full MOT. I'll need to look on the system for his meds.'

'I'll do that, I think.' Maggie swiped at the tear and sniffed.

'I'm sure we could make adjustments,' Phoebe went on, keeping her voice level and professional because she knew it was what Maggie needed right now. 'Have you noticed any other changes?'

'I did change their biscuits a couple of nights ago. Their regular one wasn't in stock and the delivery people sent a different one.'

'Maybe the change didn't agree with him? That could cause an upset tummy.'

'Of course it could.' A light flickered on in Maggie's eyes. 'I didn't think of that. Oh, my days, why didn't I think of that?' She got up from her chair at the table and went across to where the old dog lay. Bending stiffly, she fondled his ears. 'Oh, Buster, my lad, I was writing you off and maybe I needn't have done.'

'Let me have a proper look at him tomorrow,' Phoebe cautioned. 'We both know he's a very old dog.'

'Yes, yes, I know.' Maggie carried on fondling his ears. 'Thank you, love.'

* * *

The following morning, as Phoebe examined Buster properly in her surgery, she knew she was praying for a miracle. As she'd already told Maggie, he was an old dog. Mind you, saying that, apart from the osteoarthritis, he was in pretty good shape. Years of wandering around the fields of Puddleduck Farm at Maggie's side had stood him in good stead.

She listened to his heart rate, which was still strong and steady, and then focused her attention on his limbs.

'All things considered, he's in great shape,' she told Maggie, who was waiting, very patiently for her, while Phoebe ran her hands over the old dog, gently flexing his elbows and hocks.

'The crepitus isn't too bad,' she told Maggie, 'and his range of motion isn't bad either, all things considered.'

'That's because he's utterly spoiled and lives on a diet of tripe and best biscuits,' Maggie remarked.

'Has he had any more problems getting up, or making it to the garden in time?'

'No. He was fine this morning. Stiff, as always but... fine. I mean, he doesn't go charging around like he used to – but then, neither do I.' Her smile was rueful. 'We just have to adjust, don't we, Buster boy? Work within our limitations.'

'That'll be the day, at least in your case,' Phoebe said, raising her eyebrows. She paused. 'Does Buster give you any indication of being in pain at all?'

'He doesn't yelp or whimper if that's what you mean. I'm not sure he would, though. He's never been a whiny kind of dog.'

'OK.' Phoebe stroked the dog's head and told him he was a good boy and he wagged his tail in agreement. 'Well, on the good news front there's a new drug I can give him that I've been getting some good results with. It's an injection that targets the arthritis pain receptors, it's called Librela and it doesn't have the same side effects as the drug he's been on, which as you know can sometime affect their stomachs and renal systems. It should help and it can have amazing results.'

'That sounds good,' Maggie said cautiously. 'And he's not too old for it – this wonder drug?'

'No, he's not.'

'I'm paying the proper price for it, mind. I don't want any of your discount nonsense.'

'Of course,' Phoebe said, crossing her fingers behind her back.

'Let's give it a try. We can monitor him closely. I think there's life in the old dog yet. But just be aware that he won't live for ever.'

'Yes, I will. Thanks so much, love.'

After Phoebe had given Buster the shot, she lifted him down from the examining table and they both went out into reception, just in time to see Max at the desk.

He turned. 'Hi, Maggie. How's the boy?'

'He's passed his MOT,' she told him. 'Thanks for asking.'

'That's great news. Actually, I wanted to catch you,' Max continued. 'I've just booked that celebrity animal behaviourist I mentioned. He's coming on Friday at 6 p.m. to see Saddam. Assuming that's OK with you?'

'It's fine with me.'

'Will you be about then too, Phoebe?' Max continued.

'I wouldn't miss it for the world,' Phoebe said.

16

Phoebe saw Sam and Snowball first thing on Friday morning and she was pleased to see the cat looking bright and well. She examined him thoroughly.

'I think he's probably OK to have his freedom back now, Sam. He seems absolutely fine and as you know, his X-rays were all good. You've done wonders. He can come out of the crate, although maybe don't let him stay out all night for another week or so – if that's not too difficult to arrange?'

'He's usually in for his tea, so it should be OK,' Sam said. 'I just hope he's learned his lesson, and he steers clear of traffic in future.'

'Fingers crossed,' Phoebe said.

'But I know I can't keep him in,' Sam added. 'That's one thing I do know. If you love something, you have to let it go. No matter what the outcome.' He stroked the cat's fluffy black head and looked reflective. 'If he wants to go running out in front of a car again, there's precious little I can do about it.'

'I'm sure he won't be so careless again, will you, boy?' Phoebe said, and although her comment was directed towards the cat, she was looking at Sam's face as she spoke. 'Are you OK, Sam? You seem a little sad.'

He glanced at her in surprise. 'Do I? Sorry. I'm not. We should catch up properly some time, Phoebe. It's ages since we've had a pint at the Brace.' He broke off. 'I mean if that's not an issue with Rufus. Hey, why not invite him along too? I'll ask Judy. We can have a foursome.'

'Um, yes, that sounds nice.' Actually, it didn't, but she wasn't sure why. Sam looked pleased though. 'I'll suss out some dates with Judy and text you.'

'Great.'

She saw him out and then went into reception to see who her next patient was. It was odd, she knew she should feel happy for Sam. But she felt more anxious. Maybe that was because he'd looked a little strained today. Hopefully things hadn't kicked off with Judy's parents again. Sam would make an excellent husband. He was kind, reliable, selfless and fiercely loyal – what more could any future parents-in-law want?

* * *

Sam put Snowball in his cat box in the back of his car and drove home, being careful not to brake too sharply or go round corners too fast.

'Looks like it's freedom for you then, mate,' he said out loud to the cat. 'Let's hope you're going to make better choices this time. No running out in front of traffic, OK?'

There was a saying Sam had once heard, 'The definition of insanity is doing the same thing and expecting a different result.'

'Although if you manage that then you've got a lot more sense than your owner,' Sam continued his one-sided chat with Snowball.

Because wasn't that what he'd done with Judy? For some reason, he'd expected the situation with her parents to be different this time – but it wasn't. If he'd hoped they might have mellowed towards him over time – perhaps realised that their daughter's happiness was more important than class, money and a suitable marriage – then he'd been sadly mistaken. He'd only seen them once when Judy had invited them all to her house for dinner, nothing formal – just a spag bol supper. It had been immediately clear that they were not thrilled to see him.

'I didn't know you two were back together,' Sophie Barker had remarked, raising her perfect eyebrows and managing to look down her nose at Sam at the same time. 'Did you sort out your differences in the end?'

'We didn't really have any differences, Mummy,' Judy had said. 'We just drifted apart, and then lost touch.'

'One would guess there wasn't enough of interest to keep you together then,' she'd said. 'What a shame.'

She didn't sound as though she thought it was a shame, at all, and Judy's father hadn't been much better.

'You're the postie, aren't you? With that gelding over at Brook?'

How could you make the word 'gelding' sound like a personal insult? Sam had wanted to thump him. Which wouldn't have helped anything.

Judy flew to his rescue. 'Sam's not a postie, Daddy, his mother owns the post office and general stores in Bridgeford.'

'Although I do help out with deliveries occasionally,' Sam said stubbornly. He would not feel ashamed of who he was, just because these two nobs thought he should.

Snowball yowled loudly from the back seat, bringing Sam back to the present.

'We'll be home, soon, mate. You just hang on in there.'

Five minutes later they *were* home and Sam carried the cat box in and through the downstairs door of the maisonette and trudged on up the first flight of stairs to his own front door. He'd been tempted to let Snowball out at the bottom of the stairs, but there was a part of him that wanted to keep him safe for just a few more hours.

He'd never worried about his cat before. Snowball had come and gone as he pleased via the cat flaps Sam had fitted in both his front door and the main one downstairs. But the accident had made Sam feel cautious and a bit overprotective. Once bitten, twice shy. It was a pity he hadn't been more cautious about getting involved with Judy again, he thought, as back in his kitchen once more, he put the cat box down and unhinged the front gate.

'You're free, mate.'

Snowball didn't need telling twice. He shot out of the cat basket, through the open kitchen door, and headed for the stairs and disappeared. Sam winced as he heard the bang of the cat flap downstairs. He'd have a quick coffee and head back to work. He'd told his ma he wouldn't be away too long. Just a quick trip to get Snowball checked over and he'd be back. Friday was a busy day at Hendrie's.

His ma had been brilliant about having Snowball over there too. Sam half wished he hadn't let the cat out, but now he had he was reluctant to leave Snowball completely on his own, which was crazy, he knew. He'd never bothered about that before, and frankly, Snowball was unlikely to be back any time soon.

Sam sighed. He'd meant what he'd said to Phoebe. If you love something, let it go, but boy, that was one of those things that was so much easier to glibly say than to put into action.

* * *

The day passed with its usual lightning speed at Puddleduck. Phoebe didn't have time to think too much about anything – she was just relieved it was Friday and then it was the weekend. Max was covering the Saturday morning surgery too, as she was on call for the whole of the following weekend. This meant that she'd have plenty of time to get her house, and more importantly, her head in the right kind of order for Rufus's visit on Saturday night.

Half of her was looking forward to it hugely. The other half of her was terrified it was going to go wrong. Or that Rufus would cancel and it wouldn't happen at all.

She'd got some pizzas in because they were easy and Rufus hardly ever ate them at home. Emilia was a stickler when it came to healthy meals apparently. She cooked for Archie and quite often Rufus too. She cooked them Swiss specialities like polenta and braised beef and Papet Vaudois, which was a mixture of potatoes, leeks and cabbage. Foods that were, according to Emilia, very wholesome and therefore good for concentration, alertness and mental clarity.

Phoebe wouldn't have been surprised if she'd made Rufus and Archie take cold showers too – Wim Hof style. Apparently they were good for mental clarity too and lowered blood pressure. The thought of Emilia getting anywhere near Rufus's shower made Phoebe's own blood pressure rise alarmingly.

Phoebe was just getting ready to go home when Jenna, who'd just left, popped her head back around the surgery door.

'He's here. I've just seen him.'

'Who's here?' For a moment, Phoebe thought she was talking about Rufus, because he'd been so much on her mind.

'The Meow Master.' Jenna was laughing. 'That's what he calls himself. Or at least that's how he just introduced himself to Max.'

'The animal behaviourist guy? Gosh. What's he like?'

'Heavily tanned. He looks like a cross between Simon Cowell and Sherlock Holmes, although that might just be the deerstalker. But don't take my word for it. Come and meet him.'

Phoebe didn't need asking twice. Fascinated, she followed Jenna out into the yard where she saw a small cluster of people chatting. Maggie and Eddie were there, so were Marcus and Natasha. She'd thought Marcus had gone home but he must have hung around to see the celebrity behaviourist guy.

Max was talking to a man in a green tweed jacket and matching deerstalker hat. Alongside him was a slim, narrow-hipped girl with pink hair, who was presumably his assistant.

Phoebe went to introduce herself. She saw immediately what Jenna meant. All the Meow Master needed to complete the Sherlock Holmes look was a pipe.

He had blindingly white teeth too, she saw when he smiled at her. Surely they were bleached. 'Phoebe Dashwood, how nice to meet you. Thank you for inviting me over.'

'That was me,' Max said pointedly, but was ignored by the Sherlock lookalike.

'Allow me to introduce myself. I'm Lionel from Top Trainers. I'm the Canine Corrector and the Meow Master – although we do deal with other animals too, of course. This is Emma,' he added as an afterthought. 'She will be filming today's masterclass.'

Wow, Phoebe thought. How was anyone keeping a straight face? But they were. Even Marcus, who wasn't averse to taking the mickey when the occasion warranted it, although Natasha looked a bit round eyed. Phoebe didn't dare glance at Jenna. One quirk of an eyebrow and she knew she would laugh and possibly not be able to stop. Even Maggie was keeping a straight face. Mind you, she was busy signing to Eddie in that intimate language they used to communicate with each other when they wanted to have a private conversation. It was a mix of British Sign Language and their own made-up signs.

'Thank you for coming over,' Phoebe said. 'Did you have to come far?'

'Not too far. We live in Netley.'

Presumably Emma was his partner then. Phoebe wasn't sure whether to feel sorry for her or to be impressed. Don't judge a book by its cover, she told herself sternly. You haven't seen him in action yet.

'Right then, people.' The Meow Master clapped his hands together, as if summoning a group of minions. 'Let's get this show on the road. Lead me to this fiendish feline. Are we all coming along to see the show?'

'I think we might be,' Max said, looking around and compressing his lips. 'If that's OK?'

'The more the merrier. Lead on, McDuff.'

'Did you maybe want to speak to the cat's owner first?' Phoebe questioned. 'Get some inside information on his problems.'

The Meow Master was shaking his head before she even finished the sentence and Phoebe glanced at Maggie, who shrugged.

'Let the man do his job,' the old lady said, with a gleam in her eye. 'He clearly thinks he knows what he's doing.'

They walked in a straggle, albeit an eager one, across the yard to the barn, where Natasha had shut Saddam in earlier.

'I think maybe I should go in first,' Natasha cautioned as they got to the door. 'Otherwise, he might dart out when I open the door. We don't want to waste the, er – um – Lionel's time.'

She obviously couldn't quite bring herself to say 'the Meow Master'. Phoebe suppressed a snort. She didn't think she would be able to say it either. Not in all seriousness – that would definitely take some practice.

Everyone stood back obediently while Natasha nipped in first. A few seconds, later she re-emerged and beckoned them all inside. 'OK, it's safe to come in. He's down the other end asleep. But don't hang about in case he wakes up and decides to make a run for the door.'

17

Everyone did as Natasha said and a few seconds later they were all inside the oblong-shaped barn, which was a little dimmer than outside, but not much as it had several windows and a couple of skylights in the roof. The barn was where Maggie let the cats who probably wouldn't be rehomed live out their days. There weren't very many. All the cats who came in were neutered so there was no indiscriminate breeding and normally they had free range of the farm. The barn was just their sleeping accommodation and also a place to store food in the dry. It was also a great place to put the occasional cat who came in already pregnant or with a litter of kittens. They'd be safely confined in a crate and run, and it was occasionally used for other animals Maggie needed to keep a close eye on. At least the ones that didn't end up in her house.

There was a stack of hay bales at the far end almost rafter high, which were used for bedding and food for the donkeys. There were also a few scattered bales dotted around and the whole place smelled sweetly of hay. Dust motes swirled in shafts of light that angled through the skylights.

Saddam was the only cat that was restricted from having free range of the farm and that was because he terrorised the kennel dogs when Natasha was taking them for walks. He'd lie in wait for them and then pounce and Phoebe had occasionally had to deal with the results of wounds he'd inflicted. This was not very satisfactory. Not only did it make a previously totally well-adjusted dog terrified of cats, but it scared the living daylights out of anyone who might be visiting to rehome an animal. Having a large ginger tom charging towards you, obviously hellbent on mischief, was not conducive to a peaceful bonding session.

Phoebe watched the Meow Master, who had gone a little further forward than everyone else and was now standing in the middle of the barn.

'Are you ready to go with the camera?' he asked Emma, who nodded, and held up a phone in front of her.

'Excellent. OK… and three, two, one – action.'

'Hello, viewers. Today the Meow Master will show you how to deal with a fiendish feral feline who's been causing a bit of an upset for his owner.' He beamed, his teeth gleaming in his tanned face, and Phoebe could see what Jenna meant. He did look a bit like Simon Cowell. He had dark hair beneath the deerstalker. It was cut quite short and looked a little too black from what she could see of it – dyed maybe? Again, she told herself not to judge. He couldn't be much older than her – mid-thirties maybe – and he probably looked great on camera. There had to be something that inspired his 250k plus followers.

'Puss, puss,' he called, turning slowly in a full circle. 'Puss, puss, puss.'

If Saddam had heard the intruders, he didn't show it. As Natasha had said, he was flat out and fast asleep halfway up the hay bale stack about five metres or so away from the Meow Master. Only the fact that the tip of his tail twitched occasionally betrayed the fact he was even alive.

'You haven't drugged him, have you?' Phoebe asked Natasha in a stage whisper.

'Of course not. But it looks like someone has...'

'Quiet, please.' Lionel's authoritative voice cut through the air. 'Concentration is critical for this next step of my strategy.'

What was he going to do? Phoebe wondered. Sneak up on the cat? He didn't have any kind of net or other way of restraining Saddam. They all waited expectantly. This was certainly exciting. Whatever the outcome was.

Maggie and Eddie had settled themselves on one of the lone hay bales a little distance away, and were also watching with rapt faces. Max was still standing up, arms folded, his face uncertain. Beside him, also standing up and looking a little nervous, Natasha was biting her lip and Marcus, alongside her, was looking sceptical.

It seemed that Lionel's strategy did involve a certain amount of 'sneaking' because over the next few seconds he took about ten careful, exaggeratedly pantomime steps, one at a time, towards where Saddam lay.

He'd almost reached him when the cat stirred, swished his tail from side to side, and then leapt up so swiftly that Lionel, and everyone else in the room, jumped violently. Saddam was off the hay bale faster than you could say Top Trainer and heading upwards to a higher bale on the stack behind him.

Without a flicker of hesitation, Lionel leapt up after him. He was certainly agile, Phoebe observed, as a game of cat and mouse or rather cat and cat trainer along the stacked hay bales began. Saddam led and Lionel followed a couple of steps behind.

'Be careful,' Natasha called out anxiously. 'Some of those hay bales aren't as solidly stacked as they look.'

'Are you getting all this on film?' Eddie called to Emma, guffawing loudly.

It seemed that she was, she certainly had the phone pointing the right way.

'Yep, get it on film,' Lionel echoed Eddie. 'I want viewers to know that it's not always a walk in the park being a Lionel Tamer.'

'Did he just say a Lionel Tamer?' Phoebe asked Jenna in a hushed whisper. Jenna was watching with one hand over her mouth, clearly unable to believe her eyes.

'I think so,' Jenna muttered.

'We should stop this ridiculous nonsense immediately,' Max said, the only voice of reason in the barn. 'This isn't getting anywhere. He's clearly terrifying that cat.'

'No, he's not. Saddam hasn't had this much fun in years,' Maggie called out. She was bent over with mirth on her hay bale. 'Come to that, neither have I. Let him carry on.'

So they all watched as the chase progressed. Sometimes quickly with Saddam leaping out of range just as it seemed he would be caught and sometimes more slowly, as Lionel, undeterred, slowed down his pursuit.

Saddam had the advantage as he was quicker, smaller and lighter and so could also use the beams that crisscrossed the barn as stepping-stones to the next safe place. Which was always just out of reach of his pursuer.

After about five minutes of going fruitlessly in circles, Lionel abandoned the chase and went across to where Emma was standing with the camera. To give him his due, he wasn't even out of breath.

'Different strategy needed,' he said, flashing his over-white pearlies into the lens. 'As you can see, viewers, the first strategy isn't always the best one.'

'No wonder he's got thousands of followers,' Max said, shaking his head. 'If this is the kind of clip he posts.'

'You haven't seen anything yet.' Lionel shot him a glare. 'The

Meow Master never fails.' He winked back into the camera. 'Keep watching, viewers.'

'This isn't a live stream, is it?' Natasha asked in alarm. 'I thought it was just a recording.'

'Don't worry. It *is* just a recording,' Emma told her, flicking a strand of pink fringe back off her face. 'I'll edit it later. But we like to make it as "live" as possible. It's more interesting for viewers that way.'

'We should have brought popcorn,' Maggie murmured, as Lionel outlined his next strategy to the camera.

'If you can't catch your client,' he said, looking very serious, 'then you must get your client to come to you.' Another flash of his white pearlies.

'I can't wait,' Phoebe told Max in hushed tones. 'I've never seen anything like this in my life.'

'Me neither,' he whispered back. 'I'm sorry. I shouldn't have recommended him. But some of the clips did look impressive. And he had a lot of good reviews.'

'Quiet, please, in the stalls.' Lionel glanced over his shoulder and winked at them.

At least he had a sense of humour, Phoebe thought. She couldn't say she was very impressed with Lionel's tactics, but he was incredibly entertaining, and like Maggie, she knew that Saddam was fine. Saddam liked games of chase. Especially ones that he won, which was most of them.

Lionel's next strategy it seemed was to sit quietly on a hay bale, halfway up the stack, with a bowl of fishy treat cat biscuits beside him that he'd apparently brought with him.

'That's not going to work,' shouted Eddie. 'He can eat cat biscuits any time he likes.'

Lionel ignored him and began to play with what looked like a pompom on a string. It was red and blue, and he drew it backwards and forwards across the hay bale, occasionally letting it flick in the air as it caught on something. He was ignoring Saddam too. But Saddam, to Phoebe's amazement, wasn't ignoring him.

The cat, who was currently lying on a wide wooden beam a couple of metres above Lionel's head, was watching the behaviourist with curious amber eyes. Seemingly the big cat found the pompom irresistible because it wasn't very long before he got up and took a few purposeful steps along the beam, his tail swishing from side to side.

No one dared breathe as the big orange cat got closer and closer and then dropped down to a lower beam that was almost in touching distance of the behaviourist's head.

Lionel made no move to catch him, although he was clearly aware of this development because his eyes kept flicking towards the cat and he'd turned his head very slightly towards him.

Saddam stopped on his beam, still as a statue, while Lionel kept flicking the pompom, back and forth.

Lionel would have to make a move sooner or later, Phoebe thought, fascinated. But he wasn't doing it yet. He was clearly a lot smarter than any of them had given him credit for. She wondered what he was going to do when he actually caught the cat. Hypnotise him with the pompom ball, or by some other method he hadn't yet told them about. Phoebe didn't think anything he did could possibly surprise her now.

Then there was a sudden flurry of movement. It happened so quickly that Phoebe wasn't even sure who'd made the first move – the cat or the trainer. She thought it was probably Lionel, but it was mistimed. Or maybe it was just unfortunate because it seemed that Saddam had changed strategy too. For the first time he didn't leap away from Lionel but towards him. To be precise, he leapt onto his head and stayed, balanced there, all four paws static, looking like some funky marmalade cat adornment.

Thank goodness Lionel was wearing a hat, Phoebe thought, as there was a collective gasp from the onlookers. Then, in that instant of movement, the behaviourist was no longer wearing a hat. In fact, somehow he seemed to have lost all his hair too because both his deerstalker and his over-dark hair had been swept off his head by a skidding Saddam's paws and were now teetering precariously on the next hay bale.

'Cut,' shouted Lionel at the top of his voice, leaping off the hay bale and twisting from side to side frantically, as he tried to locate his headgear, without which he was totally bald. 'Cut the camera.'

It was probably too late to spare his blushes, being as she'd no doubt already got the whole thing on film, but Emma did as he said and hurried towards him, looking horrified.

There was a moment of complete silence during which time seemed to freeze frame. Phoebe was caught between shock and the urge to laugh, which she knew would be terribly inappropriate. It didn't help that she could see most of the onlookers were trying not to laugh with varying degrees of success. Natasha had her hand over her mouth. Marcus's eyes were bulging with trying to hold it in and Jenna was biting her lip.

Maggie was snorting and Eddie had given up all pretence of decorum and was now slapping his knees and rocking backwards and forwards on his hay bale and guffawing loudly. At least he had the excuse of being nearly deaf and might not be aware of how loud he was being. The only onlooker apart from Emma who wasn't either laughing or making superhuman attempts to hold it in was Max. He was shaking his head in utter disbelief.

Lionel wasn't laughing either. He'd managed to retrieve his deerstalker and what was evidently a toupee, but he wasn't making any attempt to get either of them back on his head. 'Come on,' he said to Emma. 'We're done here. That creature's beyond redemption. It's usually the owner's fault. They should have called it something sensible – like Marmalade or Pumpkin. What do they expect, calling him a name like Saddam? Everyone knows cats live up to their name. I'm not wasting any more time with it. Come on, come on, chop chop. We have to go.'

They were both at the barn door before anyone could react, although Marcus did manage to shout, 'Don't forget to send us a copy of that video for approval?'

The only answer he got was the crash of the door as it slammed behind the unlikely entertainers.

For a few moments, everyone sat still where they were and then Maggie said, 'Oh, my, I haven't seen anything so funny since Farmer Pete took me to see Les Dawson on Bournemouth Pier. *Marmalade* – I ask you!'

'*Pumpkin!*' muttered Max, shaking his head.

Then Natasha added quietly, 'Did anyone hear him say Lionel Tamer?'

Which was enough for them all to start choking with laughter again, but this time there was no holding back. Jenna collapsed on a hay bale in convulsions of giggles. Natasha and Marcus were now laughing so much they couldn't speak. Maggie joined Eddie in a knee-slapping crescendo of mirth and Phoebe and Max gave up all semblance of being sensible and professional and joined in.

Only Saddam seemed to have any sense of decorum. He was back up on his beam surveying the humans with what could only be described as total disdain.

18

After the Meow Master and his pink-haired assistant had left the farm and they'd all managed to finally stop laughing, everyone had stayed in the barn for a while chatting.

Maggie had said that she wouldn't have been surprised if Saddam had done it on purpose. 'He's always had a great sense of humour, that cat,' she'd told everyone with huge affection in her voice. 'Honestly, I know he can be a pain in the neck, but after that little stunt I think I could forgive him almost anything.'

'I'm not so sure,' Natasha said. 'He's a menace with little dogs. I know we haven't had much success with pet behaviourists so far, but I think we should keep trying.'

'But maybe he was right about one thing,' Marcus put in with a sideways glance at Max. 'Catty the Cat Whisperer and the Meow Master. Can't we at least find someone with a sensible name?'

'To be fair, I had no idea he was called the Meow Master,' Max retorted, shaking his head. 'It didn't mention that on his website. Although I think I might have seen the tag, "the Canine Corrector" somewhere.'

'I guess it could have been worse. At least he wasn't called the Pussy Perfector,' Marcus taunted mercilessly.

Max reddened and Phoebe intervened. 'Thanks, Max, for organising it. Let's just put that one down to experience.' The last thing she needed was to have those two arguing. A healthy dose of competitive banter was OK, but she didn't want things to get out of hand. It was important that her team all liked and respected each other – it made for a much nicer working environment.

Phoebe turned towards her grandmother. 'Maybe we could have one more go. I'm up for that if you are, Maggie?'

'Oh, definitely. Bring it on. I'll never turn down the opportunity for a good laugh.'

'I'll have a go at finding someone if you like,' Marcus offered and they had all agreed that this was the way forward.

In the meantime, they'd just have to keep doing what they'd done until now and shutting Saddam in the barn when the small dogs were being walked. He only chased small dogs. Even Saddam wasn't stupid enough to take on Tiny, although had he known it, the daft Irish wolfhound would probably have run a mile if he had.

* * *

On Saturday afternoon, as Phoebe vacuumed and dusted Woodcutter's Cottage – it may be tidy but there was dust everywhere – scenes from the previous evening kept flicking into her head and making her laugh. The fact that the whole thing had been videoed somehow made it even funnier, even though it was a video she was sure would never see the light of day.

Although the irony was that if it did, she was sure it would go viral and instantly become one of the Meow Master's most popular clips. The moment when Saddam had leapt onto Lionel's head and deftly removed his deerstalker and toupee would be forever burned on her brain.

It would certainly give her and Rufus something to talk about later. Although it wasn't exactly a seduction subject – Ginger Tom Removes Toupee From Bald Man's Head.

Tori didn't agree. 'Oh, I don't know,' she had said when Phoebe had phoned and given her a summary of the Friday night fiasco. 'A good sense of humour is very sexy. Laughing in bed is the key to a good sex life, apparently.'

Phoebe couldn't imagine Harrison being the laughing in bed type. But she didn't ask. Disconcertingly, Phoebe couldn't imagine Rufus being the laughing in bed type. He wasn't as dark and brooding as Harrison was, but he was definitely not one for cracking jokes either.

She hadn't told Tori but as the evening approached, she was growing more and more nervous. She felt like a virgin bride on her wedding night. She wasn't a virgin, and this wasn't their wedding night. Phoebe told herself she was making too much of it. Rufus wouldn't be having any of the ridiculous thoughts that she was.

She reminded herself about Anni's tea leaf predictions. She was going to be part of a family and she would get pregnant if she wasn't careful – that bit definitely wasn't happening. She had gone on the pill soon after she'd started dating Rufus. Being prepared was something Phoebe had always been good at.

* * *

At Beechbrook House, Rufus was sitting in his study looking at a framed photo of Rowena and Archie that he kept on his desk. It was on the filing cabinet, tucked away a bit now, not as obvious as it had once been as it had got slowly jostled out of position by other things. If you didn't know it was there, you might not even see it.

But it had been there since she'd died – a present to himself so that he and Archie wouldn't ever forget her face. It was one of his favourite pictures and one of the last he'd taken of his wife.

Rowena had her arm around a much younger Archie and they were both smiling into the camera. Her blue eyes were sparkling and a tendril of her fair hair had escaped from her ponytail and was curling around her face. Archie, more chubby faced than he was now, was also smiling. Rufus remembered taking it. About five years ago. He'd been telling them about a robin's nest close to the house, in which four eggs had just hatched out.

'We can watch the parents take food back to the nest and see them feeding their young when they're a bit bigger.'

'Can we feed them too, Dad? Please, can we?' Archie had begged. 'Can we take food to the nest?'

'No, that's the parents' job. If we take food to the nest, we'll frighten the parents away and then the babies would die.'

'No, they wouldn't because they'd have us,' Archie had pouted.

'That's not the way of it, son. It's the parents' job to take care of the babies. Not ours. They'd be very upset if they couldn't do it.'

'Just like it's our job to take care of you,' Rowena had added. 'We wouldn't want someone else to come barging in to do it, would we? That would make us unhappy.'

'What? Even if it was Grandpa?'

'Grandpa could help because he's one of the family. But we wouldn't want a stranger to be looking after you. Just like the robins wouldn't want a stranger looking after their babies. That would be very wrong.'

Rowena's words echoed down the years and Rufus swallowed. Thank God none of them had known what lay ahead.

The baby robins had grown up and flown away and Archie had watched them with the kind of awestruck wonder that children had when they were tiny. And through their son's eyes, he and Rowena had also watched with awestruck wonder. It was one of the happiest times that Rufus could ever remember.

Now, he picked up the photo – in which a young Archie, and a Rowena who would stay forever young, lived – and touched his lips to the cool glass that contained it.

'Forgive me for leaving you behind,' he said. 'I'll never ever forget you. And you will always be Archie's mother.'

He had told his father, but not Archie or Emilia, that he was going to be out all night.

'Anywhere nice?' Lord Alfred had asked. 'Not that it's any of my business.' His eyes had contradicted his words. 'But just in case I need to contact you.'

'You'd like to know what you're interrupting?' Rufus had met his gaze. 'Nothing important. I'm going to an art exhibition with Harrison – it's a family thing – and you know how he is with his family. He wanted some moral support. We'll probably have a few drinks.'

He had no idea why he was lying like a teenager, especially when it was a lie that would probably come back to bite him. But he just couldn't face telling his father what he was really up to – having only just plucked up the courage to tell Rowena.

'OK. Good.' His father had seemed mollified. 'Enjoy yourselves.'

'We will.'

Rufus had escaped, but the sense of shame he'd felt as he'd turned the Mercedes on the front and then driven out of the estate had followed him.

* * *

When Rufus had asked what time he should arrive, Phoebe had said any time after six thirty. Rufus was always prompt and today was no exception. He rang the bell at six thirty-five and as she went to let him in, having left the door on the latch, she wondered if they would ever get to the stage when they would feel comfortable walking in and out of each other's houses.

'It's open,' she told Rufus, who was holding a bouquet of flowers which were cellophane wrapped and enormous with a yellow ribbon tied around their middle.

'Is it? I didn't try.' Rufus smiled over the top of the flowers and Phoebe knew she would forgive him anything. What was it with this man who had stolen her heart so effortlessly? Though, deep down, she wasn't sure if he even wanted it.

'Come in, come in. Thank you, they're beautiful.'

In the kitchen she took the flowers from him and put them in the sink. They filled the room with their sweetness. Then she went back to kiss him.

'It's so lovely to see you, Rufus. I feel as if it's been a long time.'

'Me too. Although I don't think it has.'

He didn't have an overnight bag with him. She wondered if it was in the car. 'Would you like a glass of wine? There's some white chilling in the fridge.'

'I have some wine too. I forgot. I'll just nip back outside and get it.'

While he did that, Phoebe arranged the flowers. There were too many for one vase. So she put one on the table and took the other one through to the lounge where she put them on the coffee table.

Rufus came back with a bottle of wine in each hand. Still no overnight bag then. She tried to put it out of her mind. Maybe he didn't want to be presumptuous. Even though he had been asked.

'Shall we go and sit in the lounge, Rufus? I've lit the log burner.' Not because it was particularly cold outside but because it was cosy and romantic, and she wanted to set the atmosphere.

'I have a confession to make,' she told him a few moments later, as they sat sipping wine in her tiny lounge. 'I haven't been slaving over a hot stove all day. Although I did make the dessert.' She'd actually made a cheesecake from a Valentine's Day recipe that Tori had given her. It was salted caramel, which she knew was his favourite, and it was made in a heart-shaped tin and decorated with heart-shaped strawberries and it looked incredibly impressive and romantic.

'I imagine you've been too busy to do much slaving over a hot stove,' Rufus said. 'What's dessert?'

'Cheesecake – but it's not *just* cheesecake.'

'M&S?' he quipped.

'No, I really did make the dessert.' She laughed. 'You'll have to wait and see. How's your day been? How's Archie?'

'He's been out on a hack with Emilia. Did I tell you she'd taken up riding so she could go out with him?'

'No.' Phoebe felt a bit deflated. 'I can ride. Maybe it's something I could do with him some time too.'

Something flashed in his eyes and she knew that whatever else might happen, a family afternoon hack through the beautiful New Forest was something that was never going to happen. Although she supposed it was possible that Rufus would one day find it easier to be around horses than he did now.

'Is he looking forward to starting his new school in September?' Phoebe switched to a safer subject. 'Or is that too far away for him to be thinking about?'

'He's looking forward to the going away bit.' Rufus looked reflective. 'I sometimes wonder if I should have let him go before. I didn't want to send him away when his mum died. I wanted him to feel that I would still be around for him. That he wasn't going to lose me too. I wanted him to feel safe.'

'And he clearly does feel safe, so you must have done the right thing,' she told him now and he looked relieved.

'Part of the reason he's looking forward to going away to school is because they've got an equestrian facility, the boys can take their own pony if they wish.' Rufus paused. 'I've promised him that once he's settled in he can have a pony as long as it doesn't detract from his schoolwork. He'll need to prove that he's settled in, so we're thinking maybe the pony could be his Christmas present.'

'Wow, he'll never want to come home, will he?'

'I'm a bit afraid of that, to be honest.'

They talked a little more about the new school. It was a boarding school with the option of staying over in the holidays too. Apparently some of the boys whose families lived in other countries did just that.

'It will change the dynamics, Archie not being around in term time,' Phoebe said. 'Does that mean you won't employ Emilia?' She held her breath – he had no idea how much of a loaded question that was.

'No, there would be no need,' he said, considering it. 'Dad and I can lapse back into unhealthy living.'

'You won't have to wait until September to do that. We're having pizza for dinner.'

'Fantastic.' His eyes lit up. 'I was hoping we were. Frankly I've had more wholesome food than any man should lately.'

Hurrah. A black mark, however oblique, against his nanny. Phoebe felt as though they were conspirators in a guilty secret.

'But first, more wine,' she said, and refilled their glasses. She probably shouldn't drink too much wine, but it was definitely giving her Dutch courage.

Over the pizzas, which she cut into slices and served from a bread board at the kitchen table so they could have as much or as little as they wanted, Phoebe told him about the Meow Master and Rufus looked more and more disbelieving. 'I wonder what he'd have done if he had caught him,' he said.

'Goodness knows, but we never got the chance to find out, so we're back to the drawing board. If you hear of any animal behaviourists wanting a job, do please let us know.'

'I don't meet many in my line of work, I have to confess.'

Rufus loved the heart-shaped cheesecake. He had two pieces and Phoebe, who was still feeling too nervous to eat much, thought, he can't be as nervous as me. Or he wouldn't be eating anything.

As she carried their plates back to the sink, she was aware that she'd also drunk far more than usual and she was feeling slightly light-headed. That hadn't been part of the plan.

She put the plates into the sink.

'Can I help?' Rufus asked, and realising he'd followed and was now standing directly behind her, she turned.

'Would you like some more wine?'

'No, I don't want any more wine.' His eyes were very dark and there was no mistaking their expression.

Then they were in each other's arms and kissing with the same passion that she remembered. That breathless heady, glorious chemistry that she had begun to think was never going to go any further.

Every atom of her ached for him and she knew his need for her was just as great. For the first time, she knew he was not holding back.

It was Rufus who finally broke the kiss. 'Is it too early to go to bed? Because if we stay here much longer, I don't think we're going to make it to the bedroom.'

Phoebe took him by the hand and they all but ran for the stairs.

19

To Sam's huge relief, Snowball had come back in again on Friday evening for his tea. Sam had kept him in for the night, which he didn't think had gone down very well – Snowball had always been fairly nocturnal. On Saturday morning he had let him out again for his breakfast and Snowball hadn't been in since. It was now 10 p.m. on Saturday night and Sam and Judy were in Sam's garden, walking up and down and calling the cat's name.

Judy was shaking a packet of cat biscuits too. 'When I was small, we had a cat called Elizabeth and she always came back when she heard the biscuit packet rattling. Mind you, she was a bit of a foodie.'

'You had a cat called Elizabeth?' Sam looked at her in amazement.

'Yes. Her full name was Elizabeth Regina. Mummy named all our animals after the royal family. I must have told you that. We also had a dog called Philip Mountbatten.'

'Um, I'm not sure you did,' Sam murmured. But he couldn't say he was hugely surprised. He had nothing in common whatsoever with Judy's parents. That was patently clear.

'When I was small, we had a cat called Garfield,' he offered, and it was Judy's turn to look puzzled.

'Garfield – that's a great name.' She'd clearly never heard of the cartoon cat.

'Snowball,' Sam called again. 'Where are you, mate? I'm getting worried.'

'And I'm getting cold,' Judy said, stamping her feet on the grass to warm up. 'Shall we go in, Sam? He'll come in when he's hungry, won't he?'

'I'm not sure he'll get very hungry. He's perfectly capable of catching his own supper. But yes, let's go in.'

Five minutes later, they were back inside the maisonette and Sam made them both a hot chocolate. He was trying not to show his worry, but Judy picked up on it anyway.

'He'll be fine, Sam, I'm sure. He's got the cat flap. Shall we go to bed? We've got an early start, haven't we? I'm assuming you're still up for the Tollard Royal indoor show jumping tomorrow?'

'Yeah, I am.' Sam knew there was doubt in his voice. The plan was that Judy, who had her own double horse box, would collect him and Ninja en route to the show jumping, having already got her own horse, Delilah, ready. They were both entered for the affili-ated show jumping at eleven, which meant an impossibly early start.

'If Snowball isn't back by morning, I'm not sure...'

'Sam, don't you dare back out on me. I've been looking forward to this for ages.'

'Yes, but...'

'There are no buts. For the last six weeks practically everything we've done has centred around your cat. I know he was badly injured and I know you've had to put in a lot of care – and I respect you for that, Sam. But I'm important too. Our relationship is important.'

Her blue eyes flashed fire and Sam was taken aback. Judy rarely got annoyed, or even irritated. She was generally as laid-back as he was and he'd had no idea she'd felt like this.

'I'm sorry that you've had to work around me and Snowball,' he said, stung. 'I didn't realise you minded so much.'

It was also easier when she came to his because when they were at Judy's her mother had a habit of popping in and she never missed an opportunity to have a quick snipe at Sam. When they were at his place he could forget all about Judy's parents. There was absolutely no chance of them ever coming there. OK, so he might be burying his head in the sand, but at least it was comfortable.

'I haven't minded, Sam,' Judy said, looking slightly guilty. 'I just would like us to have some time together that didn't involve me coming here. That isn't too much to ask, is it?'

'No, of course it's not.'

'You haven't even properly confirmed that you're coming to Francesca's wedding yet either.'

That was because he was still trying to think of a cast-iron excuse not to go. It wasn't until July but a posh society wedding sounded like Sam's worst nightmare.

'Mummy and Daddy are keen for you to go.'

'Really?' That seemed unlikely but he knew he needed to meet her halfway.

'Of course I'll come.' He went and hugged her and after a moment of resistance she hugged him back. She smelled of Christian Dior and fresh air. She was shorter than him and he bent and kissed her hair. 'I don't want us to argue,' he murmured. 'I appreciate the sacrifices you've made and I'm grateful. So's Snowball.'

'No, he's not,' Judy said, beginning to laugh. 'That cat is probably two doors up from here, having the time of his life staking out some poor innocent little mouse.'

'That's cats for you,' Sam agreed. 'I should probably get a dog. They're much more loyal.'

'And even more time consuming. Besides, Snowball would definitely never come back if you got a dog.'

'Very true. I think one ungrateful cat and one horse is enough. And one girlfriend, whom I love very much,' he added, kissing her forehead this time.

'That's good to hear, although...' She raised a meaningful eyebrow. 'I think you've got that in the wrong order. Shouldn't it be girlfriend first?'

'Oh, it is, it is. Definitely.' They were both laughing now.

'Come on, let's go to bed,' Judy said. 'Fingers crossed Snowball will be back by morning.'

Sam hoped she was right.

* * *

In the morning, Phoebe woke up with a pounding headache and the dawning realisation that she was alone in bed. The space beside her was still warm though and then she heard the toilet flush and realised that Rufus hadn't done an early morning flit, after all. Phew!

She sat up in bed, her hands clasped behind her head and only the tops of her breasts showing above the duvet. She had only the vaguest memory about the end of last night – she really had drunk too much wine and she wasn't used to it – but it must have been good, seeing as she was naked but for her pants.

Hopefully Rufus was too and they could pick up from where they'd left off. A few seconds later her patience paid off and he came out of the en suite bathroom. He was wearing boxers. Well, that wouldn't take long to alter, and when he saw she was sitting up he did a double take.

'Sorry, did I wake you up?'

'I'm not sure.' She smiled at him. He had a lovely body. She felt as though she was looking at it for the first time. Annoying that she couldn't remember much of last night. He wasn't overly muscular, but he definitely wasn't flabby either. His belly was flat and there was just enough of a smattering of hair to make him all male, but not overly hairy.

Rufus watched her watching him. 'You're making me nervous,' he said, and Phoebe got the impression he was only half joking. He went round to the other side of the bed and climbed in. Then he rolled on his side and propped his head on his elbow and looked at her. For a second he looked unusually serious.

'Phoebe, I'm really sorry about last night. I...' He broke off and shut his eyes briefly, which was a relief because she had no idea at all why he was apologising. Crap, why had she drunk all that wine?

'You've got absolutely nothing to apologise for,' she said, sure that he couldn't have and just as sure that there was no way on earth she was going to tell him she couldn't remember a thing.

'We both know that's not true,' he said, opening his eyes but now staring straight ahead and not looking at her. 'All I can say is that I'm out of practice and I was a bit nervous. And it will get better. I know it will. I've never had that problem before.'

'Rufus, it's fine. Really. Don't worry.' She stroked his head as the cogs whirred frantically in hers. They had got undressed. She remembered that. They'd raced upstairs and they'd practically ripped each other's clothes off. Then they had lain side by side, looking into each other's eyes. And they'd done some more kissing, a lot more kissing, and she remembered Rufus saying that he'd like to take it slowly. That he was out of practice.

But after that, it was a blank, and try as she might, Phoebe couldn't remember a thing. She was tempted to suggest that they start practising right now, but she had an urgent need for the loo and there was that old problem of morning breath.

'Rufus, hold on just for a second.' She got out of bed. 'I'll be right back.' She darted into the loo, cleaned her teeth and then, feeling the beginnings of a self-consciousness she hadn't been expecting, she darted back into the bedroom.

Rufus was already out of bed and pulling on his trousers. 'I'm really sorry, Phoebe, but I should get back. I've promised Archie that we could go out – he's doing a school project on trees, and we're going to go and look at some of the oldest trees in the forest.'

He glanced at her face and then added, 'You could come with us if you like?'

'Um, yes, I'd love to.' Phoebe grabbed her robe from the back of the bedroom door and slipped it on. 'Would you like coffee before you go?'

He frowned. 'Er, no, it's fine. Shall I come back and get you, once I've touched base with Archie?'

'Yes, that would be great.'

A few minutes later he was gone and Phoebe walked slowly into the kitchen and put on some coffee. She felt dazed. However last night had ended, this was not at all how she had expected her morning to begin. She had brought croissants and jam and thick white bread for toast in case he preferred that and she'd got fresh orange juice and coffee. She'd envisaged them getting up late, having first worked up the appetite to eat loads.

Why, oh why had she drunk so much? That hadn't helped. Maybe Rufus hadn't wanted to make love with a half-cut woman. She couldn't blame him for that. One thing she could remember about last night was that he had stayed fairly sober.

She got some painkillers from the cupboard, popped them out of their blister packet and downed them with water. Her mobile, which she'd forgotten to put on charge last night and which was still on the kitchen table, pinged. Yawning, Phoebe went across to pick it up. There were several messages. A couple of them were from Tori last night. The earliest one simply said 'Good luck' and was followed by an emoji of a heart. Another one that had come a couple of hours later said:

Hope it's going well? I'm guessing as you're so quiet, it must be.

This one was followed by two heart emojis.

There was also one from Sam that said:

Snowball's gone AWOL. He's been out all day and all evening and I'm a bit worried. Am I overreacting? Could he hurt himself now or should everything be properly healed?

Phoebe felt a bit guilty that she hadn't answered that. Although he hadn't messaged again so hopefully the cat had returned from his wanderings.

The latest message, the one that had caught her attention, had pinged through at nine – Phoebe hadn't realised it was so late – and was also from Tori.

So... Come on then. How did it go? I thought you were going to send me a number? But if you're not up for that, just a smiley face will do.

Phoebe put her head in her hands. Bits of the end of the evening were starting to come back to her, and they weren't encouraging. She could remember a point where she and Rufus had been kissing passionately, on her bed, and then a point where they had stopped and he had rolled away from her.

She could remember Rufus looking stricken. She could

remember herself reassuring him, saying, 'It's OK, it's OK. There's really no pressure.'

Then they'd kissed some more, but she didn't think he had really touched her after that.

Phoebe clicked on Tori's message and pressed reply. She put a smiling emoji in it and then deleted it again. She had no idea what to say to her best friend. She couldn't just send her a blank message, although in many ways, a blank message would be a very apt way to tell her friend what had happened – because Phoebe knew now with a sickening certainty that absolutely nothing had.

20

Rufus didn't drive straight home. It was still not quite nine thirty. Contrary to what he'd told Phoebe, no one was expecting him this early. Although he hadn't lied about the fact that he'd promised to take Archie out.

He took a fairly circuitous route through the forest and then pulled up in a lay-by a couple of miles from Beechbrook and got out. He didn't often walk in the forest – the risk of seeing a pony or even a donkey and setting off a PTSD attack was too high. But today he had to walk and he didn't want to walk around his own land. If he rocked up too early he'd be confronted with his father's questions and Emilia's bright bossiness and he couldn't face either until he'd cleared his head.

He'd picked a plantation – there wasn't so much chance of meeting an equine in the fenced areas – you were more likely to see a deer or a wild boar. Rufus could cope with those. The bluebells were all but gone, although he could still see a few late stragglers through the trees on either side of the path. It was a beautiful blue-sky day with a hint of warmth already in the morning air, but Rufus felt wretched.

How had last night gone so wrong? He began to analyse what had happened. It wasn't that he didn't find Phoebe attractive – she was gorgeous. She was also kind, clever, amazing with Archie and Rufus knew he was beginning to fall for her. It wasn't Phoebe who was the problem.

When they'd kissed in her kitchen, all he had felt was a burning need to take her to bed. A raging chemistry that had stayed until they'd got upstairs. The chemistry had stayed when they'd hurriedly peeled off each other's clothes. It had stayed when they had lain on her bed, face to face, and it had stayed throughout a pretty intense kissing session when they'd begun to explore each other's bodies. God, she was beautiful. That's all he could think. His senses were full of her. The scent of her skin, the softness of her curves, the sound of her breath, interspersed with the tiniest of moans as their need for each other increased.

Rufus remembered opening his eyes, and in that moment, Phoebe's hazel eyes had become Rowena's blue ones. Phoebe's brown hair had become Rowena's blonde hair. Phoebe's faintly olive skin had become Rowena's English rose complexion and in that fragment of a moment, his late wife's face had swum in front of him. The face of his late wife had superimposed Phoebe's.

Guilt had smashed through him like a dark tsunami. It had been gone in an instant, but it had taken his desire with it. Or at least the physical manifestation of his desire.

Phoebe had been amazing. She'd brushed it aside as if it was of no consequence. As if it was the kind of thing that happened to people every day. But Rufus was pretty sure that it had probably never happened to her. It had definitely never happened to him. And it had shocked him to the core.

He was flicked back to the here and now by the sight of a grey lurcher coming towards him on the forest path. Just behind was its owner, a middle-aged woman, who said a cheery good morning, as their paths crossed.

Rufus echoed her words, relieved she didn't want to stop and make further conversation, as dog walkers often did on sunny days.

In between the trees, he could see gorse yellow with flowers and he could smell its coconut scent as he walked. Wasn't that known as the kissing shrub? There was a saying, when gorse is out of bloom, kissing is out of fashion, the meaning being that kissing is never out of fashion, just as gorse was never out of bloom. The memory of their kissing taunted him.

He was beginning to wish he'd never run out of Phoebe's house. He'd felt too humiliated to stay, but it hadn't been gentlemanly. She'd seemed taken aback and he wasn't surprised. Rufus knew he'd made a total and utter pig's ear of the whole situation.

When he'd woken before her this morning, he'd looked down at her serenely sleeping face, wanting only to try what they'd failed to do last night again. He'd gone to the loo, squirted some toothpaste on his finger and given his teeth a makeshift clean. But it had thrown him when he'd come back into the bedroom to find her awake. Suddenly he'd been too scared. All he could think was, what if it happens again?

Rufus gave a deep sigh. He needed to phone her. To see if he could somehow repair the damage quickly before this whole thing got out of hand. He hooked his mobile out of his jacket pocket and discovered his battery was totally dead.

* * *

Tori had followed her message up with a call. Phoebe hadn't answered her the first time but when she'd tried again half an hour later, Phoebe had finally caved in and replied.

'Phoebe, I'm getting worried. Are you OK? Tell me to bugger off if you're still in bed. Although I'm guessing you're not or you wouldn't have answered.'

'I'm not,' Phoebe said. 'I'm sitting at the kitchen table. Rufus has gone.'

'You don't sound very happy. Oh, shit. I'm sorry. Are you OK? Look, you don't need to tell me anything. I'm sorry about the messages. I was just messing about. I know you were worried. Do you want to talk – or... not?'

There was a pause.

'To be honest, Tori, there's not much to say.' Phoebe took a deep breath. 'He stayed over. We went to bed, but then we just went to sleep. Nothing happened. We might as well have been brother and sister.'

She couldn't tell Tori the whole story. She couldn't betray Rufus and anyway, she still felt too raw.

'Oh, gosh. Oh, bloody hell. I'm sorry. Did you get too drunk?'

'We definitely got too drunk. Me especially. I was too nervous to eat.' She looked out of the kitchen window at the bright blue sky outside and felt sick. 'That was a mistake. I've got a raging hangover now. But anyway...' She forced lightness into her voice. 'I've got to go because we're going out for the day.'

'Oh, brilliant. So once you've recovered from your hangovers you can go for round two.'

'Definitely.' Phoebe decided not to tell Tori that Archie was coming along too. A ten-year-old chaperone. Maybe that's why Rufus brought him along so often.

No, she was overthinking it.

'Is everything OK with you and Harrison?' she asked.

'Yes, we're going out for the day too. It's a beautiful one. Have fun with Rufus. And I will stop haranguing you for details. Some things can't be hurried.'

'You're not haranguing, you're caring,' Phoebe said, because she knew it was true. 'And I appreciate it. Bye for now.'

She disconnected the call because she had a feeling she would burst into tears if she didn't. Then she went and had a hot shower and made some more coffee.

At least her hangover had gone.

* * *

At the Tollard Royal indoor show-jumping event, Sam and Judy were enjoying themselves. It had been fun getting up at the crack of dawn and heading off in convoy with Judy. Sam to Brook Riding School where he kept Ninja, and Judy to her posh livery stables on the other side of the forest.

It was a pity they weren't actually getting their horses ready together, but Sam could never have afforded the astronomical prices that Summerfields Equestrian Centre charged and Judy had no reason to move her horses to Brook.

Part of Summerfield's package included turning out horses ready for shows, should an owner require it. Plaiting and polishing tack were all part of their platinum package which Judy had. Of course she did. But Judy preferred getting her own horse ready.

'Although it is handy if for any reason I ever take both of them,' she'd told Sam earlier. 'Saves doubling up on time. Or more. Delilah's a pleasure to get ready, but Samson usually manages to get covered in shite even if he's boxed up overnight.'

How the other half lived. Sam had tried not to feel envious. Even though he did enjoy getting ready for shows. There was something incredibly exhilarating about driving to the stables when it was barely light, catching his horse, giving him an early breakfast, then sponging off his muddy bits, grooming him, plaiting him, talking to him. Then boxing him up and driving to the show. The day ahead untouched – full of anticipation and the hope of a rosette. It was even better knowing he'd be doing the driving and competing bit with Judy.

The show jumping was going well. Judy had just jumped a clear round and Sam was up next.

To his relief, Snowball had turned up just before they'd left, which was one less thing to worry about, he thought, as he trotted into the ring on Ninja.

Since the accident that had cost him his spleen and several weeks' recovery time last summer, he had found himself worrying more than he once had about falls. He tried his hardest to keep it at bay. Worrying was too easily transmitted to his horse and that could only make things worse, but Sam knew that his hitherto cast-iron nerve was gone.

Today, though, luck was on their side, and he and Ninja also jumped a clear round.

'Which means we'll be competing against each other in the jump-off,' Judy said. 'How exciting.'

It *was* exciting – not least because competing with his girlfriend, especially when it was a small show and not too high level, usually left both of them in the mood for love.

Neither of them was the fastest in the timed jump-off. A woman who competed a lot, and whom both Sam and Judy liked and respected, jumped an incredibly fast second clear round that no one else could get near.

Judy beat Sam to second place by a whisker, but he was happy with a third-place rosette and it felt great to go home at the end of the day with two rosettes swinging from the driver's rear-view mirror of the horse box. His and hers rosettes.

* * *

Phoebe, Rufus and Archie spent the day looking at trees, which could have been boring but wasn't because Archie was so hugely enthusiastic.

She was grateful for his enthusiasm which had started as soon as they'd called at Woodcutter's to pick her up. 'Did Dad tell you we're going to look at a tree that's 500 years old?' was Archie's opening gambit.

'No, he didn't.' Phoebe had met Rufus's eyes over his son's head. Beneath the cheerful face he was putting on for Archie she could see he was strained.

'Are you OK?' she asked quietly as they drove along a forest road, and she knew that Archie had his ear buds in and was focused on something on his phone.

'More to the point, are you?' Rufus glanced briefly at her, before turning his gaze back to the road. 'I'm so sorry I shot off this morning, Phoebe. It was unforgivable.'

'It wasn't,' she said. 'You're forgiven.'

'It'll be fine next time,' he added.

There was going to be a next time then. Good. Her heart lifted.

After that, the day got better and better. They visited the Knightwood Oak, which was reputed to be not only the oldest tree in the forest but also the one with the largest trunk. It had a girth of 7.4 m. Archie had brought a tape measure with him to check and it proved to be true.

'It's still growing, you know,' Archie informed them. 'At least that's what my teacher says.'

'It certainly looks like it is.' Phoebe craned her neck to look up into the leafy green branches. She stumbled slightly on the uneven ground – maybe she wasn't quite as over the hangover as she'd thought – and Rufus grabbed her hand.

'Steady there,' he said.

She smiled at him. It was the first time she could recall him doing that in front of Archie. Not that Archie had noticed.

'And it was even visited by Henry VIII when he was out hunting,' Archie continued. 'My teacher said that too.'

'Did he now?' Rufus looked amused. 'I suppose that's very possible. Royalty used to hunt regularly in this forest.'

Phoebe remembered that Anni Buckland had said something similar. Briefly she wondered how she was getting on. They'd had no calls from her lately. Hopefully no news was good news.

Archie had wanted a picnic, but Rufus said it was still a little cold for picnics and he took them to the Forest Park Hotel which was a beautiful country inn in Brockenhurst. The kind of place with diamond-paned windows at the front and a stag's head on the wall of the bar.

'If it's warm enough we can sit outside,' Rufus told Archie. But in the end they sat inside in a restaurant area which had plush comfortable chairs and wallpaper decorated with exotic birds, squirrels and butterflies. Their table was next to the window, so they had a view over the Forest Park's extensive back lawns, which weren't that dissimilar to the ones at Beechbrook House, Phoebe thought, except they didn't have lines.

The pub was full of other dining families and couples and on the table next door to them three old ladies, who spoke with genteel voices and clearly went to the pub regularly, mistook them for a family.

'Make the most of them when they're young,' said the one who was nearest to Phoebe. 'It's the best time of your life.' Her wrinkled face was warm, her eyes bright and intelligent, and Phoebe didn't contradict her assumption that she was Archie's mum.

She knew that both Rufus and Archie were oblivious to their conversation. But it felt bittersweet.

When their food arrived, it became clear why the pub was so

popular. They'd all ordered roasts and even Archie, who could be picky, ate every scrap. The desserts were to die for. Decadent creations of spun sugar and cream and all home-made, according to the waitress who served them. By the time they'd finished, they were too full, even for coffee.

When they finally came out of the pub it was almost 4 p.m. and Phoebe felt comfortably content.

She wasn't on call, and there was no one she wanted to talk to, but out of habit she checked her phone for messages and saw that she had two.

One from Max, who was doing cover, and one from Anni Buckland.

She listened to Max's message first because that was the order they'd come in. 'Phoebe, I'm sorry to disturb your Sunday.' His plummy voice filled her ear. 'But I thought I'd better let you know that I've just done a callout to the Buckland Farm. Cindy, one of the alpacas we were treating for anaemia, has died.'

21

On Monday morning, Phoebe and Max stood in one of the consulting rooms of Puddleduck Vets in urgent conversation. They weren't yet open to customers.

After the shock message from Max the previous day, Phoebe had phoned him.

'We could do with arranging a post-mortem,' Max had told her, 'but they don't want to pay for it.'

'They can't afford to pay for it,' Phoebe had said. 'But you're right, I think if they don't object we should get that organised. I'll pay for it. We need to get to the bottom of this. We don't want any more alpacas up there dying and it should give us some more information.'

Phoebe had managed to persuade Anni that a post-mortem was the best way forward and that Puddleduck Vets would cover the cost, and the dead alpaca's body had already been removed from the farm and taken to the hunt kennels where the post-mortem would be carried out, so at least this was in hand.

Max and Phoebe were now discussing the mystery alpaca

illness. It was a mystery because so far everything they'd tested for that might be causing the anaemia had come back as negative.

'We'll have to do some more testing,' Phoebe said, 'maybe even take bloods from some of the alpacas that aren't showing symptoms.'

'Will they be happy to pay for that, though?' Max asked, his gaze meeting hers across the consulting room table. 'If they couldn't afford the post-mortem?'

'That might depend on how well they're insured. They definitely can't afford to lose any more. I'll go and see Anni today. Leave it with me.'

Phoebe drove up to the Buckland Farm as soon as she'd finished her morning appointments. Her stomach crunched with anxiety. She knew she was in danger of becoming overly involved. Who was she trying to kid? She was already emotionally involved. She'd crossed the line between professional into personal some time ago. Partly because she liked Anni and the old lady was a friend of Maggie's but Phoebe knew she should have put the brakes on earlier on the financial side. She'd already discounted Anni's bill heavily and this was something that she often did when she knew that customers were struggling.

Unfortunately, due to the state of the economy, about seventy per cent of her customers were struggling and Phoebe couldn't subsidise them all.

The effects of the economy were also echoing alarmingly at Puddleduck Pets – the number of animals that were being given up for rehoming had risen sharply in the last few months.

'People just can't afford to keep them,' Maggie had told her. 'They can't afford to feed themselves, let alone their dogs and cats. So they bring them to us. Some of them are just looking for an excuse, of course, they're poorly trained or they've grown too big and lost their puppy appeal, but lots of them aren't. Most people are decent human beings.' Her eyes had sparked with something that Phoebe had first thought was anger but had later realised was compassion. Maggie must be softening in her old age. There had been a time when she would have said the planet would be a better place if it had considerably fewer humans and more animals on it.

However, Phoebe knew she wasn't the only one who'd been subsidising the costs of other people's animals. Maggie and Natasha had a system where if an owner wanted a dog or cat but couldn't afford their veterinary costs, the sanctuary helped. Puddleduck Pets part paid for the fees from fundraising and Phoebe gave them an extra discount if they needed it. Which they often did. Sometimes Phoebe was amazed she earned any money at all.

When she got to Anni's Alpacas, she was met by a grim-faced Anni. The alpaca that had died had been Cindy, the first one that been diagnosed with anaemia by Phoebe herself.

'I try not to have favourites,' Anni told Phoebe, 'but Cindy... she was such a sweet thing.' Her voice broke and she swallowed hard. She was clearly blinking back tears. 'I'm heartbroken. I really am. Are you any further forward with knowing what's caused it?'

'Hopefully we'll know more when the post-mortem results are back,' Phoebe explained, 'and I will let you know as soon as we've got them.'

She'd explained all this last night but she knew that Anni was in such a state of shock that it probably hadn't sunk in.

'We don't have time, though, do we?' That was Nick. Phoebe hadn't at first seen him in the dimness of the hall. 'Time's the one thing we don't bloody have. We can't afford to lose another one, I know that.'

'Phoebe's doing her best, love,' Anni soothed. 'Don't get yourself worked up.'

'It was a young fit animal. How do you damn well expect me to be?'

'We need to let Phoebe do her job. She's going to take bloods from some of the others. I did tell you.'

He slammed out of the room and Anni shot Phoebe an apologetic look. 'I'm sorry. He's just upset.'

It was a difficult visit, and Phoebe was heartily relieved when it was over and she could get in her car and drive away. Thankfully the alpaca Max had seen did not seem to be at death's door. That was something. She took bloods from a few more animals and carefully packed them into her bag.

As she drove back to the practice, the memory of Anni's tea leaf reading flicked into her head. It seemed much longer but it had only been last Wednesday. Less than a week ago. Anni had predicted problems for herself just before she'd done Phoebe's reading.

Phoebe tried to recall her exact words. 'There's trouble ahead. A heartbreak of some kind.'

The prophesy, which had come true so quickly, sent a shiver down Phoebe's spine.

* * *

To her bitter disappointment, Phoebe had to cancel her next two arrangements with Rufus. Both of them because she had to work late, going out on last-minute calls, thankfully not to alpacas. One was to a dairy cow with a bad case of mastitis and one was to an old lady who had a cat with a stomach upset. The owner had mobility problems and so couldn't bring him in for a consultation, although thankfully, she was also happy to pay Phoebe's callout charge.

Every so often, memories of the night at Woodcutter's flicked into Phoebe's head. Each memory ended on the thought, 'If only.'

If only she'd realised that Rufus wasn't yet ready to take their relationship to the next level. If only she hadn't drunk so much and then maybe she could have picked up the signals. If only they'd talked about what had happened. If only Rufus hadn't needed to rush off for Archie the next day. Maybe they could have worked things out. If only they weren't both so incredibly busy. Rufus never seemed to have a spare moment either. Not seeing him was making the problem worse and when they spoke their conversation was stilted.

* * *

On the first Tuesday in June, Phoebe had a message, which on first impressions she'd thought was a wind-up from Marcus. He'd handed her a note at the end of morning surgery which said to phone a woman called Knickerbocker Gloria who had 101 guinea pigs, some of which needed attention.

Phoebe read it and then ran back into reception so she could catch Marcus before he left for lunch.

'Marcus, what's this all about? I'm not sure I've read your writing right. Does this say Knickerbocker Gloria?'

'Yes. You have read it right. That's what she said her name was.' Marcus smirked. 'It's her professional name. She used to be a pole dancer apparently in her younger days, which, judging by the sound of her voice, was about half a century ago.'

'And she told you this?'

'She did. I couldn't stop her. She sounded really proud of it.'

'And she has 101 guinea pigs?'

'Yes, she rescues them. They need nail trims.'

'What? All of them?' Phoebe shook her head. 'How come?'

'I don't think it's all of them. Sorry, Phoebe, I didn't get all the details. I was a bit distracted by her pole dancing stories.' He glanced at his watch. 'I, er, hoped I might catch Natasha for lunch...'

'OK. You go. I'll phone her.'

Phoebe was relieved when the woman who answered her call said her name was Gloria before Phoebe had to ask.

'I understand you have some guinea pigs you'd like to register with the surgery,' Phoebe said. 'How can I help?'

'First things first,' Gloria said. 'I was wondering if you did a discount for charities. Or a discount for multiple animals. Or both...' There was the tiniest of pauses and then she added meaningfully, 'Like most vets do.'

There was no mistaking the implication in her tone, Phoebe thought wearily. If she said, no, they didn't, her name would be mud and if she said, yes, they did, she'd be overrun with guinea pigs all getting manicures for free.

'That really depends on the circumstances,' Phoebe hedged. 'Are you a registered charity?'

'I am not, dear. I am a pensioner. I am also a compassionate woman who hates to see dear little guinea pigs being abandoned in cages to die or tossed out on the scrapheap as soon as their baby cuteness and the novelty factor's worn off.' She drew in a deep breath. 'Today's kids have a lot to answer for – buying a pet and then not bothering to look after it. It's shocking some of the things I've seen. And the mothers aren't much better.'

Phoebe thought of Archie. The exception to the rule. 'I'm sure that's true in some cases but there are children who look after their animals.'

Gloria carried on as though she hadn't spoken. 'I've seen some awful things, dear, I can tell you. And I don't shock easily. I used to be a pole dancer back in the day, did your assistant tell you? I've seen people at their worst. I've seen men and women, but especially men—'

Phoebe sighed and interrupted before Gloria got into full flow again. 'Our discount for multiple-animal households is ten per cent.

And I can do you a further five per cent for being a charity. How does that sound?'

'Make it twenty and you've got yourself a deal,' Gloria came back quick as lightning.

'Twenty per cent it is.' Phoebe wasn't in the mood for bartering. 'I'm going to hand you back to Marcus, to do the registering.' She looked around the empty reception and then remembered he'd gone to see Natasha.

'Second thoughts, you can register them when you come in. Did you want to make an appointment now?'

'That's why I phoned. I'll probably need a double appointment. What's your skillset like? Could you clip ten guinea pigs' claws per hour?'

'Ten?' Phoebe repeated flatly.

'Or twenty maybe? I was pretty nifty myself at claws back in the day. It only takes a second, don't it? Clip clip clip. But my eyesight's gone a bit in recent years and I don't want to hurt them. Some of them have been traumatised enough already. I thought we could sort out any other problems as we go, couldn't we?'

Very much against her better judgement but by now, deeply regretting the fact that she'd ever called her back, Phoebe agreed to two double appointments back-to-back. Five guinea pigs per appointment. Jenna could do most of them, but she'd have to do some herself.

'We can arrange appointments for the others when I come in,' was Gloria's parting shot.

Phoebe hung up before she lost her patience and said something she might regret.

'That was a deep sigh,' said Jenna, who'd just come back in through the main doors, her bag over her shoulder. She must have been out for lunch too. 'Not more trouble at the Buckland Farm, is it?'

'No, thank goodness, but please don't tempt fate.' Phoebe told her about the guinea pigs and Jenna, sweet natured as usual, laughed.

'Don't worry about them, I can deal with a few guinea pigs and a crazy pole dancer.'

'How did you know she was a pole dancer?'

'Marcus told me. He told Max too – and Max said he'd be happy to help with some claw clipping if needed. What Marcus didn't tell him was that Knickerbocker Gloria wasn't actually pole dancing professionally now. So Max, bless him, is labouring under the impression that she's a lot younger than she is.' Jenna hesitated. 'Is it just me or have you noticed that there seems to be a bit of an *edge* between our two Ms?'

'No, it's not just you. I've noticed there's an atmosphere. I thought it was just male testosterone. They both like to banter, but maybe not. Why?' Phoebe gave Jenna a searching look. 'Do you think it's more serious? You're around more than me.'

Not to mention she valued the older woman's opinion.

Jenna put her head on one side, consideringly. 'You're right about the testosterone. I think it's to do with Natasha. They both like her, don't they? Marcus has carried a torch for her for weeks, but he's too shy to do anything about it and I think he sees Max as competition. Although actually I don't think Max is.' Jenna frowned. 'What I mean is that our young super vet is too career focused to be very much interested in romance. Or at least that's how I'm reading it. He's a woman magnet for a few of our clients but he doesn't seem to notice.'

'Yes, I think you might be right,' Phoebe agreed. 'I'm not sure whether I need to do anything about it – the atmosphere, I mean.'

'Other than give Marcus a shove up the backside towards Natasha, I'm not sure there is anything you can do. I suppose we could set them up on a blind date?'

'No. There's nothing worse than being set up on a date if you're shy.' Phoebe remembered all of Tori's attempts to try to get her to date before she was ready.

'Yes, that's true. How about a work night out? When no one's on call, I mean, and Marchwood are doing the cover. That could work. And it would be a good team bonding session.'

'Yeah, maybe.' Phoebe's stomach rumbled. 'I'd better grab something for lunch. We're open again in ten minutes.'

She walked through to the back to get her sandwiches. Much as she liked the idea of a team bonding session, she had precious little time when she wasn't working as it was. She'd tried before to ring-fence her time with Rufus, but it hadn't worked. When she needed to put in extra hours, it seemed that it was always her time with Rufus that got sacrificed.

22

Rufus was very aware that when it came to himself and Phoebe, things were strained. They'd been strained since that disastrous night he'd spent at Woodcutter's.

He'd told Phoebe there would be other times but the thought of staying over there again and risking a repeat of what had happened the first time terrified him.

He hadn't seen her since their Sunday in the forest two and a half weeks ago. She had cancelled both of the arrangements they'd made since then. A sure sign she felt the same way but just didn't want to tell him. He didn't know what to do about it.

'Talk, Rufus, you must talk.' That's what Bartholomew Timms, his therapist, would say. 'Talking therapy is the way forward.'

Which was all very well, and Rufus might have done that if he was more desperate. But he didn't know who to talk with.

He certainly wasn't talking to Bartholomew about any more of his failures as a man. And Harrison, with whom he'd shared many things, wasn't the right person either. Harrison was totally loved up with Tori. Rufus had never known him so besotted with a woman.

Harrison certainly couldn't have any problems in the bedroom department.

Rufus decided he wasn't desperate enough to talk to anyone at the moment. Besides, he had begun to think that he didn't have time for a relationship, at least not one that involved sleepovers.

Over the last couple of years, Rufus had taken on more and more of his father's duties, without giving up any of his own, because unless they employed a full-time manager to work in the office, then there was no one to hand them over to. The thought of employing and training a full-time manager, whom he'd need to work alongside, filled Rufus with dread.

This meant that as well as dealing with tenants and doing the estate management, which was bigger than it had once been, thanks to the lavender crops, Rufus was also now in sole charge of the family investments, which was a full-time job in itself.

Consequently, Rufus was now doing the work of two people, but his father was fast approaching seventy and so he couldn't pass any of it back. Alfred had always been energetic and independent, but he'd been quite crotchety lately too and Rufus knew it was because he could no longer do some of the things that had always made life worth living. Like golf and shooting. No matter what else had been going on for Alfred, he'd always managed at least one round of golf a fortnight, but he hadn't done that lately.

'My arthritis is bad,' Alfred had told Rufus when he'd asked why he didn't play golf any more. 'It's getting too much to do the walking, even with a caddy. And I can't expect my friends to slow down to accommodate me, Rufus. That's not sporting.'

Rufus didn't realise quite how serious Alfred's problems were until he walked into his room one morning, having thought he'd heard him call out, and found his father sitting on his bed, half dressed. He was wearing a vest and pants but hadn't yet put on his trousers.

'Sorry,' he said. 'I thought you shouted.'

'I didn't know you were around.' Alfred waved a dismissive hand. 'I thought you were working.'

'I am.'

It was a large room, but there wasn't much in it – his father detested clutter. There were wooden wardrobes and dressing tables and the king-size bed with its wrought-iron bedstead and plain white bedding.

Alfred was sitting on one edge of his bed and Rufus found his gaze drawn to his legs, which looked mottled and swollen below the knees. He was shocked. 'Dad – that doesn't look like arthritis to me – have you seen a doctor about it?'

'I don't need a bloody doctor.' Alfred hastily pulled a sheet over his legs. 'Leave me alone, Rufus. I don't need your fussing either.'

For once, Rufus decided to risk more conflict and ignore him and he headed across to the bed.

'You can't leave it. What if it's serious? You need to get that checked out, Dad.' He sat warily beside his father. 'Seriously, you can't ignore that. How long have your legs been like that?'

'Couple of weeks, a month maybe.' Alfred huffed. 'They're sore.'

'They look sore. Will you call your doctor, or shall I?'

Alfred looked defeated. 'I don't need to. I know what it is. It's bad circulation, my grandfather had it. The medication didn't do him any good. I think it's in the family.'

'But, Dad, you don't know that. You're not a doctor.'

'My grandfather died with this.'

'To be fair, that was a long time ago. There's a lot they can do for bad circulation these days. If it even is bad circulation.' Rufus didn't know this for sure, but it seemed very likely. Both he and his father were lucky enough to be blessed with excellent health. Neither of them visited doctors very often. They did essential stuff like go for vaccinations and that was about it. Rufus hadn't even been many times with Archie.

That was Emilia's domain.

But sitting there beside his father, who he knew hadn't consulted a doctor because he was scared, Rufus felt a rush of compassion. He didn't even remember the last time they'd sat this close together.

'I'll call him today,' Alfred conceded. 'If it will shut you up.'

'It will,' Rufus said, and got up feeling relieved. 'Let me know what they say, yes?'

'Yes, don't fuss. Shut the door behind you.'

* * *

At Puddleduck Vets, Phoebe was having a stressful morning. Thanks to an emergency first thing she was running late and so was Jenna. Unfortunately, the two clients that had been left in the waiting room were Knickerbocker Gloria and Dusty Miller, who had rehomed a dog from Maggie last year. The dog Dusty had taken on was a Jack Russell called Mutley who was a vociferous barker but fortunately Dusty was deaf so that hadn't mattered.

However, as no one else in the surgery was deaf, Marcus had already asked Dusty by way of various hand signals and the use of a pen and paper if he could possibly put Mutley back in the car until someone was ready to see him.

Dusty had done this but was now back in the waiting room again and Knickerbocker Gloria, who was unaware of his hearing problem, was telling him all about her previous life as a pole dancer with great gusto and the occasional dance move demo.

Dusty Miller, who didn't often let on he was deaf because he was embarrassed about it, was nodding and smiling and occasionally laughing, presumably directed by the expression on Gloria's face. Encouraged by his reaction, Gloria was getting more and more colourful with her descriptions. She was also getting louder and louder.

Both Dusty and Gloria were sitting in the waiting room reserved for the owners of cats and other small animals, which was the furthest away from the entrance door and opposite the second consulting room.

Until recently, it had also been occupied by a new customer who'd brought in her Siamese cat, Oscar, for a routine check-up. Oscar had yowled periodically from his cat basket, and his owner had grown more and more po-faced at the antics of Knickerbocker Gloria and Dusty and had eventually got up from her seat and left.

Phoebe had been oblivious to any of this until she'd gone into reception between appointments and been enlightened by Marcus.

'Oh, my goodness,' she said. 'Do you think she'll come back?'

'I don't think so. I did try going after her. She was waiting for Max. But she was here quite early. He's running a bit late too. When he's done, I'll mention it. If anyone can sweet talk her into coming back, he can.'

He beckoned her over and lowered his voice. 'There's also a man waiting to see you. He said he didn't have an appointment and he'd just wait until you were free. He's sitting in the corner at the end. You can't see him from here.'

'Did he give a name?'

'Hugh Lawson. He wouldn't say what it was about. I think he said he was a vet.'

Phoebe did her best to hide her shock and Marcus looked at her curiously. 'Do you know him?'

'I do. He's my ex,' she said in hushed tones. 'I can't even remember the last time we spoke.'

'Ah! Do you want me to get rid of him?'

'No. But please could you tell him I won't be able to see him until lunchtime, possibly later. Hopefully he'll get tired of waiting.'

'Got it,' Marcus said. 'OK. Will do.'

'Thanks. Do you know if the post-mortem results on the alpaca came through. That's what I came out for. They're due today and Max and I are going to discuss them when we get a second.'

'Yes, they came through. And I printed them off.' He glanced around the reception desk area. 'Ah, they're still on the printer there, look.'

'Thanks, Marcus.' Phoebe picked them up as she passed. She glanced at them and felt her heart sink. Nothing abnormal found, seemed to be the overall conclusion. Shit!

Fortunately, she didn't have to see Hugh directly because Jenna went and got Knickerbocker Gloria before she could frighten off any more customers and brought her and two cat boxes full of chirruping guinea pigs through to the consulting room.

Phoebe wasn't sure what she'd been expecting but it wasn't the petite woman with vibrant crimson hair, topped by a green beret, who appeared. Knickerbocker Gloria was a colour-clashing nightmare. She also wore a gold sequinned jacket with heavy shoulder pads over a brightly patterned short dress. Black fishnet stockings completed the ensemble and it was hard not to look at them because the dress was very short. Phoebe dragged her eyes up to her client's face, even though Gloria's outfit was obviously designed to be eye-catching.

As well as the crimson hair, she had crimson lipstick to match. She did not look as though she was short of money and fleetingly Phoebe felt cheated.

She might not have enough money to spend on her rescued guinea pigs, but she obviously didn't stint on clothes. Her artfully tasteless outfit dripped designer labels and Phoebe had learned a thing or two about designer labels since she'd met Rufus. That gold sequinned jacket definitely hadn't come from any high street shop.

She supposed they could all be from charity shops. Phoebe was still feeling too shocked at the news that Hugh was sitting in her waiting room to get hung up on Knickerbocker Gloria's clothes for long. Putting on her most professional voice, she said, 'I'm Phoebe Dashwood, and these must be your rescued guinea pigs.'

'Not much gets past you,' Gloria quipped sweetly and Phoebe gritted her teeth. 'This is Fuzzmeister, Pork Chop, Snickerdoodle, Pipsqueak and Miss Tiggywinkle Fairy-Toes.'

From the other side of the examining table, out of sight of Gloria's eyeline, she saw Jenna's lips twitch. Definitely best not to make contact with her vet nurse's eyes or they would both lose all semblance of professional dignity.

'Right,' Phoebe said. 'If you'd like to get them out one by one, we'll make a start on claw clipping.'

To her relief, apart from their long claws, the guinea pigs were all in good shape.

'They have the run of the garden,' Gloria said with satisfaction, 'so as much grass as they can eat. I round them all up at night in case of predators. They're all used to being handled too.' She picked up the one who'd just had its claws clipped and put it on her head on top of the green beret. 'See what I mean. No hands.'

The guinea pig, who looked as though it was used to such antics, sat peacefully on Gloria's head.

'Maybe we should put it back, just in case it falls.' Jenna stepped forward and Gloria cackled with laughter.

'Don't worry. I've got lightning reflexes. I'd catch it before it hit the floor. Comes from years of dancing. I used to be a pole dancer, you know. Back in the day. Oh, my goodness, the tales I could tell you.'

'How fascinating. Maybe another time, though.' Jenna always

managed to say what she wanted to without ever sounding sarcastic or patronising. She smiled sweetly.

'It's come back in, you know.' Gloria was totally unfazed. 'Very popular. Only they call it pole fitness, these days. That's the woke name. You couldn't call it pole dancing these days without getting flack from the PC brigade. Oh my. Those were the days, though.'

Finally, they were finished. Ten guinea pigs clipped and happy, and Jenna showed Gloria out.

'Oh, my God, I thought I'd seen it all,' Jenna said, as she came back into the consulting room. 'But now I think I really have.'

'Yes, I know. I wonder if she had her hair that colour back in the day. What colour was that anyway?'

'I think they call it Look At Me Scarlet,' Jenna said and lowered her voice, presumably in case Gloria was still lurking on the other side of the door. 'Did she mention she was a pole dancer?'

'Stop it.'

They both snorted with laughter.

When they'd recovered their composure, Jenna said, 'Moving on. Who's that hunky man sitting in the waiting room? Is he waiting for you or Max? He was there when I got Gloria.'

'Me.' Phoebe had almost managed to forget Hugh, but now he crashed back into her head. 'I was hoping he might have gone by now. He's my ex. We used to live together in London and work together at the same vet practice. I have no idea why he's here.'

'Ah. Sorry.' Jenna looked at her keenly. 'Do you want to find out? Or would you rather not have to speak to him? I could tell him you've had to go out on an urgent call if you like?'

It was the second opportunity she'd been offered to get rid of Hugh, Phoebe thought wryly. But again she said no.

'If I don't speak to him, he'll just come back. He's pretty persistent.' She sighed. 'But I'm certainly not going to make our clients wait even longer than they have already. That's for sure. So he'll have to hang on until I'm free.'

It was just after one thirty when she finally got to see Hugh. Everyone else had gone out to lunch but Jenna had said she'd be in reception eating her sandwiches – just in case Phoebe needed rescuing.

'I won't, but thanks,' Phoebe told her gratefully.

She showed Hugh into the bigger of the two consulting rooms and stood facing him across the examining table. If he'd been anyone else, she'd have apologised for keeping him waiting but if he'd been anyone else, he'd have phoned and asked if he could call round at a convenient time.

'This is a surprise, Hugh. Were you just passing? I thought you'd gone back to London.'

'I did for a while, but I decided to come back to the area. I've had enough of city life.'

He still looked like a city boy, Phoebe thought. The shirt, the expensive coat, the designer stubble. He'd always said he preferred the buzz of the metropolis to the quiet backwaters of country life. It had been thanks to Hugh that she'd gone to London in the first place. He was still as attractive as he'd ever been too. Dark hair, dark eyes. But it was weird, how he was no longer attractive to her. It was like looking at a stranger.

'Actually, I came to offer you my help,' Hugh continued, meeting her gaze.

'I don't need your help, Hugh.'

'Really? Deaf pensioners, ex-pole dancers and clients who leave in a huff because they don't like their company. Not to mention a mystery illness killing alpacas. I'd say you do need my help, very much.'

23

'The bloody cheek of the man.' Tori looked as outraged as Phoebe had felt, a few hours earlier. 'Did he really say all that?'

'That was just his opening gambit,' Phoebe told her. 'He had a lot more to say than that.'

They were sitting in Tori's office at *New Forest Views*. Tori hired office space in Bridgeford, and the premises wasn't a million miles from Hendrie's Post Office and General Stores where Sam worked. Tori could have worked from home, but she liked the buzz of an office, and she shared the space with an advertising company, which meant it was cheap.

At the moment the office was empty – all of the advertisers, and also Tori's assistant editor, Laura, having already left for the day – and Phoebe and Tori were now sitting on office chairs on wheels, sipping coffee. Phoebe had gone round to see her best friend after work, partly because she was desperate for a chat and partly because she didn't want Hugh to know where she was now living.

He had left Puddleduck Vets just after lunch, but she wouldn't have put it past him to have parked up somewhere close by and then followed her back to Woodcutter's. Hugh was incredibly persistent when he wanted something. And he hadn't been impressed when she'd sent him packing.

'What did he actually want?' Tori said now, her green eyes wide as she leaned forward expectantly. 'I thought he'd given up chasing after you a couple of years ago. Is this the first time he's been in touch?'

'Yes. Thankfully it is.' Phoebe blinked a few times. 'He's living in Lyndhurst apparently and he's been working as a locum at a surgery there for someone who's been on maternity leave. But she's back now and so Hugh thought he'd come along and see if I needed any help – of the veterinary kind, that is.'

'The bloody cheek of the man,' Tori said again. 'I know I'm repeating myself but I'm actually flabbergasted that he'd even think you'd say yes.' She tucked a strand of red hair behind her ear, leaned forward on her chair and raised her eyebrows. 'I mean, this is the same Hugh you lived with in London for six years. The same Hugh who thought it would be a good idea to start an affair with your mutual boss, hence causing you to lose your job, your home and him all in one fell swoop.'

'Put like that, it does sound outrageous.' Phoebe giggled. 'Yes, it's the very same Hugh. I can't believe I'm laughing, but actually that's how "over him" I feel. Which is one good thing, I guess.'

'That's because you're a strong and independent woman.' Tori said up straight again on her chair. 'Whereas Hugh is a rat of the highest order. Not to mention you have a lovely man already. Did you send him packing?'

'He went eventually. Yes.' Phoebe paused. 'Actually, he didn't just want to do locum work for me. He wanted to buy in – to sink some money into the practice – is how he put it.' She found herself bristling at the recollection of Hugh's calmly worded offer, which she now repeated back to Tori. She could practically recite it word for word – it was burned on her brain.

'You obviously need some financial help, Phoebe. And I can provide it. There are absolutely no strings attached. I'm aware that there won't be any romantic entanglement between us. This is business only.'

'Wow.' Tori shook her head. 'That man is unbelievable.'

'It goes without saying that I'm not considering it, but the trouble is, he hit a nerve on the financial front. We're not struggling but the business isn't as profitable as I'd hoped and some months we do actually only just break even.'

'What? But why? You're always so busy.'

'I think I need to be more hard-headed,' Phoebe said slowly. 'I've been doing a little bit too much work at discounted prices. Because lots of people can't afford the full prices. And I don't want the animals to suffer.' She told Tori about Knickerbocker Gloria and her guinea pig sanctuary.

'Unfortunately, she's not the only client who's given me a sob story lately and then asked for a discount and I always fall for it. I'm too gullible, that's the trouble. In fact, I'm not sure that word hasn't got round. We've had a few people do it. Although I do know that a lot of them are genuine cases.

'Take the Buckland alpacas. I know they're genuine because Maggie put us in touch and vouches for them, but unfortunately I can't seem to get to the bottom of what's wrong with their alpacas. One died recently and we had the post-mortem results back today and they didn't show anything abnormal. Neither have all the tests we've done since then. Anni and Nick can't afford to lose any more alpacas, though. I'm so aware of that.'

'And you can't afford to go bust trying to find out what's wrong with them. Oh, Pheebs. I had no idea. Why didn't you tell me?'

'Because we've hardly seen each other, I guess. I know I get too emotionally involved. I need to set better boundaries. That's been difficult with Anni. I like her a lot. It didn't seem a big deal to pop by and see how the alpacas were doing. Then it progressed into me having a home-made scone or two when I went. And then one afternoon she ended up reading my tea leaves.'

'Your tea leaves. Okaaaay...' Tori looked fascinated. 'I didn't know people still did that.'

'Anni has Romany ancestry. You'd know what I mean if you met her. You can see it. She has the gorgeous dark hair and sloe eyes. Apparently her grandmother, Madam Kesia, read the palms of celebrities on Scarborough seafront. Anyway, Anni still reads tea leaves. She told me you didn't need any particular gift to do it, it was something you could learn.'

'And so you had yours read?' Tori stirred her drink.

'Yes, it sounds a bit crazy when I say it like that. But at the time I was just having a scone with her, and tea obviously, and afterwards she upended her cup in her saucer and read her tea leaves and then she asked me if I'd like mine done.'

'I would have done the same in your shoes,' Tori said, totally caught up in the story. 'Did she see anything interesting?'

'Well, when she did hers she was a bit sad. She said there was a heartbreak ahead in her life, and the thing is, Tori, that prophecy or reading or whatever you want to call it came true. Her favourite alpaca, Cindy, who she'd hand reared from tiny, well, she was the one that died. And it didn't happen very long after that reading.'

Tori's hand flew to her mouth. 'Gosh. That is heartbreaking.' Her eyes shadowed. 'What did she tell you?'

'Nothing at all that she said to me has come true. Although I suppose you could read things into it. She saw an A which she said meant there was someone significant in my life whose name began with A.'

'Archie,' Tori said immediately.

'Yes, I thought that too, but the thing is you could pick any letter of the alphabet and find someone significant in your life whose name began with that letter, couldn't you? Apart from Z or X maybe.'

'For someone who describes themselves as gullible, you're incredibly cynical when it comes to all things clairvoyant.'

'And for a cynical journalist, you're incredibly idealistic when it comes to affairs of the heart.'

'Touché,' Tori said and they both grinned.

'Any advance on A? What else did she see in the tea leaves?'

'She said I was going to have success in a venture, which I was hoping meant Puddleduck Vets, and, well, I've just told you how that's going at the moment.'

'Yes, but success isn't just financial. There are other types of success. Did she say it was financial?' Tori pressed.

'She saw a crown, which sounds pretty financial to me. She also saw a house, which signifies a family and me being part of one, which is fairly general. Oh, and she also saw a baby. She said that if I wanted to avoid getting pregnant, I should make sure I was very careful. Chance would be a fine thing. I barely see Rufus – both of us seem to have 24/7 jobs which make having a relationship impossible... What?' She broke off. Tori was looking shocked. Her eyes had clouded and she was biting her lip.

'What did I say?' she repeated.

Tori took a deep breath and then another slow sip of her drink. She looked at Phoebe over the rim of her cup. 'I haven't had a chance to tell you – because I wasn't 100 per cent sure until recently. But it's me who hasn't been as careful as I should have been. Strictly speaking, it's Harrison too, of course. But it's me who's pregnant, Pheebs.'

It was Phoebe's turn to be flabbergasted. 'Pregnant, oh, my God, Tori. How do you feel? What did Harrison say? How much pregnant?'

'I'll answer the easiest question first. I think I'm about twelve weeks.'

'Twelve weeks.' Phoebe did some swift calculations. 'But that means you were pregnant when we went to the Brace.'

'Yes, I know. That's why I didn't drink anything. I wasn't 100 per cent sure then, to be honest. And besides, Phoebe, you'd just told me that you'd never slept with Rufus, I thought that me telling you I might be pregnant would be like rubbing salt in the wound.'

'It wouldn't have been but that is so sweet of you.'

'I know. I'm like that.' Tori grinned. 'Cynical journalist but sensitive and empathetic friend.'

Her words were so utterly true that for a second Phoebe didn't speak. Tori had obviously assumed that the problems with Rufus were all sorted. Now was definitely not the time to tell her they weren't.

Also, it hadn't escaped her that Tori didn't look very thrilled about being pregnant.

'Is everything OK?' she asked gently. 'What did Harrison say about it?'

'Those questions are definitely trickier.' Tori got off her chair and went across to the coffee machine. 'Everyone told me I would go off coffee if I got pregnant. But I haven't. Do you fancy another one?'

'Yes, please.'

She came back with two mugs, handed one to Phoebe, and sat back down again on her office chair. 'I'm frankly still processing the whole thing. I've never had any plans to have kids. As you know, I've never been the maternal sort. And if I was, then I definitely wouldn't have started now. Harrison is positively anti-family. He had a pretty crappy childhood and he doesn't speak to his family any more. Not at all. His view on having kids is similar to mine. We did discuss it one drunken evening. It was after a condom broke.'

She winced. 'We were fine that time, as it happened, and I went on the pill straight away afterwards. I've been on the pill ever since.' She paused. 'After that first scare, Harrison mentioned that maybe he should get the snip. That's how anti having kids he was. But I said the pill was ninety-nine per cent effective. And he said he trusted me not to bugger it up. And I haven't, Pheebs. I may have taken one late occasionally but I was totally mystified when I got pregnant.'

She had tears in her eyes and Phoebe felt a rush of compassion. 'It's not necessarily anything you've done, but ninety-nine per cent means that the occasional woman will get pregnant. I think we just assume ninety-nine per cent means we're fine.'

'Yeah. I should have known I'd be the unlucky one per cent. I should have asked you before.' Tori wiped her eyes and Phoebe got up and went to hug her friend.

'Did he react badly when you told him?'

'I haven't told him yet.' Tori pulled back from the hug, rubbed her forehead and shut her eyes. 'I just can't bring myself to say it because I think I'll lose him if I do. I kept thinking that if I didn't mention it, then it wouldn't be real.'

She cupped her stomach gently with her hands and glanced downwards. 'And I know I'm not showing yet and I haven't gone off coffee, but I'm having morning sickness like you wouldn't believe. It's definitely bloody real.'

'You have to tell Harrison,' Phoebe said gently, 'because it's not going to get any easier and it's not going to disappear, is it? And it's not something you should be dealing with on your own.'

'I know.' Tori's eyes filled with tears and she swiped them away. 'I'm over-emotional – bloody hormones. Just ignore me.'

'I'll be here – 100 per cent here, whatever you decide.'

'I know that too.'

In the end, Tori had phoned Harrison and said she had something she needed to talk to him about and could she go to Beech-brook, and so she and Phoebe had driven over there in convoy. Beechbrook House and Puddleduck Farm were a stone's throw from Woodcutter's Cottage, which was in the same direction.

'I'm in all evening,' Phoebe had told Tori before they'd gone their separate ways. 'I mean, if you want to come over afterwards or anything.'

'Thanks, I'll let you know. If you don't hear from me, it's prob-ably good news. Or very bad news. And I don't want to talk to anyone.'

'Think positive,' Phoebe had said.

Tori hadn't dropped in afterwards, but she had sent a text to Phoebe at just before midnight saying Harrison had been really shocked and still was, but at least they were talking and to watch this space. Phoebe, who'd been wide awake, and worrying a little, had sent back a row of hearts and a crossed fingers emoji.

She wasn't just worrying about Tori and hoping she was OK. She was also still processing the fact that Hugh had come round and wondering if he was likely to come back. She made a mental note to talk to her staff about it and prime them all to say she wasn't available to see him if he did.

And Rufus was also on her mind, as he so often was. They had no plans to meet up this coming weekend. She was on call, but she could have done something. It was Rufus who'd said he was too busy to meet. He'd also said his father wasn't feeling too well and he wanted to keep an eye on him. Phoebe hadn't argued. After all, she'd cancelled on him twice lately. Maybe he was just fed up with being let down.

Or maybe it went deeper than that. Phoebe knew that Tori wasn't the only one who preferred to bury things rather than face a problem head on. OK, so it was true that her work was hugely important and it did take priority but she and Rufus hadn't talked about what had happened or rather hadn't happened when he'd stayed over. It was the elephant in the room, and the more that time went on the harder it got to say anything.

There was a part of her that wanted to race round to Beech-brook and tell him he was top of her priority list. That seeing him and Archie was one of the things she looked forward to doing the most. But she didn't do this. And she knew she would have done once. Things were changing between them and not for the better.

24

The next couple of weeks passed peacefully. On the plus side, Jenna and Max were doing Knickerbocker Gloria's next couple of appointments and on the minus side, the blood samples she'd taken from the extra alpacas also came back clear. So she and Max were no further forward in getting to the bottom of the matter.

To Phoebe's relief, Hugh did not make any more appearances. At least none that anyone mentioned. She had told everyone that if he did, they were to say she was not on the premises. Maggie said she'd set Tiny and Buster on him if he as much as set foot on Puddleduck Farm.

Phoebe hadn't seen Maggie for a proper chat lately, despite the fact that she was at Puddleduck Farm every day. This was partly because Eddie had been around a lot and every time she saw Maggie, she was with him. Phoebe quite often glimpsed them in the distance, arm in arm as they strolled down to see the donkeys, or neddies, as Maggie called them, with Tiny and Buster trotting along beside them. Those injections were doing wonders for Buster. They'd given him a new lease of life. Eddie had given Maggie a new lease of life too. Phoebe had never seen her so relaxed and happy and she didn't want to gate crash their time.

However, Phoebe wasn't that surprised when Maggie came into Puddleduck Vets one lunchtime, when she was alone in reception, inputting notes into the computer. Her grandmother leaned her elbows on the reception desk and her chin on her elbows and said, 'Are you avoiding me or something? I've not seen you for weeks!'

'It's not weeks. But I know what you mean. It is a while. Two ticks. Let me just finish this.'

'Pah, that's the trouble – you're always working.'

Phoebe pressed finish and swivelled on the reception desk chair to face her grandmother. 'I'm sorry. I know I am. How can I help?'

'I don't need any help. I'm fine. But I just thought I would check you were. How's Rufus?'

Oh, my God, her grandmother had a knack of getting straight to the heart of things without even trying. Phoebe felt like a rabbit caught in the headlights. 'Um, fine. I think. I haven't seen much of *him* lately either.'

'It's not just me then.' Maggie's gaze softened a little. 'That's more serious, though, isn't it? You need to make time for the love of your life.'

In her pocket, Phoebe heard her mobile buzz with a text. 'I expect that's him messaging me now,' she quipped.

'I hope he does more than just message you.' Maggie glanced towards the plate-glass entrance doors of Puddleduck Vets where outside the sky was the brightest of blues. 'Summer will be gone before you know it. Had you noticed we're having the most glorious June and you are in danger of missing it all? It's the longest day tomorrow.'

'I'm not missing it. I'm out on farm calls too much to miss the summer.'

'Yes, but that's work, not play.' Maggie paused and went on idly, 'The lavender looks beautiful next door. I never thought I'd say it but some of those new eco-crops are very easy on the eye.'

'Yes.' Phoebe knew she was blushing. She hadn't been up to Beechbrook House lately and you couldn't see over the high walls that enclosed the estate. She hadn't actually seen the lavender in bloom. As Maggie had no doubt guessed.

'I've had to cancel a couple of arrangements with Rufus lately, but you're right, I need to make Rufus more of a priority.'

'It's not just Rufus you need to prioritise, darling. It's you! Living the dream only works if you don't have to kill yourself to do it.'

Phoebe nodded. She felt oddly vulnerable. She had never thought of it like that.

Maggie cleared her throat. 'And I heard that Hugh was sniffing around the other day, wasn't he? Fingers crossed he'll have the good sense not to come back.'

Phoebe raised her eyebrows. 'Because you'll set the dogs on him.'

'Or Eddie. He may be an old man, but he could see off the likes of City Boy Hugh. Did I tell you he took up kickboxing when he retired?'

'Kickboxing.' Phoebe looked at her in amazement. 'I thought he walked with a stick.'

'That's because he injured himself kickboxing.' Maggie giggled like a girl. 'I don't think he's going to go back to it, but he's still got a whiplash tongue on him when he gets going. And there's always my baseball bats.'

They both laughed now. 'Can I come in for my tea after work one night, Gran?'

'Only if you stop calling me Gran. But darling, seriously, you don't need to ask. Puddleduck Farm is your home just as much as it's mine. Come in anytime. Bring Rufus and Archie.'

'I will. Thanks.' In her mind's eye, Phoebe had a brief cosy picture of Rufus and herself and Archie, all sitting round Maggie's table, eating her amazing home-made soup and chewing on great hunks of bread and butter. It was interrupted by the sound of the door opening and Jenna, Marcus and Max all came back from lunch at the same time.

Maybe they'd been out together. Phoebe hoped so. Team bonding. Even if they did have to do it without her.

'Ah, Maggie.' Max strode across to reception. 'It's good that you're here, because this concerns you too.'

'It does?' Maggie looked worried.

'Yes, we've been discussing behaviourists,' Marcus joined in. 'I've tracked one down this time. Another guy but this one's got a degree in psychology and a qualification in animal behaviour. And he hasn't got a silly name.' He glanced at Max slyly. 'Peter Good. He's an independent and his company is called Good Behaviour.'

'Showing a distinct lack of imagination,' Maggie scoffed.

'Yes, but at least he might be sensible and offer some sound, practical advice,' Marcus said enthusiastically. 'Shall I book him?'

'Is he expensive?' Phoebe asked.

'No,' said Jenna and Max in unison. Then Jenna continued, 'He does a similar thing to the last one. He offers a free half hour and if you like him, you sign him up.'

'But there's no obligation,' Max added.

'I guess it can't hurt,' Maggie said. 'We don't have to hire him and if he does seem sane and/or have a modicum of skill, then at least we'll have someone we can recommend to our re-homers.'

'And our clients,' Phoebe said, inspired by her staff's enthusiasm. 'Yes, I'm definitely up for that. Although I might not be able to attend the demonstration,' she added quickly, aware of Maggie's glance. 'I've got quite a lot on at the moment. But I totally trust you guys to make a judgement.'

* * *

The message that had come through on Phoebe's phone turned out not to be from Rufus after all. It was from Tori.

Is it OK if I come round to Woodcutter's after work? Say if it's not. Just want a quick chat.

Phoebe had texted back:

Of course it's OK.

Since Tori's text saying that at least she and Harrison were talking, she hadn't been in touch. Phoebe had sent just one message, asking if she was OK, and had got a message back that said:

Yes, we're getting there.

Phoebe hadn't pushed her for more.

They'd always had the type of friendship that went in spurts. They could switch from full-on communication for days or sometimes weeks, to long silences. Neither of them were needy friends. They both knew that the other was there, and would come at the drop of a hat if asked.

It was a relief, though, to see that Tori was smiling when she arrived at Woodcutter's that evening.

She breezed through the door, in a cloud of red hair and perfume. 'I'm sorry, Pheebs. I should have called round before but it's been deadline time at the mag and Laura had a sick child so it was all hands on deck. It's been mad. I'm so sorry.'

'Stop apologising and come and sit down. Is coffee still OK?' She glanced without thinking at her friend's tummy.

'Yes, it is. And yes, I'm still pregnant. But oh, God, Pheebs, it's been a rollercoaster of emotion. I can tell you.' She paused in the middle of the kitchen. Her face was alight and yet serious as well. She looked different somehow.

'I'm having a baby,' she said softly. 'It's odd, you know. They were wrong about the coffee, but they were right about the maternal hormones. I want this baby so much. Even though I never thought I wanted it at all. And I knew it didn't matter if Harrison was on board or not. I knew I was going to have it.'

'That's brilliant. I am so pleased.'

Phoebe made their drinks and carried them through to the snug back room. They sat by the wood burner that was still full of ash from winter fires that Phoebe hadn't had time to empty, and they held hands across the coffee table.

'So how is Harrison? How does he feel now?'

'He's OK. I think at first he was really shocked. Like me, he'd trusted that it couldn't happen. But he also knows me well enough to know that no way would I have been careless. Or done it on purpose, heaven forbid. He knows I don't have a single maternal bone in my body. Didn't have,' she amended softly, cupping her tummy once more. 'Bloody hell, Pheebs. It is weird how things can change. We went for the scan yesterday. Harrison hates hospitals, and I'm not so keen on them myself, but there we were in this poky little room, looking at this screen of wriggly lines and listening to our baby's heartbeat. Our baby which we'd created – part of him and part of me – and we were both just utterly blown away.'

For a second, her face looked so serene that Phoebe felt a bit blown away herself too.

'That sounds amazing.'

'It was.' She paused. 'He'd come round to the idea before that, but not that much longer before, only a couple of days. It was fear, Phoebe. He was afraid that he wouldn't be a good dad. He'd had such a bad relationship with his own father that he didn't think he'd be able to be a good dad himself. But I think he'll be a great dad. He's kind and gentle and patient.'

Phoebe, who'd seen none of those attributes in Harrison, nodded uncertainly and Tori caught her look.

'I know he doesn't seem like that at face value, but that's only because he has the same sort of social phobia thing going on that Rufus has. How is Rufus anyway?' She finished her coffee and put her mug back on the table. 'I'm sorry, this has all been about me, me, me.'

'Of course it has, you've got big news. Where are you planning to live?' Phoebe changed the subject deftly.

Tori didn't seem to notice. There was a faraway look in her eyes. 'We're not sure yet. Not at my flat – babies and stairs aren't a very good mix, are they? We've thought about staying at Beechbrook but that's not ideal either. Although it is in some ways. It's a tied cottage so Harrison gets it thrown in with his job rent free and it's obviously very handy for his work, but it's also very small and has a spiral staircase, which isn't very practical either.'

'Does it really?' Phoebe drove past the little gatehouse property, the front of which echoed the façade of the big house, all grey stone and chimneys, every time she visited Rufus and Archie, but she had never been inside. 'Are you going to get married?'

'I think we will. Yes.' Tori giggled. 'Listen to me. I never believed we'd end up having this conversation, Phoebe. I thought it would be you who got married first. You who ended up wearing some gorgeous white dress and drifting up the aisle with Mr Tall, Dark and Handsome. You're the one that has the serious relationships, not me. Not that I'm going to be doing any drifting up any aisle until after the baby's born. I'm starting to show and I am not going to be a pregnant bride.' She paused for breath, but not for long. 'I'd ask you to be my chief bridesmaid obviously and we both want you to be godmother to our baby. We've discussed all the important stuff like that.'

Phoebe blinked back tears. It was amazing to see her best friend so happy. And maybe she had misjudged Harrison after all.

'I always thought it would be you who did it first,' Tori said. 'Do you remember when we were all small? You, me, Frazier and Sam, and we had that mock-up wedding in the barn at Puddleduck Farm and we argued about who would do what?'

'Of course I remember.'

'You said I had to be the bridesmaid.' Tori's eyes sparked with amusement. 'You were the bride and you made your brother be the vicar and stand at the top of the aisle made out of hay bales.'

'Well, I couldn't marry my brother, could I?' Phoebe said.

'No, you married Sam. I always thought you might marry him for real one day.'

'I didn't.'

'But in real life it was Frazier who got married first and had babies. And then it was me.' Tori's eyes misted a little. 'I reckon Sam will be next,' she carried on blithely. 'I heard on the grapevine that he and Judy are living together now at his. I can't see them living in sin for too long. Sam's definitely the marrying kind.'

'Wow, I hadn't heard that.' Phoebe remembered with a jolt that she never had followed up Sam's invitation to go for a drink as a foursome. No wonder she wasn't up to date on his news. She swallowed the prickle of unease that rose in her throat. Where had that come from?

'That's brilliant for Sam,' she said brightly.

Tori grinned. 'Oh, my God, Pheebs, I was so sad last time I saw you, but now I'm so happy.'

'And I'm very happy for you,' Phoebe said. 'And for Sam.' And she meant it from the bottom of her heart.

Although later, when Tori had gone home, Phoebe couldn't

shake off the ache of envy in her heart. Her two best friends were settling down and it was brilliant, of course it was, but she felt as though she was the odd one out. The one who'd been left behind.

25

'You look absolutely beautiful.' Sam's voice was husky as he stepped back a pace to take in Judy's dress. It was pale blue, made of some kind of shimmery material and it hugged her curves, as protectively as a lover's arms.

'Thanks. It's fun dressing up, isn't it? It makes a nice change from breeches and Barbours, don't you think?' Her eyes were sparkling with fun. 'I have to say, you scrub up quite well yourself.'

Sam was in his only suit – the one he dragged out for funerals and weddings. It was black and had cost a fortune about fifteen years ago and fortunately it still fitted him and was still vaguely in fashion, he hoped. He wasn't at all sure it was up to the occasion, which was the wedding of Judy's cousin, Francesca. Not just a wedding, Judy had told him happily. But the society wedding of the year.

Sam had contemplated buying a new suit when he'd first agreed to go. But he knew he couldn't afford anything expensive, and a cheap suit wouldn't have fitted the occasion either. Because of this, he'd almost said no. It was only because Judy had said that her parents really wanted him to go that he'd agreed at all.

Why her parents wanted him to go was beyond Sam. But he was pleased that they did. Maybe they were finally starting to accept him as their daughter's partner. He really hoped so because he knew he couldn't fight them. He wanted a future with their daughter but he wanted them to be happy too. He couldn't ask Judy to make a choice between him and her parents. It just wasn't fair.

The wedding was taking place at a church on the outskirts of Brockenhurst and from there the whole wedding party would transfer by car or carriage, depending on how they'd arrived, to Rhinefield House, a very grand country house hotel, set in forty acres of its own grounds in the heart of the New Forest.

Rhinefield House itself had featured in several D. H. Lawrence novels apparently and there were also links with Wordsworth, the poet. Sam wasn't unaware of Rhinefield House – it was hard to be unaware of it if you'd been brought up in the New Forest, but he'd never been there, although they were open to the public for cream teas. Sam would rather have gone to one of the many independent tea shops in the forest for a cream tea if he fancied one than to have sat at Rhinefield House amongst the nobs. It would have been cheaper too.

Still, the day of the wedding was finally here, and he was determined to make the best of it. He and Judy had had the luxury of a lie-in because they'd both arranged for someone else to take care of their horses. Judy just had to send the livery stables a text – full livery was part of her package anyway. Sam had a reciprocal arrangement with one of the other livery owners – they saw to each other's horses if either of them couldn't get there.

'We can go in my car if you like?' Judy had said as they got ready to leave. The wedding present had already been delivered to the venue. Apparently that happened a lot these days to avoid the nuisance of people turning up with gifts and not knowing where to put them.

'No, it's fine, we'll go in mine,' Sam said. 'Don't worry, it's clean. I had it valeted yesterday.'

He'd actually put it through the car wash in Bridgeford, but he'd vacuumed out the inside himself.

'Fine,' Judy agreed without fuss. It was only when they were halfway to the wedding that Sam wondered if maybe they'd have been better going in Judy's electric BMW. She'd probably have preferred to arrive in that than his old Subaru Forester. He berated himself for second-guessing everything. It didn't make a blind bit of difference what car they turned up in. It wasn't all about money.

Oh, yes, it was, Sam thought as he parked his car at the end of a row of shiny electric models and top-of-the-range hybrids. He felt a little like he'd entered a Thelwell pony into a class of thoroughbreds.

Judy didn't comment. Maybe it was just him, being super aware. Super self-critical. He was good at that. A few minutes later, they were mingling outside the church with the other guests. Once more, Sam felt slightly out of place. He didn't know anything much about fashion, but the smell of money was unmistakable. The flamboyant hats, the jewels, the expensive scents, the plummy voices and the smoothly tanned limbs of the women. It reminded Sam of a time he'd been to the races and had been trying to find the mate he'd gone with and had inadvertently stumbled into a private box. Everyone had turned and stared at him. Then a guy in a top hat had shouted, 'I think you're in the wrong place, mate. The lavatory's the other way!' Everyone had laughed and Sam, humiliated, had backed out of the door, apologising.

No one shouted this time, but he could feel lots of eyes on him and Judy. Quick sharp gazes that fell on him and Judy and then flicked away. They were too well bred to stare. But the feeling was exactly the same as it had been at the racecourse.

Judy reached for his hand and squeezed it. 'Hey, are you OK?

Come on, I want to introduce you to people. It's OK, they don't bite. There's Auntie Maud. We'll start with her. She's horsey. And she's in a group with Mummy and Daddy. Perfect.'

To Sam's relief, it wasn't long before they could stop the chitchat, which to him felt painfully difficult, despite the horse element.

Judy's parents were polite but not warm, as Sam was introduced, and he was aware when he was talking to Auntie Maud that a woman standing next to Judy's mother leaned in close and whispered something Sam couldn't hear and Judy's mother looked at Sam, nodded and looked pained.

It was much better when the ushers began to round people up and they all trooped into the big old church. It felt easier sitting on a pew in the muted light of the stained-glass windows amidst the heavy scents of the flowers dotted around in giant vases.

The wedding wasn't so different from any other he'd been at. There were the same oohs and aahs as the bride came down the aisle, the train of her dress carried by several bridesmaids. There were the same words solemnly pronounced by the vicar, the same beautiful vows. The same slants of sunshine filled with dust motes angling through the stained-glass windows to light the faces of guests. There was the same music, although at this wedding they did have a choir too, their high voices blending with the more sonorous sound of the organ.

Then finally the ceremony was over and they were spilling back outside into the sunshine amidst the jangling of bells. Such a joyous sound, Sam had always thought. The sound of hope and optimism.

There seemed to be more than one wedding photographer, both were women. One was darting around taking informal shots, while the other bossed people into groups and took the more formal line-ups. Sam was not asked to join any groups, at which he was heartily relieved.

Then finally it was back into the cars and across the forest to Rhinefield House.

'Wasn't that beautiful?' Judy chattered as he drove. 'Didn't Francesca look stunning? That dress cost her eighty thousand pounds. Not that price is that important,' she added hastily, as she caught Sam's gasp of shock. 'It's just that if you have lots of money I guess you just would spend more on your wedding dress, yah?'

Judy never said yah usually, but an hour or two in the company of her relatives and it was back in her vocabulary.

'She did look beautiful,' Sam said. 'It was a lovely wedding.'

He was really tempted to suggest that now they'd done the important bit they could perhaps skip the reception and just head off for lunch at a nice country pub instead. If he was going to do it, he'd need to do it soon. They were close to Rhinefield Ornamental Drive which was one of the most beautiful parts of the New Forest, bordered on either side by ancient woodland. They weren't far away from the venue.

He didn't suggest this, although he was beginning to wish he had as he joined the procession of flash cars going up a long drive that was bordered by azaleas and rhododendrons. The azaleas were in full bloom. It was like driving along an avenue of pink and purple. Stunningly beautiful.

Sam tried to relax. These people may be posh and rich, but they were just people with the same fears and emotions and anxieties as anyone else. They were the same as him beneath their finery and flash cars.

At the top of the drive he followed the signs that said wedding party and he realised that they were being diverted from the car parks and driving up to the hotel itself. Was that so they could witness the full effect of its grandeur? The building was magnificent, no one could dispute that. It was grey stone with turrets and dozens of chimneys. An imposing square arch led to the front entrance door. Grandeur on a huge scale.

Sam realised why they were being diverted a few seconds later as the Mercedes in front of him stopped and its occupants got out and the driver handed over his keys to a man in a liveried uniform. Bloody hell, even the valet was posh. Their cars were clearly going to be parked by the hotel staff.

When it was his turn, the guy in the uniform took his keys, bent to look into the driver's seat more than a little disparagingly to Sam's sensitive radar, and then lifted what looked like a stalk of hay from the driver's head rest. 'Sorry, sir. I'll just dispose of this for you, sir.'

He wrapped it in a serviette and put it in his top pocket while Sam's face burned as though it was on fire. Sam would have given anything for the earth to have swallowed him up. The car behind him, and probably the one behind that, would have seen the whole thing. Not only had he dared to turn up in an ancient Subaru Forester, he'd turned up in one unfit for a valet to drive.

Judy was pretending not to notice, but Sam wished he had listened to his instincts and suggested they skip this bit. It wasn't just Thelwells and thoroughbreds, it was like taking a pit pony to the Horse of the Year Show and expecting no one to bat an eyelid.

From that point on, the day got worse and worse. Maybe he was being too sensitive, Sam thought, but it seemed to him that he was eyed with, at worst, suspicion and, at best, surprise, by practically everyone he met.

For the lunch – he had no idea why it was called a wedding breakfast – he and Judy and her parents were sat on a family table with a couple of Hooray Henrys who turned out to be Judy's old friends from school. One of them worked in hedge funds in the city and the other had a father who owned a small island in the Bahamas. They talked of wintering abroad and of visiting places that Sam had never heard of. He knew it was only a matter of time before someone asked him what he did.

When it finally came, Judy intervened before he could answer. 'Sam's in the civil service,' she said.

'Postal service, isn't it?' her mother corrected and several eyebrows raised.

He forced himself to keep smiling. To keep sitting in his chair, being polite to these hideously obnoxious people. He forced himself to swallow down his anger and also his surprise that Judy had felt the need to lie about what he did.

By the time their food arrived, which was about 4 p.m., the Hooray Henrys were quite drunk. They obviously hadn't driven themselves here and neither had Judy's parents. They were all laughing uproariously at in-jokes and talking about people they knew – but who Sam obviously didn't.

Both of the guys were getting increasingly friendly. At one point, where there was a lull in the conversation, Sam heard the one who was sitting on Judy's other side lean in and say, 'I'd have thought you'd have been married yourself by now. Do you know, there was a time when I thought I might be the lucky chap.'

Judy just laughed and said, 'In your dreams, Claude,' but Sam felt a sting of discomfort. She had never said they'd been close in that sort of way.

The discomfort was followed by an awareness that he was being watched. Sam felt a prickling sensation in that way that you do when someone is studying you. He glanced across the table and his gaze locked with Judy's father's. There was something in the man's eyes. A smug kind of triumph. And in that moment Sam knew why

Judy's parents had been so keen for him to come to this wedding. Not because they were softening towards the idea of him being with their daughter. But the exact opposite. They wanted him to know that never in a million years could he fit into their world.

26

On the same Saturday that Sam was at the wedding, Phoebe was at Buckland Farm. She had nothing new to tell them, but they had two more alpacas with symptoms and they were getting desperate.

So was Phoebe. 'I'm going to get a second opinion,' she told Anni, as they made the now familiar journey up to the alpaca field. 'Don't worry, it won't cost you anything.'

'How won't it?' Anni glanced at her anxiously. 'You can't keep subsidising us, Phoebe. I know you have been. But you've got a business to run.'

'It's OK. I've called in some favours.' Phoebe brushed the older woman's concerns aside. She'd already been speaking to Seth and he'd promised he'd call by the next time he was passing. Which she hoped might be today.

Phoebe could have sworn there was more grey in Anni's jet-black hair every time she saw her. And she felt partly responsible. She should have suggested a second opinion before.

The alpacas seemed more unsettled than usual. They were all up in the top field which was bigger and slightly less parched than the bottom field, but they weren't grazing peacefully, they were milling about. Maybe they knew that her presence meant more prodding and poking, more nasty needles, Phoebe thought, but just as she was about to voice this to Anni, Anni shouted, 'Hey. Hey, *you*... What do you think you're doing?'

Alarmed, Phoebe followed her gaze and saw what Anni had seen. High up in the top field, there was a man moving in and out of the alpacas. A man with a bag. Seth was her immediate thought, but she was surprised he hadn't come by the house. That would have been the usual protocol. She shielded her eyes against the sun, which was shining directly into them.

It didn't look like Seth. Seth was short, nimble, jockey sized, and this man was tall. Oh, my God, was this sabotage? Had someone been doing something to the alpacas? Several scenarios, each one more outrageous than the last, flicked through her head, but in the next instant things moved forward quickly.

As she and Anni quickened their pace up the slight incline, the biggest of the alpacas, a black male called Charlie, clearly decided that attack was the best form of defence. Instead of aimlessly milling, he was now actively pursuing the intruder. And his body language was not friendly.

The man, who was clearly aware of the change of mood in the herd, abandoned whatever he'd been doing and began to run across the field in the direction of the five-bar gate with Charlie hot on his heels. The field was stock fenced so it would have been harder to get over that than the gate in a hurry, and the man was certainly in a tearing hurry. Being pursued by an angry male alpaca was not something any sane person would brush off as a minor inconvenience. It was urgent and dangerous.

Phoebe gasped. 'Oh, my goodness, should we be doing something?'

They'd been almost running, but now Anni slowed and put a hand on Phoebe's arm.

'Good old Charlie. Looks as though he's sorting out the situation. That's not your vet with the second opinion, is it? He's got quite a turn of speed on him.'

'No, that's not Seth.' Phoebe bit her lip. The man reached the gate just in time and half jumped and half climbed it, before landing in a crumpled heap on the other side.

Charlie skidded to a halt by the fence, and, as Anni and Phoebe got closer, they could hear the man on the ground groaning.

'Hopefully he'll have broken something,' Anni said with satisfaction.

For once, Phoebe found herself agreeing. Whoever the guy was, she couldn't think of a single good reason why he'd be skulking around a herd of alpacas. 'Shall I call the police?' She got out her phone.

'Let's see what he's got to say for himself first, shall we?'

They arrived breathlessly at the gate. Charlie, having succeeded in chasing the threat out of his field, had now retreated to a safe distance. On the other side of the gate, the man, still groaning, rolled over and half sat up.

Phoebe got the shock of her life. Oh, my God, it was Hugh. There was a graze on his face and he had a cut lip and what looked like a mouthful of dirt which he was now trying to wipe away. He must have face-planted the ground, which was rock hard, in his haste to get over the gate. It had been a dry June and the earth was parched and cracked.

'What the?' She stared at him in confusion. 'Hugh. What the hell are you doing here?'

Hugh didn't speak straight away. He rubbed his mouth and then spat something out. 'I think I've broken a tooth.'

'You know this guy.' Anni looked at Phoebe with her eyebrows raised. 'Did you ask him to come up here?'

'Yes, I know him and no, I didn't.' Phoebe took a step closer. She felt as though she'd stepped into some alternative reality.

'Then he's trespassing,' Anni said with some satisfaction, 'and yes, I think you should call the police. This had better go through the official channels...' she turned back to Hugh, '...because if my Nick gets hold of you, you'll lose more than a bloody tooth.'

'I'm a vet,' Hugh said, straightening his shoulders from his position on the ground, and looking up at Anni as if that explained everything. He scanned the area for his bag which had somehow survived the chase and was now lying on the grass a few feet away. 'And you've had problems with anaemia – correct?'

'How do you know that?' Anni said sharply.

'Yes, I'd like to know that too,' Phoebe echoed. 'And you still haven't told us what you're doing here.'

'I saw the alpaca post-mortem when I came into the practice.' Hugh looked at Phoebe directly now. Then he blinked a few times and clearly deciding that being on the ground put him at a disadvantage, he got slowly to his feet and leaned heavily on the five-bar gate. His nose was bloodied too, Phoebe saw. If he'd been anyone else, she might have felt sorry for him. But he'd crossed a line this time.

'I was passing when I saw your car parked under the Anni's Alpacas sign and I put two and two together.' He reddened and Phoebe knew that he was regretting the last half hour. He knew he'd gone too far, and, despite his protestations of innocence, he felt guilty.

Phoebe also knew Anni deserved an explanation. She wasn't just a client, she'd become a friend too.

'Hugh is an ex of mine,' she told her, feeling her own face flame.

'An ex who doesn't want to let go.' Anni interpreted the situation instantly. 'A stalker kind of ex. That's a police situation, I'd say.

Throw in the trespass too and you'd have a reason to get out an injunction to stop him bothering you.'

Hugh put his hands up – palms forward. 'Hey, no police. I'm not a stalker. Phoebe, you need to tell her I'm not a stalker.'

'But I'm not sure that's true. And you're definitely a trespasser, Hugh.' She unlocked her phone.

'No. Look. Hear me out. Please. I think I know what's wrong with your alpacas. I've seen it before. It's Mycoplasma Haemola-mae. It's textbook.'

'Don't you think I've tested for that, Hugh? It came back nega-tive.' Phoebe sighed. 'I am not stupid.'

'I know. I know you're not. But there was a case on a farm I went to a few years ago.' He paused to rub more earth from his chin and only succeeding in making it worse and smearing dirt across his cheekbone. 'It took us ages to get to the bottom of it. And in the end we found out that the best way to diagnose is to perform a blood smear on a slide as soon as you take the blood – like here and now, I mean. Not in the lab. You'll identify it then under a microscope.'

Phoebe hesitated, her thoughts racing.

'Could he be right?' Anni's question snapped her back to the present.

'Yes. Yes, it's possible. I've got my portable microscope. I'll do it now. Will Charlie be OK if I go into the field again?'

'I'll take care of Charlie. But who's going to take care of this bloke? The police or Nick?'

'I can take care of myself, I'll go.' Hugh went to walk a few steps, but he was limping heavily and his face screwed up in pain. 'Shit, I've done something to my hamstring.'

'Maybe that'll teach you to think twice next time you're plan-ning on poking your nose in someone else's business,' Anni said crisply.

'I was trying to help.' Hugh was starting to sound aggrieved again. 'And I haven't had so much as a thank you.'

'I'd prefer it if you checked with me first about whether your help was required,' Phoebe said quietly. 'I mean it, Hugh. Don't follow me again. And please don't think I won't involve the police. Because I will if you carry on turning up like this. Just go.'

He didn't answer. He knew he was beaten and neither of the women spoke as they watched him limp the long way back along the road, to his car.

'Was I too harsh?' Phoebe asked Anni. 'Should I have offered to go and get my car? That did look painful.'

'On the contrary.' Anni narrowed her eyes. 'You're too nice, Phoebe. And I'm not a bit surprised that men fall in love with you and then stay in love with you.'

'They don't.'

'They do,' Anni said. 'There is more than one suitor in your life. I saw it in the tea leaves. Remember?'

'Suitors, stalkers – not a lot of difference there,' Phoebe said lightly and Anni nodded thoughtfully.

'You're so cynical for one so young. Although I can see why, having met your ex. He hurt you badly, didn't he?'

'Yes, but it was a long time ago.' Phoebe sighed. 'I'm over Hugh. I have been for ages.'

'Good job.' Anni rubbed her hands together. 'Right then. With a bit of luck some good will have come out of this little fiasco. How quickly can you tell if he's right about that thing? What is it again – in layman's terms? And more to the point – can you cure it?'

'It's a nasty bacterial disease,' Phoebe said. 'We can find out pretty much straight away once we look at the slides under a microscope. And yes, if it is that, we can hopefully cure it.' She looked into Anni's eyes. 'I'm going to phone Seth – he's the vet I asked for a second opinion. Please don't get your hopes up too much.'

27

'Funnily enough,' Seth said, once Phoebe had explained Hugh's hypothesis, 'I did do some research after you phoned me, and I think Hugh may be right. Mycoplasma is hard to diagnose. It's such a transient thing because it's cyclical and it's not uncommon for PCRs that go to the lab to come back negative. So yes, perform a blood smear on a slide as soon as the blood is taken and if it is Mycoplasma then you should be able to identify it under a microscope.'

By the time Phoebe had finished speaking to Seth, Hugh had gone. She was hugely relieved about this. Him turning up at her surgery had been bad enough but him turning up at Buckland Farm and wandering around amongst the alpacas had really spooked her. What had he been planning to do anyway? Surely he'd not planned to take a blood sample himself. He could have been struck off for less.

She didn't have time to think about it now. She went and got the samples, fetched her microscope and did exactly what Seth had told her.

Her heart hammered and her hands were clammy as she

studied the sample. A few seconds later, she found to her incredulous delight that Hugh was right. Finally, they had the answer.

Hugh being correct was a huge relief, Phoebe thought, as she went to break the good news to Anni, but it didn't get him off the hook.

'I'm so sorry about that little fiasco, Anni, but we do now have a confirmed diagnosis.'

'So the trespassing vet was right. Does that mean you can cure it?'

'Yes, we can. And yes, he was, although I wish he hadn't gone about it the way that he had.'

'I think he learned his lesson,' Anni said, letting out her breath in a huge sigh of relief. 'I'll never forget him nosediving over that gate. I'll give Charlie some extra treats later.' Her voice sobered. 'Where do we go from here?'

'The anaemia is caused by a type of bacteria so I'll need to give your whole herd a long course of antibiotic injections. With luck, you shouldn't lose any more.'

'When can you do it?'

'I'll come back up with Max later today if that's OK with you?'

'Of course it is.' She paused. 'Phoebe, if ever you need any help to – well, see off men who've become a nuisance, you just let me know and Nick will be more than happy to oblige. He's pretty nifty – if you know what I mean. Back in the day, he was known as Nifty Nick and he hasn't lost it... I do hope you don't mind me saying that, but I feel that our relationship is a bit more than just professional now, isn't it?'

'Yes, it is. And of course I don't mind you saying it. Thank you for that, and Max and I will see you in a while.'

Phoebe drove back to the practice. What with Kickboxing Eddie and Nifty Nick on her side, no stalker would stand a chance, she thought, suppressing a smile.

But another thought had also struck her. It was interesting that Anni hadn't known she didn't need protecting. Anni hadn't asked if she already had a protector either. She had been dating Rufus for ten months and no one really knew that they existed as a couple.

When she got back to Puddleduck Vets, she relayed what had happened to Marcus and Jenna, and asked them about the post-mortem results. 'Have you any idea how Hugh managed to see them? He came in on the same day that we were doing Knicker-bocker Gloria's guinea pigs.'

Marcus frowned. 'Ah, yes, I do remember. It was that really hectic day. That woman with the Siamese cat walked out. She took offence at some of the things Gloria was saying to the deaf guy that was here. Dusty Miller. Oh, shit, and I did go after her too. I thought I might be able to smooth things over. I'm pretty sure I left the post-mortem results on the printer. I'm so sorry. I should have put them out of sight.' He looked stricken.

'Marcus, it's fine. You didn't do anything wrong. They would have been out of sight to any normal customer.' Phoebe glanced at the printer, which was on the shelf, alongside the reception desk. 'Hugh would have had to lean over to get a look at them.'

'I was only out of reception a few minutes, I swear. And I was only just the other side of the door.'

'Hugh could have taken a photo of them,' Jenna said. 'Sneaky beggar.'

'Yes.' Phoebe shook her head. Hugh had always been a little bit obsessive. And he'd used that trick of seeing her car parked some-where and assuming he could turn up and talk to her, before, but actually following her to a client's and then trespassing on their land and trying to get involved in one of her cases – that was breaking new ground.

It bothered her. Why would he go to such lengths?

It was just as well she wasn't seeing Rufus this weekend though because by the time she and Max had finished administering antibiotics at the Bucklands', it was quite a late night. Thankfully she didn't have any other calls. And she was even more thankful that Hugh didn't make any reappearances, so she didn't need to call in the services of Nifty Nick, her Buckland bodyguard, or Kick-boxing Eddie.

On Sunday morning, she caught up with Maggie at Puddleduck Farm. Maggie was having coffee with Eddie in her kitchen but when Phoebe popped her head over the half-open stable door, she got up and came across.

'Hello, stranger. Is this a social visit or are you after some advice on getting rid of stalkers?'

'Wow. News travels fast. You've been talking to Anni. Is nothing a secret round here?'

'We may have had a little chat.' Maggie was unfazed. 'Not that I needed to talk to Anni – I already know the story of Hugh photographing the post-mortem. That man needs a serious talking to.'

'And I've done that already.' Phoebe met her grandmother's steely gaze. 'I don't think he's dangerous, Maggie. He knows he overstepped the mark.'

'Does he, though?' Maggie ushered her into the kitchen. 'Come and have a cuppa and a chat. Eddie can read his paper in the other room. Can't you, Eddie?' She made shooing motions with her hands and Eddie rolled his eyes.

'Girl talk, is it?'

She nodded and he folded up his paper and got up with good grace.

'He doesn't need to go on my account,' Phoebe protested but Eddie was already heading for the door that led through to the rest of the house.

A few moments later, Phoebe and Maggie were sitting at the

kitchen table and Phoebe was breathing in the scents of coffee, toast and dog – they must have only just had breakfast and the dogs were sprawled on the floor. Tiny was snoozing peacefully and Buster was chewing a ball by the Aga.

'He's doing so well,' Phoebe said, glancing at the black Lab. 'He's got a whole new lease of life.' She looked at Tiny. 'Does that wolfhound ever do anything? Every time I see him, he's asleep.'

Tiny opened his eyes. He knew they were talking about him with that sixth sense that dogs have, even though they hadn't mentioned his name.

'He prefers to take life at a steady pace,' Maggie said. 'He's a sensible chap.' She poured them both a mug of coffee and pushed one across the table. 'Pity I can't say the same about Hugh.'

'No.' Phoebe stared into her coffee. 'It was a shock seeing him yesterday, I must admit.'

'Yes, I bet. Anni said he took quite a tumble.'

'He did. I'm hoping that will put him off doing anything like that again. What?' she asked, seeing that Maggie was shaking her head.

'It sounds like he's on too much of a mission. Do you know what he's doing back in the area?'

'Not really. When he came into the surgery, he told me he'd been working as a locum at Lyndhurst, but that came to an end. He's living there too, I think.'

'Lyndhurst is a far cry from London. Could he have fallen out with his parents? It seems odd that he'd give up that flash flat in Greenwich otherwise.'

'I suppose he could have done. But why come here?'

'Because he knows you were one of the best things to ever happen to him and he's egocentric enough to think he can get you back if he proves his worth. That's what that alpaca thing was all about, I'm sure.'

Phoebe looked at her in surprise. 'Do you really think he wants me back? It's been ages since we split up.' She hesitated. 'I've never really seen Hugh as egocentric. He's pretty insecure underneath that calm exterior.'

'Low self-esteem and an ego the size of a planet,' Maggie said. 'It's not as uncommon as you might think. Hugh's spent his whole life trying to impress his father, and if he has fallen out with him then it makes sense that he might think he could try to impress you instead.'

'Get you and your amateur psychology,' Phoebe teased, but her grandmother's theory did have a ring of truth about it, she had to admit. She'd never thought that a big ego and low self-esteem could go hand in hand, but the description summed up Hugh perfectly.

'Does he know you're going out with the lord of the manor?' Maggie asked. 'If he knew that, he'd probably stop. Men like Hugh look up to the landed gentry.'

'I doubt it.' Phoebe laughed ruefully. Even if Hugh had been following her for a few days, he wouldn't have seen any signs of her and Rufus interacting. She gave a deep sigh.

'Tell me to mind my own if you like,' Maggie said. 'But you're not acting like a young woman in love...' She let the sentence hang in the air.

'No, to be honest, I don't feel like one.'

'You and Rufus haven't sorted out the work/life balance thing, I'm guessing.'

'No, but I'm not even sure if it is that any more. I keep thinking that if we were really good together, we'd make time for each other.'

'Yes. You probably would.'

There was another silence, although it was never quite silent at Puddleduck Farm. Outside there was birdsong and the distant sounds of barking, and closer by there was the ticking of the clock and the sounds of Tiny and Buster breathing.

Maggie went on softly. 'I don't want to pry, so all I'm going to say is that in my experience communication is at the heart of a good relationship. If you can talk to each other, you can resolve pretty much anything.'

'Yes, I think you're right.' Phoebe thought of her grandmother and Eddie. They'd overcome the huge obstacle of his partial deafness by creating a whole new language.

She and Rufus didn't even have any communication difficulties, or at least not physical ones. Surely they could overcome the few issues that they had. They just needed to talk.

Phoebe sipped her coffee. 'I'd better make a move, thanks, Maggie.'

'Puddleduck Therapy Services are always available,' Maggie said, giving her a mock bow, but her eyes were serious. 'Good luck, darling. And you will let me know if you have any more trouble with Hugh.'

'I will.' Phoebe was tempted to go straight round to see Rufus now but she restrained herself. Impulse visits never worked very well. He might be out somewhere with Archie and even if he wasn't, she'd have to get past bloody Emilia. And she might get a callout and have to dash away again.

No, she would ring him later. They could arrange to go out for dinner one day this week. It would be a school night – Archie didn't break up for another week – so it would just be the two of them. They could have a proper heart to heart with no interruptions and nothing and no one else to distract them.

28

Sam and Judy hadn't spent Sunday together. They'd gone their separate ways first thing. Sam had gone off to see to Ninja at the crack of dawn. He'd only arranged cover for his horse for one day, and Judy had stayed in bed at his place.

'There's no need for you to get up,' he'd told her when the alarm had gone off and he'd tugged on his old yard jeans. 'I won't be long.'

But when he'd got back from the stables just over an hour later, she'd been gone. His bed had been neatly remade and there was a note propped up by the toaster.

Things to do, people to see. Catch up later. Jx

Sam had moved around his large oblong kitchen, making coffee, and putting on more toast and feeling an odd disquiet.

Snowball had purred around his legs, meowing for his breakfast. Thank goodness there had been no more problems with his cat. But he wasn't at all sure about his relationship.

After they'd got back from the wedding yesterday, he and Judy had had their first real big row. It had started in the car as he'd driven them back. Judy was in that relaxed slightly loose-tongued mood that she got into after drinking. Not that she was drunk, but she'd had two or three glasses of wine spread across the day and Sam was stone cold sober, having drunk nothing but sparkling water.

'You don't seem very happy,' she had said, as they drove out of Rhinefield House at around six thirty, Sam having finally managed to track down someone to find his car.

'I'm not,' he had said tersely. Not happy was an understatement. There was a cold anger spreading up through him. For the last hour or so of the reception it was all that had been holding him together.

'Why, Sam? Didn't you enjoy the festivities?'

'I didn't enjoy the feeling that I didn't belong there, no.'

'Oh, Sam, I think you're being oversensitive. It was just a party. No one thought you didn't belong there. Mummy and Daddy especially asked that you should go.'

He had gripped the steering wheel tight, feeling his back lock with tension. He'd been about to explain that the reason they'd invited him had been nothing to do with them *wanting* him to be there and everything to do with wanting to show him he *didn't* belong there, but one quick glance into Judy's bemused eyes had stopped him.

She would not understand. She would accuse him of having a chip on his shoulder.

Instead he asked her, 'Why did you tell your friends I worked in the civil service?'

'Because you do.' She looked at him in astonishment. 'The post office is part of the civil service.'

'But why not just say I work in my mother's general stores and that I help out behind the post office counter when it's busy?'

'Oh, Sam, you're splitting hairs. You don't need to be specific about what you do. People just ask out of politeness.'

Politeness – that was a joke. 'Are you ashamed of what I do, Judy?'

'No. No, of course not.' Her voice had become sharp with embarrassment, and he had known in that moment that she was ashamed. She hadn't wanted to tell her rich friends that her boyfriend had such a humble job. It might not matter when it was just the two of them, but it mattered when they were out socially. And it had struck Sam in that moment as they drove through the forest that they didn't do anything usually that involved each other's friends. Socially their worlds didn't overlap. They did a lot as a couple, but Francesca's wedding was the first thing they'd ever done where one of them had gone into the other's world.

'It strikes me that it's you who is ashamed of what you do,' Judy had said, and Sam had looked at her in shock.

'I'm not,' he said tightly. 'I'm perfectly comfortable with who I am.'

When they'd got back to his maisonette, the argument had carried on. Judy had accused him of being cool towards her old friends.

'It might have helped if you'd told me that one of them had wanted to marry you,' he'd shot back.

The argument had turned into one about jealousy. It seemed that Judy thought he was overprotective, and just hadn't liked her having male friends. But Sam knew it wasn't that. In the end, they'd both apologised to each other and they'd made up in bed. The chemistry between them had always been amazing.

But it was very telling, Sam thought, that Judy had eaten her breakfast and had left before he'd got back from seeing to Ninja. He was pretty sure that she had nowhere else to be that Sunday. At least nowhere that she'd mentioned the previous evening anyway. The whole thing had left him with a deep sense of sadness. He'd always worried that their backgrounds were too different for them ever to mesh properly.

But he had thought they could get over that if they talked about problems as they arose. For the first time, he wondered if that was possible, and his doubts rocked him.

* * *

Phoebe started Monday morning feeling happier than she had for weeks. Last night she and Rufus had finally caught up and it was he who'd phoned her. He'd suggested they have dinner out on Wednesday night and that he hoped it might be possible that they spend the whole of the following weekend together as Archie would have broken up from school for the summer recess and was going on a sleepover the Friday and Saturday night with his friend, Jack.

A sleepover wasn't something that Archie did very often but apparently Jack had stayed over a few times at the manor house lately, while he and Archie plotted their guinea pig breeding enterprise, and this was his parents' way of saying thanks. There was an added appeal in going to stay with Jack because they were a multi-pony household. Both Jack and his elder sister, Kate, had ponies and Kate was more than happy for Jack to ride hers. So the two boys could go hacking in the New Forest.

'I'll be lucky if he ever comes back,' Rufus had told Phoebe with a wry smile in his voice. 'But I'm so glad he's making like-minded friends. Jack's also going to the same school he is in September, which makes me feel so much easier about sending him away. They're going to do pony summer camp together too. I'm not going to see much of him for the next few weeks.'

Rufus had sounded lighter than he had for ages and it had been contagious. It helped that she was feeling confident about the alpacas too, Phoebe thought, when she got to work on Monday.

It was a little soon to tell, but she was sure they'd turned a corner with their diagnosis. And Monday turned into the kind of day where everything fell into place. There were no awkward customers, and no awkward animals, and a farmer who'd been dragging his heels on paying came in and settled his account in full.

Jenna was in a very good mood and even Max and Marcus were chatting amenably. Phoebe had started to think she'd imagined the tension between them.

'Peter Good is coming over tonight,' Max told her when they broke for lunch. 'Just in case you're about?'

'Peter who?' She looked at him, puzzled.

'The Good Behaviour guy – he's the behaviourist Marcus found.'

'Yes, of course.' She smiled across at Marcus, who had relaxed his dress code because it had been a hot June and was today wearing a white shirt without a tie and brown cord trousers, which weren't part of a suit – he'd finally taken her at face value and realised he didn't have to be suited and booted every day.

He beamed back. 'Jenna and I have high hopes of him, don't we, Jenna? She knows someone who had a snappy Shih Tzu and Peter sorted him out no problem.'

'Sounds promising,' Phoebe said, although secretly she wasn't so sure. A snappy Shih Tzu was probably a doddle compared to Saddam.

Peter Good was due to arrive at five forty-five and Phoebe had said she'd be out as soon as she'd caught up on paperwork, but to let her know if she was needed before then. Marcus was apparently going to give him a full debrief before they went anywhere near Saddam's barn. Deep down, Phoebe doubted that Peter Good was going to be much more use than any of the others had been so she wasn't altogether surprised when 6 p.m. came and went and no one called in to see if she was about.

But it was a shock when the next thing she became aware of was raised voices just outside the surgery doors. Phoebe got up from the office chair and went outside to see what was going on and walked straight into a row that appeared to be going on between Max and Marcus.

'You must have given him the wrong time,' Marcus was saying. 'Or the wrong directions. I wouldn't put it past you.'

'That's totally ludicrous. Why on earth would I do anything like that?'

'Because you want me to fail.'

'Of course I don't want you to fail. I'm not as petty as you are.'

'I am not petty.' Marcus sounded outraged. 'And if you're not petty, why did you tell Natasha that we were meeting by the barn and tell me that we were meeting up at the house?'

'That was a misunderstanding.'

'Misunderstanding my eye.' Marcus glared at Max and Max glared right back, seemingly unrepentant. Brown cords and white shirt squared up to designer label man neither of them seemed aware that Phoebe had just turned up. They were too locked in on each other.

Phoebe cleared her throat and they both turned to look in her direction.

'Is there a problem, guys?' she said in her most authoritative voice.

'He's the problem,' Marcus said instantly. 'Changing the plans. Saying different things to different people. I had this whole thing perfectly under control!'

'I thought Maggie was going to be here,' Phoebe said, looking around the yard as if she might conjure her up. 'And Jenna...'

'Jenna had to go on. She had a message from her husband,' Max filled her in.

'And Mrs Crowther said she'd stay at the house in case Peter Good didn't realise there was a side gate that he could use to go around the back.'

If he didn't realise there was a side gate, there was no hope for him, Phoebe thought, but decided not to say. There was enough friction out here already.

'It's pretty pointless us standing around arguing,' was what Phoebe did say. 'Marcus, why don't you go and see if Natasha needs any help, and Max and I can go up to the house to see if there's any news.'

Marcus didn't need telling twice, he went with good grace, and Max fell into step beside Phoebe.

'Are you two OK?' she asked him as they headed round to the Puddleduck Farmhouse. 'Only I have to say I do sense an atmosphere sometimes.'

'I'm sorry.' Max stared at his feet and then back up at Phoebe. His eyes were apologetic. 'It was unprofessional of me to get involved in an argument. Marcus is angsty because he thinks I'm interested in Natasha, which, as it happens, I'm not.' He sounded affronted. 'She's way too young for me.' He shrugged. 'But there's none so insecure as a man who thinks you're chasing a woman he's too shy to ask out.'

Phoebe nodded. 'OK, but please try to keep the peace with him at work. And maybe you could clear the air with him regarding Natasha – you are the senior member of the team.'

'Absolutely. I'll apologise.'

Phoebe knew he would. He was a nice guy, Max Jones.

By the time they'd got to the farmhouse and discovered there was no sign of Peter Good and then they'd all gone back to the barn, Maggie included, in case he'd turned up there, the tension had blown over.

As they stood in a small group outside the barn, Marcus said, 'Maybe I'd better check he hasn't messaged me.' He got out his phone. 'Ah,' he said. 'He has just messaged. He's been unavoidably detained. Well, he had a breakdown and he's waiting for the RAC. He's asked if he can reschedule.'

'Tell him no,' Maggie said crisply. 'None of us have the time to wait around for people who may or may not be any use even if they do arrive.'

Phoebe nodded. 'That's fair comment.'

'Sorry, guys.' Marcus looked chastened. 'I thought I was onto a good one there. If you'll excuse the pun.'

'It's not your fault.' Max's voice was conciliatory. 'It might be better if we had a behaviourist closer to home anyway. What do you think, Phoebe?' He was standing with his hands in his pockets and he glanced at Marcus. 'Didn't you say you'd be interested in doing a course? Would that work for you, Phoebe?'

'Yeah. I'd love to.' Marcus looked at him in surprise and then at Phoebe. 'Would that be OK? I'd do it in my own time obviously. And I can pay for it.'

'The practice can pay for it,' she said, shooting a grateful glance at Max. He'd obviously taken her earlier words to heart, and he'd hit on exactly the right resolution. 'Why don't you have a look at some courses?' she said to Marcus. 'When you think you've found something suitable, show me, and we can go from there.'

'Will do, boss.' He glanced back at Max. 'Cheers,' he said quietly.

A little later when everyone had dispersed, Phoebe and Maggie wandered up to the neddie field – to check on Diablo, Roxy and Neddie. 'You look happier,' Maggie said, as they reached the donkeys, who were swishing their tails in the evening sun. 'All sorted with Rufus now?'

'We're getting there,' Phoebe said, glancing up across the sloping fields towards the strip of woodland that had been planted to hide Puddleduck Farmhouse from view of Beechbrook House. 'Thank you for asking. How are things with you and Eddie?'

'They're lovely.' Maggie's eyes softened. 'I never thought I'd find anyone I wanted to be with again. After your grandfather, I mean. And I wasn't looking. Obviously. Romance was the last thing on my mind.'

'I'm so pleased for you both,' Phoebe said.

'It just goes to show that it's never too late.' Maggie's lips twitched as they stood beside the donkeys. It had been a warm day and they were some time off sunset – but the evening sky that arched above them was the softest of pastel blues, and the air had a hint of gold that held all the romance of a sunset. All of its promise and all of its hope.

29

Phoebe's meal with Rufus on Wednesday night was all that she'd hoped it would be. They went to a Thai restaurant near the cathedral in Salisbury that Rufus had told her came highly recommended.

'Sometimes it's good just to get out of the forest, don't you think?' he said, as they walked, hand in hand, along the city streets towards the restaurant with the cathedral spire never far from sight.

Phoebe agreed that it was, although she suspected her reasons were different than his. For her, it was a change to swap fields and trees and the sound of birdsong for concrete streets and the sounds of traffic. But for Rufus she was pretty sure that getting away from the forest spelled anonymity. He was unlikely to be recognised walking through a city or bump into anyone he or his father knew at one of the dozens of restaurants. He could be himself.

The Thai was very good. They ate tapas, which suited them both, fragrant aubergine bao buns, with pickled cucumber and peanut satay sauce, crispy pepper squid, spare ribs and duck rolls. The little dishes kept on coming and somehow it was easier to chat when they were both sharing than eating a more formal meal. The soft candlelight and white linen tablecloths added to the atmosphere and the tables were spaced out enough so there was no chance of eavesdropping by other diners.

Their conversation grew gradually more intimate. They stopped talking about work and began talking about each other and about the relationships they'd had.

'I dated a little bit at uni,' Rufus told her, 'but really I only ever had one serious girlfriend and that was Rowena.'

'Your late wife,' she murmured, not wanting to break the spell. He rarely mentioned Rowena and she didn't want to stop him.

'Yes. We clicked immediately and we got married and I don't think there would ever have been anyone else were it not for...' His dark eyes grew darker. '...the accident.'

Phoebe waited for him to go on and after a while he did.

'Yes, as you know, I was there. And it's been very hard to get over it – to move on. I didn't expect it would be easy. But I didn't expect it to be this difficult either.' He reached for his serviette and she saw that his hand shook slightly. She felt a deep well of compassion for him.

'You don't have to talk about it, Rufus, if it's still painful.'

'I think I do. I think...' He paused and wiped his mouth and put down the serviette. 'I think that I must if we're to have any chance of a relationship that's to be more than friendship.'

Rufus closed his eyes and then opened them again. There. He had said it. He was on the way to talking about what Bartholomew Timms had said he must and this girl, this lovely girl, was looking at him with nothing but compassion in her eyes. And maybe it wasn't the right place – a Thai restaurant in the middle of a city he had always loved – but it felt like the right place. No one could hear. No one was looking their way. It felt safe and anonymous.

'I would like our relationship to be more than friendship,' Phoebe said softly, and he reached for her hand across the table.

'That's good then.' It sounded so trite, even as he said it, but he was so new to this. His dating skills were rusty. His relationship skills were rusty. He felt like one of the old pieces of farm machinery on his land that had been left too long outside and had rusted quietly to a point where no one really thought it would work again but had left it there, just in case.

He was a rusted out old tractor. The metaphor made his head ache. All at once he felt awkward and desperate to change the subject. 'Tell me about you?' he said quickly. 'Has there been anyone serious for you?'

'I lived with a guy in London called Hugh. He was a vet like me, and we lived in his father's flat in Greenwich Park and we worked at a city practice. Looking back now, I'm not sure I would have called him the love of my life. We were both so focused on our careers. It's hard work qualifying as a vet and then getting established and we were both fixed on that track. So life was good. We were a partnership and we were committed to each other.' She hesitated. 'Or at least I thought we were.' Her eyes shadowed. 'Then I discovered that he was having a fling with our boss, Melissa. It was just before Christmas three years ago and so I ran away. I ran back here.'

She looked at him now. 'And I stayed here. And you know the rest. I set up the practice at Puddleduck Farm.'

'And he didn't follow you and beg you to come home?'

'No.' Again she hesitated and for a moment Rufus thought she was going to say something else. But she didn't.

He took a sip of his sparkling water. He had driven them tonight and she'd agreed to one glass of wine but he never drank when he was driving. 'I thought for a while that there was something going on between you and Sam Hendrie,' he said.

'There was a time when Sam wanted there to be. But we have never been more than friends.'

Rufus felt another layer of resistance melting away. Maybe

Bartholomew Timms was right. Maybe there were things that could be resolved by talking. It felt like it now, sitting here like this with her. Phoebe wasn't Rowena. But she was one of the loveliest women he'd ever met. He wanted her but he needed to be sure.

If he was going to settle again, find a mother for Archie, then it had to be the right person. Everything had to be perfect. He couldn't afford to get this wrong. He couldn't afford another disaster. His father had said to him once – a few months back when Rufus had told him he was taking Phoebe to dinner – 'Are you sure, Rufus? Do you really want to get involved with a Crowther? Look at the history.'

Rufus hadn't agreed with him. He had railed against the history. They were four generations away from that poker game that had started the bad blood between the two families, but his father's words had certainly had an impact.

'You look miles away.' Phoebe's voice brought him back to the present.

And to Rufus's relief, the waiter arrived at the same moment. This was a destructive train of thought and he needed to stamp on it.

'Sorry.' He smiled at her, a completely open smile.

Phoebe was torn. It had been a long time since she'd seen Rufus open up like this. In fact, maybe it was the most of himself he'd ever shown her – and she was already feeling guilty that she hadn't returned the compliment. She should have told him about Hugh's recent reappearance in her life. But she knew she hadn't because she was scared it would put him off.

Rufus's confidence was so terribly fragile. If she told him that Hugh had showed up twice lately, offering to come back into her life, even though he had insisted it was no strings attached, and even though Phoebe had told him very firmly to leave her alone, then Rufus might back off again. He might retreat into that faraway place he so often did. Put up the barriers again. Phoebe didn't think she could bear it if he did.

So she kept quiet. She would tell him at the weekend. But only after they'd made love. Was that terrible? Phoebe wrestled with herself. She was sure that Tori would say she was overthinking things. She probably was overthinking things. But she had never had a relationship like this. One that she thought might go the distance. It was true what she had told Rufus – she and Hugh may have lived together, but they had never really got that close to being permanent. Their lives had run along parallel lines and when she looked back on it, she thought that this was probably just because they were going in the same direction. Maybe Melissa hadn't caused the ending as she had thought back then. Maybe Melissa had just been the catalyst. If at any point their paths had diverged, maybe they'd have split up anyway.

She asked Rufus how much he saw Harrison, wondering if his closest friend had told him about the baby, and it turned out he had. Rufus's face softened as they talked about how happy the couple seemed at the prospect of having a family and getting married. Phoebe felt warmed by his enthusiasm. Maybe they were finally on track for becoming closer. A proper couple. Maybe talking more had been the answer all along.

Although they didn't talk much on the drive back home. Rufus had seemed to clam up as soon as they left the restaurant. She hoped he wasn't regretting the confidences he'd shared. As they left the lights of the bright city for the inky darkness of the forest, Phoebe wondered if Rufus was overthinking everything as much as she was. When he dropped her off at Woodcutter's, he said he wouldn't come in for coffee.

'I ought to get back. Dad hasn't been so good lately, and I don't like to leave him too long.'

'Oh, I'm sorry to hear that.'

'Don't worry. He's under the doctor's care and he's taking medication but I'm still a bit concerned.'

'Of course.' She stepped back at the same moment that Rufus bent to kiss her and his lips grazed her forehead instead of her lips.

'I'm really looking forward to us spending the weekend together, though. Dad's health allowing, of course.'

So he was still giving himself a get-out clause then. Phoebe ignored it. His eyes held a promise and she knew that hers would be reflecting one back at him.

'Me too.'

'See you on Friday, Phoebe. Sweet dreams.'

She watched him walk back to his car, parked alongside hers in Woodcutter's two parking spaces.

It was going to be OK, said a little voice in her head.

Were relationships really meant to be such hard work? said another voice. Phoebe ignored it. Tonight had been a good start. Real life wasn't a fairy tale. Real life had its ups and downs.

30

Real life had its ups and downs. Nowhere was this more apparent than in a vet's surgery, Phoebe thought the next day as Thursday began with a bang. In a literal way. A woman whose pug she had recently treated stormed into the practice, crashing the glass door behind her, to say that she'd been overcharged.

Phoebe was seeing a patient at the time, with Jenna assisting, but she'd almost finished and all she could hear from the other side of the door were escalating voices. Marcus's voice and that of a very cross female.

She caught Jenna's eyes across the examining table. 'I'll go,' Jenna said.

Phoebe nodded gratefully, but when she'd finished with her patient and caught up, the woman had gone.

'What was that all about?' she asked Marcus, who was sitting in reception. Jenna was now on the phone.

'Basically, she found a cheaper price online for the drugs we'd prescribed and she wanted a refund.'

'Did you give her a refund?'

'She didn't actually bring the prescribed drugs back. I think she'd used them all but she wanted us to refund the difference in price between the ones she'd bought from us and the ones she could get cheaper on the internet. The internet ones weren't that much cheaper actually and she didn't seem to get that she'd need to pay for a private prescription which would pretty much cancel out any savings. She wasn't listening to me. Jenna sorted it out.'

Jenna finished the call she was on. 'It wasn't Marcus's fault. He was spot on about the prescription. But this is a sign of the times. She's not the first person who's accused us of overcharging because they've found drugs cheaper online.' She paused. 'They're not always from reputable companies unfortunately. And there's a big market in counterfeit drugs.'

Phoebe sighed. 'Yes, it's certainly a sign of the times.'

'Also...' Jenna was frowning. 'I've just been talking to Mr B. Remember him? The man with the Kunekunes?'

'Where there's a WiFi there's a way,' Marcus prompted helpfully. 'He had an unhealthy obsession with cameras.'

'How could I forget!' Phoebe had a vivid recollection of a rather pompous voice, a man who'd been paranoid about cameras in her surgery. 'Why? Does he have a problem with a Kunekune?'

'Yes. But it's not quite as simple as that. He called earlier and Max has gone out. Apparently Max diagnosed mange, but Mr B wants a second opinion.' Jenna shook her head. 'Honestly, Max is more than capable as I've just told him, but he wants you. He said he wants the best care and he's talked to you and you're the only one who will do.'

'Right,' Phoebe said. 'OK. I guess I should go then.'

'Sorry,' Jenna said.

'It's fine.' Phoebe was in such a good mood after her night out with Rufus that she could have taken on the trickiest of customers and remained smiling.

Which was just as well, as it happened. Half an hour later, she found herself driving up an unmade lane in Godshill not a million miles from where her parents lived. The house, which was called The Conifers, although there was no sign of any, was at the end on the right-hand side.

She saw Max's car parked opposite it as soon as she got there. He was sitting in the driver's seat doing something on his phone and when she approached he slid down the window.

'I stayed to warn you,' he said cheerfully. 'That man is totally bonkers.'

'Dangerous bonkers?' Phoebe asked, instantly wary.

'No, I don't think so. But there's nothing wrong with that Kunekune that an avermectin won't cure. He doesn't believe me.'

'What does he think it is?'

'Greasy pig disease at the very least. I've told him that it's unlikely to be that as it mostly affects piglets in humid climates and I know we've had a hot summer but it's not terribly humid. Not to mention, that Kunekune definitely isn't a piglet.' Max, who rarely got irritated, shook his head. 'He won't have it, though. He insisted on calling you.'

'Where is he now? Mr B, I mean, not the pig.'

'He's just coming out of the house now.' Max grinned and in true pantomime style said, 'He's behind you,' before sliding the window back up rather niftily, Phoebe thought, as she turned around.

Mr B was striding across to the car. He was very tall, was Phoebe's first impression. And skinny too – wasn't there a saying, 'Never trust a skinny chef,' and he had black hair and matching bushy eyebrows and a rather bulbous nose.

'Ah,' he said. 'Ms Dashwood, I presume,' and he held out his hand.

Phoebe felt she had no option but to shake it and his grip was surprisingly firm.

'I appreciate you coming out here. It isn't that I think your junior vet is incorrect, but I'd really just like to see someone more senior.' He beamed, clearly pleased that he'd got his own way. 'So if you'll follow me.'

Phoebe did as he said and she heard the car door slam behind her. Max had decided to come too then. A part of her was quite relieved.

Mr B led them around the back of the house and down the garden where there was a gate that led onto a small paddock area, which was more earth than grass. There was a brick-built pigsty in one corner, along with the faint but unmistakable smell of pigs.

'I was lucky enough to find excellent accommodation for Portia and Percy,' Mr B said. 'The owner of this house used to keep pigs.'

Portia and Percy were not in situ, though – they were both on the other side of the pigsty, snouting around on the ground. Both of them were brown and black spotted and the larger of the two gave a welcoming grunt as he saw Mr B and began to amble across.

At least they were tame enough to catch. That would make her job easier, Phoebe thought.

A few seconds later she was able to confirm Max's diagnosis. 'I do agree with Mr Jones that this is a mild case of sarcoptic mange,' she said. 'Distressing, but very curable. And also quite infectious. You'll need to keep an eye on Portia too.'

'So it's definitely not greasy pig disease?' Mr B asked.

'No.'

'Sarcoptic mange. You're 100 per cent sure?'

'I am,' Phoebe said.

'Can it infect humans?'

'It has been known to cause problems,' Max said, with rather too much glee in his voice, Phoebe thought, although he was keeping a perfectly straight face.

'Ughhh.' Mr B took a sharp step backwards. 'How do I prevent cross infection?'

'My advice would be to wear gloves when you're handling Portia and Percy,' Phoebe said. 'Our usual treatment would be to give two injections of an avermectin which is a drug used to treat parasitic diseases, two weeks apart.'

'We'd also recommend that you remove any bedding and treat the accommodation block – superb as it is...' Max gestured towards the pigsty, '...in case this was the source of the mange mites.'

'Could it have been that?' Mr B's eyes widened. 'My landlady didn't mention anything like this.'

'It's unlikely for mange mites to survive off the host very long,' Phoebe said quickly. 'But yes, I'd agree with my colleague. It won't hurt to thoroughly disinfect and clean their living area. As part of the treatment plan.'

'Wear gloves for that too,' Max added. 'Marigolds are good.' He was clearly enjoying himself far too much.

'Oh, I won't be doing it myself.' Mr B wrinkled his nose fastidiously. 'That's a sous chef's job. But rest assured, it will be done.'

A few minutes later, having administered the first injection and had an assurance that Mr B would come down to the practice to pick up the insecticidal spray and to settle up, Phoebe and Max were back at their cars.

'Marigolds!' Phoebe said, trying not to smile. 'It can't be transferred to humans.'

'I have heard of a case where a dog with mange set off a skin irritation in its owner,' Max said, unrepentant. 'So you can't be too careful. Mind you, I couldn't believe it when he said he wasn't doing the cleaning himself. Do you think he'll really manage to get his sous chef to do it?'

'Would you argue with him?' she said, as she put her bag back into her car. She turned to smile at Max. 'The things you have to do to get a Michelin star these days.'

Mr B was as good as his word and came down to collect his prescription and pay his bill later that day.

Phoebe was out on a call, but when she got back Marcus filled her in.

'Did he use a debit card?' Phoebe asked curiously. 'Did you find out what his actual name was?'

'He paid cash,' Marcus said. 'And he left you a tip too. Twenty quid.'

'I hope you charged him for two callouts,' Jenna said.

'Actually, I did. So at least we didn't make a loss. I'm toughening up in my old age,' Phoebe said.

They both nodded approvingly.

But Phoebe couldn't help feeling a warmth towards Mr B. He might be totally bonkers, but he loved his animals and clearly wanted the best for them. And anyone who did that would always be OK with her. She hoped he managed to get the Michelin star for the hotel where he was working.

* * *

On Friday afternoon, Phoebe started getting butterflies, which happened when she was anxious about something. It wasn't work. Every appointment had been routine. So she knew it was about Rufus. Or more specifically about attempt two of them spending the night together. There was a part of her that was terrified.

What if Rufus cancelled? What if Archie didn't go to Jack's for some reason? What if Rufus's father was ill? What if Rufus was ill? What if he turned up and there was a repeat of last time?

She and Tori had been in regular touch about Tori's pregnancy with Tori sending her excited messages about how things were progressing. Phoebe had also told Tori that Rufus was coming to stay for the weekend and, as it got closer, how nervous she felt and had received a succession of reassuring texts across the day in response to every one she sent her.

Don't overthink it.

It'll be great.

Just relax.

Don't drink too much.

That last one definitely wasn't happening. Phoebe had no plans to drink anything at all. Even if Rufus did.

At just after 5 p.m. she got a WhatsApp message from Archie, which turned out to be a picture of a grey pony tied up in a stable yard. It was accompanied by one word in capital letters.

WOW.

Archie had clearly got to Jack's and was happy. That was one less thing to worry about, Phoebe thought.

She'd contemplated leaving work early but that would just give her more time to worry so in the end she'd left at the usual time. Then she'd driven home to Woodcutter's, had a long hot shower and as the water had rolled over her body she'd closed her eyes and imagined the night ahead.

She had changed the sheets for her best Egyptian cotton ones, her only Egyptian cotton ones, as it happened, because they might be lovely, but they needed ironing, which was one of her pet hates.

She had also lit a candle in her lounge. Lavender and Pumpkin Pie scented.

Tori had bought it for her online because, having done some research, Lavender and Pumpkin Pie scent was the one that forty per cent of Americans found the most aphrodisiac. 'Rufus isn't American,' Phoebe had pointed out but Tori had shrugged this off.

'He's a man, though. And I couldn't find a British equivalent. Apparently it drives men wild.'

When Phoebe had carried out a sniff check earlier, she'd decided it was a nice smell. Spicy with undertones of lavender. It would be interesting to see what effect it had on Rufus.

He'd said he would call round at seven, having picked up some takeaway pizzas en route, and at just before seven, her doorbell rang.

Phoebe checked her hair in the hall mirror, and smoothed her fingers down over her dress, also bought especially for the occasion, and opened the door with a welcome on her lips.

But it wasn't Rufus, standing there. It was Hugh. Her heart sank.

31

For a moment, Phoebe thought she must be hallucinating. No way. She blinked several times and stared at her ex who looked as if he were dressed for a night out, although his face still looked bruised and the cut on his lip wasn't quite healed. 'What are you doing here?'

'I was just passing and I...'

'You weren't just passing. This road doesn't go anywhere. Have you been following me?'

Hugh looked shamefaced and Phoebe swore. Behind him she could see Rufus's car coming up the unmade lane. There were only two parking spaces. She was in one and Hugh had just parked his BMW in the other. Rufus would have nowhere to park. Although that was the least of her problems.

'You need to go,' Phoebe told Hugh. 'I'm expecting my boyfriend. As you can see.' She gestured and Hugh glanced behind him to where the silver Mercedes had just pulled over on the other side of the road.

'Flash boyfriend,' Hugh said, making no attempt to move as Rufus got out of the car and then reached into the back seat, presumably to get the pizza boxes. The waft of takeaway pizza drifted across.

'Not a very flash dinner, though,' Hugh remarked. 'Hang on a minute, don't I recognise him? Isn't that Rufus Holt?' Pleased with himself, he looked back at her. 'You're dating the lord of the manor. Bloody hell. No wonder you're not interested in me.'

'Get off my property.' Phoebe's voice was louder and sharper than she'd intended it to be and Rufus glanced across, alerted by the sound, and saw them for the first time. 'Go now, Hugh. I've had enough of you turning up uninvited. I'm serious.'

Phoebe didn't think she could feel any more awkward. Rufus was hurrying across.

'Are you OK? Is this man bothering you?'

'Yes.'

'No.'

Phoebe and Hugh spoke simultaneously.

'I think you should leave.' Rufus looked Hugh up and down and her ex, who had always disliked confrontations, nodded and took a step back, holding his hands high, palms facing towards them.

'OK. I'm going. No need for a situation.' He moved swiftly past Rufus, calling back over his shoulder, 'I wanted to know about the alpacas, that's all.' He was still limping too, Phoebe saw, as he crossed the road back to his car.

Rufus glanced at Phoebe questioningly.

'Come in, I'll explain. Sorry about that.' She could feel herself trembling with a mix of shock and guilt and humiliation. Of all the things she'd worried might happen, this had not been on the list. She knew her face was flaming red and her heart was thundering in her ears.

Why hadn't she told Rufus about Hugh when they'd gone for the Thai? Then at least this wouldn't be so out of the blue. Now, whatever she said, it would look as though she'd been lying to him.

'I take it you knew that guy.' Rufus put the pizza boxes on the kitchen table. 'Is he someone you work with?'

'He's someone I used to work with.' For a second, Phoebe wondered if she could leave it there but she knew she couldn't. Rufus wasn't stupid and there was the small matter of her own integrity.

'That was Hugh,' she told him, leaning both her hands on the back of a kitchen chair and meeting his curious gaze. 'The man I used to live with in London.'

'The vet,' Rufus said. 'The one who had an affair with your boss.'

'Yes.'

'Did you know he was in the area?'

'Yes. It's not the first time he's turned up unexpectedly.'

'He's turned up here?' Rufus's voce had gone a shade more serious. 'Does he want you back? Is that it?'

'This is the first time he's been here. I didn't think he knew my address.' Phoebe told him the whole story while their pizzas grew cold in their boxes and she knew she was talking too much, babbling, trying to find a reason why she hadn't told him before, when the real reason was that they'd drifted so far apart lately that she hadn't dared risk it.

She could see that he was closing down by the second, although when she reached for his hand across the table, he didn't move away.

'I'm so sorry I didn't tell you, Rufus.'

'I wish you had.' His eyes were slightly distant. 'What did he mean about alpacas?'

She told him.

'And was he right?'

'Yes, he was. And I was grateful. He probably saved the herd.'

'But you didn't tell him that was the outcome. Or thank him.'

Phoebe looked at the floor which she'd just noticed could have done with a wash. There was a muddy boot print by the door. One of hers after a callout. But it looked like it could have been a man's. She felt as guilty as hell and also as though she was under interrogation. She'd never seen this side of Rufus. But he was right, she hadn't told Hugh that his impromptu and unasked for diagnosis had been correct. And she certainly hadn't thanked him. She had been too cross with him for interfering.

'No. I hadn't told Hugh about the outcome.' She paused. 'You sound as though you think I should have done?'

'I don't know what you should have done, Phoebe. I've never been in your situation.'

Of course he hadn't. He'd had a wife whom he'd adored, who had tragically died. He'd never been in the position of fending off an ex who wouldn't take no for an answer. All of the lovely closeness that they'd built up over the Thai meal had evaporated. And his comment had stung. Phoebe cleared her throat. The last thing she wanted was a row with Rufus. It was time to change the subject.

'I had a WhatsApp from Archie earlier. He sent me a picture of a grey pony.'

Rufus flinched, and Phoebe remembered too late that this was the last image he'd want in his head.

'What I mean is that he looked happy,' she mumbled. Oh, my God, how had they reached this point? The evening that she'd had such high hopes for seemed to be disintegrating in front of her eyes.

'He's in his element over there.' Rufus was flustered. Visibly, he pulled himself back together. 'I'm sorry. Shall I – reheat the pizzas?'

'I'll do it.'

They reached for the box at the same time and their hands collided and Phoebe felt herself blinking back unexpected tears. Once that collision would have resulted in an embrace but instead they had both jumped apart.

'I'll be right back,' she said, and hurried out of the room and up to her en suite bathroom where she splashed water on her face, reapplied make-up and took a moment to gather herself. She would have given anything to be able to turn back time and begin the evening again. But in her version, Hugh wouldn't have appeared.

Also, in her version, Rufus wouldn't have been cross-questioning her. Wouldn't have been looking at her as though she were a stranger he had only just met.

As she went back down the narrow stairs into the kitchen, she heard the ping of the microwave. She should have told Rufus to use the oven – they'd be soggy. Phoebe swallowed. Soggy pizzas didn't seem that important right now.

Rufus was sitting at the table, reading a text on his phone. Phoebe hoped Archie wasn't sending him too many horse pictures. But he wouldn't be, of course. Archie knew better than that, bless his little cotton socks. At least Archie was having a lovely weekend in his equine haven.

They ate the pizzas, which weren't too soggy. Rufus refused a glass of wine, but accepted a glass of sparkly elderflower he'd brought with him. Phoebe knew it was going to take a miracle to transform the evening into something resembling romantic. It was definitely going to take more than the Lavender and Pumpkin Pie candle, which she'd lit in the lounge earlier, to get them in the mood. She'd planned that they'd take chocolate and cherry cheesecake in there – it was another of Rufus's favourite desserts from M&S. But they hadn't ventured in yet. Lucky that candle had twelve hours' burn time.

But her hopes of the candle were dashed a little while later when Rufus went to use the downstairs cloakroom and came back asking her if she knew there was a strange smell coming from her lounge.

Phoebe went and blew the candle out then came back and

offered him cheesecake, which he refused on the grounds that the pizzas had been bigger than he'd realised.

Phoebe made them filter coffee. It was still only eight thirty. Rufus had had two more text notifications on his phone which he hadn't looked at. Presumably this was from politeness. Phoebe wondered if he was worried about Archie settling at Jack's. She was about to tell him that he should check his phone just in case when it rang.

He looked at her. 'Do you mind?'

'Of course not. Go ahead.'

Phoebe listened to the one-sided conversation, which was terse and grew increasingly more so as it progressed.

'No,' Rufus said. 'No, he didn't. OK. OK, yes, call them. Ignore what he says. I'll be there.'

He disconnected and looked at Phoebe.

'Is everything OK?' Clearly it wasn't. She bit her lip. It sounded as though Archie might be homesick, bless him.

'No, I'm afraid it isn't,' Rufus said. 'That was Emilia. My father's taken a turn for the worse. She's sent me a couple of messages too. But I thought at first she was panicking unnecessarily. Now I'm not so sure. I'm afraid I'm going to need to head back.'

'Of course. I totally understand.' Phoebe got to her feet. Rufus was already on his.

'Is there anything I can do to help?'

'No. But thanks.' Rufus looked at her. 'I'm sorry this evening hasn't worked out.'

'It's fine,' she said, realising the disappointment she'd expected to feel was missing. She felt a little numb, but, to her surprise, the main emotion swirling around her body as she saw Rufus out barely two hours after he'd arrived was relief.

* * *

Rufus was feeling both guilty and worried. Emilia had known he was coming to Woodcutter's tonight – his nanny had overheard him talking on the phone to Phoebe about getting pizzas. Rufus was very aware that Emilia didn't like Phoebe and did her best to disrupt any plans he made with her.

Because of this he'd been half expecting some kind of interruption, which was why he hadn't responded to Emilia's earlier messages. There had been four altogether. But when she'd finally phoned, she'd sounded genuinely panicked.

'Your father – he is on floor when I walk past. He is moaning. He says I am not to call the ambulance. I do not know what to do.'

That's when Rufus had told her to ignore him and call them. Now he drove back as fast as he dared across the forest. Fortunately, it wasn't far from Woodcutter's to his. As he sped up the long drive that went up to Beechbrook House, his mind conjured up several scenarios, each one worse than the next.

His father had been evasive about what the doctor had said, saying only that he'd been put on medication. But what if it wasn't working? Or it was the wrong dose – that probably took a while to get right. Or what if Alfred had stopped taking it and was having some kind of reaction? He wouldn't have put it past him, he hated pills.

Rufus felt guilty that he hadn't responded to Emilia's first message. But he'd been so sure she was crying wolf. And of course he'd so much wanted this evening to be perfect, but it had started so badly anyway. It had unsettled him when Phoebe's ex had turned up. But the news that it wasn't the first time and that she hadn't told him had rocked him much more.

When they had gone to the Thai, he'd poured out his heart to her, and yet she hadn't felt able to mention Hugh. He felt betrayed. He knew he was probably overreacting. It wasn't Phoebe's fault that her ex had turned up on her doorstep – and yet...

Rufus had always thought that Phoebe was totally honest and straightforward. What you saw was what you got. But he hadn't forgotten that business with Sam, Archie's riding instructor. There had been a time he'd thought something was going on between him and Phoebe because Sam had told him there was. Phoebe had later told him there wasn't. But one of them hadn't been entirely honest and after tonight Rufus was struggling with the thought that it might be Phoebe.

His head hurt thinking about it.

He skidded to a halt on the gravel outside Beechbrook. The ambulance wasn't here yet, neither was Harrison's car. He must be out with Tori. Rufus ran inside and Emilia met him in the hall. Her face was white. 'Rufus, thank you. He is upstairs. The ambulance is coming.'

Rufus took the stairs two at a time. Alfred was on the floor on the upstairs landing.

'What are you doing here?' He did not look pleased to see his son. 'I've told her. I'm fine. I don't need any help.' There was anger in his voice, but he was also breathless. That was odd. Rufus didn't know if he was in pain or embarrassed.

'You're lying on the floor, Dad.' He hunkered down beside him.

'I slipped.'

'But you haven't got up.'

Alfred's face was almost as grey as Emilia's. 'I'll get up when I'm ready.'

Rufus closed his eyes. That stubbornness he knew so well because he'd inherited it himself. It would kill Alfred if he wasn't careful.

'Thanks, Emilia,' he said in a quick aside to her. 'But I can take it from here.'

She nodded and looked relieved and then withdrew. It must have been horrendous, not knowing what to do. Again, Rufus felt a rush of guilt. Why hadn't he taken her messages at face value? What the hell had he been thinking, putting his own pleasure above his family's? The guilt bit deep.

He sat beside his father, wishing he knew what to say and feeling incredibly relieved that Archie wasn't here. He would have hated Archie to witness his grandfather being carried off in an ambulance. Thank heavens for small mercies.

32

Phoebe's eyes pinged open the next day at her usual getting up time, which was just before seven. Her first thought was that something bad had happened the previous night and her second thought was that at least it hadn't involved alcohol. She didn't have a hangover. As she lay there in bed, the events of the previous evening replayed in her mind.

Hugh's arrival. Then she and Rufus and their stilted, awkward evening and then finally his disappearance into the night, responding to Emilia's phone call. Phoebe hoped his father was all right. There had been no word from him after he'd left.

She checked her phone. Still no messages from Rufus, although there was one from Tori.

I hope it went well. How did he like the candle? Give me a ring if you want to chat. But if I don't hear from you for a couple of days I'll assume you're still in bed.

This was followed by a winking emoji.

Phoebe didn't answer Tori's message, but she sent one to Rufus.

I hope you're OK. I hope your dad was OK. Please let me know when you get a moment. Px

Then she got up slowly and went into the bathroom. She was beginning to wonder if she and Rufus maybe just weren't meant to be. She cleaned her teeth, splashed water on her face, met her own sad hazel eyes in the mirror, and then went back to bed, where she curled up and pulled the duvet up around her chin.

In a different life, Rufus would have been here too. But he wasn't here. And he hadn't messaged her. For all she knew, he was sitting at home, wondering if it would be crass to finish their relationship by text.

She had wanted them to be a couple so much. She had fantasised and dreamed about it and there was no doubting that the chemistry had been there at the start. When he had asked her out to dinner that first time, Phoebe had been over the moon by a good few hundred air miles.

It had felt as though all of her birthdays and Christmases had come at once. Not because he was the lord of the manor to be, not because he was the most eligible bachelor in town. But just because he was Rufus. Because there had been something between them from the very first moment they had met.

Even though in that first moment they had both been angry, she remembered. She had been trespassing on his land, trying to retrieve Maggie's donkeys after a storm, and he had seen only danger – his PTSD triggered by the donkeys.

For most of the time she had known him, they had clashed, Phoebe thought. And when they hadn't been in direct conflict, they had missed each other entirely. Either she had gone towards him and found him going the other way, or he had come towards her and found she was somewhere else.

A new relationship surely shouldn't be this difficult. A new relationship should be the time that you were head over heels, giddy with love, and so wrapped up in each other that you hardly had time to get out of bed – not to put too fine a point on it.

That was what it had been like for Tori and Harrison. But it had never been like that for Phoebe and Rufus. There had always been so much else to contend with. Not least his family.

Phoebe had accepted that Rufus had a son, she'd adored Archie from the outset. If it had just been Rufus, Archie and herself, she knew it would have been OK. But it wasn't just the three of them. There was his father, Lord Alfred, who Phoebe knew wanted as little to do with her or her family as possible. Then there was Emilia, who'd done her best to get rid of Phoebe from day one. There had been Sam and now there was Hugh, her ex.

And that was before you even started on their jobs. Rufus's job and his responsibilities extended far beyond working hours and so did Phoebe's. There had never been time for their relationship to naturally develop. There was too much else that came in front of it.

Phoebe felt a tear run down her nose. She couldn't remember the last time she'd felt so bleak.

Her phone pinged with another message, then another, then another, then another and she reached for it eagerly.

But it wasn't Rufus. It was Archie sending more pictures of horses. Then another message. But a written one this time.

Did Dad tell you I'm getting a horse when I go to school in September? Jack's mum and dad are going to look at some with me. Don't worry. Jack and I will make sure the guinea pigs and rabbits get good homes before I go. If it's a mare I shall call her Enola after Enola Holmes.

Phoebe felt more tears coming. That was so typical of Archie, thinking about the guinea pigs even when the prospect of finally owning a horse, a long-held dream of his, was on the horizon. He was one of the few children she had ever met who was totally dedicated to his pets' care.

Enola was a good name too. She had a vague inkling Enola Holmes was Sherlock Holmes's fictional sister, who solved crimes with the help of her big brother. Right up Archie's street. He must have outgrown *The Incredibles* now then. Kids moved on fast.

Adults could learn a lot from kids, Phoebe thought, with a sense of renewed purpose. She sent him a message back.

That's brilliant news. I'll look forward to hearing more. Have a fabulous weekend.

She added a smiley face and got one back, almost immediately.

Why was it so much easier to communicate with Archie than it was with his father? Oh, the irony.

But Archie's message had galvanised her into action. Phoebe decided she'd had enough time lying in bed feeling sorry for herself. She threw off the duvet and got up for the second time.

Saturday stretched ahead of her – the Saturday that she and Rufus had planned to spend together – well, maybe that could still happen. But whatever happened, she needed to know if they had any chance of a future. She couldn't carry on like this – jogging along in this limbo land – feeling that she was neither in a relationship nor out of one. She had to know where she stood.

She picked up her mobile and then decided against phoning Rufus. She would go round to Beechbrook House and see him. It was still barely 8 a.m. But by the time she'd had breakfast and coffee, it should be a more appropriate time to call at the big house. Oh, my goodness, was that how she saw it? Phoebe didn't know whether to laugh or cry when she realised that yes, it was. That was exactly how she saw it.

* * *

Rufus had not had a good night and he was feeling utterly exhausted. He'd finally followed the ambulance to the hospital with his father the previous evening at around ten. The two paramedics had been worried enough to take the old lord in for a thorough check over.

'He's on heart medication,' Rufus had told them and it had been at this point that he'd discovered that his father had lied about going to the doctor. He'd never been to the surgery at all, and he wasn't on any medication.

In the end, after a very long wait, Lord Alfred had been diagnosed with fairly advanced heart failure, by a doctor at the hospital, who'd told him wearily that it hadn't been helped by being ignored.

To Alfred's chagrin, the doctors had said that it would really be best if he stayed in for some more tests to check for any further damage that ignoring his condition may have caused and Rufus had insisted that his father complied. Rufus had finally left the hospital alone around 3 a.m.

He'd slept fitfully and his dreams had been fragments of mixed-up scenes from the past. Hospitals, riding accidents, Rowena, his father, and Phoebe.

It had been a relief to wake up and then reality had crashed back in and he'd remembered the past twenty-four hours' events and had immediately phoned the hospital. It was at times like these that he was relieved they still kept a landline. His mobile battery was totally dead. He was told that his father had spent a peaceful night and that his condition was satisfactory.

What did that even mean? Rufus made himself coffee and was drinking it when Emilia came into the kitchen.

'How is he? How are you?' Her eyes were worried as she stood opposite him, hugging her arms around herself and looking vulnerable. Emilia didn't often look vulnerable. She was one of the most capable women he'd ever met. But he knew he shouldn't have put her in the position he had. Technically, with Archie away, she shouldn't even have been on duty.

'Dad is fine,' he told her gently. 'I'm sorry I wasn't here last night. Would you like some coffee?'

'Yes, please.'

He poured her a cup from the cafetière, realising he didn't even know whether she took sugar or not.

'You won't be put in that situation again,' he told her. 'I'm going to be around more. Dad has a progressive illness and he's going to need me.'

Emilia looked horrified and for a moment he didn't realise why. Then she spread her hands wide to encompass the kitchen, and beyond. 'You cannot do all this by yourself. You need more help – or you will be sick too – like your father.' She paused. 'In Switzerland we have saying, *Wer zwei Hasen auf einmal jagt bekommt keinen*. It means, he who chases two rabbits at once catches none.'

Rufus smiled despite himself. 'Yes, you're probably right.' He rubbed his eyes. 'I know things need to change. Both of us have been trying to do too much. I'll sort it.'

The problem was, Rufus didn't really know what needed to change and right now he was too tired to think about it.

* * *

Sam was working in the post office section of Hendrie's Stores, as he often did on a Saturday morning, but planning a lunchtime escape. He took money, weighed parcels, helped a pensioner fill in a form, and exchanged banter with customers, but a part of his mind was elsewhere.

He and Judy had split up five days ago and he was still trying to process it. Her cousin's wedding had been the catalyst, but Sam had a feeling that the credits had been coming up for weeks.

That was something he'd heard a customer say once when she'd confided that she and her boyfriend had finally decided to go their separate ways, and it described the situation perfectly. 'It was a mismatch from the start,' she had told Sam. 'But I guess neither of us wanted to acknowledge the truth.'

Lord knows Sam could relate to that now. He'd hoped that if his and Judy's feelings were strong enough then they could fix anything. But he knew now that it wasn't true. There were some things love couldn't fix.

Sam would never forget that look Judy's father had given him across the table at the wedding. The smug triumph in his eyes.

'Sam. Have you heard a word I've said?'

He jumped, realising his mother was speaking to him now, and that she sounded exasperated.

'Sorry, Ma. No, I was miles away.'

'So I saw. You've been on a different planet all week. Is something wrong?'

Jan Hendrie's eyes were concerned, as she pulled up a chair next to her son behind the counter. The shop was empty for the first time that morning. The busy period over, at least for now.

'Judy and I decided to call it a day,' he told her. 'It's been coming for a while.'

'Ah. I thought it was something like that. I am sorry. I don't mean to pry.'

'It's OK, Ma.' He sighed. 'It was on Monday. It wasn't all that unexpected, to be honest. I think we'd both been living in La La Land.'

Not that this had made it feel any better when they'd finally admitted to each other that it wasn't working. That had been after a long night of talking. It had all been strangely calm in the end. Sam had hated the fact that her family had been right. Love didn't always conquer all.

'It's never easy to end a love affair.' His mother began tidying papers on the counter. His family didn't do big talks about feelings and he knew she was searching for the right words to say.

'I'm OK,' he said. 'Sorry if I've been distracted.'

'I think I'm the only one who's noticed. You're a good actor.' She stopped fiddling with the papers and touched his arm. 'Why don't you get off a bit earlier? It's nearly midday. I can cope here.'

'Are you sure?'

He met her soft gaze.

'Of course I'm sure, you great daftie. Get off to the stables and take that horse of yours out. It's lovely out there. Get some sun on your face.'

'Thanks, Ma.'

'Go on.' She made shooing motions with her hands. 'Get off before I change my mind.'

Sam grabbed his coat and blew her a kiss from the door.

33

Phoebe's stomach crunched as she drove the short distance to Beechbrook House. It was just after eleven and already the most beautiful summer's day they'd had so far. The sky was a perfect cerulean blue with not a cloud to be seen and it was warm enough to drive with the windows down. It was not a day for heartbreak. She'd still had no word from Rufus, but it had struck her that if his father was seriously ill then they might both have had a very late night.

She turned off the road with its high wall that bordered Beechbrook House and drove beneath the archway with its full-size stag straddling the top and onto the quarter-mile driveway up to the house. Maggie had been right. The lavender fields on either side of her were now a vast expanse of lilac. Row upon row of lavender bushes stretched off into the distance left and right like some endless wave breaking beneath the sunlit sky. It was breathtaking and the smell that drifted through the open windows was intoxicating. Phoebe breathed it in. Wow.

Rufus's foray into eco-crops was a resounding success, at least as far as this stage of the process went. She wondered if he was still as blown away by the beauty of the lavender fields as she was. Or did he take it all for granted, seeing them every day, as he must do?

In another reality, she and Rufus would have walked hand in hand through these amazing lilac carpets as they once had walked through the bluebells. They'd have chatted easily and laughed and been spellbound by the beauty of their surroundings, and the romance of that made Phoebe's heart ache because they had never done that. Not once.

Maybe she could suggest it today. They could resolve their problems by walking hand in hand through the lavender fields. She knew she was in danger of drifting into fairy tale land again and real life wasn't like that. There were storms as well as sunshine. It was very hard to remember that on a day that was as perfect as today.

As always, it was a surprise when the end of the driveway opened out into a wide turning circle, in which there was a fountain on a circular pond that was smothered with lilies. Rufus's car was in its usual place, but his Land Rover was missing. It was possible that Harrison was out somewhere on the estate in the Land Rover.

Phoebe walked past the fountain with its two tasteless white cherubs towards the imposing façade of the house. The parapet, the twelve paned windows overlooking the front and the numerous chimneys were all familiar to her now. They didn't feel as intimidating as they once had.

But she still felt nervous as she went towards the flat-roofed porch with its steps leading up to the great oak door. Please let it be Rufus who answers, not Emilia.

A few seconds later, her prayers were answered. Rufus, looking very tired and slightly dishevelled, pulled back the heavy oak door.

'Phoebe?'

'I... is this a bad time?'

'Er, no. Come in.' But he sounded so surprised that she regretted turning up on spec. Some of the sunlight flew from the day and it wasn't only because she'd just stepped into the dimness of the ancestral hall.

Rufus went straight into his office, which was just off to their right, and Phoebe, feeling as though she was a prospective employee about to be interviewed, followed him.

'Is your father OK?' she asked as they both sat down on leather chairs, Rufus straight-backed in his and Phoebe perching on the edge of hers.

'He's in hospital, but he is OK. It turns out he has a heart problem, which would have been more treatable if he'd sought some advice about it sooner.' Rufus sighed. 'He doesn't like doctors. He told me he'd been to see one, but he hadn't.' He rubbed at his temples, a tight little gesture. 'They're going to do some more tests and see what needs to be done from this point on. I'm sorry, Phoebe, I'm so tired I can't think straight.'

'No, of course you can't.' Reacting on impulse, she got up and went across the room and hugged him. For the briefest moment, he tensed beneath her touch, stiff as a board, and Phoebe felt as though, even now, he was backing away from her. Even now he was treating her as if she were a stranger.

'I'm so sorry,' she said, feeling her own throat tighten at his rebuff. She let go of him and stood back a pace. 'Is there anything I can do to help? Just say it.'

For a long moment, there was silence and then Rufus said quietly, 'I don't know what to do next. I'm going to talk to Harrison. I've already been talking to Emilia and I'll need to talk to Father too. But I do know that something has to change.'

He planned to talk about his problems to everyone but her,

Phoebe thought, feeling rebuffed for the second time. He was still looking at her as if he didn't really know what she was doing there. She bit her lip. He wasn't the only one. She was beginning to wish she hadn't come. This was no time for a conversation about their future. She could see in Rufus's face that his priorities lay elsewhere and while she knew this wasn't surprising in the circumstances, it didn't mean it hurt any less.

'The thing is, Rowena, I don't really know where to go from here.'

Phoebe looked at him, aghast. His eyes were very dark, and he wasn't looking directly at her, but at some place in the distance. She didn't think he was even aware that he'd just called her by his late wife's name.

No, he couldn't be because he carried on speaking, his voice low. 'I haven't been fair to you, have I?' He glanced back at her again. 'The truth is that all of this has been terribly bad timing, Phoebe.'

He hesitated, but at least he knew who he was talking to now. 'Neither of us really have time for a relationship, do we?'

Phoebe took a deep breath. God, this was so much more painful than she'd expected. Especially in view of the fact that she'd more or less come to the same conclusion herself.

'Are you saying you'd like us to call it a day, Rufus?' She was amazed there was no tremble in her voice, because there was a huge one in her heart.

'I think so. Yes. I'm so sorry. I know it's not fair on you. You're bright and you're beautiful.'

Phoebe stood up. 'It's OK, Rufus. We don't have to do the whole, it's not you, it's me, routine. We really don't.'

He half rose, and then stood up with his arms at his sides, looking awkward. Phoebe hesitated. If he'd have said something, even in that moment, something that showed her he wanted to try, that he really truly cared about her – them as a couple – then she would have stayed.

'I think it's for the best, if we cool things off for now,' was what he finally managed.

Phoebe knew there was nothing more to be said. Cool things off! She would have laughed if that wasn't so tragic. Things couldn't get any cooler than they'd been these last few months. In that moment, looking into his stony face, she thought, good God, I've done it again. I've picked a man who finds it impossible to emotionally connect.

She had to get out of this stuffy little office, the place where Rufus spent all his time, before she broke into pieces. She knew there was sure as hell nothing more to say. The mixture of pain and anger was like a hot hard lump in her chest.

Trying to muster the shredded remains of her pride and her heart, she went across the room, half blinded by tears. Rufus made no move to stop her opening the door. And no move to follow her.

In the hall she thought she saw Emilia dart back into the shadows of the big old house. That was someone who'd be pleased they'd split up. Phoebe didn't care what Emilia thought. But then an image of Archie's dark eyes and enthusiastic little face jumped into her mind, and new pain surged in her. She hadn't realised until this moment just how much she loved that little boy. In the last few moments, it wasn't just Rufus she had lost, it was Archie too.

On the way back down the drive, Phoebe finally gave way to her feelings and the tears came fast and furious, blurring her vision so that the lavender fields were blinding in the sunshine, and she had to slow down to avoid veering into their midst. In every romantic movie that Phoebe had ever seen, this was the point at where the tragic hero would realise he was in love with the beleaguered heroine, he would rouse himself from his apathy and chase after her, vowing his love for her, usually at an airport or a train station or in some place like that where a big reunion would take place.

For God's sake. Phoebe gripped the steering wheel tight and shouted out loud, even though there was no one to hear, 'This is not a fucking fairy tale.'

She was tempted to go straight round and see Maggie next door, because her grandmother never judged. Even though she'd had doubts from the outset about Rufus because of the bad blood between their families, Maggie would have just given her the biggest hug and plied her with coffee and love.

But Phoebe felt too raw to see anyone. It was too soon. Like a wounded animal, she needed to be alone. She would do what she always did when she wanted to think or process things. She would find somewhere to park up and she would walk in the forest. Let all of her emotions out into the green, verdant peace of nature.

Within minutes, she was on the forest road, heading for her favourite walk. She wasn't driving very fast, there was a part of her that knew she shouldn't really be driving at all because she was definitely not in full control of her senses. But she had to put as much distance as possible between her and Beechbrook House. Her mobile beeped and her heart leapt despite herself – Rufus?

Phoebe realised her phone had fallen into the passenger footwell. With one eye on the road, she slowed down, and leaned across to rescue it. Which meant that she was only going about twenty, fortunately, when the deer leapt straight into the path of her car.

Phoebe had swerved to the left before she was fully aware of what had even happened. She hit the raised verge and then the car was off the road and lurching sideways, as it bumped at speed along uneven ground. Jolting violently in her seat, Phoebe felt her head bang hard on the steering wheel before the car drew to an abrupt halt at an oddly tilted angle.

She hadn't hit the deer. That was a blessing. She'd had a fleeting image of it racing into the forest, but she had hit her face. Hard. Shocked, Phoebe touched her hand to her cheek and felt something sticky. Blood. Not surprising when she'd just nosedived the steering wheel. Her nose hurt a lot and she was bleeding profusely. Brilliant. The perfect end to a perfect morning. She reached across for her phone, which was still in the footwell. Dear God, why hadn't she just stopped in the first place? Why had she taken her eye off the road? The good news was that her phone was charged and she had a signal, hence, the text, which wasn't from Rufus but her mobile provider, telling her she had a bill.

The other good news was that she was pretty sure she hadn't knocked herself out when she'd hit her head. She hadn't even been going fast enough for the air bags to deploy. That was probably a blessing too. She'd seen what a mess they could make of a car.

The bad news, Phoebe thought, as she took in the full implications of her situation, was that she wasn't going anywhere now. Her Lexus was stuck in a ditch, the two left-hand wheels in and the two right-hand wheels out. She could not just drive off again, presuming it would even start.

She needed to phone for help. Rufus. No, not Rufus. It might be stupid, stupid pride, but she didn't care. She was not going to ask him for help. Not after the way they'd just parted. Not if he was the last person on earth. No way.

Tori then. Phoebe tried her mobile and got a tinny voice. 'The number you have dialled is switched off.' She swore, before realising it would be pointless to phone Tori anyway. She needed someone who could offer practical support. Preferably someone who could bring a tractor and tow her out of this ditch.

Sam. She needed Sam. He didn't have a tractor personally, but with luck he'd be at Brook Stables where he spent every Saturday afternoon. They would definitely have one. Her fingers were shaking so badly that she could barely find his number and she realised that she was going into shock.

That was all she needed. She held the mobile to her ear. It was now sticky with her blood, but suddenly that didn't seem very important. At least it was ringing.

'Please pick up, Sam,' she said as the phone rang and rang. 'Please, please pick up.'

34

Just at the point that Phoebe thought the phone was going to ring out unanswered, Sam picked up.

'Hello, stranger,' his familiar warm voice filled her ears. 'What can I do for you?'

'Sam, I need your help, I've just crashed my car, I'm in a ditch, are you at Brook, I think I need a tractor.' She knew her words were running into each other, over each other. She felt sick now too, it was no longer just the shaking. She was starting to babble with shock.

'OK. Slow down. Can you tell me exactly where you are? Do you need an ambulance?'

'Um. No. I don't think so.' She could hear her own ragged breathing. 'I bashed my nose. I don't think it's broken.' Where was she? She looked out of the window. 'I'm on a back road off the A31. Not a million miles from the Blackwater Arboretum. Do you know where that funny cottage is? The little pale green one with the five chimneys – we used to think a witch lived there when we were kids. I'm a little way up the road from there. But opposite side.'

'I know it.' She heard his sharp intake of breath. 'I'm minutes away from you, as it happens. OK, Phoebe, strange question, but do you think you're up to getting on a horse? I'm out on Ninja. We're heading towards you now.'

'A horse. I don't know. Yes, probably.' The situation was turning steadily more unreal or perhaps that was her state of mind. Phoebe thought she could hear the jingle of a bridle in the background and the soft thud of hooves, or perhaps she just imagined she could. The power of suggestion.

'I'm going to stay on the phone, OK, don't worry. We'll be there very soon.'

She wasn't imagining the faint backdrop of hooves, which was louder now. Sam must have quickened his pace. She laid her head forward on the steering wheel, feeling too sick to do any more.

'Phoebe, are you still there?' He sounded breathless. He'd definitely quickened his pace. 'Talk to me, please.'

'I'm still here. I'm fine.'

'We can't be more than a few hundred yards away. Are you in or out of the car?'

'In.'

'Can you smell petrol?'

'No.'

'Are you sure?'

'Pretty sure.'

'Look out of the window. Look towards the direction of the witch's cottage.'

Phoebe looked. Nothing. This was such a quiet road. Not even another car had passed since she'd gone into the ditch. For a horrible couple of moments, she thought that he'd gone to a different place. Another witch's cottage. That they weren't on the same wavelength. That they'd somehow miscommunicated.

And then she saw a horse coming full pelt down the side of the witch's cottage and then slow down to a fast trot as it got to the grass verge at the side of the road and then halt as Sam shielded his eyes against the bright sun and looked in her direction. Immediately, he broke into a more controlled brisk trot and less than half a minute later, Sam and Ninja stopped beside her. Ninja's bay coat was wet with sweat and he was blowing heavily as Sam dismounted and led him towards the car in one fluid graceful movement.

Never in her life had she been more pleased to see someone, Phoebe thought, wondering for the first time if she could get out of the car at this angle, or whether it would make more sense to slide across and get out of the passenger door.

Before she'd got any further with this train of thought, Sam had opened the driver's door. The shock on his face, even though he quickly masked it, told her she didn't look much better than she felt.

'Jesus Christ, Phoebe, I think you might need an ambulance.' He was hunkering down beside her. Ninja, alarmed by the scent of blood, danced back to the limit of the reins away from the car. Fortunately, the grass verge was wide enough for him still to be off the road.

'I think it's stopped bleeding. I could probably use a wet wipe.' Phoebe took her cupped hand away from her face.

Sam leaned closer. 'Before you move, are you hurt anywhere else?'

'No, I don't think so. Just my nose.' She couldn't help it. Shock, relief and the trauma of the morning's events welled up inside her and she burst into tears.

'Hey, hey, it's OK.' Sam put one arm around her, while still holding Ninja, and he squeezed her shoulder gently. 'Everything's fine. The calvary's here, don't worry, sweetheart.'

'Oh, Sam.' The smell of wax jacket and horse filled her nostrils. She still had a sense of smell. That was a miracle.

'Are you able to get out of the car?'

'Yep, I think so.'

'Lean on me.'

She did as he said and was surprised that she didn't collapse at his feet. She was definitely on the wobbly side, but it felt good to be out of the car. To let someone else take control. 'I guess I look a state.' She glanced at her hands which were covered in drying blood.

'I have to say, I've seen you looking better.' He clicked his tongue and gave her a half smile. 'But hopefully it's nothing a wet wipe wouldn't cure.'

'I've got some. Or something similar in my vet bag. It's in the back. Can you get it, Sam, please? I can't go anywhere like this. And I can't leave it in the car.'

'No worries.'

A few moments later, he'd fetched the bag, found the wipes and handed them over. 'Maybe do it in the wing mirror,' he said.

She bent to do as he said and dabbed at her face and winced. Jeez, no wonder he'd looked shocked just now. She was covered in blood.

'That does look sore. Are you going to need any stitches?' Sam asked.

Rather miraculously, Phoebe discovered when she'd cleaned off some of the blood, there weren't any actual cuts on her face. Her nose had taken the brunt of the bashing. She examined it carefully. She already had the beginnings of a black eye.

'I actually don't think so.' Phew. It felt good to be doing something constructive.

'Small blessings,' Sam said. 'Right then, here's what I propose.' Sam took control again as she stood up. 'We'll go back to Brook Stables where we can get you cleaned up properly with soap and water. There's a first aid kit in the office. I'll organise someone to come and tow your car out of this ditch. You're right. It'll need a tractor. Then I'm going to drive you to hospital. Just to be on the safe side.'

'I don't need a hospital.'

Sam was wise enough not to push the point. 'Maybe you can decide that bit later. First things first. Back to Brook. You can ride Ninja.'

'We can't both ride Ninja.'

'No. I'll be leading him. We really aren't that far as the crow flies. Ten or twelve minutes, even if we walk slowly. I could phone and get someone to come and pick us up, but they'll have to drive the road way round. Cutting across the forest would probably be quicker.' He paused, his eyes were gentle. 'You OK with that? Do you need to phone anyone and let them know what's happened before we go? Maggie? Rufus?'

Rufus? Phoebe wondered what he'd have done in these circumstances. What he'd do or say if she phoned him. Well, he certainly wouldn't have been her knight in shining armour on a horse! It was Sam who'd come riding in on a white stallion. Well, actually, a bay gelding, but the result was the same. Oh, the irony. She began to laugh.

Sam looked worried. 'You definitely didn't hit your head?'

'No, no, I'm fine. It's all superficial. I've had a traumatic day. And if I didn't laugh, I'd cry. I'll tell you later.'

He raised his eyebrows but didn't pursue it. 'OK. Do you need a leg up on Ninja?'

'Please. It's been quite a while since I've ridden.'

He linked his hands together and bent close to the horse's near side to make her a step and Phoebe put her left foot into it while Ninja stood still patiently. In the next moment she was up on the horse. Instinctively she found the offside stirrup. To her surprise it was all coming back more quickly than she'd expected. Maybe it was like riding a bicycle. Once learned, you never forgot it.

It was still a relief though when Sam took hold of the reins from the ground too. Being on a flighty thoroughbred, however well behaved, while she felt this vulnerable wasn't her first choice of safe places. It struck her in that moment that Sam was one of the few people in the world who she trusted enough to relinquish responsibility to. That was a revelation.

'Have you got your car keys?' Sam asked. 'And is there anything else you need from the car before I lock it up? I'll bring your vet bag.'

'No, I've got my phone in my pocket. Are you sure about the bag? It's heavy.'

'I'm sure. I'm a big strong lad.' Sam gave her a lopsided grin. 'It's all that tossing of hay bales I do.'

'I didn't think it was the pen pushing at the post office,' she shot back. She couldn't believe they had slipped into banter. Half an hour ago she had felt as though her world had been knocked off its axis and ending up in the ditch had been the final straw.

But after ten minutes in Sam's company, the whole world felt brighter again. He was a very good person to have around in a crisis, Phoebe thought, as he grabbed her vet bag and locked up the car.

They set off, Sam on foot, Phoebe on Ninja, along the grass verge. She had the reins now, but Sam was holding on to them too, and a few seconds later they'd retraced Sam and Ninja's steps along the side of the witch's cottage and back into the forest that, fortunately, Sam knew like the back of his hand.

Phoebe remembered that Sam had always been great in an emergency. Although the last drama they had both been in had been his, when he'd fallen off Ninja during the show jumping at the New Forest Show last year.

'How did—'

'How are—'

They both spoke at the same time and Sam gestured for her to go first.

'I was just going to ask how you were, since your accident,' Phoebe said. 'Are you fully recovered now?'

'Good as new,' Sam said. 'With the addition of a cool scar.'

'And no spleen,' Phoebe replied. 'That's not exactly good as new. Aren't there implications for your immune system not having a spleen?'

'Supposedly, but I haven't noticed any so far.' He brushed her concerns away. 'Lots of people manage fine with no spleen. Enough of me. How did you end up in a ditch?'

'The short version is that I swerved to avoid a deer.' She hesitated, wondering how much more to tell him.

'And the long version is...?'

What the hell, Phoebe thought. She knew she would tell him sooner or later and actually Sam was a good person to confide in. He was discreet and empathetic and sensitive.

'Rufus and I split up this morning. I'd just left Beechbrook – it was all a bit traumatic and I'd decided to drive out and go for a walk to clear my head, but... I suspect that I wasn't concentrating as much as I should have been.'

She told him how they had seen less and less of each other, how busy they both were and how Rufus had finally ended it.

There was something very peaceful about riding through the sunlit forest with the sound of Ninja's hooves on the sandy track and the backdrop of birdsong and the arch of blue sky above it all. Everything felt muted and numbed, even her nose didn't hurt so much any more. The shock of crashing her car had passed and the air smelled of warm pine forest and summer.

Sam listened without interrupting and at the end of it he said, 'And how did you feel? Did you want to carry on?' His voice was very even and gentle. 'Or did you agree with him that it was over?'

'If you'd asked me that an hour ago, I'd have said that it was his choice, not mine. But to be honest, that's probably not quite true. I've known it hasn't been working for months. It hasn't been working since we started out really.'

It was a relief to finally say it, Phoebe realised. She'd been trying so hard to deny what was patently obvious for so long that she'd lost sight of the truth. She and Rufus had never worked out when it came to the mish mash mix of real life. They had only ever worked in a surreal and beautiful fantasy, most of which had been in her head.

'I am sorry, though,' Sam said. 'Break-ups are never easy, no matter how much you think they're the only solution, are they?'

'No,' Phoebe said. 'But I'll get over it.'

'You will.' He was staring straight ahead so she couldn't see his face. 'It's an annoying old cliché, but time does heal most things.'

'I'm glad you and Judy are happy this time round,' Phoebe added. 'Tori told me a while back that she had moved in – we weren't gossiping. She was just happy for you.'

'Sadly, Tori was misinformed,' Sam said, and Phoebe heard a slight tension in his voice. 'We did talk about moving in together, but it didn't happen.' He paused. 'To tell you the truth, Judy and I have split up too. It's still a bit raw, to be honest. It only happened on Monday.'

'Oh, Sam, I'm so sorry. And there was me blathering on about me and Rufus. Selfish, selfish, selfish.'

'You've never been selfish.' Sam glanced up at her. 'Bizarrely, from what you've said, I think Judy and I were probably in the same situation as you and Rufus. As you know, I've always had my doubts that we had a future. That's why we split up last time. But I thought that maybe it would be different this time around.'

'What made you realise it wasn't?'

'The short version is that we went to a very posh wedding. I'll tell you the long version next time we've got a few hours to spare.'

Phoebe realised that they were on the track that led up to Brook Stables. He'd been right, they'd been ten minutes from the stables as the crow flew. She'd never have believed they were that close.

'Maybe, after today's over, we can have a drink, Sam. And we can catch up properly,' Phoebe said.

'That sounds like a plan.' He smiled up at her. 'Now maybe you should get ready for a few raised eyebrows. Those wet wipes were good, but you do still have a nice black eye coming out on that side.' He touched his right cheekbone. 'Second thoughts – maybe make that both sides.'

'You say the sweetest things,' Phoebe quipped, and Sam laughed.

Phoebe joined in and by the time they'd ridden into the yard at Brook Stables, which was, to Phoebe's embarrassment, chock-a-block with both youngsters and adults in riding hats, about to go out on a hack, they were both laughing so hard they couldn't stop.

Thankfully, although they drew a few stares, everyone was too polite to comment. It was still a relief, though, to be able to slip down off Ninja's back, and to follow Sam and his horse into the welcome dimness of a nearby loose box.

35

Phoebe lost the battle with Sam about getting herself checked out, although she did manage to persuade him that going to a walk-in appointment at the urgent treatment centre would be just as good as him driving her to A&E and them both waiting for hours on end for an overstretched triage nurse.

He insisted on driving her to the urgent treatment centre where a doctor confirmed there was no permanent damage to her nose, but yes, Phoebe had two lovely black eyes coming out.

While they were waiting to be seen, Sam organised a tractor to tow the Lexus out of the ditch, which, to Phoebe's relief and delight when she saw it again, turned out to be none the worse for its unofficial off-road excursion.

Sam also insisted that he drive her back to Woodcutter's later that day, despite her assurance that she could drive herself. 'I can get a taxi home from there,' he said. 'Or Pa would probably come out and pick me up. Seriously, Pheebs, I know you think you're OK, but don't forget what the doc said, "Best not to drive for twenty-four hours if you can avoid it. Just to be safe."'

She gave up arguing and she was secretly relieved when he drove her back home in her Lexus. He was right. The events of the day had caught up with her.

At Woodcutter's Cottage she sat in her kitchen while he made them both hot chocolate and Phoebe thought that there was nothing so comforting as being made a hot chocolate by someone who knew exactly how you liked it.

'Do you have any hot water, Pheebs?' he asked, as she sat cupping the mug's warmth in her lounge. 'I can run you a bath if you like.'

'That sounds amazing. Thank you.'

A few minutes later she closed the bathroom door while Sam went downstairs to call a taxi, having decided that would be better than dragging out his father, and then she undressed and lowered herself into the deliciously scented heat of a bath full of bubbles.

'If the taxi comes before you're out of the bath, I'll shout goodbye from the foot of the stairs, and I'll make sure the door is latched behind me,' he'd said.

'Thank you, Sam.' She'd given him an impulsive hug and he hugged her back. 'I don't know how I'd have got through today without you.'

'It's what friends are for, isn't it?' He'd been the first to break the hug and step away and Phoebe had felt a sense of loss.

While she lay in the bath, luxuriating in the scented bubbles, she could hear him on the phone, presumably to a taxi firm. She didn't hear the front door close, but when she got out of the bath fifteen minutes later, wrapped herself in a fluffy robe and went downstairs, it was a surprise to realise he hadn't left.

He'd fallen asleep on her sofa, his phone lay beside him, and he was snoring quietly. So she wasn't the only one who must be worn out by the day's events. Or maybe it was the emotion. It must have affected him, too. Certainly it hadn't been how he'd been expecting to spend his Saturday, that was for sure.

For a few moments she watched him, asleep on her sofa, her gaze running over the familiar lines of his face. The face she had known all her life. Deeply tanned from his time spent outdoors but handsome by anyone's standards. He had a strong profile, a strong jaw, even in repose – his face reflected how he was, Phoebe thought. Strong, loyal, compassionate. She felt her heart jump a little in her chest and in that moment she was aware of something new in the room, no, it was something new in her. She had an overwhelming urge to be back in Sam's arms. To be wrapped up in another one of his hugs, to feel the strength of his body next to her.

She blinked a few times, trying to clear the new and confusing feelings that were sweeping through her. Jeez, what was this? What was happening? She must still be in shock.

Then he opened his eyes, and for a few seconds he was looking straight into her gaze and they both jumped, as if they'd both seen something neither of them had expected, and Phoebe thought, no, this isn't possible. The jolt of chemistry, that bolt of charged emotion – that just didn't happen with friends.

Sam broke the gaze. 'Hell, I'm sorry, Phoebe. I must have fallen asleep. I had the phone on repeat dial for a taxi company. The first one I tried said nothing for another hour.' He sat up, groping around for his mobile.

Phoebe went across the room and sat beside him. 'But you haven't got through?'

'No, they were permanently engaged. I'll try them again.' He avoided her eyes as he pressed buttons to unlock his phone.

'Stay here tonight, Sam. You don't have to go home.'

'What? Why?' He still didn't look at her. 'Do you feel vulnerable being on your own? Maybe I could call Maggie for you...'

'I don't want Maggie. I want you to stay in my bed with me. I want...' She leaned in a little closer and for the briefest of moments, she saw the answering want in Sam's blue eyes, before he leapt off the sofa, faster than a cat dancing on hot bricks, and stood up.

'I can't do this.'

'Why not?' Phoebe caught his hand very lightly. 'Sam, please just sit down for a second and tell me why you can't. Tell me how you feel.'

After the tiniest of pauses, he sat down again, but he put a gap between them, this time, and she didn't try to breach it.

'OK. I'll try.' He met her eyes. 'You've had a very tough day. You're very likely still in shock, Phoebe, so whatever you think you're feeling now, it's very likely a result of you still being in shock. Nothing more.'

'I don't think it is.' She gave a half smile. 'And I have a medical qualification.'

'That's for animals.'

'There is some cross-over, and there are no side effects of shock that make you feel like you want to take someone to bed. Not unless that feeling was already present.'

'Oh fu...' Sam shut his eyes. '...I mean, flip.'

'I think you had it right the first time.' Phoebe felt the beginnings of a giggle and she snorted.

Sam wasn't smiling. This time it was he who took her hand. 'I rest my case. Inappropriate laughter is a sign of shock.'

'It's not inappropriate,' Phoebe said. 'Actually, on second thoughts, yes, it is inappropriate. What's on my mind is totally and utterly inappropriate.'

'Phoebe, stop,' he implored, edging away to make a bigger gap on the sofa between them. He took a deep, slightly ragged breath. 'OK, let me tell you how I see things. Will you please just hear me out? Properly, I mean. Without interrupting.' He put up his hands.

'And please stay where you are.'

She nodded, and made a zipping motion across her lips and got the barest glimmer of a smile back from Sam.

'OK. This is how I see it.' He was breathing a little too heavily. He was definitely stressed. 'If we do ever spend the night together, it will be when both of us are (a) in a perfectly sober and sane state of mind, and (b) because we've both decided that we want to move our relationship to a different level. It won't be because we're just looking around for comfort.' His face was flushed. 'I can't do that, Phoebe, my love. I can't do that to you. And I can't do it to me. No matter how much the idea appeals right at this moment, which believe me, it bloody does. More than you'll ever know. But I can't do it because it would be disastrous for us, for both of us. Does that make sense to you?'

He blinked and Phoebe saw that his eyes were sparkly with unshed tears, and she had to swallow hard on the sudden ache that filled her own throat, because she knew he was right.

'Right then.' He went on quietly, 'I know I said to you a little while back that my feelings for you were changing and that I wanted more than friendship.'

That was true. He had.

'Well, I don't feel any different now. I've been in love with you for perhaps most of my life. I've tried not to be, but there it is. Every other woman I've dated, even Judy, has been a second choice – an attempt to move on and face reality. But none of it has worked. That's my cards on the table, Phoebe. Every last one of them.' His Adam's apple bobbed and she knew it wasn't easy for him, laying himself bare like this.

'Have you finished now?' she asked him quietly. She felt impossibly moved. It was hard to speak, even though he had now spelled out in black and white his own emotions.

'I've finished,' Sam said, 'except to say, that if you wake up tomorrow or the next day and realise I was right – that all these emotions were just a side effect of shock, then we can forget this conversation ever happened.'

'And if I don't?'

'Then we can talk again and...' He broke off. 'We can talk some more.' He sniffed the air. 'What is that spicy smell? Have you been burning candles in here?'

She got up and went across to the mantelpiece. 'Lavender and Pumpkin Pie scented. Do you like it?' She brought it back to the sofa and handed it to him.

Sam breathed it in. 'It's very pleasant. Although I do think it's hard to beat the smell of woodsmoke and red wine and newly bathed Phoebe.' He caught himself. 'Sorry. I'll stop there. I'd better go, sweetheart. While I've still got enough willpower to make it out of the front door. I'll phone Pa – I'm sure he'll come out. I'll phone him from outside. If there's any problem, I'll come back in.'

'You don't have to wait outside. You can wait in here. I'll go and get dressed.'

They both stood up, a two-person distance between them, and Phoebe hugged the robe around her.

'Thank you, Sam. Whatever this is that I'm feeling, I don't think it's going to vanish overnight. Is it OK if I ring you tomorrow?'

'Of course it is. Tomorrow or in a few days. However long it takes. And, whichever way it goes, if there is anything else I can do to help, you will let me know that too.' His steady gaze met hers. 'I value your friendship enormously, Phoebe.'

'And I yours. Thank you, Sam.'

When she came downstairs for the second time since her bath, this time dressed, Sam had his coat on and was standing by the door.

'Pa's on his way. How are you feeling? Physically, I mean,' he added quickly.

'Tired,' she said. 'And that is a side effect of shock.'

'I'll give you that.' He winked.

Ten minutes later they both saw his father's car drawing up outside and Sam went out into the evening sunshine to meet him. Phoebe, feeling conscious of her battered face, waved him off from the window.

Sam's dad was lovely, both of his parents were, but she wasn't in the mood for facing anyone at the moment. All she wanted to do was to curl up on the sofa for the rest of the evening and watch something inane on television. Whichever way you looked at it, it had been one hell of a day.

* * *

As Sam climbed into his father's car, his head was spinning a bit. He certainly hadn't expected that ending to the day and there was a tiny, selfish part of him that was already regretting that he hadn't taken Phoebe at face value and stayed over for the night.

But it was only a tiny part of him that regretted it. He knew he'd made the right decision. The *only* decision that he could make. Integrity was a bloody hard taskmaster sometimes, he thought, knowing almost immediately that it wasn't just integrity that had stopped him leaping into bed with Phoebe. It was love too. Love was an even harder taskmaster.

'You OK, Sam?' His father's voice interrupted his thoughts and Sam became aware of his gaze. 'You look like you've got the whole world on your shoulders. Are you still worried about Phoebe? Because I'm sure your mother wouldn't mind if we took her back to ours for the night – or to Maggie's even if you're worried.'

'I don't think we'd get her to go, Pa. She's too flaming stubborn and independent. But thanks for the offer.'

'You're probably right, son.' Ian Hendrie shrugged his shoulders. 'Women – huh – life would be so much simpler if they were more like men. I bet she was trying to push you out of the door as hard as she could, wasn't she?'

Sam smiled at the irony. But he didn't have the energy to contradict his father. It had been a tricky enough day already.

36
————

Phoebe woke up on Sunday morning after an incredibly vivid dream that had featured herself, Rufus and Sam on a fairground carousel, the kind which had exotically painted horses that galloped in endless circles to an accompaniment of tinny music. They were all riding different horses. Hers was blue and white, Sam's was red and white, and Rufus's was gold plated with a candy-pink bridle. The dream was accompanied by strange emotions, as dreams so often are, and the overriding one was loss.

Phoebe sat up in bed. Rufus on a horse! She wasn't going to even begin to try to untangle that dream. She reached for her phone.

There was a message from Sam.

Hope you slept well.

There was a message from Tori.

Are you two still in bed? Call me! xx

Phoebe realised with a shock that Tori must still think she was so deeply immersed in her planned weekend with Rufus that she hadn't had time to even respond to messages. She decided she would speak to Tori later.

There were also three missed calls from Rufus and a voicemail which had been left late last night.

'Phoebe, Harrison just told me he saw your car in a ditch. Please call me and let me know you're OK.'

He sounded very worried. Phoebe felt a flicker of gratification. He still cared about her on some level then. But oddly she didn't feel the rush of relief to hear from him that she'd have felt just twenty-four hours earlier.

She messaged Sam.

I slept well, thanks, yes. Hope you did too. xxx

Then she phoned Rufus. He answered immediately. 'Phoebe, where are you? Are you OK?'

'I'm fine.' She told him what had happened and heard his indrawn breath as he realised she'd been driving back from seeing him when she'd just missed the deer.

'I'm so sorry. Was it because of us, because of our...' He hesitated. '...discussion?'

'Maybe a little.' She wasn't going to lie. 'But the reality is I just wasn't concentrating. I'm OK. No permanent damage – I wasn't even going fast enough for the air bag to deploy so my car is fine too.'

'I'm so glad you're all right.' He sounded it.

Phoebe changed the subject. 'How's your dad?'

'He's still in hospital. Hopefully he'll be coming home tomorrow or Tuesday. It turns out he's been ignoring the symptoms of a heart condition and now he's gone into full-blown heart failure.'

'Oh, my goodness.' It was Phoebe's turn to be shocked.

'He'll be OK,' Rufus reassured. 'Heart failure sounds dreadful, but it just means his heart isn't working as well as it should. It's treatable with medication. As long as he does what he's told and takes it easy. Which is difficult for him.'

'Like father, like son,' Phoebe said softly.

'Yes.' There was no denial in his voice, just a quiet acceptance. 'I am sorry for how it's turned out, Phoebe. Archie and I will miss you.'

'And I'll miss you both too,' she said, feeling a fierce stab of loss at the thought of not seeing Archie again – weirdly that mattered more than not seeing his father. 'Rufus, I hope we can still be friends. Archie is welcome at Puddleduck Pets any time he wants to see the animals, and if ever he, or you, have questions about any of Archie's animals – I don't just mean in my vet capacity, I mean as a friend – then please don't hesitate to call me. Just because our relationship hasn't gone in the direction we'd hoped, I don't want Archie to think he can't still call me and text me.'

There was a little pause before Rufus said, 'I really appreciate that. Thank you.'

'I mean it.'

'I know you do.'

'And I hope your dad is feeling much better soon.'

'Thank you.'

They said their goodbyes and Phoebe felt light, as if she had somehow become freer in the last few minutes. At least mentally she felt light. Physically she felt sore. Her face was tender and bruised and her hope that the two black eyes might have come to nothing was smashed as soon as she glanced in the bathroom mirror. She looked like the victim of domestic abuse. Thank goodness it was Sunday and she didn't have to go anywhere. Not that she imagined she was going to look much better tomorrow for work. It was going to take more than a splash of foundation to cover this lot up.

When she came back into the bedroom, her mobile was ringing again. This time it was Tori. She snatched it up, but before she could speak, Tori launched into a tirade.

'Phoebe, thank God. I've been worried sick. Harrison just told me he saw your car in a ditch yesterday. Are you OK? What happened? Where are you?'

'I'm fine. Calm down.' Phoebe cut through her friend's frantic questions. 'Sorry, I was just about to phone you.' Harrison had a lot to answer for, she thought.

She explained what had happened, from the moment Hugh turned up at the same time as Rufus, to Rufus being called away by Emilia on Friday night, to her visiting him at Beechbrook House and then her hasty departure and Sam rescuing her. Tori listened and sympathised in all the right places and Phoebe felt a huge rush of affection for her best friend. 'I'm so sorry I didn't phone you before. It's all just happened so quickly and my head's all over the place, to be honest. How are you? How's bump? How's morning sickness?'

'Bump is fine.' Tori's voice softened. 'Morning sickness is easing. I actually feel amazing, to be honest. Like a proper glowing mother to be.'

'That's brilliant.'

'I know. We need to meet soon to catch up properly. How was Sam? I heard a rumour that he and Judy had split up too. Did he mention it?'

Tori's romance antennae must be working overtime, Phoebe thought. She hesitated, and then said, 'Yes, he did. He told me that he's OK with it. Sad but OK.'

'Bless him. I guess the two of you got to exchange notes on each other's break-up stories when you were in the urgent treatment centre then?'

She was definitely fishing now, and Phoebe murmured noncommittally but didn't enlighten her. It wouldn't have seemed fair when she hadn't yet spoken to Sam.

Having exchanged a promise that they would meet for coffee after work on Thursday, they finally stopped chatting and said their goodbyes.

Phoebe's thoughts turned back to Sam. She hugged the warmth of her feelings tight to herself. One thing she was totally sure about was that she still felt the same way about him as she had last night. That sea change of emotions that had swept through her like a tsunami had settled today into calm. But the way she felt held true.

Maybe she had just needed to open her eyes all along and see what was in front of her. And yesterday her eyes had been opened, first by Rufus's indifference, and secondly by landing in a ditch and knowing that when she was really up against it, there was only one person she wanted to call.

The events of the last twenty-four hours had shaken her. The shock of knowing that she and Rufus were over had paled into significance against the shock of realising that she did, after all, want to go to bed with Sam. For most of her life she had shut her mind to the possibility that they could ever be more than friends. She had denied she'd found him attractive on a personal level. She had pushed her jealousy about him and Judy to one side and convinced herself she was just envious that he was settling down before she was, but on some level she had known it wasn't quite as simple as that. After all, she hadn't felt envious of Tori settling down, she'd just felt thrilled for her.

But yesterday she had realised that while Rufus had been a beautiful fantasy, her feelings for Sam ran much deeper. If she was honest, it had been a long time before yesterday. It had started at the New Forest Show last year. Her mind flashbacked to the panic she'd felt when he and Ninja had hit the jump and Sam had lain unmoving on the ground. All she'd cared about then was making sure he was OK. She had been the first person to reach his side.

Sam had pushed her away, insisted that Rufus and Archie needed her more than he did, which had been true in that moment. But Phoebe knew that if he hadn't pushed her so hard in Rufus's direction, her real feelings for him would have surfaced sooner.

It had hit her again yesterday when she'd seen him sleeping on her sofa. As she'd watched his unguarded lovely familiar face, she'd felt overwhelmed with love for him. She had ached to be back in the security of his arms, but as a lover, not a friend.

As the last vestige of her denial had been smashed, Phoebe had been left facing the truth and the truth was that she couldn't imagine a life without Sam.

She wished he had stayed last night and yet she was relieved that he hadn't. The timing had been all wrong. Her very wise friend had been spot on about that. They were both on the rebound. But Phoebe was pretty sure her feelings were real, and were here to stay.

* * *

Sam had seen to Ninja and was giving a riding lesson at Brook Stables to a child with cerebral palsy who showed a lot of promise and clearly loved horses when Phoebe's reply to his text had come through. He didn't look at his phone until he'd finished the lesson, helped the child to dismount and had handed him back to his proud parents. Then he opened Phoebe's text.

I slept well, thanks, yes. Hope you did too. xxx

He couldn't stop smiling. Not because of the words, but because of the three kisses at the end. In all the time he had known her, Phoebe had never ended a message to him with anything other than an emoji. It was usually a smiley emoji, or a winking emoji, or a sad emoji. She had never ended a message with three kisses.

He'd been shocked by her revelations yesterday and he couldn't second guess it. He would find out soon enough if she still felt the same. They both would. Either way, he hoped he'd done enough to make sure their friendship continued. Because their friendship, as he'd told her, was hugely important to him.

* * *

On Sunday afternoon, Phoebe called round to Puddleduck Farm to see Maggie. She had rung first in an effort to spare her from the shock of seeing her bruised face without warning, but true to form, Maggie hadn't answered the phone.

The first person Phoebe saw at Puddleduck was Natasha. She was talking to a couple who were obviously hoping to rehome a dog. A small fawn-coloured Pomeranian danced around on the end of a lead that the man was holding while the woman bent to pet it. Phoebe wondered if it was the same one that had come in at Easter. They didn't get many Pomeranians into the sanctuary.

Phoebe hung back until the conversation ended and then Natasha turned in her direction. 'Oh, my goodness, what on earth happened to you?'

'You should see the other guy,' Phoebe said, and filled her in on the ditch incident, missing out the bit about splitting up with Rufus.

Natasha made sympathetic noises, although Phoebe could tell there was something different about her, a kind of glee bubbling up through her concern.

'What's going on?' she asked. 'Wasn't that the Pomeranian that was given up by that old lady whose grandkids were allergic?'

'Yes, and they were the parents of the grandkids.' Natasha was almost bouncing up and down on the spot with excitement. 'They're taking it back again. Apparently their old mum's been lost without William and they're going to work round it. They came in a couple of weeks ago to ask me to please make sure he wasn't rehomed. The whole family have just been away to Disneyland, but they came back yesterday. You see, there are some happy endings.'

'Great news,' Phoebe said, feeling a warmth stealing through her. 'Is that it or was there something else?'

Natasha leaned in, even though no one else was in the vicinity. 'I'm seeing Marcus. We're keeping it very low-key, in fact no one else knows, but it's going great. I really like him.'

'That is even better news,' Phoebe said. 'I'm so pleased for you both.' She paused. 'Is Maggie around?'

'She and Eddie are up at the top field with the neddies, I think.' Natasha gestured and Phoebe thanked her and went up towards the top field.

As she got closer, she could see both her grandmother and Eddie in the field, but there was something odd going on. Eddie appeared to be on the ground, kneeling in a patch of dirt and Maggie was trying to pull him up. Good grief, what on earth was happening? Phoebe broke into a run.

A few moments later, she arrived breathless beside them.

'Hey, what's happening? Is everything OK?'

Both Eddie and Maggie turned towards her, clearly startled.

'What are you doing here?' Eddie spoke first.

'And what on earth have you done to your face?' Maggie's eyes widened. 'Dear God, have you been in a fight?'

'I bashed my head on my steering wheel. That's all. I'm fine. More to the point, what's Eddie doing on the ground? Did he fall?'

'No. I did not fall.' Eddie sighed with exasperation. Then he drew the shape of a heart in the air. And to her utmost embarrassment, Phoebe caught up with what was going on.

'Oh, my God. I've just interrupted a very special moment, haven't I?'

'Yep,' Maggie said. 'You broke straight into the middle of a romantic scene. Eddie's just proposed marriage.' She screwed up her face in a frown. 'Although to be fair your timing's quite good. I've already said yes and he's having more trouble getting up than he did getting down.' She hesitated. 'Maybe if we get hold of one hand each, we can haul him up between us?'

37

On Monday morning, Phoebe, Max, Jenna and Marcus held a swift impromptu meeting in reception before they opened to discuss the week ahead.

'I think it might be better if I don't see any new clients until my face heals,' Phoebe said. 'I don't want to scare them off, do I?'

Max agreed and they swiftly rejigged the appointments so that Phoebe was only scheduled to see clients she knew well.

'Max's specialist subject is charming new clients,' Marcus put in, but there was no edge to his voice, just affection.

Things had clearly settled down between the two men, Phoebe thought, even if no one but her did know about Marcus seeing Natasha. He was starting his course in animal behaviourism this week too. Marcus, who Phoebe suspected struggled with self-esteem, had found a focus in both his personal and professional life. She was thrilled for him.

On Monday evening, Phoebe called Sam, who sounded delighted to hear from her. 'Hey, you. How are the bruises?'

'Um, looking worse, feeling better.'

'Good. And how are you feeling in other ways?' His voice

sobered just a little. 'I meant what I said, Pheebs. If it's just friends, that's fine with me.'

'And what if I still feel exactly the same and I don't want it to be just friends any more?'

'That would be great too.' His voice was very even. 'But the ball is totally in your court.'

'So would it be OK if I came round right now and ravished you?' she hedged.

'That's very tempting, but...' She heard his intake of breath. 'In the interests of us having the whole of our future ahead of us, I think we should take into account that rebound relationships don't always work.'

'You mean, you think we should wait.' She felt a crashing disappointment. This was crazy – having taken years to decide that she wanted a full-on relationship with Sam, she didn't want to wait another second. She wanted him now.

'At least a month,' Sam said.

'A month!' she exclaimed. 'I can't wait for a month.'

'OK, a fortnight.' There was laughter in his voice.

'A week,' she bargained, 'and you have yourself a deal.'

He laughed out loud this time. 'OK, how about you come to mine for dinner next Saturday and we can negotiate timings then.'

'Done,' Phoebe said, before he could change his mind.

* * *

At Beechbrook House, Rufus was sitting in his office feeling empty, but also more clear-headed than he'd felt for weeks. Ending things with Phoebe had been the right thing to do. He just wasn't in the right state of mind for a relationship at the moment. And even though it hadn't really got off the ground, it had been a relationship of sorts. And it had been difficult and painful for both of them.

In another time, another place, it could have been perfect. Phoebe was beautiful, strong, clever, and he knew Archie adored her, but he had also realised in recent weeks that their relationship couldn't work out in practical terms.

Rufus knew that if there was going to be another woman in his life, she would have to be a wife. She would be by his side full time, and one day she would be Lady Holt. And old-fashioned as it might be, she wouldn't be running a vet practice, 24/7. She would be like Rowena had once been, an equal partner with an independent income. She wouldn't need to work for a living, at least not outside of the estate that he owned, and Rufus had known, soon after day one, that Phoebe would never willingly step into that role.

His feelings for her had muddied the waters but he had known, his body had known, that there was no future. It had thrown him seeing Hugh at hers – but in a way it had clarified everything too.

If he let her go then Phoebe could move on. Maybe not towards Hugh, who still obviously wanted to be with her. That had been crystal clear, but at least she would be free. Then Rufus could concentrate on what mattered most. His family, his son, his father, and his obligations to all of the men who'd gone before him. All of the men who'd lived in his ancestral home and kept it safe, before entrusting its care to the next generation. You didn't hear much about that in modern society. But it still ran through Rufus. As a child, he remembered his father saying, 'If you cut me in half, you'd find two things at my core, running through me like two bright colours running through seaside rock. And those two things are duty and responsibility.'

It was the same for Rufus.

A noise disturbed him from his thoughts and he realised his father had come into the office, leaning heavily on a walking stick with an ornate handle, fashioned in the shape of a hound's head. It was the first time he'd got up since Rufus had picked him up from hospital this morning, and he'd never seen him using a stick before.

'Hi, Dad. Should you be up? How are you feeling?'

'I'm OK. Don't fuss.' There was a small silence, then he continued. 'I... I think I owe you an apology.'

'No, you don't.' Rufus looked at him in surprise.

'Yes, I do. I shouldn't have lied to you about the doctor. I caused so much fuss.'

'It's fine, Dad. Seriously.'

'It's not. It won't happen again, and I apologise.' His father sat heavily on a chair. 'That's something I don't do enough... Apologise.' He gave a wry smile. 'I didn't want to accept that things have changed. I'm getting older. I've been too proud and that's not always the way forward.' He looked at his son. 'What are you doing in here working? I thought you were seeing the vet – Phyllis?'

'Phoebe. No. We decided to call things off. On Saturday.'

'I see.' There was a little silence. His father cleared his throat. 'Probably for the best in the long run.'

'Yes.'

'Where there's an ending there'll be a new beginning, eh, son?'

'Yes. I guess there will.'

'The boy's growing up. He'll be off to summer school in a week or so. Then he'll get his pony and be more independent and then in September he'll be away to big school. It will be different then too.'

Rufus closed his eyes. There was another little silence. Rufus was about to break it when his father said, 'I'm proud of you, Rufus. Do you know that? I don't say that often enough either.'

Rufus met his father's gaze. It was hard to speak. 'I don't think you've ever said it.'

'Well, it's true.' His father fidgeted with the handle of his stick. 'Don't forget that, son.'

Rufus got up and went around to where his father sat.

He touched his father's shoulder and then his father gripped him by the arm and squeezed tight. They wouldn't hug. Rufus could count on one hand the number of times they'd hugged in his life. But this was enough for now. It was a very good new beginning.

* * *

As the week progressed, Phoebe's bruises slowly began to heal, and so too did her heart. She'd thought she might feel sad about Rufus, that there might be some lingering regrets, but there weren't. On Thursday night she caught up with Tori for a coffee at Woodcutter's.

'Ironically, I think I'll miss Archie most of all,' she told her friend, 'but Rufus said he's fine about us keeping in touch, and Archie's off to boarding school in September. He can't wait – it's a school where he can take his own horse. That's quite a draw.'

'I bet it is. And that's nice of Rufus. I'm sure Harrison would bring Archie over to Puddleduck Pets too before he goes. Not that he can't walk from next door.' Tori grinned. 'Does Sam still give him riding lessons?'

'Not so often, but I think he does occasionally, yes.'

'Another opportunity to see him then, maybe.' Tori raised her eyebrows. 'And while we're on the subject of Sam, what's going on there? I know you're holding out on me. You're looking far too sparkly for a woman who's supposed to be heartbroken.'

Phoebe felt herself blushing under Tori's eagle-eyed scrutiny. 'Tell me about the baby first – is it a boy or a girl – and when is Harrison making an honest woman of you? It's ages since we've caught up.'

'OK.' Tori cupped her tummy. 'Well, we're having a little girl. We've been talking names. I want to call her Vanessa Rose after my grandmother and Harrison's just so blown away that he's having a daughter I think he'd agree to anything. Like I said before, we're not getting married until after the birth. Possibly next summer, possibly the one after. Neither of us feels the need to rush into it. We just want to be together. It's such a great feeling, Phoebe. I'm so happy.'

'And I'm so very pleased for you.' Phoebe reached for her hand and squeezed it. 'Vanessa Rose is a beautiful name.'

'Your turn,' Tori pressed.

'OK, you're right. I'm not heartbroken about Rufus. I think we've both known for a while that it wasn't going to work. Rufus was just braver about admitting it than I was.'

'And Sam?'

'Sam and I – have – um – decided to be more than friends.'

Tori squealed with excitement. 'No way. Oh, that's brilliant. I had a feeling that was happening. Call me telepathic. So how did that come about? Was it the bang on the head?'

'No, it was not the bang on the head.' Phoebe giggled. 'Or maybe it was. Maybe it knocked some sense into me. I don't know. I don't care. All I know is that on the day he came and rescued me and took me home and ran me a bath and looked after me, something changed. I suddenly saw him through new eyes. It was a complete shock to me, to be honest.'

'The only thing that shocks me is that it's taken you so long to see it.' Tori's green eyes sparkled. 'It's a classic trope in all the best romcoms. Childhood friends become lovers. We often don't see what's right under our noses though, do we?'

'I've always been a slow learner when it comes to romance. But oh, my God, it feels lovely, Tori. And a bit scary. I'm going round for a meal with him on Saturday.'

'Just a meal!' Tori teased and then looked guilty. 'No, don't tell me. I don't want to know. It's none of my business.'

Phoebe giggled. 'You don't want me to send you a number between one and ten then?'

'Absolutely not,' Tori said. 'I want my two best friends to have a lovely evening together and not to worry about anything else. But you will keep me posted on how it pans out – you know, in a general way.' She blushed and put up a hand. 'Sorry. You do whatever feels comfortable. The only thing I care about is that you're both happy.'

'I'm feeling pretty happy at the moment,' Phoebe said.

She didn't tell Maggie about Sam either when she went round on Friday night, having been summoned for tea, although she did tell her about Rufus and that it had ended by mutual agreement. Because it had really, Phoebe knew that now. They had both known it wasn't going to work.

Luckily Maggie was too distracted baking to notice there was anything else on Phoebe's mind. There was in fact a bit of a party atmosphere at Puddleduck Farm because Maggie and Eddie certainly weren't keeping their engagement quiet.

On the side by the Aga was a cake with, 'We're engaged,' iced in blue on the top.

'Aren't you guys supposed to keep that for your engagement party?' Phoebe asked, laughing.

'Consider this an impromptu engagement party,' Maggie said. 'Your parents are coming round in a minute and hopefully Frazier and Alexa if they can get a babysitter. We can't afford to hang around at our age. We're getting married in November.'

'This November? That's an odd month for a wedding.'

'Or possibly this December,' Maggie said. 'Eddie quite fancies a Christmas wedding. There are advantages. I won't be the only one wearing long sleeves. I'm sure your mother will be up for that too.'

'When did you tell my mother?'

'Yesterday,' Maggie said. 'We could hardly keep it a secret once you'd stumbled across us in the neddie field, could we?'

'I'm sorry about that.' Phoebe caught her grandmother's gaze and saw her eyes flash with amusement.

'You're forgiven. On condition that you come up for your tea, just the two of us, when all this has settled down a bit, and tell me all your news. And, of course, that you stay for my engagement party.'

She brushed flour from her hands, rinsed them at the sink, picked something up from the side and came back to where Phoebe had settled herself at the table. She held out her hand. 'What do you think?'

Phoebe stared at the small but sparkly diamond ring on her finger. 'Oh, wow. It's beautiful.'

'Isn't it?' Maggie beamed.

'And of course I'm staying.' Phoebe eyed the cake. 'You don't think I'm going to miss out on home-made cake, do you? Is it Victoria sponge?'

'It is.'

'I wish you'd told me it was an engagement party, I'd have bought you both a present.'

'We don't need presents at our age. All we need is the love and support of our families,' Maggie said in a voice that was unusually soft, and her eyes teared up.

She sniffed a few times and cleared her throat. 'Flaming hay fever,' she complained.

But before Phoebe could ask her if hay fever was a new thing because she'd never had it before, the barking of the dogs heralded the arrival of the rest of their family.

38

Phoebe phoned Sam on Saturday lunchtime after morning surgery.

'Sam, what time do you want me later?' Why did that question feel so loaded? She could feel herself blushing a little.

'Whatever time's convenient. Sevenish?' Sam's voice was as warm and lovely as ever. No innuendos there.

'Great. I've got a couple of things on my list, this afternoon, but sevenish is perfect.'

The first thing on Phoebe's list was phoning Hugh.

As she'd expected, he was surprised to hear from her, and even more surprised, she realised, feeling slightly guilty when she thanked him for helping her to cure the mystery alpaca disease.

'That's OK.' His voice was coolly polite.

There was a small silence. Hugh broke it.

'I wish you well, Phoebe, with your new relationship.'

For a second she thought, how does he know about Sam? Then she realised he was talking about Rufus, but she didn't correct him.

'And I won't be bothering you again,' he added. 'I was wrong to follow you. It was a case of I didn't know what I'd got till it had gone. And I thought maybe I still had a chance, but I've realised that I don't. You've moved on, haven't you?'

'I have,' she told him. 'But I wish you well, too, Hugh, and maybe we can be friends, one day in the future. Purely platonically,' she added, in the interests of being crystal clear.

'I would like that,' Hugh said, and she disconnected, feeling as though she'd finally said goodbye to an older part of her life.

The second thing on Phoebe's list was a follow-up call to Buck-land Farm. It was lovely to arrive and see Anni open the door with a smile on her lips. This vanished swiftly when she saw Phoebe's face, which was now a fading montage of yellow and blue. 'My, oh, my, what happened to you?'

Phoebe told her and Anni listened sympathetically, and a few minutes later they were walking up to the alpaca field.

'How have they been?' Phoebe asked. 'Any more problems?'

'None whatsoever. It's as though they have a new lease of life. But you can see that for yourself.'

And indeed Phoebe could. Three or four of the herd were racing around their paddock, kicking up the dry earth and clearly running for the sheer pleasure of running in the afternoon sunshine. The thud of their hooves was like a welcome symphony.

'Isn't that a beautiful sight, love?'

'Yes, it is.'

For a moment, the two women stopped to watch. 'There's a lightness in them all,' Anni said. 'You can see it, can't you?'

'Yes, you can.'

'You seem lighter too.' Anni glanced at her face. 'You've resolved something on the love front, haven't you? And the trespassing vet has finally let go.'

'You're right on both counts, yes.' Phoebe wasn't surprised that Anni knew.

She'd always seemed to know stuff, despite her insistence that she hadn't inherited the clairvoyant gene.

All of her tea leaf predictions had come true. The heartbreak she'd foreseen for herself, certainly, that had been Cindy. But several of her predictions for Phoebe had also come true. The crown that had predicted financial success. There was no doubt that Puddleduck Vets' finances had picked up lately. This was partly due to the fact that Max now spoke to all new customers, and he was much more discerning than Phoebe had been about what was a sob story and what was a genuine case of hardship. Phoebe was also no longer offering a new customer discount. The practice was too busy already.

Then there was the pregnancy. OK, so it had been Tori who'd got pregnant, not her, but there had been a pregnancy. Phoebe remembered the A – had that been Archie? He'd undoubtedly played a big part in her life. Or had it been an upside-down V all along? V for Vanessa, the name of Tori's unborn child. Phoebe's heart banged in her chest. Of course.

As for the big heart that stood for much love or many suitors, Anni certainly hadn't been wrong there either. Phoebe drew in a breath.

Anni turned and studied her face for a moment. 'You've chosen the right one.'

Phoebe blushed and didn't answer, not that it had really been a question.

'There's a thing about alpacas that not many people know,' Anni went on quietly. 'When they mate, the sire hums. Some of the males are very gentle, some are rough. Some are indifferent, some are almost tender, but each alpaca is also different when it comes to the hum. Each male hums their own tune.'

'Wow.' Phoebe looked at her in astonishment. 'Really – that's amazing.'

'It's true.' Anni clicked her tongue. 'Men are a different breed, of course. I don't think many of our human males hum while they're mating.' Her eyes sparkled with merriment. 'But they definitely all have their own tune, don't they?'

Phoebe dropped her gaze, feeling suddenly shy. Then she looked back at the alpacas, who'd stopped careering around and were now milling in and out of the apple trees. It looked as though there would be a bumper crop this year. The seasons moved through their cycle, from blossom to the tiny fruits, to the full-blown crop that would be ready for harvest in another couple of months, but were currently at the stage that was so full of promise. Like new love, Phoebe thought.

Forty-five minutes later, Phoebe was parking outside Sam's. He'd moved his car onto the street so she could have his off-road parking space. Typical Sam, she thought, as she rung his bell.

He buzzed her in and a few moments later she'd run up the flight of stairs and he let her in the front door of the maisonette. She felt breathless and it wasn't just the stairs. She was like a cat on hot bricks. An appropriate analogy, she thought, as she passed a purring and sleek-looking Snowball, who no longer had the slightest of limps.

'He looks well.'

'He is. Thanks to you.'

'And you – nursing him back to health.'

'Teamwork. Would you like coffee or hot chocolate? Or something cold? I think I've got juice.'

'I brought wine.' She put it on the breakfast island in his kitchen and it clunked loudly. Solid wood. When Sam had bought this place, his father had helped him refurbish it and everything had been done properly.

Or maybe her senses were on super high alert. There was no maybe about it. She felt as though she had no top layer of skin. All her nerve endings were exposed and jangling. Every sound was super loud. She could hear her own breathing.

'Have you had a good day, Sam?'

'I have, thanks. Busy.' He got wine glasses down from a cupboard and orange juice from the fridge, but he'd stayed across the other side of the kitchen. He hadn't even given her a peck on the cheek, which they would normally do.

Phoebe went across the kitchen. 'Sam, you were right about not staying over last week. All of the rebound stuff that you said.'

'It's OK.' He hushed her with a look. 'Our friendship is more important to me than anything else.'

'No, no, that's not what I mean. I don't want friendship. Well, I do, but not just friendship.' She caught his hands, realising hers were clammy. 'Oh, God, I'm just going to say it. It's taken me longer to realise it than you, but I love you too, Sam. And I want to spend the night with you. This night. Every night from this day forward – that's if you want to spend any nights at all with a clammy-handed woman with two black eyes.'

'Oh, I do, I do.' His eyes widened as if he couldn't quite process her words, and for a moment she was lost in the blue of them. That deep, beautiful blue she knew so well. Then he was holding her, drawing her into his arms, and his touch was so tender, yet so very strong. No longer the hug of a friend but something more serious. Phoebe had never dreamed that Sam's touch would feel like this. Very briefly she laid her head against his shoulder and he stroked her hair. She breathed in his faintly citrus aftershave and the scent of his neck, the scent of Sam.

When she lifted her head again to look up into his eyes, she saw they were a different colour this close up. The exact colour of the sky just before dusk on a perfect summer's day.

Sam was a couple of inches taller than she was in her flatties. But he only had to bow his head the smallest bit to kiss her, and she kissed him back eagerly. He tasted of sunshine and toothpaste, and she wanted to carry on the kiss for ever. But it was Sam who broke it, opening his eyes and holding her gaze.

'I have two questions.'

'Fire away.'

'I have pizza if you're hungry, are you?'

'You know me. I'm always hungry. What's the other question?'

'There's something else I'd much rather do first. So I was wondering if you'd prefer pizza for dinner or pizza for breakfast?'

Phoebe realised they were standing beside the door that opened to the second flight of stairs that led up to his bedroom. It was shut, or at least pulled to. Sam had his back to it. 'Pizza for breakfast sounds perfect to me.' Phoebe reached behind him, twisted the handle, then pulled him through the door to the stairs.

A few moments later, they were kissing again, but this time they were sitting on the edge of his king-size bed. Phoebe knew this was a kiss there was no coming back from, a kiss there would be no interrupting. She let herself fall into its warmth and its passion, because there was not a single doubt left in any part of her. Every inch of her wanted Sam and she could feel that every inch of him wanted her. They had waited a long time for this moment, but she felt as though they had both, finally, come home.

When they woke up the next morning, after a night which Phoebe knew she would never forget, for all of the right reasons, one of the first things she did was to send Tori a one-word text. All it said was...

Eleven!

ACKNOWLEDGMENTS

Thank you so much to Team Boldwood – you are amazing. Thank you to every single one of you who works so hard to bring my books to my readers in paperback, audio and digital.

As always, my special thanks go to Caroline Ridding, Judith Murdoch, Cecily Blanch, Shirley Khan and to Alice Moore for the gorgeous cover.

Thank you to Rhian Rochford for her veterinary knowledge, without whom this book would be a lot harder. Thank you to Vanessa Hobbs, for her suggestions about the Meow Master, to Vicky Daddo and Sam Styles, for their amazing help on all things alpaca. Thank you to the Dunford Novelists for your perceptive comments.

Thank you to Gordon Rawsthorne for his enduring support. He endures a lot!

Thank you, perhaps most of all, for the huge support of my readers – without whom it would be pretty pointless writing novels. I love reading your emails, tweets and Facebook comments. Please keep them coming.

ABOUT THE AUTHOR

Della Galton is the author of more than 15 books, including the *Bluebell Cliff* and *Puddleduck Farm* series. She writes short stories, teaches writing groups and is Agony Aunt for *Writers Forum* Magazine. She lives in Dorset.

Sign up to Della Galton's mailing list for news, competitions and updates on future books.

Visit Della's website: www.dellagalton.co.uk

Follow Della on social media:

 facebook.com/DailyDella

twitter.com/DellaGalton

instagram.com/Dellagalton

bookbub.com/authors/della-galton

ALSO BY DELLA GALTON

The Bluebell Cliff Series

Sunshine Over Bluebell Cliff

Summer at Studland Bay

Shooting Stars Over Bluebell Cliff

Sunrise Over Pebble Bay

Confetti Over Bluebell Cliff

The Puddleduck Farm Series

Coming Home to Puddleduck Farm

Rainbows Over Puddleduck Farm

Love Blossoms at Puddleduck Farm

Boldwood

Boldwood Books is an award-winning
fiction publishing company seeking
out the best stories from
around the world.

Find out more at
www.boldwoodbooks.com

Join our reader community
for brilliant books,
competitions and offers!

Follow us
#BoldBookClub

Sign up to our weekly
deals newsletter

https://bit.ly/BoldwoodBNewsletter

Printed in Great Britain
by Amazon

41982837R00178